THE

CURSE

OF

THOLGOR

Trilogy
The Last light

Book I

The Curse of Tholgor

F. Dubay

ISBN : 9798265149183

Foreword

Enter Nalorëa. An ancient world where magic still exists, at the very heart of the universe of **Ilmarë**. Across the vast continent of **Veyanor**, unfolds the adventure of **Akennor** and his companions — drawn, against their will, into a fate far greater than their own.

This world is inhabited by humans, dwarves, elves, and dark races long believed to have vanished forever. Its very essence is naturally inspired by the work of **Tolkien**, of whom I have been an ardent admirer since my youth.

I believe my favorite tale is that of **Beren and Lúthien** — a forbidden love, an impossible quest to reclaim an object, while the true treasure lies in unconditional love itself.

Many of the names of characters, places, and spells come from **Quenya** and **Sindarin**, sometimes derived, sometimes entirely reimagined in their spirit.

I have also drawn inspiration from other worlds that left a mark on me, such as **The Forgotten Realms** and the adventures of **Drizzt Do'Urden**, not to mention the countless hours spent wandering through **Baldur's Gate**. Fragments of those worlds, emotions, and memories have naturally found their way into my writing.

When I was a child, my father used to tell me stories before I fell asleep. He invented them anew every night, and they existed only for a fleeting moment.

Sometimes I would beg him to tell them again, but they were never the same — each story lived only once.

Now it is my turn to carry a head full of stories. Perhaps I write so that they may live on after me, escaping the silence of time.

It is my way of passing something down, of offering a legacy — however modest — a fragment of dream, of darkness, and of light.

Chapter 1 – A Dream

The air was cold and heavy. Darkness reigned supreme, only a distant glow allowed shapes to be discerned. Stopping on the edge of a carved stone ramp, she narrowed her eyes, forcing them to pierce the shadows.

A ball of fire burst from the ground and shot toward her. She fell backward, breathless, heart pounding. The projectile struck the stone behind her in an explosion that shook the ramp and sent debris raining down. A smell of sulfur filled the air.

Recovering, she rose again and tried once more to pierce the gloom. Countless tiny red lights, glowing like embers, moved across the ground in every direction.

The sky roared in anger, lightning struck and wrought havoc, which also allowed her to better see her surroundings: the impacts had ignited blazes, like streams of fire winding across the earth.

Shocked, she saw things that seemed impossible, born of a nightmare. Abominations, half-man half-beast, emerged from the flames: protruding jaws, curved fangs, pointed ears.

But they were not the most frightening creatures. To her great astonishment, undead beings animated by a damned life advanced with guttural roars.

Some were almost reduced to skeletons, others half-decayed, brandishing swords, a red glow burning in their sockets.

A piercing scream tore the sky, making her hair stand on end and the hairs on her arms bristle. A great winged shape emerged, black, spewing an unreal fire of phosphorescent green.

The battle raged with unheard-of brutality. Stunned, she watched, when the sensation of being watched made her turn her head.

A purple light, laced with black filaments, rose toward the heavens. Amidst the clamor of combat, a dark figure rose. His red eyes pulsed, shifting between demonic flashes and bloodshot human gazes. Bald, with a face furrowed by deep wrinkles, he opened a gaping mouth lined with sharp teeth. A terrible, dark force emanated from him.

Strangely, she felt an intrusion into her mind. Panicked, she screamed, shaking her head as if to drive away the presence. Then a voice split the darkness:

"Illawen, my darling… gently, what is it?"

She found herself in her lover's arms, nestled in his embrace, reassured by his tender kisses. Yet the images did not fade. Even with her eyes closed, the scene continued to swirl behind her eyelids, etched into her mind.

"Come now, I think you've had a terrible nightmare. I've never seen you like this."

Panicked, her eyes wild, breath short, it took her a moment to regain her composure.

"Just a nightmare… I hope. It was terrifying. Hold me tight."

Her heart pounded frantically, haunted by the dark silhouette in the distance, it all seemed so real. She had not experienced anything like this for a very long time, and a deep unease swept through her mind, her breathing grew faster.

She nestled against him, which reassured her, but she could not close her eyes for the rest of the night.

But what could it possibly mean? she wondered inwardly.

Chapter 2 – Arrival and Departure

It was a beautiful day, the first morning of a well-deserved rest. The second year of training at the academy was finally over, and Akennor savored the joy of being back home. Not that he had hated his classes, but the last few months had been so grueling that he felt drained. At last, he could enjoy a respite.

He rose from his cozy bed, far more comfortable than the spartan cot at the academy that had felt like sleeping on the floor. Pulling aside the opaque brown curtains, he gazed out at the landscape: fields stretching as far as the eye could see, the gentle relief of plains and small hills, bordered by the dark edge of a dense forest.

How he had missed his family and this land! At the academy, no visits were permitted. The institution did not want apprentices distracted by the outside world.

His gaze swept across the room: everything was just as he had left it. Near the window stood a large oak chest with heavy black hinges, filled with fine clothes and a few precious items. A wide candle rested on the nightstand, to the right of a simple wooden bed. Opposite, a dresser held his everyday garments; on it lay a large bowl of water and a towel for his morning wash.

At the back of the room stood a wardrobe, and on the floor to the left of the bed lay his academy gear:

black pants, a dark blue long-sleeved shirt embroidered with the school's emblem — two crossed swords, a war hammer raised before a shield — and the inscription *Huorë ar Astara*, "Courage and Loyalty," in the old Elvish tongue.

His swords, still sheathed in leather scabbards, lay on the dirty laundry, while a pair of tall boots waited at the foot of the bed.

The night before, too weary, he had not taken the time to tidy up. At the academy, such negligence would never have been tolerated: the threat of a reprimand was enough to energize even the laziest apprentice.

Akennor attended the prestigious school of Lurtarg, named after a great warrior. This centuries-old institution taught every style of combat, as well as the art of survival in any climate or situation. Renowned throughout the kingdom, it imposed strict discipline and prided itself on producing the finest warriors in the world. From its ranks emerged warlords, army captains of great cities, and law-keepers in rural lands.

Akennor was about to begin his third and final year at the academy. He was proud to have been chosen to study there — his elder brother had gone before him and had passed the entrance trials with flying colors. He still remembered the day of the exam: nervous, obsessed with the idea of success, he had felt the weight of his brother's achievement on his shoulders. But beyond that pressure, he had nourished since childhood a burning dream: to become a great warrior.

This passion had grown from the admiration he felt for his father, whose tales of adventure had fascinated him.

And the past year had been extraordinary for him: he had excelled in unarmed combat, survival, and weapon handling. In the second year, each student had to choose a specialization: Akennor had opted for the straight sword and the ambidextrous style — one blade in each hand. Few warriors mastered this demanding art, geared almost exclusively toward attack.

The memory made him smile as he dressed. Tall and lean, with a robust body, square shoulders and muscular legs, Akennor possessed a physique made for combat.
He pulled on his old brown work trousers and a beige linen shirt, buckled a worn leather belt around his waist, and laced up his rough leather shoes. After washing, he left his room, walked down the corridor, and descended the polished wooden staircase. The aroma of a hearty breakfast welcomed him, and his stomach growled with pleasure.

The whole family was gathered around the large dark table. Torhon, his father, sat in the place of honor. As Akennor approached, he noticed deeper lines on his father's face. His brown hair was veiled with gray. But his small blue eyes still shone with unyielding pride.

His father was a sturdy man, shorter than his sons. His tanned skin contrasted with Akennor's pale complexion. He had passed on his facial features to his sons, and above all that distinctive straight nose. His parents kept a small farm that provided for the family's needs.

They grew a few rare plants with medicinal properties, as well as barley and wheat. Two cows gave milk, calves were raised each spring for meat, and chickens provided eggs.

Torhon worked tirelessly so that his family would lack nothing, and he loved his children more than anything — his greatest achievement, he often said. Before meeting their mother, he had led a youth of adventure and wandering, without a home.

Then his eyes fell on his mother. Akennor thought he resembled her more, with her light gray eyes, dark hair, and even her more delicate features.

His mother, Illawen, was a woman of great beauty: tall, slender, graceful, with a natural charm. Her long, straight black hair framed an oval, delicate face. Time seemed to glide over her without leaving a mark.

When Torhon drank, he liked to boast that he had "brought his wife back" during one of his adventures. Judging by his mother's reaction and the sparkling glint in his father's eyes, Akennor had always suspected some truth in the tale. Yet every time, some event interrupted the story, and he had never learned the full truth.

His father had lived a thousand adventures before meeting Illawen and settling down to start a family. On stormy days, he told those tales to his children. When he saw his brother, Akennor thought:
Kallo looks more and more like father as he grows older.

To Torhon's right sat Kallo, his elder brother. Shorter, stockier, with short brown hair and dark blue eyes. His square face and straight features conveyed quiet strength. His brother combat specialty was the war hammer paired with a shield, a style demanding both strength and endurance.

But beneath his burly exterior, Kallo was jovial, generous, always ready to help anyone in need. He truly had the soul of a knight. Akennor was still descending the stairs when his mother spotted him:

"Good morning, my boy! How are you? Did you sleep well? Not too tired from the trip?" she asked cheerfully.

"Good morning, mother. Yes, I slept well… I'm fine," replied Akennor with a yawn.

"There's nothing like a real bed, eh? " laughed Kallo. "At Lurtarg, it takes a week to get used to those bunks!"

"How many eggs do you want? And some sausages, toast? " added his mother.

"Uh… I'll take two eggs, two sausages, and two slices of bread, please."

The food at home was nothing like that of the academy. There, meals were decent but bland, gulped down hastily in the endless line of students. Here, everything tasted like a feast.

"You slept in! Any later and you'd have missed us. I'm leaving soon for Elenshae. It's been a month now since I started as a city guard," he announced proudly.

Elenshae was a large port city, southwest of their village. The most important city in the region.

"You started earlier than planned!" exclaimed Akennor, taking the plate his mother handed him. "Why?"

Beginning earlier delighted Kallo: since his promotion, he had repeated constantly that he wanted to serve Elenshae's safety, and nowhere else. His patience and perseverance had been rewarded.

"Well, there's trouble these days," said Torhon in a graver tone. "Caravans no longer pass without being attacked. Convoys now have to be escorted by guards from Elenshae and Kementári to keep the link between the two cities."

Kementári was a major city, a week's ride eastward, in a mountainous region. Rich in mineral deposits, it had a mixed population of men and dwarves. Akennor had never set foot there, but he had heard many tales of its unique landscapes.

"There are also rumors of war with the kingdom of Foranor," added Kallo.

Foranor... Akennor shivered at the name. It was a closed, self-sufficient realm, trading little and discouraging travelers. Their warriors were formidable and inspired fear. The kingdom's neighbors respected its power as much as they dreaded it. The last battles with Foranor had taken place more than a century ago, but they had been frightfully savage.

"And as if bandits weren't enough," Torhon continued, "barbarian tribes are also attacking convoys... even raiding isolated villages," he said in a voice heavy with restrained anger."

Akennor knew his father well: Torhon hated feeling powerless in the face of a crisis. He ate hungrily, but his eyes stayed fixed on his father and brother.

Between two bites, he managed to ask:
"Since when have the troubles started?"

10

"Darling, don't talk with your mouth full," his mother teased with a smile. "Don't they teach you manners at the academy?"

"The manners we're taught are to fight and survive," Akennor retorted with a mischievous grin. "The rest is considered a waste of time."

"What a reply!" laughed Illawen. She carried some dishes to the kitchen, then called over her shoulder: "I'm counting on you all to help me, nonetheless!"

"Yes, dear," answered Torhon. Then his face grew darker. "The first attacks began a few months ago. They are multiplying, intensifying. As for Foranor… relations have always been tense. Whether the rumors of war are true, only the rulers know for certain. And these days, they aren't very talkative about it."

Akennor knew his father was well-informed. Torhon played a role in managing the village and the region; he was regarded as an important figure. He even occasionally spoke with Elenshae's leaders.

"Anyway," concluded Kallo, "that's why I was called earlier than expected. I'll take the guard post in the city, while the more experienced soldiers escort the convoys."

With that, he stood.

"Excuse me, I need to finish preparing my things. We're leaving soon."

He exchanged a meaningful glance with his father, who simply nodded. Then Kallo disappeared up the stairs. Torhon rose as well to fetch his gear. Illawen returned to her seat, but her face betrayed a shadow of sadness.

"Is something wrong? " asked Akennor, worried.

"No… it's fine. Don't worry," she answered with a faint smile.

Akennor wasn't convinced. Something troubled her, and she refused to say more. He placed a hand on hers, trying to reassure her.

"Don't worry too much, I'm staying here for now."

"Sometimes life brings surprises we cannot control, my dear," she said softly.

Akennor raised his brows, doubtful. He wondered what she truly meant. But already, his mother's melancholy vanished, replaced by a spark of cheer.

"But look at this beautiful sunshine!" she exclaimed. "What a magnificent day. And you, what will you do?"

"I was planning to see my friends," Akennor replied eagerly. "We're meeting at our usual spot."

He finished his plate, stood, kissed his mother.

"Thank you, mother, it was delicious."

Then he turned to his father, who was returning from the next room with a large sack over his shoulder.

"You're going to accompany Kallo to Elenshae, aren't you?"

"Yes, I am. We're leaving with Krent and his son Brumir: he too starts in two days."

"Do you want me to come with you?" asked Akennor.

"No thank you, son. It won't be necessary. We are four for the trip, and Krent and I will return with a convoy."

"All right. Be careful on the road, above all, he said, glancing at his father." Torhon merely nodded.

Akennor bounded upstairs, heart light at the thought of finally seeing his friends. In his room, he took his belt with its two sheathed swords. He also grabbed his gear for sleeping under the stars: an old canvas for rain, a few threadbare wool blankets, his flask, and a small set of pans.

A sweet nostalgia came over him. It had been so long since he had used all this… and the thought of wandering again filled him with simple, genuine joy.

He longed to see his companions again, to tell them of his adventures, the gossip of the academy, and above all to hear their own stories. They had been a close-knit band since the village elementary school. Education there wasn't compulsory, but most parents deemed it essential for their children to know how to read, write, and count.

That influence came from Elenshae, which for generations had always favored learning. Five years of schooling formed the foundation: reading, writing, arithmetic, a bit of geography, basics of construction and farming, plant knowledge, and an introduction to forest survival.

Among his friends was Sheila, an apprentice mage already skilled in the occult arts. Akennor recalled her radiant smile, her mischievous laugh that always brightened their meetings. Life, however, had not spared her: born into a poor family, she had learned to survive by stealing. Yet despite her hardships, Sheila retained a fiery temperament.

Then came Darian, driven by a deep desire to help others, unable to tolerate cruelty or injustice. That was why he wanted to join the Order of Calaista, founded during the great war against demons and bringing together clerics and paladins, warriors of faith and virtue.

Akennor wondered if he had grown even stronger, and remembered his piercing blue eyes. Darian cherished his companions like the brothers and sisters he had never had. His tenderness for Sheila was obvious, though he vehemently denied any attraction, swearing his heart belonged to another.

Finally, he longed to see Shaya again, the liveliest of the group. Her gentle, ever-smiling face, her overflowing zest for life made her presence indispensable. She loved nature with a fervor almost sacred, convinced that man could never stand against its forces.

Akennor tightened his belt, donned his coat, and left his room. In the hallway, he met his brother, dressed in his old clothes but proudly carrying his shield and war hammer.

"Just arrived, already leaving again," Kallo teased. "You're going to meet your friends, I suppose?"

"Exactly. We arranged to meet at our usual place," Akennor replied, excitement in his voice.

"On the round hill, isn't it?" insisted Kallo, narrowing his eyes.

"Don't try! It's a secret. No one could ever guess where it is," said Akennor with a mischievous wink.

For years, Kallo had tried to discover the mysterious place. Out of curiosity, he had even attempted to follow them, but his schemes had always failed: spotted and shaken off each time.

"Eager to return to duty?" asked Akennor.

"Yes. My leave has done me good, but I love the atmosphere with my comrades," Kallo replied, stroking the haft of his hammer. "And there, we'll have more chances to see action. How I'd love to crush the skull of those highwaymen, those bloodthirsty barbarians… and better still, an orc!"

14

"An orc? But they no longer exist!" exclaimed Akennor. "They were exterminated in the wars of the Great Deliverance!"

"They say a man returned alone, the sole survivor of a convoy. Traumatized, he spoke of monsters that had attacked them.

From his description, some think they were orcs. But most called him mad: he screamed uncontrollably and had to be locked up."

"Well... in that case, his testimony is doubtful," Akennor replied, skeptical.

"Some believed him," Kallo insisted. "They want to shed light on this story."

A deep voice then rang out at the foot of the stairs:

"Kallo! Are you ready? Krent and his son are waiting for us."

"Coming!" he answered.

Kallo descended at once, followed by Akennor. He smiled when he saw his best friend with his father. Kallo thought the two looked very much alike, sturdy, slightly stout. Their dark brown eyes carried a proud, fearless look. Their round faces with a childlike air were framed by long reddish-brown hair.

Kallo grinned at the sight of his friend.

"Hey, Brum! How are you?" he exclaimed, hugging him.

"Yeah!" replied Brumir with a broad smile. "I hope we'll finally see some action!"

"Don't worry about that, children," said Illawen with an air of resignation. "Soon, you'll see enough blood to sicken you."

Images from her nightmare flashed befor her eyes.

"Come now, my dear, don't be so pessimistic," Torhon replied soothingly. "Things will get better. And besides, they are young, full of vigor. They just want to burn off their energy. I was like that, back in the day!"

"That's exactly what frightens me…" murmured Illawen.

A brief silence fell. Their eyes met, heavy with unspoken words. Akennor felt a distance grow between his parents and wondered what he could do about it.

"So I'll be doing the dishes alone, it seems," Illawen sighed.

"Oh, sorry my dear! I'll make it up to you, I promise," Torhon said with a wink.

"All right… take care of yourselves, boys," she said, turning to Kallo. She embraced him tightly and kissed his forehead. "I'm proud of you, my son. I love you so much."

"I love you too, mother. Don't worry. I'll come back as soon as I have leave, in about a month and a half. I'll tell you everything I've seen."

"Well, we must go now. We'll be back in about five days, my dear," said Torhon, kissing his wife.

Kallo adjusted his pack, swung it onto his back with one motion, then held. He adjusted his pack, swung it onto his back with one motion, then held out his hand to Akennor. He grasped it firmly, man to man.

"Take care of mother. And don't go off on too many adventures!" Kallo warned.

The whole family knew Akennor would not stay more than a few weeks at the farm. Routine chores would bore him soon enough, and he would quickly give in to the call of adventure.

"Don't worry," he replied with a mischievous smile. "I'll be as good as gold… as always. Like my big brother, such an inspiring example."

Kallo rolled his eyes, laughing. He was hardly better than Akennor when it came to chasing after adrenaline.

"Still as witty as ever, huh?" he said, shaking his head. "Let's go, father."

With those words, the travelers crossed the threshold. The sky, cloudless, shone brilliantly at its zenith. They turned one last time to wave to those they left behind, then set off toward Elenshae.

Akennor lingered a moment. In the doorway, his mother stood motionless, a fragile silhouette frozen in the light. Her eyes followed her eldest son until he disappeared over the horizon. Akennor felt she was hiding a secret, and promised himself he would one day uncover it.

He returned to his room, made his bed — a habit painfully acquired at Lurtarg —, took his backpack, and went back downstairs.

"Ah, there you are!" Illawen said with a radiant smile. "I prepared something for you to snack on along the way."

She handed him a small bundle. — Ressen cakes, a family recipe. They'll give you strength. I knew you would leave early."

Akennor hesitated, a twinge of guilt tugging at him. — "Maybe I shouldn't leave you alone…"

"Come now," she answered softly, "I can defend myself. And besides, the neighbors aren't far. Go, find your friends, they're waiting for you."

She kissed his cheek and walked him to the front door.

"I won't be gone long, he promised. I'll be back tomorrow. We just want to camp for one night."

"All right, have fun," she said tenderly.

He went down the porch steps, waved one last time to his mother, then set off westward, toward the village of Dal'norsa.

To the north rose the Kalandor range, vast and formidable, its jagged peaks like teeth tearing at the sky. The eternally white summits gleamed in the sunlight. Akennor and his friends had already ventured to the foot of those mountains, but had never dared climb higher: they feared the heights and lacked the proper gear.

After a short while on the main road, he left it for a narrow path strewn with leaves and branches. This trail, halfway between the house and the Ford Crossing bridge over the Norsa, led straight to the village.

Here, the trees were ancient. The forest, though less dense than in the past, flourished with abundant flora. Forage plants, sometimes as tall as a man, crowded the undergrowth. Akennor loved this lush forest, teeming with animals and fragrant with a thousand scents: wildflowers, ferns, resin. The air remained surprisingly light, never stifling. Many plants had medicinal virtues that Illawen knew well.

Akennor quickened his pace, thinking of his friends who must already be waiting. He hated being late; it always made him feel indebted to others.

Each turn of the path stirred memories. Here, a large oak branch at shoulder height: he remembered it at the last moment and ducked quickly to avoid it. How many times had he hit it? A small scar above his left eyebrow bore witness — a souvenir of a mad dash to catch up with Sheila.

Further down, he narrowly avoided the root of old Brunt, so named in memory of the village elder, as wrinkled as the bark of the hollow tree it belonged to. Soon he reached the Watcher's Rock, so named by him and his companions.

Massive and silent, it seemed to guard the entrance to their secret passage near the Norsa River. The murmur of water gliding over the rocks reached his ears like familiar music.

He walked to the riverbank. Before him rose a sheer cliff of the Kalandor range: a wall of stone, tall as ten men, standing at right angles. It looked as though the mountain had been cleaved by the blade of a god.

The Norsa's crystal-clear water revealed its bed even in the deepest pools. At his feet, one of those pools reminded him of fishing trips and summer swims. A few large boulders jutted out, frozen in the current.

After one last glance at the landscape, he turned back toward the Watcher's Rock and slipped behind it. Concealed by the polished stone, a narrow passage opened, known only to four people: himself and his friends. More than a path, it was a track, made nearly invisible by vegetation. Subtle signs carved into tree trunks guided the attentive eye.

As he advanced, Akennor noticed trampled grass, broken branches: his companions had passed this way. His heart tightened with impatience, and he quickened his pace.

Soon, the low roar of a waterfall reached his ears. Moments later, he stood before the torrent: water tumbled furiously between sharp, slippery rocks. Fortunately, its clarity revealed its depth and hidden traps.

Spotting a narrow stone ledge, Akennor edged onto it, fingers clutching the damp wall, moving slowly sideways.

It was the most dangerous, most arduous step. Holding his breath, he pressed on, the thunder of the falls pounding his ears, icy spray lashing his face.

Ahead, the gap between rocks and the liquid curtain appeared. Just a few more steps...

His left foot slipped, he nearly toppled, but caught himself just in time. With one last effort, he crossed the narrow opening and emerged into a rocky hollow, just behind the cascade.

There, the roar of the water thundered endlessly, amplified by the damp walls. Drenched to the bone, he allowed himself a brief respite, caught his breath, then pressed forward.

The passage carved into the rock was but a natural fissure: narrow, slippery, steep on either side, offering barely a few handholds. He advanced cautiously, each step measured, each movement deliberate.

He disliked this part of the path — the most secret, for no one outside their small group knew of it. But above all, he hated being underground. The heavy air made him feel suffocated. He clenched his teeth, focused on not slipping, avoiding the fall that would break an arm or a leg.

Several times, he nearly lost his balance. In the past, such missteps had earned him painful bruises. This time, however, he held firm. Step by step, he pressed on and, finally, reached the other side of the crevice.

Chapter 3 – The Dark Master

The air was freezing. A dry, biting wind lashed Drendor's emaciated face, carved with deep wrinkles that revealed the outline of his skull. His black eyes fixed on the horizon, to the south, toward warmth and joy — everything he despised. There lay the world that had rejected him, the one that had turned him into this malevolent being. His only comfort was to feed that hatred, to constantly nurture the desire to destroy, to dominate… or perhaps both. Deep down, what he truly sought — perhaps even without realizing it — was to share his suffering with the entire universe.

Once, Drendor had been a man. But he had long ceased to think of himself as such. Now, he saw himself as a superior being, corrupted and powerful. Thin and wiry, he possessed a disturbing charisma: despite his ugliness, he knew how to impose his voice and command obedience. His greatest strength lay in the art of manipulating minds, chaining others' wills to his own.

His face bore the marks of damnation: a broken nose, hooked like a vulture's, dominated skeletal features covered in greenish skin, cracked with crevices. From this grotesque appearance radiated palpable malice. His thin lips, corpse-like pale, stretched for a moment into an icy smile — a promise of torment to come.

He dreamed of the future, obsessed with absolute power. For a very long time, this insatiable quest had condemned him to an eternity of damnation. By twisted and unholy means, he had managed to suspend the effects of time and forever ward off the grasp of death. The price had been terrible: his soul, his humanity. But he cared little. Now, he was close to his goal. No one suspected it, and even if his enemies discovered his designs, it would already be too late.

In his mind, the devastated world to come was taking shape: ashes, blood, slaves thrown to the orcs and ogres, playthings for the demons of hell. He already saw himself seated on that throne of ruins, master of a universe bent to his cruelty.

His gaze swept across the barren lands surrounding his fortress. The trees there were almost entirely black, their few leaves charred as if burned from within. Around the walls, no grass grew, save for venomous brambles and thorns with purplish hues. Further away, vegetation timidly returned, but these dead woods never erased the mark of evil.

Construction of the fortress had begun centuries ago. When Drendor had discovered these cursed lands, feared by men, he had known at once he had found the perfect place, a landscape mirroring his soul. With the help of orc tribes, survivors of the wars of the Great Deliverance, he had set out to build his sanctuary upon the ruins of an ancient forgotten citadel. Delving into the foundations, he had sought to reproduce its form, guided by fragments of tales torn from antique grimoires. In his eyes, he had succeeded. And he was proud.

Some black stones came from the original edifice: smooth, hard as the purest rock. But they reflected no light. Dull, matte, they seemed to absorb the world's brightness, as though cursed themselves.

The fortress rose, massive, bristling with towers of uneven heights. Yet from afar, no matter the angle, only the central tower seemed to dominate the sky, the others vanishing into the illusions of its treacherous architecture.

Upon the ramparts, at regular intervals, stood immense spikes of black iron, like sharp fangs turned toward the clouds. The entire fortress looked like a gaping maw ready to tear the heavens apart.

To crown this vision of horror, Drendor loved to impale prisoners there. The tortured bodies remained stuck upon those iron lances or hung from wooden stakes fixed to the walls, until their flesh rotted and gave way under its own weight. The ground at the foot of the walls was littered with blackened corpses and broken skeletons, exhaling a nauseating stench no wind could disperse.

A thick mist permanently stagnated at ground level, hiding traps, poisonous brambles, and venomous beasts. Some creatures, the most abominable, had been shaped by Drendor himself, spawned by his black magic. Sinister creaks echoed endlessly, hisses and indistinct howls filled the air — enough to drive anyone mad who lingered too long.

"Soon… yes, soon," he muttered to himself, his eyes gleaming with a sickly glow.

"The whole world will look like this: my domain."

After centuries of waiting, preparation, and relentless labor, the time was finally approaching.

"Forgive my intrusion, master."

The strong, cavernous voice echoed in the maleficent air. Drendor emerged from his thoughts and slowly turned toward the one who dared disturb his reverie.

"I bring joyous news, the imposing servant continued, his eyes sparkling with dark delight. A message has come from team number six. They have found the last one's trail. They know where he hides and are heading there even now."

A heavy silence followed the declaration. Then a dreadful smile stretched across Drendor's lips, revealing his sharp teeth. A chilling laugh burst from his throat, rolling like wicked thunder:

"At last! Eighteen years I have searched… and now!"

Indeed, for many long years he had hunted the last element needed to fulfill the prophecy. The announcement thrilled him more than anything.

"It was a brilliant idea, master, to send your agents to the four corners of the world! "

The orc resumed fervently.

Drendor nodded curtly. In truth, he had dispatched a hundred teams of four, scattered like shadows across the continents. All searching for the missing fragment, the final obstacle to his victory.

"More than an idea," he murmured coldly, "it was a necessity."

"The time for my glory is finally near," declared Drendor sharply, "and great measures had to be taken… even at the risk of arousing my enemies' suspicions."

For him, the word "enemy" in truth encompassed all living beings capable of loving life in any form. But in particular, he meant the Order of Calaista — those paladins and priests sworn to defend the light.

"Humbly, my lord, I believe the surprise you are preparing for them will remain sealed until its final unveiling."

A cruel sneer brushed Drendor's lips.

"Yes... I believe so too."

He valued this lieutenant more than any other. Maultarg had become his right hand the day he had slain his predecessor in a fit of uncontrollable rage. That day, Drendor had recognized in him a raw, pure hatred, worthy of his service.

Maultarg was a fearsome warrior, a being without scruples, without remorse, without the slightest pity. A predator who lived only to destroy. And Drendor loved that murderous energy. Half-man, half-orc, he inspired terror as much through his appearance as his brute strength.

His face, stern and hollowed, was framed by long black hair. His eyes, a blue so dark they seemed to absorb the light, exuded a chilling coldness. His features betrayed his mixed heritage: a jaw less heavy than an orc's, a face more slender, almost human... but a squashed nose recalling that of a pig, and rounded, misshapen ears. An abomination in the eyes of men — and he knew it. Their contempt had only fueled his hatred.

His rage, when unleashed, was so extreme it froze his enemies' blood even before battle. Selfish and merciless, he nonetheless remained loyal to Drendor. For he was clever enough to know that alone, he would never attain the power he now enjoyed, nor that promised by his master's coming ascension.

"It is time," Drendor's icy voice cut suddenly, bringing Maultarg back to the present. "Gather the lieutenants. We will review the plan… and begin troop deployment."

Maultarg hesitated:

"So soon, master? But the last one has not yet been caught, unless…"

He stopped dead. Drendor's expression froze his blood: his eyes, filled with such black hatred, seemed capable of killing with a mere glance.

"AND SO WHAT ?!" Drendor roared. "It is only a matter of days. The troops will take weeks to deploy."

"When the ritual is completed, everything will be ready at the same time, and the surprise will be total. If you are too foolish and stupid, then never oppose me again… or I will rip your head off, is that CLEAR ?!"

He punctuated his words with a stinging slap across Maultarg's left cheek. The half-orc seethed with rage. He had to summon all his reason not to retaliate. Not worth it, he told himself. For now, Drendor is stronger. But it won't always be so. One day, I will find your weakness… and I will destroy you.

Regaining control, he rubbed his cheek lightly and forced an air of resignation mingled with contempt.

"I am sorry, master. I had not seen it from that angle… but now that you enlighten me with your cruel genius, I can only be impressed."

Appeased, Drendor straightened and ordered:

"Summon the generals and lieutenants. At once."

"LIMZI! … LIMZI! … Come here immediately!" thundered Maultarg's powerful voice.

Dry, quick footsteps echoed in the stairwell behind. A scrawny little being appeared on the threshold of the door leading to the balcony. He measured barely a maïca in height. His triangular, inverted face was topped with pointed ears and a sharp nose. It was Limzi, a swamp troll.

This race of creatures, petty and malicious, compensated for their small size with boundless cruelty. Forced to serve in order to survive, swamp trolls preferred to place themselves under the orders of merciless masters. They found sordid satisfaction in watching tortures, executions, and their lords' intrigues. Their servitude was thus reinforced by their unreserved adoration.

Panting from his run, Limzi hurried toward Drendor. Maultarg had called him, but, true to habit, he went straight to the dark master.

"Yes, master… what can I do to serve you?" he squeaked in his shrill little voice.

Drendor leaned slightly over Limzi.

"Limzi, go immediately and warn all the lieutenants and generals of my army. I want to see them at once, as quickly as possible."

He fixed his black gaze into the little creature's eyes.

"You know I do not like waiting… don't you?"

A shiver ran down Limzi's spine. He remembered the day he had lost the use of his left eye, having forgotten an errand for his lord because he had lingered to watch a torture session.

"Yes, yes, master! Oh yes, Limzi remembers… Limzi goes right away!" he squealed before darting like an arrow toward the stairs leading to the lower floors.

He had to hurry: two generals and three lieutenants to warn… and he had no idea where each of them was.

Drendor turned to Maultarg, a cruel smile on his lips.

"Let's prepare the instructions. I believe Limzi will not dawdle this time."

"Good!" replied Maultarg with a guttural laugh. "I already feel the excitement… soon the intoxication of battle will consume me."

Drendor placed his left arm on the half-orc's shoulders, and together they took the spiral staircase.

Meanwhile, Limzi was dashing headlong through the fortress's shadowy corridors. His first destination: the chambers of Gauldrom, supreme general of Drendor's forces.

Gauldrom was a gigantic orc, stocky, with muscles of steel. An undisputed master of the axe, he wielded his weapon with unmatched precision and brutality. This axe was no ordinary weapon: according to legend, it had belonged to a demon of the underworld. Forged by a dwarf who had bargained with evil forces, the weapon was said to hold the very soul of the demon within.

The axe head, forged in a forgotten metal, was tinged a dark red like dried blood. Ancient runes were engraved upon it, so mysterious that no mage, even the wisest, had ever deciphered them.

Gauldrom was feared by all. His rages were legendary, his touchiness extreme. Paranoid and hungry for respect, he could make his own soldiers tremble with a mere frown.

He respected Drendor, but did not entirely trust him. Still, he admired his tactics and ambitions; by staying at his side, he ensured his own thirst for power would be sated.

Limzi reached the heavy dark wooden door, stained with dried blood and hacked by axe blows. The frail creature shivered and knocked timidly.

"What is it? RAAARGN! " roared Gauldrom. "I said I was not to be disturbed under ANY circumstance!"

Limzi heard heavy steps approaching rapidly, like rolling thunder. For a moment, he thought of fleeing at full speed, but he restrained himself: it was, after all, his master's order.

The door slammed open. Gauldrom's face was twisted with rage. Limzi hurried to deliver the message, his voice trembling and quavering:

"Th-the… the master wants to see his commanders right away, in the throne room."

Gauldrom's chamber contained a large bed at the far left, near the outer wall. A vast table covered with numerous maps stood in the center. The rest of the room was filled with training devices, targets, and shelves lined with weapons of every kind.

Gauldrom seemed to ponder, then bellowed:

"Why the hurry?"

"Limzi doesn't know, general, but it seems very important."

"All right, filthy parasite, I'll go."

He turned briefly to shut the door. Limzi took the opportunity to slip away like lightning.

He was afraid of this orc general and had no wish to prolong the conversation, nor give him a reason to end his miserable existence.

The little troll now sped toward Trumakara, the second-in-command. He was a hideous troll, vicious and treacherous.

His skin was covered with small green scales, his nose long and pointed, his eyes yellow and bulging, his teeth long and sharp, and his coarse black hair stood on end like spikes.

He was willing to do anything to win a battle, for glory and for status. Trumakara had already tried to discredit Gauldrom in Drendor's eyes, but the plot had backfired: the orc had discovered the scheme and had nearly killed him. If Drendor had not intervened, the troll would have been history.

He bore a deep grudge against the orc for humiliating him and would one day make him pay… but only after the events to come. The dark sorcerer had indeed warned him: he was to keep quiet and do nothing that might hinder operations.

Trumakara feared Drendor far more than Gauldrom. The great troll was neither courageous nor strong despite his size. On the other hand, he was agile and very quick, which had allowed him to escape many perilous situations. His weapon of choice was the two-handed sword, which he wielded with ease but without true mastery.

His true strengths lay in deceit, strategy, intrigue, manipulation of others, and of course his vast knowledge of magical potions.

He was concocting a particularly violent and insidious poison when he heard a faint knock at his door. Trumakara lifted his head slightly and, in his shrill voice, called:

"What is it? I'm busy… I hope it's important!"

Trumakara was an expert in the art of making deadly poisons. He supplied them to his soldiers to coat their weapons. Trolls were more effective with ranged weapons, like bows and crossbows, but their legendary clumsiness limited their accuracy.

Trumakara believed that any blow struck should be fatal. To compensate for this lack of dexterity, poison was the perfect solution: if the wound inflicted by an arrow did not kill immediately, the poison would finish the job.

The troll general's chamber was furnished with a large iron bed, countless shelves crammed with his own potions or elixirs concocted by ancient evil sorcerers, catalogued in manuscripts and grimoires.

A vast table, covered with vials and strange ingredients, took up almost all the space, while another, near the bed, served him for writing his recipes, military strategies, and journal.

He rose carefully, avoiding knocking over the small glass vials scattered on the table, and walked to the door. Trumakara spent his days experimenting with all kinds of brews: poisons, antidotes, but also potions aimed at solving his race's greatest weakness. For years, he had worked on an antidote that would make trolls resistant to sunlight, whose rays burned them horribly. So far, his results had only been partially successful.

"Ah, Limzi!" he said in a warmer tone.
He liked the sadistic little creature, naïve and fond of gossip. Trumakara could easily manipulate him for his purposes. He had already used him to spy or steal objects.
"What can I do for you?"

Limzi, who loved to feel important when entrusted with missions, lifted his head, blinked, and declared:

"The master wants to see everyone, right away, in the throne room, General Trumakara."

"Hmm... Then it must be very important, probably linked to the coming operations. I'll go."

Finally, he thought to himself. His plans, matured for many moons and revised countless times, were about to take shape.

"Goodbye, general," said Limzi as he darted off again.

Limzi now headed toward the inner courtyard, where the soldiers were training. As he approached, he heard the voice of the one he sought: Gromurh.

Gromurh was an orc, Gauldrom's second lieutenant, and the only one the latter trusted even a little. He was a young orc, tall and robust, wielding his two-handed sword with impressive dexterity. He was in charge of training the soldiers in combat.

"Come on, you maggots! Higher with the sword, shields straight! What is this bunch of WRETCHES? AAAARGN!"

Limzi stepped through the door just as Gromurh stormed at the soldiers to give them a lesson. The first, too slow to parry, received a sword blow in the gut. Gromurh tossed him aside like a rag doll and charged the second. This one managed to block the tremendous strike aimed at his flank, but staggered, unable to parry the next attack that split his skull in two.

With a kick, Gromurh freed his blade and rushed toward the others, who had already taken to their heels. They leapt over Limzi, who was delighted by the bloody spectacle, and disappeared into the corridors of the fortress.

"Cowards! COWARDS! Come back so I can cleave you in two, you worthless dung-eaters!"

Limzi shook himself, recalled his lord's wise words, gathered his courage, and stepped into Gromurh's path.

"Excuse me, but the MASTER demands to see all his lieutenants immediately. I'm sorry, but it's urgent, lieutenant."

The little creature trembled from head to toe before Gromurh's rage-twisted face. He thought he was witnessing the last moments of his miserable life, but the orc calmed and said:

"All right, I'll go."

Then he lifted Limzi off the ground and brought him close to his slobbering maw.

"Listen well, filthy shoe scrap, you didn't see anything, got it?"

"But of course, Gromurh, of course…" whimpered Limzi, trembling.

The orc hurled him through the open doorway.

"Get lost, you rat."

Limzi landed heavily against the wall. His shoulder ached, but he shot off like an arrow toward the quarters of Kassef. This sadistic and perverse human sometimes abducted women for his own pleasure. The minds of those poor wretches would break, leaving them in a semi-vegetative state.

Apart from the pleasures of the flesh, Kassef loved battle and blood. He came from a barbarian tribe that haunted the hostile lands west of Kementári. He was a handsome blond man, with green eyes and a perfectly chiseled face.

Tall, strong, and well-built, he was an outstanding warrior, wielding his war hammer with formidable efficiency. This magical weapon he had stolen from a dwarven adventurer who had strayed too close to his camp.

Limzi knocked softly at the door.

"Yes, come in," said Kassef in a rather calm tone. He was less irritable when his primal appetites were satisfied.

Limzi entered timidly and approached the bed that occupied the center of the room. Three young women, completely naked, lay there. Many times, Limzi had spied on Kassef in the throes of debauchery, through a small hole hidden in the patterns of an obscene tapestry.

Kassef's room contained that enormous bed, a simple small table, and a wardrobe for his clothes. The barbarian spent most of his time with his tribe. He only came to the fortress to receive instructions and give his reports. During his absence, his women were put to other tasks in the citadel.

"Forgive me for disturbing you, sir Kassef, but the Master demands everyone immediately, in the throne room."

Kassef nodded.

"All right, I'll go, little one."

"Now off you go."

Limzi turned and headed for his favorite place: the torture chamber. It was located on the lowest level of the dungeon, near the cells of the unfortunate prisoners. A nauseating stench lingered permanently there. Rats scurried everywhere, gnawing at remains — most of them human and dwarven.

Bones piled up in the corners of cells and corridors. The walls and floor, damp and slimy, were partially covered with mold and fungi.

Limzi loved this atmosphere. He spent most of his time in the dungeons, watching punishments, listening to prisoners' screams… and even harassing them. He quickly covered the distance to the chamber and gently pushed open the heavy iron door.

Cartaraug, a medium-sized troll with green, scaly skin, bulging green eyes, and hair standing in a fan like Trumakara's, was the last lieutenant — but also the chief torturer. He was seated at a table, working on his instruments.

This chamber was undoubtedly one of the most terrifying in the fortress. Numerous machines stood there, designed to inflict the worst torments. No one had ever managed to remain silent within its walls. The acts of cruelty there were so abominable that all captives eventually longed for a quick, painless death.

Cartaraug, pitiless, took genuine pleasure in torture. He almost reached ecstasy when his victims begged him to stop. This incredible sensation of absolute power was, he often told himself, a delight.

The troll suddenly turned his head toward the intruder, then relaxed and even gave him a smile.
"Ah, hello Limzi! How are you? It's been a while. Things are rather quiet these days, aren't they?" Feels almost as if time has stopped… he said in his raspy voice.
"I think that's about to change, the little troll said triumphantly. The Master wants to see everyone, now!"

Cartaraug leapt to his feet and rubbed his hands in satisfaction.

"At last, a bit of action! About time, I was getting bored."

It felt to him like an eternity since the last time he had played torturer. The cells were nearly empty: barely one or two prisoners still survived, and Drendor reserved them for himself. At that thought, Cartaraug considered asking to attend the torments orchestrated by his lord.

For, as cruel and pitiless as he was, all of it was nothing compared to Drendor. The torturer dreamed of learning from him.

"It's in the throne room," Limzi added.

"Well then, let's go. Let's not keep him waiting."

Limzi and Cartaraug set off quickly and soon arrived before the throne room. It was a vast, circular hall, plunged entirely in darkness. No windows let in light.

Six stone columns, each carved with the grimacing likeness of demons, formed a circle around the central throne, midway between it and the circular wall. Two torches fixed on each column, and others set along the wall, gave off a flickering glow. Usually, those on the wall remained unlit, but tonight they all burned, casting dancing shadows.

On the great stone table before the throne lay countless maps of the known world. It was here that Drendor gathered his commanders to devise his plans… but the table also served as an altar during rites of dark magic.

The throne itself had been carved from a block of absolute black rock, said to come from infernal regions.

Dark energies emanated from it, chilling any who dared gaze too long. Its sides were covered with abhorrent engravings: human figures tortured, mutilated, frozen in eternal agony.

Cartaraug entered first, followed closely by Limzi. All the others were already there, seated around the table.

Drendor rose.

"Well, Limzi, well… but I expect a faster time next occasion. Now go, and don't get clever. Understood?"

The little troll timidly nodded and slipped away at once, without asking for more.

The dark sorcerer sat down again and swept the assembly with his cold gaze.

"Well. I suppose most of you are beginning to find the wait long… and unnerving."

Gromurh slammed his fists on the table, interrupting his lord.

"I can't take it anymore! I'm going mad… I'VE HAD ENOUGH!" he shouted.

Drendor turned toward him with a gaze dripping malice.

"ENOUGH! I will not tolerate such insubordination."

The dark sorcerer made a sharp gesture while muttering incomprehensible words. At once, Gromurh clutched at his throat, choking as if an invisible force were strangling him.

His face flushed, his bulging eyes betrayed his agony, then he collapsed to the floor, convulsing and gasping. After a few moments, Drendor released his grip.

"I spare your life… for now. I need each of you. But I swear: if you defy me again, I will reserve for you a torment a thousand times worse. Do you hear me? … IS THAT CLEAR?"

The sorcerer's words rang in the hall like thunder, amplified by the echoes of the stone walls, chilling the assembly to the bone.

Gromurh, trembling, got up painfully. His voice, hoarse, came in a whisper:

"Sorry, Master… yes, it's very clear."

Drendor stared at him a moment longer, then turned his attention to the others.

"Good. Maultarg has just informed me that a team has found the trail of the last one we seek."

He paused, studying each of his lieutenants in turn.

"I will recall the teams whose missions are complete. They will not return here, but to our hideouts near Elenshae and Kementári."

His gaze fell on Kassef.

"You will return to your people. Keep pressing the tribes, I want the raids on villages and caravans to intensify."

The barbarian nodded, but added gravely:

"All right… but I must tell you that the forces of Elenshae and Kementári are beginning to organize escorts to protect the caravans. The last raids cost us dearly… we suffered heavy losses."

Drendor gave a cold smile.

"Yes, I know. And that is perfect. The authorities of those cities suspect nothing. They are wasting their strength in the worst way, diverted from what truly awaits them. You must continue to convince them of the necessity of the attacks."

"Yes, I believe I can manage that without trouble if I have more gold," Kassef said confidently.

"Gold is but a tool to serve my ends. Very well, take what you need — but do not take me for a fool, Kassef."

"Do not fear."

Trying to deceive the dark sorcerer was surely the last thing Kassef would ever attempt. He would never dare do anything to anger him; he cared too much for his life of debauchery.

"Good. While the barbarians continue to harass and create diversion, the troll troops, presently north of Elenshae in the mountains, will prepare to strike first. Cartaraug, you will go join them and begin giving them their orders."

"Yes, master. When should I leave?"

"As soon as this meeting is over, prepare your things and go."

Cartaraug nodded his approval.

"Next, Gauldrom and Gromurh, you will leave for the Morgrunt camp and prepare the troop movement as quickly as possible, for you have a long march ahead."

"Maultarg and Trumakara, you will remain here for now. We will finish the final details and you will leave just before the final ritual. I will join you with our new allies and the Black Guard for the final crushing...!"

All burst into sadistic, contagious laughter.

"We will crush Elenshae first, for it is the most powerful, and it is also a strategic point because of its seaport. Then Kementári will fall, encircled. Then part of the troops will turn back to destroy Foranor."

"Forgive me, my lord, ventured Gauldrom, but what if the team fails in its attempt? Not that I wish it, but..."

Drendor flushed with fury at the thought and struggled to restrain himself. After all, Gauldrom was a proud warrior and a good general — a precious asset.

"They will not fail. Failure is not an option. If they ever do, I swear they will suffer the worst torments I can imagine — and you know I have a great deal of imagination."

A deadly silence hung around the table. Everyone looked at one another, but no one dared say another word.

"Well. If all is clear and there are no more questions, go execute my orders."

They rose and left in silence and haste, each lost in thought. Once they had all departed, Drendor went to sit on his throne and, with a gesture, extinguished the torches on the circular wall, then rekindled them in a ghostly green glow.

Four dark shapes emerged from behind the throne and stood before the sorcerer. They were the Black Guard, powerful necromancers who assisted him in rituals and experiments of magic. Three were men and one an elf who had renounced his kin for darkness.

"You witnessed the entire meeting? asked Drendor."

A voice that seemed to come from beyond the grave answered:

"Yes, master. And the preparations are almost complete. We will be ready in time."

"Good. Very good. The key is coordination. Now leave me: I must think."

The four hooded forms departed quietly, soundless, as if gliding on a cushion of air. They disappeared behind the throne through a secret door known only to them and Drendor, leading to their chambers and laboratories.

Chapter 4 – The mercenaries

The weather was splendid. The sky had just turned completely dark and the stars shone with a bright sparkle.

Dresden advanced with his band: Deidre, Aaron, and Parthe. All humans, all mercenaries drawn by the lure of profit. For months they had wandered from village to village, chasing every lead, every rumor. Dresden was convinced they were finally close to their goal. He hoped so with all his soul: he had already sent a report to the Dark Master. And he knew what awaited them in case of failure… or if their information jeopardized Drendor's plans.

The monastery suddenly appeared, at the turn of a bend: a square, massive building, built of carved stone blocks. A courtyard surrounded it, enclosed by a wall as tall as a man. The sloping roof rose toward the sky, and from its center emerged a three-story tower.

The main door was shut, protected by an iron grille. Beside it, an old bell hung on the wall, a relic meant for visitors.

The four riders dismounted and, out of sight, improvised a plan.

"So… how do we go about this?" Aaron asked nervously.

Dresden glared at him, annoyed. This incapable fool never ceased to astonish him: thin, cowardly, he only kept his place thanks to his skill with bow and crossbow. A valuable asset at a distance, but otherwise… dead weight.

"According to the last witness interrogated…" Parthe began.

Dresden turned toward his companion.

At least this one knew how to be useful. Cunning, agile, a former thief of the Colimport guild, he had survived a childhood of abandonment and wandering. Together they had shared many missions — and forged a blood loyalty.

"… almost everyone has gone to pray. There should be only a few guards and one or two priests left in the monastery."

Deidre observed the thief. Taller, slimmer, his long chestnut hair framed a closed face. His blue eyes remained cold, but behind that calm she sensed constant vigilance. She respected that composure, that self-control he maintained in all circumstances.

"Yes, Dresden added. The man in charge has his quarters in the East Wing."

An assassin from the same guild as Parthe, he had grown close to him over the course of their missions.

"It shouldn't be too complicated."

"Unless the witness lied, even under torture," Aaron objected.

Deidre shrugged. To her, Aaron was nothing but a burden: unremarkable appearance, cowardly attitude, as dull as his face.

"No," she said calmly. "I cast a truth spell during the interrogation. He could not lie."

Dresden then turned his gaze on her. She didn't look impressive at first glance: a round face, long brown hair, dark eyes. But he knew that a formidable intelligence and a hidden darkness lay behind that ordinary mask. Her spells had saved their lives more than once. He had already had her in his bed, and she, on her side, did not hesitate to use her charms to get what she wanted. Yet a part of her always unsettled him

"Listen." Deidre met his eyes… muscles taut beneath the leather, a square face framed by a dark beard, and brown eyes so intense they seemed to cut straight through her.

She had shared his bed more than once—sometimes out of play, sometimes out of desire—and she relished teasing his quick temper. Yet she knew he could be as brutal as he was captivating. A man to be desired, but one to be forever mistrusted.

Dresden continued in a sharp voice.
"Here's what we'll do. We observe the grounds and the surroundings. We spot the sentinels, note anything suspicious, and meet back here when the moon reaches this position, Dresden pointed. If there's a guard, we eliminate him.
Then we enter through a first-floor window: Parthe will take care of that. He'll detect the traps, then deal with the priests."

His gaze swept over the group. Parthe simply nodded, calm and focused. Deidre gave an enigmatic smile, her eyes gleaming with a troubling light. Aaron lowered his eyes, his sweaty hands clutching his bow.

He turned his head toward the thief.

"Parthe, kill them in their sleep, if possible. No alarm."

The assassin nodded.

"No problem."

"Aaron, you follow him, but from a distance. You intervene only if things go wrong. Understood?"

"Yes, understood," Aaron confirmed.

"Deidre, you're with me. We'll go straight to the old man in charge. You'll cast a spell to silence him, stop him from resisting… you know what I mean?"

"Perfectly, chief."

"Good. We wait a little longer, just to be sure everyone's in a deep sleep, then we begin our round."

The four mercenaries split up in opposite directions, moving closer to the stone monastery. Each watched attentively.

Later, they regrouped at the designated spot.

"Report," Dresden demanded.

"I spotted a guard on patrol, Parthe said. He's very discreet, hard to follow. Sometimes inside, sometimes outside, and he picks his routes at random."

"Nothing to report," said Aaron.

"I saw nothing, but I felt a presence watching," Deidre added.

"I also noticed a lookout, Dresden confirmed. The best would be to wait for him to come out. Aaron can bring him down with an arrow."

"All right, I can do it, Aaron replied without hesitation."

"Good. Go with Parthe and comeback once it's done."

"Understood, the two men answered."

A long moment passed when suddenly, a shadow appeared out of nowhere, between Dresden and Deidre.

"Damn, Parthe! Deidre swore. You scared me half to death, I almost screamed."

"It's done, the thief announced coldly. Aaron shot him — one dart in the throat and another straight to the heart. The man didn't have time to raise the alarm, he barely realized what was happening."

"Excellent. Let's go, enough wasted time," Dresden ordered.

The plan unfolded as expected. Parthe and Aaron went to murder the remaining guard and the sleeping priests, while Dresden and Deidre soon found themselves in the room of the master of the place. They woke him with a knife at his throat and bound his hands and feet to a small wooden chair. Slowly, Dresden removed the gag they had placed in his mouth.

"Sorry for the intrusion, old man, but we want some information."

Meanwhile, Deidre was already searching the papers in the adjoining office.

The old man replied firmly:

"You couldn't simply come to the office decently if it were just a question? No, then it is much more than that, am I wrong?"

Discreetly, he had drawn a small blade from his sleeve and was beginning to cut his bonds.

"Let's just say we're in a hurry, we want a true answer without raising suspicion... and we like to act this way. No lies: we are crooks," Dresden replied with icy calm.

"According to our sources, about nineteen years ago, you were entrusted with the guardianship of a child. Since you are not an orphanage and did not wish to attract attention, you must have confided him to others."

"I have absolutely no idea what you are talking about, retorted the old man, lifting his head."

"I see… So all our research, these months of effort, all those clues leading here, all the people we had to kill… all lies? Is that your version?" Dresden asked, still perfectly calm.

"Yes, exactly."

One of the cords gave way.

But suddenly, Dresden exploded: he slapped the old man so violently that his cheek split open, blood spurting.

"You old fool! You know very well. Do you think to deceive us? You have no idea of the powers at play. So will you speak, or die in atrocious suffering? It's your choice. But without an answer, we will not leave."

The priest locked his gaze on Dresden's. Another cord snapped, and the last was nearly broken.

"I know who you are… and especially to whom you belong. But I am not afraid. Not of you, not of pain, not of death. Know this: Drendor is nothing but an evil, selfish being who seeks only his own interests. To him, you are nothing but a worm."

Dresden flinched. How could this old man know? He turned away for an instant, searching for a way to make him talk. But Ardoras seized the chance: the ropes fell to the floor. Swift as a serpent, he grabbed his chair and smashed it over Dresden. The mercenary collapsed, stunned.

The commotion alerted Deidre. Ardoras was waiting. As soon as she entered, he pronounced an incantation:

"*Úlévima!*"

The sorceress froze, paralyzed. Dresden, half-unconscious, writhed on the ground. Parthe rushed in. The priest, a disciplined former warrior, still quick despite his age, seized his war hammer and raised it with a savage roar. Parthe barely dodged: the blow would have crushed his ribcage. But the force of the impact sent him rolling to the ground. Ardoras lifted his weapon to finish him.

A *click* sounded. The old man's eyes widened: an arrow had lodged in his throat, another pierced his heart. He dropped his hammer and collapsed, dead.

"Well done, Aaron. Lucky you were here. What a foolish old man, Parthe muttered."

Dresden staggered to his feet, furious.

"How can we make him talk now? Was it really necessary to kill him?"

"He was about to kill Parthe, I didn't have time to think!" Aaron defended himself.

Dresden swallowed a bitter comment, then roared in rage. So much effort for nothing! Their lives depended on this, they had to find another lead.

"We must explore another trail," he finally said.

"Perhaps in his office," Parthe suggested.

"That's what Deidre was searching when he paralyzed her," Aaron reminded him.

They ransacked the room. Soon after, Deidre regained her freedom and joined them.

"I found an interesting chest. Parthe, it's your turn."

She pulled a small silver chest from a cupboard and set it on the desk. Parthe examined it.

"A trap, probably. I've seen this kind of mechanism before. We must act with caution."

He took out a long metal tool and set to work. A bead of sweat formed on his forehead. The others moved back. Then, a click: the lid opened, intact.

"You're a master, Parthe," Dresden exclaimed.

Deidre leaned in at once. The chest contained only papers. But one of them made them smile.

"A small village, nearby," she said.

Their eyes gleamed.

"It's only a matter of days now, Dresden declared. Let's sleep here for a while, the place is clean. But first, let's see the kitchens."

"I'm starving," Parthe added.

Chapter 5 – The Reunion

Akennor climbed over the last rocks. The familiar voices of his friends already echoed, while the roar of the waterfall faded behind him. He was the last to arrive.

Sheila, deep in conversation with Darian and Shaya, turned her head and saw him. At the sight of him, her heart skipped a beat: his fine features, short black hair, and eyes that seemed to pierce the soul… She smiled, overwhelmed with happiness; she could have melted on the spot.

Sheila stood up at once:
"Akennor! Finally! I've been waiting an eternity for you!"
He saw her run toward him, her full lips curved in a radiant smile. Her brown, intense eyes shone with a joyful light. Akennor found her enchanting: even more dazzling than in his memories.

She threw herself into his arms, immediately followed by Shaya and Darian. The four embraced, moved. Akennor pressed her against him, breathing in the delicate scent of her long hair.

When the wave of tenderness subsided, Darian said:

"A little later, and we would have gone searching for you."

"Yeah, we thought maybe you hadn't managed to get past the waterfall, like the time you fell into the basin and lost all your gear," Shaya added teasingly.

Akennor lowered his eyes, a little embarrassed.

"Ah yes, the time I almost drowned... I remember it well, what a great day," he replied with a smile.

Since that incident, he had always harbored a certain fear of water.

"That's why we were worried," Sheila concluded. "So, what's your excuse for being late?"

She crossed her arms, a smile on her lips. Her outfit — fitted trousers and a sleeveless leather jerkin — highlighted her figure, which Akennor could not help but notice.

"I... maybe overslept a bit," admitted Akennor, embarrassed. "And then, my brother left earlier than expected for Elenshae."

He sat down on his usual rock near the fire pit.

"Let's just say the last few days at the academy were exhausting. I was worn out."

"Exhausting... did they ask you to think with your head instead of your muscles?" Sheila mocked with a laugh. "No wonder you're tired, that's not your habit!"

Everyone burst out laughing.

"Ha! ha! ha! Very funny. Well, we did learn how to neutralize a mage," Akennor retorted.

"And how do you do that?" Sheila asked, curious.

"The surest way is to stop him from speaking. A dagger to the throat, or cutting out his tongue, and he can't cast a spell."

He looked at her intently. His words carried a tone of playful humor: he liked to tease her, and she knew never to take his jabs seriously.

"Easier said than done! You still have to aim right," Sheila chuckled. "By the way, wasn't your brother supposed to leave at the end of summer?"

"Probably recalled earlier because of the troubles with bandits and barbarian tribes," Darian answered.

"Exactly," Akennor confirmed. "Well informed, for someone who's supposed to stay out of things."

"Ah! I have my sources," Darian said with a smile.

"Our mentor told us before leaving. He urged us to be careful during the summer."

Shaya chimed in mockingly:

"So, you're the one helping your father on the farm?"

Akennor rolled his eyes.

"Ah damn…"

The others burst into laughter. He hated farm work and often found excuses to avoid it. But this time, he wouldn't get out of it. Besides, he would feel guilty leaving his father to do everything alone.

"We'll come give you a hand," Darian added resolutely. "That way, we'll still have time for our expeditions."

"Thanks," Akennor replied sincerely.

"Speaking of expeditions," he continued, "anyone have an idea? Because I've got nothing. Feels like we've done everything in the region."

They exchanged resigned looks and nodded silently.

Then Sheila spoke up:

"I heard about a temple dedicated to a long-forgotten god."

She paused, capturing their full attention.

"The story goes back to very ancient times. The god of the temple was good and caring toward his people. But after a period of great turmoil, his subjects became corrupt and wicked. They turned away from him. In anger, he cursed them: those present in the temple were walled in alive, and the others died in dreadful ways."

"Charming. And what's the point?" Shaya asked.

"According to legend, a powerful artifact was kept there."

"Do you know what it is?" Akennor asked, interested.

"No, unfortunately. It was just a small passage in a large book I stumbled upon by chance. I tried to find more information, but without success."

"And was the location mentioned?" Darian asked curiously.

"The passage was vague: it said the temple was south of a branch of the Kalimdor mountain range, near Lake Narya."

Sheila thought back to that forgotten book, lost amid the immense library of sorcery. Old and worn, it spoke of myths and legends, tracing the evolution of religions since the dawn of time.

"I figured it might be the Split Cliff. So, we might be in the right area."

"But unless we find more clues, it's going to be very hard to locate," Akennor added.

"Anyone else have an idea?"

"We could explore the mountains or the forest," Shaya suggested. "Better than doing nothing at all."

"Okay, I'd vote for the mountains. I want some fresh air," Akennor exclaimed.

"Good. We'll see tomorrow then," Darian concluded.

"Who starts? I can't wait to hear what you've been doing this year." They all looked at each other in turn.

"We should maybe finish setting up camp and preparing dinner first. The sun is almost down," Akennor suggested.

"All right, let's do it!"

They got up and finished arranging the camp. Darian and Shaya went to gather firewood, while Sheila prepared the two chickens that would cook slowly over the fire.

Akennor worked on his old canvas: he fixed two wooden poles and set it up next to Sheila's, both facing the fire. The shelters, side by side at a safe distance from the flames, would serve as protection against bad weather or the night chill.

But in summer, they often skipped this tedious setup. Akennor's canvas had special value: his father had crafted it with his own hands, and inspired by this model, each companion had made one.

Once his setup was complete, Akennor spread his blankets and joined Sheila by the fire. A skilled cook, she always knew how to make the best of modest resources. She usually prepared the group's meals. This diligent, warm side contrasted with her fiery temperament. Akennor sat by her: he especially cherished those moments of conversation with her.

"What are you cooking for us? Can I help?" he asked.

"No thanks, I'm done. Just need to put it on the fire. One roast chicken on the spit with a special 'Sheila' sauce, and another in pieces cooking in a pot with vegetables and malt liquor sauce."

"Mmm… sounds great." Akennor's stomach growled; he was eager to taste the meal.

He watched Sheila attentively as she finished her preparations. The firelight highlighted her features, casting golden reflections in her hair. For some time now, Akennor had wondered if he should take the leap — open his heart to her and seek a deeper bond.

The thought haunted him, but fear held him back: what if she turned away? What if, instead of love, he found only silence, shattering their precious closeness?

This dilemma gnawed at him. Every time he looked at her, his thoughts tangled and his heart raced, torn between the ardent desire to draw near and the unbearable fear of losing her.

Cracking branches and voices broke Akennor's reverie. Shaya and Darian returned, arms full of firewood.

"That should be enough for the evening," Darian said with satisfaction, dropping his load by the fire.

Akennor arranged the wood in the stone circle. Once done, Sheila placed her cauldron and the spit with the other chicken.

"Just need to light it," she announced.

"*Ruinë!*"

Sheila pointed at the pile of wood, and it ignited instantly. The group sat back around the fire. With a knowing smile, Shaya pulled from her bag a bottle filled with light brown liquid.

"Anyone want a little brandy? It's good. I borrowed it from my father's stash."

"Gladly," Akennor said, holding out his iron cup.

"Me too," Darian said.

"Thanks, but I'll stick to my malt liquor," Sheila replied, grabbing her half-empty bottle from the cooking. "I've brought a few more if you want some."

Darian lifted his cup, gulped a large swig… and coughed violently, nearly choking.

"Ha! Not bad… but damn strong!"

The others' laughter rang out, mingling with the crackling fire.

"After a few sips, you won't feel it anymore," Shaya joked.

"So, who starts? " Darian asked eagerly.

"You should," Akennor replied.

"Yeah, go on!" Sheila exclaimed.

"You're dying to," Shaya teased.

She knew him best: Darian, her best friend, had an irresistible charm that melted hearts. Tall, muscular, with blond hair brushing his shoulders and blue eyes sparkling with mischief, his perfectly sculpted face gave him the look of a hero. Shaya bit her lip without realizing it.

Darian took a deep breath, pride shining in his eyes.

"This second year has been incredible. I've learned techniques of meditation, breathing, even exercises to calm the mind. And, of course, the combat methods of the paladins."

"My teachers say I'm progressing well. They make me study sacred texts, learn to pray, even read the stars to guide myself at night. I also had philosophy classes... and honestly, they opened my mind."

He lowered his voice slightly.

"Next summer, I'm leaving on a pilgrimage, to a temple of Calaista. It'll be far and isolated... I'll spend the whole season meditating, training, and learning spells. It's exciting... but also intimidating."

"All summer?" Shaya exclaimed. "So, we won't see each other for a whole year!"

At these words, Akennor noticed a strange light in her eyes, but chose to remain silent.

"Yes..." Darian replied. "But once that stage is complete, I'll be transferred to a monastery. I don't yet know which. If my results are excellent, I'll get to choose. If not, it'll be assigned."

He smiled faintly, tinged with regret.

"It's a shame… but everything has its good and bad sides."

Shaya sighed.

"Maybe… but we'll miss you terribly."

Her face darkened for a second before she straightened, masking her feelings.

"Well then, who's next?"

"I'll go," Sheila said, stirring her chicken over the fire.

"My second year… let's just say it was pretty intense," she began with a sly smile.

"I learn fast and I have talent, but… I need to control my temper. They say it throws my spells off balance. My offensive ones are stronger, but my defensive ones weaker."

She rolled her eyes with a sigh.

"So, for months, I've been meditating. And it's working. But I'll have to do it all my life."

She brightened.

"But I did learn new spells this year! Some defensive ones, but especially offensive ones. And they also initiated me into elixirs, potions, and antidotes."

She shrugged.

"Very useful, though a challenge for me, since it takes research and patience. Not exactly my favorite thing, as you can imagine."

"Next summer, I'll be free," Sheila announced. "But after, I'll have to serve a mage… one or two years, maybe more. I don't yet know with whom or where."

"You'll likely stay around here," Shaya smiled encouragingly. "Most mages live in Elenshae."

"Yes, true… but you never know," Sheila replied with a hint of doubt. "Let's say I hope so. Okay, who's next?"

Akennor stared into the flames. The thought of their paths soon diverging weighed heavily. In a few years, they would likely be scattered across the world. The idea clenched his heart with painful nostalgia.

"Me then!" Shaya exclaimed, full of enthusiasm.

Darian stared at her intently. He had missed her so much. His best friend, his confidante.

He loved their long conversations, their unique bond. Everything about her seemed charming: her curly chestnut hair, her almond-shaped brown eyes, her round, ever-smiling face.

She straightened, her eyes shining.

"My training is a bit special… I'm destined to become a druid. My mentor says I have great potential, and that makes me really proud. I can spend long moments meditating, listening to nature, feeling the elements around me. It focuses on animals, and the forces of earth, water, sky, fire, even lightning. Later, I'll learn more advanced spells. And who knows? Maybe I'll become a priestess of Kemen, god of earth and elements. If so, I'll be sent to Kementári."

She smiled dreamily.

"At first, it was hard to meditate so often and so long. But now… it brings incredible peace. You feel the force of nature everywhere."

Her tone grew more determined:

"I'd like to specialize in mastering the elements. Few druids in the world can, but they're tremendously powerful."

"And feared by many," Darian remarked.

"Perhaps," she replied with a smile. "But I do it because I love it, not for power. Come on, Akennor, your turn now. No backing out."

He grinned and began, pride gleaming in his eyes.

"I chose dual combat. Not the easiest… at first, it was a real puzzle. Both arms had to move together, my parries and strikes perfectly synchronized."

He mimed his words with a gesture, as if still wielding his weapons.

"I had to train hard, with special exercises just for that. I even asked for help from a specialized teacher. But it paid off."

His smile widened.

"I won the weapons competition, all categories. The medal is in my chest at the academy. I'll show you as soon as I can."

"I suppose you'll join your brother after your training?" Sheila asked, raising an eyebrow.

"Maybe… but nothing is certain," Akennor replied, shrugging. "I could work anywhere: in the cities, even in the service of a king. But… if I had the choice, I'd rather stay here, with you, in this region."

The sun had long since dipped below the horizon, and the smell of roasting chickens filled the air. When all was ready, they sat around the fire. Sheila uncorked a bottle of wine and served each of them.

"This is excellent, Sheila. You're really amazing, Akennor complimented sincerely between bites."

"Fantastic!" Darian exclaimed.

"Yes, amazing. You should show me some tricks," Shaya teased.

Sheila laughed, flattered.

"Thanks, everyone… it's true, I did well."

The rest of the evening passed pleasantly. They drank a bit too much and stayed up until dawn, exchanging scary stories, legends, and epic tales.

The next morning, waking up was hard for all: they had overindulged. Though they each had their own tent, the girls had chosen not to sleep alone: Sheila shared

Akennor's, and Shaya Darian's. When they opened their eyes, the sun was already high in the sky.

"Ugh, my head…" Darian groaned.

"Tell me about it, Akennor muttered," his mouth dry and sticky.

A heavy silence fell, broken only by the crackling embers. Then Darian lifted his head:

"We're not staying here all day."

"You're right," Sheila added, still tired. We should pack our things and get what we need from the village.

With that, they gathered their gear and set off toward the village.

It was a small, simple village, whose inhabitants lived mainly from farming. In the center stood the market square, bustling with traveling merchants and local farmers selling their produce.

Around this square rose a few notable buildings. There was the village's only inn, standing diagonally, halfway between the market and the temple of Kemen. On the other side of the square, an armorer offered weapons and armor of all kinds. His selection was limited, as was the quality, but he also provided forge services, repairing farm tools and shoeing horses.

Right next to the armorer stood a small, dark, dilapidated magic shop. It was run by a solitary old woman, little liked by the villagers. Discreet, she rarely spoke to anyone, and no one really knew her. She sold potions of her own making, healing elixirs, antidotes, and concoctions that enhanced certain abilities. One could also find a few magical artifacts — staffs, cloaks, grimoires — sold at exorbitant prices.

Finally, near the temple of Narya, a row of adjoining houses lined the central square, while to the south of the market stood other homes.

Between these quarters and the main square lay the village elementary school, the one the companions had attended as children.

Besides the market and shops, the village also had its community hall, the mayor's office, a small jail, and the office of the peacekeeper. Between the inn and the blacksmith, a general store sold clothing, food, sweets made by the merchant's wife, as well as a multitude of everyday items.

Sheila and her companions finally reached the village after a long walk under the dense forest canopy. Their footsteps echoed on the planks of the old bridge near the mill, which spanned the Norsa River. They then followed the paved road leading to the inn.

The building stood proudly before them. It was one of the very first constructions in the village, over a century and a half old. With its two massive stories, thick beams, and dark stone, it dominated the surroundings. The inn measured nearly fifteen *maicas* long and twelve wide.

The *maica*, the elders often explained, was a unit created by the master blacksmiths themselves, based on the standard length of a sword blade. Replacing older, imprecise measures, it had gradually imposed its regularity into daily life.

In the past, the inn had served many functions. The rooms were often empty. Its steeply pitched roof was pierced with dormer windows, and each room had one, both at the front and the back of the building.

A wide gallery encircled the inn, supported by solid wooden pillars set at regular intervals, rising up to the roof. The walls were made of rough stone blocks.

The group climbed the steps to the main door and crossed the threshold. The interior proved warm and welcoming. Portraits of the region's pioneers and murals depicting heroic deeds hung on the walls.

At the west end, a large hearth stood. During great celebrations, it served as a rallying point, and game was roasted there.

Large tables occupied the center of the hall, but outside those occasions, they were replaced by round tables seating six.

Opposite the entrance stretched an imposing counter, about half the building's length. One could sit there to drink or chat with the innkeeper, a jovial and friendly man. Behind him, shelves covered the entire wall, stacked with bottles of various spirits.

The inn was almost empty. Bobby, the village drunkard, dozed with his head on the counter, while in the back, the old sorceress read in the shadows, a brownish cup in hand. The companions paid her no attention — out of habit and unease — and headed straight for the bar.

"Hey, hello, youngsters!" called a warm voice.

It was a large, corpulent man with a thick mustache covering his upper lip. His hair was now salt-and-pepper, and he bore a prominent belly. His small eyes and round cheeks gave him a friendly look.

A hardened bachelor, he had never taken a wife nor had children, and slept in one of the inn's rooms. On busy days, he was helped by the blacksmith's wife.

"It's been a while," he said cheerfully. "If my sources are right, you've only just arrived, haven't you?"

"You're right, Josey," Darian replied with a smile.

"Nothing escapes you," Akennor added.

"So, what can I do for you?"

"We'd like to know something," Shaya asked sweetly.

"I'm listening," he said attentively.

"You who know so many stories, perhaps you could enlighten us," Sheila said with a smile.

Josey puffed out his chest, flattered.

"Do you know where Lake Narya is? They say it's nearby, near the mountains… but our information is very vague."

Josey frowned and thought for a moment.

"Sorry, kids, but no, that name means nothing to me. If the lake is around here, it surely goes by another name now. I know this region well, and that name doesn't ring a bell at all."

Josey was indeed the best-informed man in the village. He had many contacts, and people confided in him easily. The number of travelers he had met made him a true source of knowledge.

"Thanks anyway, Josey," Akennor concluded.

"So, what do you plan to do this summer?" the innkeeper asked curiously.

"We'll wander in the forest,"Akennor replied, exchanging a look with his friends, "and maybe go as far as the northern mountains, on my father's lands."

"Very well! Enjoy your youth, my friends," Josey advised.

After thanking him, they headed for the exit.

But as they were about to step out the door, a sharp voice rose behind them:

"Lake Narya, eh? Looking for the temple of the damned, are you? The angry god who cursed his people…"

It was the sorceress speaking, without lifting her eyes from her book. At her words, a shiver ran down the companions' spines. They exchanged silent, uneasy glances.

Akennor, heart pounding, dared to approach. The old woman's face was deeply lined, her nose hooked, her lips thin, her thick white hair strangely silky. Her features radiated age and mystery. Usually reclusive in her shop, *why was she in the inn?*

"Excuse me…" he murmured timidly. "What do you know of this legend?"

The sorceress raised her head.

"Probably what you already know. Few writings exist about what happened." She set her book down and fixed them with her deep, intense blue eyes.

"It is a place where darkness never lifts. Presences lurk in the shadows. Many have perished there… but the evil remains."

She paused, her voice deepening.

"That place is cursed. It should remain sealed, forgotten forever. Great curses reign there… but also great power that lures the foolish and the ambitious."

"Do you know where it is?" Sheila dared ask, curiosity in her voice.

The sorceress opened her eyes wide and looked at each of them in turn, as if to probe their souls.

"You… you all have potential. Perhaps one day you will go there, to face the darkness and banish it forever. But not now… no. You are not ready."

Without another word, she reopened her book and resumed her reading, as if nothing had happened.

"That's it? You won't tell us where it is?" Sheila protested, incredulous.

The old woman slowly lifted her head.

"Return when the time has come… when you feel ready. When I sense you are ready. Then I will tell you."

Her eyes gleamed one last time, and she concluded solemnly:

"Safe travels, my children."

"Come on, let's go. She doesn't know more than we do," Darian muttered, clearly annoyed.

He had always wondered where the old woman had come from and what had driven her to settle in their village.

The companions left the inn. Josey gave them a final wave, to which they responded with a knowing look.

"I need to stop by my house to pick up a few things," Darian explained. "And let my parents know so they won't worry."

"Me too," Shaya added.

"Same for me," Sheila said. "My parents are away, so I'll take the chance."

"In that case," Akennor said, "I'll head home too. Join me as soon as you can."

"Perfect. See you soon," Darian concluded.

They went their separate ways, each to their home. Shaya and Sheila lived in the village center, Darian near the temple of Kemen, and Akennor took the road to his family home. Moments later, he arrived. His mother was working in the vegetable garden, where the crops were beginning to grow.

Illawen straightened up when she saw him.

"Ah, hello Akennor! Did you have a good evening yesterday?" she asked with a smile.

"Yes, it was very nice. We talked almost all night... waking up was hard."

He stepped closer to kiss her. She wrinkled her nose with a laugh.

"You didn't just talk... you had a few drinks, didn't you?"

"Doesn't happen often, Mom."

"I know. And anyway... it's normal, you're young."

"I won't stay long," Akennor explained. "I came to grab a few things, then we'll head to the mountains."

"Good... wise choice. You'll go through our lands?"

"Yes, exactly. I'll get ready before the others arrive." Akennor smiled at his mother and went inside.

A little later, his friends arrived together. Akennor waited for them on the porch, chatting with his mother.

"Hello, Illawen," Darian said politely. "How are you?"

"Very well, thank you," she replied kindly.

They exchanged a few words, then soon after, the group bid farewell to Akennor's mother and set off across the fields.

For that first night, they decided to stay close to the house, to watch over the lands until Akennor's father returned. He appreciated that his friends had accepted this precaution.

They found an ideal spot on a small hill, in a grove amid the fields. By the time the camp was set up, the sun was already sinking below the horizon. Later that evening, four riders entered the village of Dal'norsa from the south. They quickly rode through the streets, easily spotting the house they were looking for, before heading to the inn to rest and eat.

"What a dump," Deidre grumbled as she dismounted.

"Yeah, but just think — it'll all be over soon. We're close to the goal," Dresden retorted.

"About time, I'm sick of this too," Aaron added.

"Shut it!" Parthe ordered. "Let's get inside, have a drink, it'll clear our heads."

They agreed and entered the inn. About twenty customers were inside: some chatting with the innkeeper, others laughing loudly in the back, and a ragged man slumped asleep over the counter.

The band sat at a table, while Parthe approached the bar. Sitting at the counter, he overheard a conversation between Josey and a few men. The innkeeper, busy, motioned for him to wait. But suddenly, Parthe's face froze. He stood abruptly, muttered that he had forgotten something, and hurried back to his companions. Josey shrugged and resumed his conversation.

Leaning over the table, Parthe whispered:

"We need to leave. Now. I'll explain on the way, but we can't waste time. Let's slip out quietly."

The others obeyed without question. Once outside, Parthe told them what he had overheard. Without delay, they mounted their horses and set off westward.

Chapter 6 – The Abduction

They lay on their backs, gazing at the stars in a sky still cloudless.

"What a beautiful night," said Akennor, looking at the stars.

"It's incredible, isn't it? I wonder what they really are," Shaya mused. "We're only supposed to study the stars next year. I can't wait."

Darian yawned so wide it nearly dislocated his jaw.

"Excuse me, but I can't take any more. I'm going to sleep. Will anyone stand watch?"

"No, I don't think it's necessary. We're on my father's lands, let's take advantage of it to rest," Akennor decided.

The others agreed and followed Darian's example. They were all tired from the previous night. The young companions decided not to pitch their shelters: the weather was fine, warm, and the sky was clear, with no threats. They would sleep under the stars. They let the fire die out on its own and soon fell into deep, restorative sleep.

*

Dresden and his band galloped at full speed down the black road.

"From what I've heard," Parthe shouted over the pounding hooves, "his father has a farm not far from here.

They must have taken the path through his lands toward the mountains."

Parthe had a hunch and ordered:

"Slow down. I see a house and a barn nearby. Better to cut across the fields."

"Already there?" Aaron asked, surprised.

"Maybe not. But it's more discreet than the road. Let's try to stay unseen."

"I agree. Let's go," Dresden said, steering his horse aside.

They slipped silently between the young crops like four shadows. A small flame on a hill caught Aaron's eye.

"I see firelight up there," he said, stopping.

"It's them!" Dresden exclaimed. "Finally!"

"Parthe, go see what they're doing."

Parthe obeyed at once, dismounted, and vanished into the night. Dresden and the others waited in silence. Shortly after, Parthe returned.

"They're all asleep. This is the moment."

*

Akennor's sleep was restless: fear, despair, and loneliness pierced his soul. The world wavered, rivers turned to blood, and the earth split open into infernal abysses. Voices cried for help, others wailed in sorrow.

Suffering engulfed Akennor. A sinister echo — a malevolent voice speaking in an unknown tongue — laughed and resounded in his dream. He writhed, struggled to escape, clenching his eyes shut.

Suddenly, he woke with a start, gasping, drenched in sweat. As he opened his eyes, a shadowy figure lunged at him with sword in hand. His warrior reflexes saved his life:

he rolled aside, seized his blades, and shouted for his friends to wake.

Dark figures were attacking Shaya. Two of them gagged and bound her as she struggled and cried, but no sound could escape.
Darian and Sheila awoke in shock.

Akennor roared a battle cry and engaged his foe. Caught by surprise but already alert, he resisted fiercely. Though shaken by the ambush, his intense training quickly helped him regain the advantage.
He struck in rapid succession. Dresden barely managed to parry. Akennor attacked with both blades, then diverted his left at the last moment to strike Dresden's right shoulder. Dresden deflected the second blade but still took a deep wound.

Furious at the treacherous attack, Darian seized his war hammer and charged at Parthe, who was carrying Shaya. As he raised his weapon, a click rang out, followed by sharp pain in his side. A slender figure stepped into the firelight, crossbow in hand.

Another bolt threatened Darian, when a woman's voice, full of rage, shouted:
"Templa pilini!"

A ball of blue, crackling energy smashed into Aaron, hurling him through the air. Sheila, shaken and her heart racing, ran at Parthe, who was already fleeing with Shaya. A green flash streaked the sky — Sheila collapsed to the ground. Aaron staggered to his feet, dazed, but managed to follow Parthe.

Deidre rushed to aid Dresden, who was in trouble. Akennor parried a strike aimed at his stomach, pivoted, and slashed Dresden across the chest and right arm.

Dresden screamed in pain and dropped his sword. Akennor turned on Deidre, but she was faster.

"Sirpë!"

Roots burst from the ground, seizing his arms and legs. The bonds tightened, forcing him to drop his weapons. The harder he fought, the stronger they held. Suddenly, horses neighed: Parthe and Aaron were back with the mounts.

Dresden, wounded, picked up his sword and hauled himself into the saddle. The mercenaries vanished into the night at full speed, Shaya bound on Parthe's horse. Akennor watched his friend disappear. Why had they attacked? Why Shaya?

Darian was first to rise, blood pouring from his side. With his good arm, he cut Akennor free.

"Who were those bastards? Why did they take Shaya?" he cried.

"I don't know, but they knew what they were doing," Akennor muttered.

He thought of Josey, the talkative innkeeper. Only he — and Akennor's mother — knew where they were.

His heart clenched. Please, let nothing have happened to her…

"Oh, my head… Sheila groaned. That bitch… Wait until I get her. She'll pay for this."

"Let's see my mother. If she's safe, we'll take horses and chase them."

Relieved, Akennor found Illawen awake, waiting.

"What happened?" she asked, horrified at Darian's condition.

"We were attacked by four strangers… they took Shaya," Akennor explained.

Illawen gasped in shock.

"What?"

"We must leave immediately, Mother. We can't lose their trail."

"Yes, but I must tend to poor Darian first. It will only take a moment. Come with me, Darian."

In the kitchen, she cut his shoulder to remove the bolt, then smeared it with a viscous green ointment. Darian screamed in pain.

"It's a family recipe," she reassured him. "It fights infection and neutralizes most poisons."

"It was poisoned?" Darian asked shakily.

"No doubt. But you'll be fine now."

She dressed the wound tightly until the bleeding eased. Soon after, Darian returned with her, pale but determined.

"We must go. If we delay, they'll be too far ahead."

Akennor hugged his mother tightly.

"I love you, Mother. Don't worry, we'll bring her back."

"I love you too. Be careful. She handed him a flask of thick green liquid. Take this, you'll need it."

They saddled the horses and rode off into the night.

Their second stop was Shaya's parents' house, across from the magic shop.

A two-story home with a balcony over the front door. Shaya's father, a bald man with a wooden leg, answered, confused at their late arrival. Her mother, round and kind-faced, joined him quickly.

"What's going on? Where's Shaya?" she demanded.

Akennor explained:

"We were attacked by four black-clad strangers… they took her. I think she was their target."

The parents froze. Tears welled in her mother's eyes.

Her father's voice trembled:

"I must tell you something. Eighteen years ago, a priest of Calaista brought us a child."

"He was a distant cousin, and I was his only living family. I knew him well; we used to see each other often before he entered the monastery."

Her mother stood behind him, listening in silence.

"He didn't tell me who her parents were. He only asked me to be very discreet, because she was in danger."

"He couldn't keep her at the monastery — too many people coming and going, too great a risk the secret would get out."

"Only he, my wife, and I knew."

"I didn't really believe his fears... I knew he tended to exaggerate. Years went by, and we thought the threat was behind us... perhaps it had never truly existed."

He pulled his wife into his arms. Shaya was their daughter in every way that mattered.

Darian spoke again:

"A priest of Calaista, from the monastery not far from here?"

The father nodded.

"But... that's my monastery," Darian said, stunned.

Then a chilling thought crossed his mind. He went pale.

"If they knew where she lived... and only the priest knew..."

"That means they went to the monastery first," Akennor concluded.

"Oh no... not that..." Darian breathed.

"We don't have a moment to lose," Sheila said.

"We'll find her, I swear it," Akennor told Shaya's parents.

"Bring my baby back!" the mother cried. "She's all I have!"

Those words broke the young warrior's heart.

"Come now, Marya, they'll do everything they can…"

"Good luck, Be careful."

Eyes brimming, the father gently led his wife back inside. The companions mounted at once and headed south, toward Darian's school. One encouraging sign: four sets of hoofprints led the same way.

They sighted the monastery in early afternoon. They had galloped through much of the night and morning. Exhausted, they saw that the tracks continued on, but the kidnappers were nowhere in sight.

Akennor and his companions tied their horses to a tree near the main gate. Darian went toward the building, with Akennor and Sheila close behind. They soon found a guard's body facedown, a crossbow bolt buried in his throat.

They didn't linger: the monastery door stood wide open. Inside, all was quiet.

"I don't like this…" Akennor murmured.

Deaf to everything, Darian rushed for the east wing. They found the priest dead, lying in his blood.

At the sight of his murdered mentor, Darian cried out in rage and threw himself toward him.

"NO! It's unjust! It's unjust!"

He collapsed to his knees, head bowed, as a flood of tears streamed down his face.

Total incomprehension, the feeling of a soul torn apart, smothered him. A dull, invisible pain crushed his spirit. His friends came closer, silent, respecting his grief. It was too much… far too much for him.

The apprentice paladin was shattered, his heart pierced by unseen blades. Helplessness gnawed at him.

A dart pierced the victim's throat.

"That bastard's work again…" Darian cursed, clutching his shoulder.

"He plays support," Akennor explained. "He strikes from a distance, or when the others are in trouble."

He looked at Sheila.

"They have attack patterns. They're rather clever."

"Indeed, Sheila agreed. We'll have to be careful if we cross them again."

Akennor tried to keep a cool head despite the horror of the scene. Overwhelmed, Sheila fought to swallow the anger rising in her.

Darian pulled himself together and got to his feet with difficulty. His eyes were red, his cheeks still wet.

"Are you all right, Darian?" Sheila asked softly.

He didn't answer. She stepped closer and embraced him.

Suddenly, something glittering on the floor by the wall caught Darian's eye. He gently moved Sheila aside and approached.

"What is it?" she exclaimed.

Akennor turned. Darian held a small object in his hand.

"Some kind of badge," he said, intrigued.

The symbol depicted a skull with two large horns at the brow. A dagger pierced the skull and a serpent plunged through the mouth, emerged at the back, and coiled over the crown. Its head drooped a little toward the forehead like a sinister coronet.

"Have you ever seen this symbol?" Darian asked.

"No, never," Sheila said.

"Me neither," Akennor replied. "But it doesn't bode well."

"What do we do?" Sheila asked.

"We follow their trail without hesitation," Akennor said firmly.

"But we don't know who they are, where they're going, or whether they have allies…"

Darian resumed:

"If they want to move quickly north or south — which seems the case since they aren't heading east — they might try to take a ship at Elenshae."

"I agree," Akennor said.

"Then I suggest we stop first at the headquarters of the Order of Calaista. They might help us… and tell us what this symbol means."

"And it's almost on the way to Elenshae," Sheila approved.

"Yes, but first, let's eat and rest. We'll need our strength to continue," Akennor said.

The companions agreed. The adrenaline had faded, leaving only fatigue and hunger.

Akennor led the horses inside the monastery grounds. Darian carried his mentor's body to the rear courtyard. Sheila went to prepare a simple meal.

Akennor helped Darian build a pyre. They laid the old priest's body upon it, then those of the guards. The fire was lit.

Darian sat for a long time, staring into the flames devouring one of the beings he respected most.

"It's a great loss, not only for me. Many admired him. They'll pay for this," he said, his voice tight with rage and sorrow."

"I'm with you. We'll hunt them down — every last one."

They remained silent until Sheila called them.

They ate without pleasure, only to regain strength. Then, exhausted, they lay down, hoping for sleep.

Akennor told himself the bandits must have wounded to tend as well… They wouldn't be able to get very far.

*

"Enough!" Dresden roared. "We stop for a moment — I can't go on…"

The gash he had taken hurt terribly. Deidre had bandaged him quickly, but the wound still bled. Dresden was weakening.

Aaron was suffering too: a stabbing pain twisted his side. He would never have believed a magical projectile could hurt so much — and yet he had taken several in his life.

Parthe and Deidre were uninjured.

"Yes, all right, Parthe said. We must have outdistanced them… if they're even following us."

But if they are, they'll have had to stop too. They may have a wounded man, even a dead one.

"They're following us, in my opinion," Deidre said. "Their reaction was too quick."

They stopped in a clearing at the edge of the forest. The horses were tied up. They settled Shaya, still bound, near a rock a few *maicas* from the fire.

Deidre redressed Dresden's wound.

"He's pretty skilled, that youngster, isn't he? And not bad-looking, too," she taunted.

"Yeah… skilled, so-so. I'd have finished him off," Dresden growled.

"Don't make me laugh," Parthe said. "I saw your duel. You were outmatched."

"Shut it…" Dresden shot back. "I'd like to have seen you there."

Parthe, clear-eyed, knew he'd have struggled as well. Unlike Dresden, he acknowledged the strength of their enemies and adapted to it.

"We have to admit we underestimated them," he said. "Aaron's hurting, and that was only a novice who hit him…"

"Yeah, well. We couldn't have known. Anyway, they don't know who we are or what we want. Once we reach Elenshae, we'll be out of reach," Dresden concluded.

The others agreed. The drop-off point was unknown to everyone… including themselves.

They relaxed a little and prepared a quick meal. The mercenaries lay down early. Tomorrow promised to be harsh. Shaya remained tied all evening. Deidre removed her gag to feed her, but Shaya tried to bite. She got a slap, and the gag went back on.

She understood none of what was happening. She remembered the dark shapes pinning her to the ground. She had glimpsed her friends during the fight — Akennor wounding their leader, Sheila furious, Darian running to help… then nothing. Blackness.

She had struggled like a madwoman, but Parthe had knocked her out. When she came to, she was bound across a saddle, her nose over the ground racing past beneath her.

She cried.
Why her? Why take her?

She had tried to tell them they were mistaken, but Deidre had answered there was no mistake. She would soon learn why.

Shaya felt wretched. She hadn't even been able to defend herself. She hoped her friends would come to her rescue, but feared they'd get hurt for her sake. In her heart, she knew they would do anything for her. She closed her eyes and tried to calm the panic clawing at her. She sought refuge in meditation, hoping a solution would come.

*

The sinister voice laughed again. Akennor heard it more and more clearly — as if it were drawing closer. He ran in the dark... without moving forward. Despair choked him. He woke with a start, drenched in sweat, almost more tired than before he'd fallen asleep.

Has he was the first awake, Akennor let his friends sleep a little longer. They all needed rest. The young warrior prepared a breakfast to take with them and woke the others.

"Up! Come on, my friends, time to go."

Sheila and Darian struggled to their feet. It was still night; dawn was far off.

"Did you manage to sleep at all?" Akennor asked.

"Not really," Darian groaned.

"Me neither. One nightmare after another," Sheila said.

"Ready?" Akennor asked. "Darian, do you know the way?"

"I've never been there, but I know the route. By the main road it's long. Crossing the Black Forest would save time… but it's riskier."

"And after that?"

"After that, a path leads straight to the stronghold. It's not complicated."

"Then we take the shortest way," Akennor said.

They checked they had forgotten nothing, then set off toward the looming shadows of the Black Forest.

Chapter 7 – The She-Wolf and the Sage

The entrance to the forest was relatively close, and it would take them about a day to cross. This path through the woods was the shortest, but also the least traveled, for it was far more dangerous than the main road. The bandits had preceded them. The horses' tracks were clearly visible despite the harsh terrain.

"They passed this way," Akennor confirmed.

They were on the right trail.

"It's the fastest path. Makes sense for scoundrels trying to escape," Darian said.

"Come on, let's hurry. The tracks aren't very old."

Despite the forest's density, the first rays of sunlight filtered between the branches. The Black Forest was well named: thick, dark, composed almost entirely of tall conifers. A lone traveler would have had difficulty passing between the trees, they were so close and thick.

Stories told of people once smothered in their sleep by trees whose quiet had been disturbed — the trees' branches wrapping around them in anger. Other tales said that during certain phases of the moon, travelers who ventured into the forest never returned.

Darian recounted these kinds of stories for much of the morning. Then they fell silent, listening carefully to the sinister sounds of the woods.

The deeper they went, the heavier the shadows grew, until the light nearly vanished. They stopped around early afternoon to stretch their legs and eat a quick meal.

Sheila found the spot where the kidnappers had spent part of the night. The coals of a small fire were cold, and they searched in vain for clues.

Quickly mounting again, they pressed on, determined to leave the forest before nightfall. None of them wished to spend a night within it.

At one point, Akennor thought he saw a gray blur in the distance — something resembling a wolf. A large wolf. He blinked and rubbed his eyes: the vision vanished as quickly as it had come. Perhaps, he thought, he was only imagining things.

Darian had said that weary travelers could suffer hallucinations, even lose their minds. Akennor decided to keep it to himself. His friends didn't need more worries.

After a ride that felt endless, the forest's edge suddenly appeared ahead. The sun was already descending — another day was nearing its end. At the forest's exit was a perfect spot to camp: a natural hollow at the foot of a small hill, surrounded by large boulders. Darian went to fetch firewood. Akennor set about unpacking their blankets. Sheila began preparing food. As he untied the blankets, Akennor saw the great gray-white wolf again.

He shook his head. Once more, it was gone. These visions were becoming annoying — they were out of the forest now, couldn't they leave him alone?

Sheila prepared a small stew with meat she had taken from the monastery's kitchens.

"That hits the spot. Delicious, Sheila," Akennor said, patting his stomach.

The sky was now completely overcast, clouds covering the stars.

"Tomorrow will likely bring rain," Darian said.

Suddenly, Akennor's warrior's ear caught a familiar sound: the faint metallic clink of weapons. He leapt up, blades drawn. Out of nowhere, an axe flew toward him, which he parried with his swords.

All around, bestial cries and roars erupted.

"We're surrounded!" Darian cried.

"Aure!"

Sheila gasped, startled, her voice trembling. She cast a spell to light the area. A glowing orb rose into the air, then burst into countless small lights that floated above them.

Hideous faces appeared in the glow, as if stepping out of nightmares: humanoid creatures with dark green skin. They were broad and muscular, with long, horned fangs jutting from their lower jaws, and pig-like snouts.

Darian stood dumbstruck.

"Orcs — they're ORCS!" he cried.

He remembered reading about them in class: bloodthirsty monsters thought to exist only in tales and ancient legends.

The horde charged the three companions, snarling.

"Dûlu sairina!"

Sheila raised her hands, and a great transparent bubble enveloped her for protection.

Akennor leapt into the fray, unleashing a terrifying war cry. The first monster fell quickly — unable to block his fatal strike, it lost its head.

The second did not last much longer. Akennor parried effectively, created an opening, and drove both his blades into the heart of a third orc. Darian's rage, fueled by his determination, burst forth in a cry that stunned his opponents for a moment.

Taking advantage of their shock, he smashed one's skull with his hammer. Another he struck in the ribs so violently that, though it blocked with its arm, it was hurled backward, landing helpless on its back — where Darian finished it with a crushing blow to the head.

Sheila hurled a magical projectile at another attacker. The orc was blasted into the air, slammed into the ground, and lay stunned.

She rubbed her hands together.

"Carnë-narë!"

She shouted, and her hands burst into flames. Screaming, she hurled herself into the melee with her short sword, igniting as many monsters as she could. The beasts shrieked in agony, writhing and clawing to extinguish the magical fire. Though the companions fought bravely, the orcs were numerous, and they would soon be overwhelmed.

Akennor slashed one's leg, then severed its head. Now a great orc stood before him, wielding a two-handed sword. He struck first, but the creature parried. His second blade lunged at the orc's belly, but again it blocked — this one was more skilled. So Akennor shifted to close combat, both blades flashing. The orc defended, but Akennor pivoted, dragging his right arm low across the creature's abdomen. Its belly split open, entrails spilling onto the ground, filling the air with a foul stench.

Akennor prepared to strike another foe when an arrow whistled through the air and buried itself in his shoulder. The impact was brutal, the pain searing. He struggled to remain conscious. Another orc charged, axe raised, ready to end him.

But before it could strike, the wolf Akennor had glimpsed earlier sprang from the shadows. With powerful jaws, it tore into the orc's throat, clawing its chest savagely.

Darian, too, was struck by an arrow in the leg, halting his advance. Only Sheila's quick spell saved him from being crushed, her projectile blasting the orc aside.

But she paid for it — an enemy's blade cut across her belly. Their new ally lunged upon this foe, leaping onto its back and snapping its neck with a sickening crack.

Akennor dealt with the hidden archer. Though wounded again by a final clumsy arrow to his thigh, he pressed on, decapitating the grimacing orc with a skilled maneuver.

Darian crushed yet another foe despite his injury. The orc tried to block with a wooden shield, but Darian's hammer shattered it, flinging the creature down, where he pounded its chest until it was still.

"Úlévima!"

Sheila's powerful voice rang out. Her spell froze the last attacker, and she slit its throat. They regrouped by the fire. Around fifteen orc corpses lay mutilated or charred on the ground. Akennor's blades dripped with their dark red, almost black blood.

"They ambushed us. They must have been following… and we saw nothing."

"Good thing you came to our aid, noble beast."

They looked at the wolf: a great gray beast with a near-black mane.

Could it be? Akennor wondered, recalling what he'd seen earlier in the forest.

The gray of its fur faded to white along its belly. Its ears and tail stood proudly, radiating strength and assurance. The companions were intrigued — what was this creature doing here, and why had it intervened on their behalf?

The wolf sat before them, unmoving. Then a thin mist swirled around it. The fog thickened, the form blurred, grew larger, and transformed. Instinctively, the companions gripped their weapons, unsure of what to expect.

Suddenly, the mist dissolved. Where a majestic wolf had stood now appeared a strikingly beautiful young woman. Her skin was pale, her long, wavy jet-black hair framing a flawlessly sculpted face. Her deep blue eyes shone, her nose was small and perfect, her lips full. Her body was equally flawless: tall, slender, with graceful curves. She stood as tall as Akennor.

She wore pale gray trousers and a matching fitted tunic, with a darker gray hooded cape. If Akennor and Darian looked on with admiration, Sheila was filled with jealousy. *Why is he looking at her that way? What does she have that I don't?* The sight pierced Sheila's heart.

She regarded the stranger with both contempt and curiosity.
"Who are you?"

The woman lifted her head suddenly, her silky hair rippling back from her face.

"My name is Milenna," she said with a slight bow.

"I've been watching you since you set camp."

"You weren't following us through the forest?" Akennor asked. He clearly remembered glimpsing the wolf earlier.

"No, not at all. I had been tracking the orcs for days. I outpaced them, looking for a place to ambush them. I loathe those monsters. Then I saw you, and decided to observe instead."

"When I saw you in trouble, I stepped in," she added with a smile, clearly satisfied with the sight of so many orc corpses.

"Thank you, you saved us," Akennor said gratefully.

"Oh, it was my pleasure."

Her eyes sparkled with satisfaction.

"But you three are wounded! she exclaimed. Come with me, my home is nearby. Quickly — orcs often poison their arrows. We must not waste time!"

"Let's go," Darian agreed, clutching his leg.

They hastily packed and mounted their weary horses.

The mounts balked, and Darian, impatient, drove his spurs harshly.

"Come on, move, you wretched beast!"

"ENOUGH!" Milenna shouted angrily. "That is no way to treat a loyal animal."

Akennor quickly defended his friend.

"Forgive him, we've endured much these last days. We're all at our limit."

Milenna seemed to understand. She whispered strange words to the horses, and they obeyed at once.

"Let them go. They'll follow me."

She shifted back into wolf form and trotted west. The companions, awestruck, followed despite their pain.

Not long after, they reached a rustic stone house with a pitched wooden roof, radiating warmth and comfort.

"Come in, Milenna said. My father, Svealëdor, will tend to you. I'll stable the horses."

Inside, the main room glowed with the light of a stone hearth. At the far end stood a large wooden table; two comfortable armchairs flanked the fire.

An old man approached — his hair nearly white, his beard long over his round belly. Short and stout, his face was kindly.

"Oh heavens, you're terribly injured! My name is Svealëdor. Please, come in. Quickly, lie down in the beds next door."

His voice was gentle and warm.

Akennor dragged himself to the bed the old man indicated. Sheila lay down on another. Darian nearly collapsed, and Svealëdor had to help him to a small chamber.

Milenna soon returned.

"I found them nearby. They were attacked by the orcs I told you of."

"I guessed as much, my dear. Come, help me."

He handed her a flask of pale blue liquid and a white cloth.

"See to that one first, he said, pointing to Akennor. I'll tend the young woman, then the last."

Exhaustion overtook them. Darian felt better once laid down in a soft bed. A faint candle glowed by his side.

"Ilfümë!"

At the word, the youths fell into a deep, dreamless sleep. It was a sleep without dreams or nightmares, deep and restorative. Akennor slowly reopened his eyes.

He felt reinvigorated. A faint tightness lingered in his thigh and shoulder. A soft white bandage covered both wounds.

He turned his head to the side and saw Sheila, fast asleep, bundled in cozy-looking blue sheets. No sound came from the small chamber at the back. Akennor tried to get up. He sat on the bed. His wounds burned like bites.

He also realized he was wearing only his underclothes, and wondered who had undressed him… Grimacing in pain, he stood with difficulty. Leaning on the bedframe, he began to get dressed.

Akennor searched for his weapons, but in vain. He hated not knowing where his swords were. He moved to the room where Darian rested. The latter still slept, peaceful beneath a green blanket pulled up to his neck. His clothes, freshly laundered, were folded neatly on the small chest at the foot of the bed.

Akennor turned back and followed the short hallway leading to the main room. The old man was seated in an armchair, while Milenna occupied the one near the front door.

They both turned as Akennor approached.

"How are you, son? Well rested?" Svealëdor asked cheerfully.

"I should hope so, after an entire day of sleep," Milenna replied offhandedly.

"What ?!" Akennor cried, visibly outraged that he had slept so long without being woken. An entire day… lost, he thought angrily. They couldn't afford to waste a moment — his friend's life depended on it.

"Come now, my child," said the old man, rising to offer him his seat. "What troubles you?" Svealëdor asked with concern.

Akennor sat heavily in the comfortable chair. He was weary, despair gnawing at him. *How will we ever succeed?* he wondered, anxious.

He slowly raised his head, looking at Milenna and Svealëdor. He sighed, then began recounting: how they had been attacked in the night, their meeting with the adoptive parents, the massacre at the monastery, then the forest crossing and the battle against the orcs.

Akennor told it all with detachment, as if he were relating a story he had only heard.

"Have you any idea who they are?" Akennor asked, staring straight into the old man's eyes.

Svealëdor shook his head.

"I truly don't know. There aren't enough clues."

Then Akennor remembered the badge found at the monastery. Rising suddenly, wincing in pain, he went to retrieve it from Darian's bag.

"I'll be right back," he told them.

A few moments later he returned and placed the insignia in Svealëdor's hand. The sage, intrigued, lifted it close to his eyes, turned it over, inspecting every side.

"Hmm… this symbol is familiar, yet I cannot place it."

He paused briefly, then continued:

"I am sorry, my child, but my memory is failing me."

He handed the badge to Milenna, who scrutinized it in turn.

"If I've forgotten what this symbol represents," said Svealëdor, "I do know where you might find the answer… and very likely, aid as well."

Akennor's eyes widened — the old man had his full attention.

"There is a fortress not far from here. It is the headquarters of the Order of Calaista, a gathering of Paladins."

They will certainly be very interested to know who murdered Ardoras, for he was one of their own, and among the Order's most respected.

"That is where we were headed, for Darian is an apprentice paladin, and Ardoras was his mentor."

Svealëdor's face clouded with sorrow and understanding.

"It must be so hard for him: a friend abducted, a teacher slain… I knew Ardoras myself. I spoke with him several times. He was a good and wise man. Such a premature death is truly grievous."

"I will accompany you to the fortress," Milenna declared firmly. "I too wish to know what this means."

She handed the badge back to Akennor.

"Gladly!" Akennor accepted. "Your help will be invaluable, and I am already grateful."

Footsteps sounded. Sheila, followed by Darian, appeared, looking still drowsy.

"Ah, good morning, young ones! How are you?" the old man asked.

"I ache all over," Sheila said with a grimace as she sat at the table.

"I'm a little better," said Darian. "My shoulder still hurts, but my leg is fine."

"The arrows were large, but not poisoned. Healing is usually faster in such cases. But your shoulder wound is nasty, Darian. I stitched it to help it mend," Milenna said, rising.

The sun was nearly set. A faint orange glow lit the room through the window. A delicious smell of stew filled the air, wafting from a second hearth in the kitchen.

The kitchen opened directly onto the main room, with no dividing wall, though a stone partition separated it from the back chamber. Cabinets and shelves laden with jars lined the wall.

The old man stood and announced:

"You must be very hungry. Come, let's eat and continue our talk."

Milenna set plates and utensils as Akennor and his friends took their places. Svealëdor placed the heavy iron cauldron on a slab in the table's center. A metal ladle protruded. He filled their bowls.

"It smells wonderful!" Sheila exclaimed. "And I'm starving! By the way, how long were we asleep?"

"Yes, how long?" Darian echoed.

"Nearly a whole day," Akennor replied wearily.

Sheila and Darian exchanged a look.

"What ?! But we should have left already!" Darian cried, leaping to his feet.

"Sit back down, my child. You were in dire need of rest and care."

Darian obeyed at once. He was weak, and rising so suddenly had left him dizzy.

"Speaking of care, Akennor," the old man continued, "while going through your things, I noticed a green potion... and it intrigues me."

Akennor raised his eyes, chewing a piece of meat. Where is this going? he wondered.

"What intrigues you, exactly?" he asked.

"I wonder where you got such a potion," Svealëdor replied.

To Akennor it was merely a healing potion like many others. He swallowed a mouthful of vegetables.

"Well… it's just a healing potion, like those found everywhere, I suppose. Perhaps a bit different, since it's homemade. My mother alone knows the recipe."

Svealëdor's eyes widened with interest. The others listened closely, intrigued. Only Milenna and Svealëdor truly knew the potion's properties — and its origin.

"Hmm… Do you know where your mother comes from?" the old man asked, stepping closer.

Akennor, seated at his right, looked up at him. The question struck him as strange. He realized he had no idea of his mother's origins. He remembered asking once, but she had always evaded the answer.

He looked at Milenna and the old man, puzzled.

"No, I don't. Nor do I think my brother knows… Why this sudden interest?"

"You see, Akennor, this potion is unique. It follows a recipe known only to a mysterious, distant people," Svealëdor said gravely.

"I once saw such a potion with a great sage who knew of that people. It was long ago… centuries, it seems now. I was young, wandering in the far western plains."

Svealëdor spoke with nostalgia, the weight of years pressing on him.

"Barbarians attacked me, but a powerful mage came to my aid and healed me with this very potion. That elixir can neutralize even the deadliest poisons, cure fevers, hasten healing, and soothe pain."

"Even that mage did not know how to make it. He had obtained it during a journey to a far-off land. He told me little, only that it lay far to the south, deep within vast, unexplored forests."

His gaze grew distant.

"What matters more to me is that land itself, rather than the potion."

He fixed Akennor intently.

"Never before had I heard of a member of that people living among us."

Akennor was stunned. His father had spoken true: he had brought his wife back from one of his journeys.

So many questions filled his mind. He longed to return and confront his mother with the truth. But Shaya needed them — they could not abandon her. Perhaps he would never learn his mother's secret. The thought pained him deeply.

"Today, I am too old. Even if I knew where this people live, I would not have the strength to go," Svealëdor admitted.

"Oh, Father, you exaggerate. You're still strong," Milenna said.

"I always thought your mother a little mysterious… but now I begin to understand," Darian added.

"Yes, interesting indeed," Sheila said. "But not relevant to our cause right now." She looked at Akennor and Darian in turn. "We should leave quickly. We can't be far now, right Darian?"

Jolted from his thoughts, Darian answered:

"No, not much farther. Half a day's ride at most, to the southwest."

"Exactly. The path straight ahead will lead you directly there."

"I had heard the orcs were exterminated… Yet we just faced a well-armed band. Do you know anything about this?" Akennor asked, remembering past talks with his brother.

Svealëdor nodded gravely.

"The history of the orcs goes back long ago. Legend says they were created by a demonic prince named Morthag, forged from volcanic ash mixed with elven blood. He poured his malice into them, making them his pawns, soldiers to conquer the world of men."

All listened intently.

"Long ago, demons walked this land. They created monsters to aid them: orcs, trolls, goblins, even entire races of dragons sworn to evil. A titanic war followed — the War of the Abyss... Evil was subdued, the demons banished forever to their infernal world. Then came the Wars of the Great Deliverance, of which you may have heard. Their goal was to annihilate all abominations born of darkness and their masters."

"As you saw yesterday, the purge was not complete. The orcs have clearly survived... and now they return. For centuries, none had seen one. For about a year, Milenna has encountered them — and hunted them relentlessly."

"They're cunning and sly, hard to spot," Milenna added.

She explained how, about a year earlier, she had first sighted three of them — silent, watchful. Svealëdor had urged her not to attack, to wait until they revealed their intent... then strike. She had obeyed, tracking them, until their numbers and activity grew. The resurgence troubled her deeply.

"They're preparing something, I'm certain. But what?" she said darkly.

The companions pondered in silence, convinced harder times lay ahead. They had to find their friend before it was too late. Akennor finished his stew with a last spoonful of sauce.

"Thank you, Svealëdor, that was excellent. But we must leave without delay. We've already lost precious time. Every second counts."

The others agreed, thanking Svealëdor warmly for his hospitality, and Milenna for saving them.

"Milenna will accompany us to the Order's fortress," Akennor announced.

Sheila received the news with some reserve, though she acknowledged the value of Milenna's help.

"Perfect! We'll need her if we face more of those wretches," Darian said. "By the way, Milenna... how do you explain that wolf transformation?"

Milenna blushed at the question.

"I am a druid — close to nature and animals. The wolf is my favorite. One day I found a text explaining how to shapeshift. With Svealëdor's help, I learned. It's long and perilous... but worth it. I can nearly do it at will, though it drains me greatly."

"I, however, do not shapeshift," the old sage said with a smile, sensing the question. "I am just an ordinary druid.

When at last they were ready, Svealëdor gave them provisions, a vial of healing potion, and a strong antidote.

"Good luck in your quest, and be very careful."

Once more, Akennor and his companions thanked him. Then they mounted up.

Milenna lingered with Svealëdor.

"You're leaving with them, aren't you?" the old man asked, his voice breaking though he forced a smile.

Milenna remembered her nightmares of arms dragging her into the earth... and a gray-eyed stranger pulling her free.

"Yes. I feel I must go. When I saw that badge, I recognized an ancient evil... like an imprint I know."

Sadness filled her — leaving the man who had been a father to her was painful.

"I understand. Your time has come to fulfill your destiny. Go, and be safe. I am proud of you," Svealëdor said, embracing her tightly.

It was hard to let her go. After all, she was his daughter — though not by blood. He had taken her in as a baby, entrusted to him by a powerful mage just before his death.

Tears welled in his eyes. An oppressive feeling came over him — that he might never see her again.

"I will return," she promised with resolve.

"Go now… they await you."

He kissed her one last time on the cheek and returned inside heavily, the years weighing on his shoulders. Alone, he wept. His beloved daughter was leaving for the unknown. His heart ached.

Milenna mounted Kintaro, her proud black stallion, as tall and spirited as his rider. They set off at a trot, lanterns swaying with their staffs, the narrow path forcing them into single file, swallowed by shadows.

Chapter 8 – The Order of Calaista

They arrived within sight of the imposing fortress. The sun was just... of the ground, thus isolating the castle like a fortified island.

Two massive, slender square towers rose in the center, at equal distance from the ramparts.

They seemed to spring from an imposing fortified building... now revealing the silhouettes of the guards posted on the ramparts. The journey had taken place without incident and almost entirely... more so because their wounds were not completely healed. Large banners, proudly fluttering in the wind, bore the symbol... silver war hammers set before a coppery shield.

When they reached the main gate, a guard shouted to them:
"What do you want?"
Darian stepped forward to answer him.
"I am an apprentice paladin at the monastery of Calaista not far from here and we have come to report an attack and the murder of Ardoras."
A few moments later, the massive iron drawbridge lowered with a chorus of screeching hinges and clattering

chains. The group crossed the metal bridge and was greeted by two armored guards. Their armor was made of solid steel plates covering their shoulders, arms, thighs, and legs. Across their chest, they wore a breastplate engraved with the symbol of the Order.

Beneath this protection, they wore dark blue tunics. The soldiers stationed on the ramparts carried a crossbow and a war hammer, strapped to a wide black leather belt secured by a clasp at the thigh. Inside the walls, the companions halted their mounts and dismounted.

Two young squires promptly took the horses and led them to the stables. The inner courtyard, vast and well-kept, was carpeted with neatly trimmed green grass. The stables stood to the right of the entrance, just beyond the guard posts occupying each corner of the fortress.

Before them rose the main building, from which two towers soared. Broad steps stretched across the length of the edifice, forming a wide staircase that led to the main entrance. Tall stone columns, carved in the likeness of armored knights, priests, or mages, rose from the ground to the sloping roof.

"Come, follow me. I will take you to the head of the Order. He wishes to speak with you."

The guard was young, likely a recent arrival, but he was tall and broad-shouldered. He seemed proud to be here, serving such an honorable institution. The group followed him, escorted by another guard bringing up the rear.

They climbed the staircase, crossed the main door, and entered a long corridor at the end of which a staircase appeared. At last, they reached a dark red wooden door, its frame beautifully engraved with runic symbols—likely magical—whose meaning they did not know.

Their guide gently pushed the door open and invited them inside. The walls were lined with books from floor to ceiling, carefully protected behind tall glass cabinets.

At the far end of the room, a large window covered with a magnificent lattice of polished wood formed an entire wall. A few *maicas* away stood the wooden desk of the leader. He was an old man, his face marked with deep wrinkles. His heavy eyelids drooped over pale blue eyes that still sparkled despite his years. A salt-and-pepper beard reached the base of his neck, while his equally gray hair fell in thick locks across his shoulders.

He seemed robust despite his age. When he saw the young people, he rose from his wooden chair upholstered in dark blue fabric embroidered with the symbol of the Order.

"Welcome, my children. My name is Orendil. What brings you here?"

"Tell me."

Orendil glanced at the guard.

"You may leave us now, Samuel, thank you."

The latter bowed and slipped away silently, taking the other guard with him.

"According to what I've been told…"

The elder continued, inviting them to sit on one of the couches, covered with the same fabric as his chair and placed perpendicularly to the desk.

"You bring bad news?"

The old man took his place on the couch facing them. This time it was Darian who spoke. He recounted everything that had happened since their attack in the middle of the night.

Akennor, Sheila, and Milenna remained silent, letting Darian speak, while pondering recent events. Orendil took on a dark, sorrowful look at the announcement of the massacre at the monastery.

"What a misfortune…" he murmured, eyes vacant.

"I am going to send men at once to set things… you did well to burn the bodies," said Orendil, grateful.

"I understand you didn't have time to do more."

Akennor handed the badge to Darian, who showed it to Orendil.

"We found this at the scene. Do you know what it might mean?"

Orendil examined the object closely, turning it over on all sides.

"This symbol looks familiar… I've seen it before, somewhere, but I couldn't say when, or where, nor exactly what it represents."

The sage strained to remember, but part of his memory seemed out of reach. The companions were bitterly disappointed by this. They had so hoped to obtain answers that would let them move forward…

They were still in the dark. Sheila was beginning to lose patience. She knew her dearest friend was in the hands of dangerous fanatics. Akennor felt frustrated, powerless before the situation. Darian felt weary and discouraged, overwhelmed by grief.

Milenna, though she did not know the victim, felt a deep sadness. She kept telling herself they must not give up: there had to be a way.

"But if I have forgotten," Orendil said suddenly, "the books will surely reveal it. Come, follow me: I will lead you to one of the oldest libraries in this world."

The companions rose at once, hope shining in their eyes. The group therefore, guided by Orendil, made their way to the Order's library, which held countless knowledge and lore.

Some manuscripts and volumes dated almost to the dawn of civilization—more than five thousand years. The library was located in the fortress cellars. An ingenious ventilation system kept the rooms dry and at a stable temperature, thus ensuring the preservation of these treasures of knowledge.

Orendil gave instructions to the guards and went down with the young adventurers to the library. Darian was excited at the thought of entering this sanctuary of knowledge.

Sheila had heard of it and dreamed of one day being able to do research there. A spiral staircase led down to the main room. Numerous magical torches lit the place constantly.

The library's five levels had been carved directly into the rock. A wooden lining covered the stone, and the space between wood and rock was padded with dried plant moss to block out moisture.

Each floor measured about fifty square *maicas* and was about two and a half *maicas* high.

The works were classified first in chronological order, then by theme, and finally alphabetically. The group went down to the lowest level, thinking what they sought would likely be found in the oldest works available — and that they had to start somewhere.

Orendil suggested they each take several books and leaf through them to speed up the search. He also pointed out several volumes dealing with demonic sects, accounts predating the great War of the Abyss, as well as old works recounting the very founding of the Order of Calaista.

A long portion of the day went by. Orendil and the companions skimmed rapidly through the books, hoping to find the symbol, but it was in vain. Had he only dreamed he had seen that dreadful symbol before? Orendil was beginning to grow old, and his memory was no longer very reliable. He had to write a great deal to be sure he forgot nothing.

Soon, he told himself, I will have to find a successor. It was a task Orendil would devote himself to as soon as he returned to his study.

He would take a few years to train his replacement, so that he would be well prepared for the heavy responsibilities that awaited him.

Orendil rose from the small reading table and made for the stairs, tired. The day must already have been well advanced.

He turned his head: a canvas hanging on the wall caught his eye. It showed a son killing his father, while a demon, lurking in the shadows, watched the scene with sick delight. Orendil stopped dead. The memory returned as if a key had just unlocked his mind. It was linked to what he was searching for. Orendil thought back to that day. He was young then, newly appointed a priest of Calaista.

He had begun a study of ancient languages, now known only to a few scholars.

Orendil walked toward the last row at the back, where the oldest manuscripts were kept, and where the apprentice paladin he had been had consulted many volumes. His hand ran along the books on a shelf that came to mid-chest. He seemed to feel tingling at his fingertips, and a shiver ran down his spine.

Then his hand stopped almost mechanically on a large book whose cover was red as blood. How could he have forgotten this book, this legend?

"We're wasting our time!" Darian burst out angrily. "This leads nowhere—we're wasting our time! Every passing moment plays against us."

"All right, Darian. We've spent enough time here. I'm for leaving," Sheila added.

"Yes, at least we tried to understand what it was. We're not going to go through every book in this library, after all " Akennor added.

Orendil came back to them, the much-sought book tucked under his left arm.

"Here is the manuscript dealing with the damnation of Tholgor."

The companions widened their eyes. The old man sat, found the page on which the symbol appeared, then resumed his tale. They looked in turn at the illustration in the book, and all recognized the badge's symbol. A shiver of dread ran down Darian's spine.

"This story goes back a very long time. Nearly two thousand five hundred years ago, a great kingdom prospered to the north of the lands we know today, beyond the Foranor."

The sage continued.

"You will no doubt say that no map mentions lands north of the Foranor—and that is true. These accursed lands have long been erased from maps... and from the memory of men. Upon those lands, then, prospered a kingdom ruled by a king noble and good to his people. This king had two sons, Thalion the elder and Oriador the younger.

Thalion was more wily and underhanded. He manipulated people and was ready to do anything to achieve his ends. By contrast, Oriador was just, loyal, and good, toward his parents, his friends, and his people. Yet the two children had been raised with the same love and attention. They had grown up in a serene family atmosphere, despite power and wealth.

When the great king noticed his eldest son's straying, he tried many times to bring him to reason, but in vain. One day, Thalion found in ancient books of magic passages about the infernal worlds and the means to summon creatures from the depths of the abyss. This led him to meet the prince of demons: Morthag."

Orendil took a short break before continuing.

"The latter enchanted him with dreams of infinite powers. He helped the young man perfect his enchantments to allow demons to come into this plane of existence. One evening, when the moon was full, Thalion came to see his father. The good king had punished him so that his son would understand and return to the right path.

The son came to his father saying he was sorry. He had come to ask his forgiveness. The king, astonished and filled with sudden joy, then believed his son saved. But his joy turned to terror when he caught sight of Morthag lurking in the room's shadows.

His son's face then appeared in the light, like that of a disfigured demon, bearing horns on the head. Thalion savagely murdered his father by stabbing him, then tore out his heart and devoured it. Tholgor was born. Oriador arrived in the midst of it and screamed in terror and anger. A rage no being had ever known filled him. He rushed at his brother, raining blows. Tholgor was wounded during the fight, but managed to escape through a passage to the abyss opened by Morthag."

"That's horrible!" Sheila exclaimed in spite of herself.

"Cursed be you, traitor to your father, your mother, your brother, your people and yourself! May you endure the worst torments for eternity." Shouted Oriador.

"Then the younger son took his father's body, knelt, and held him up in his arms. In a voice filled with sorrow and anger, he implored the gods to grant him the means to fight his brother and the demons of the infernal planes."

The young adventurers were incredulous before the sage's tale. They had never heard of this story.

"In answer to Oriador's plea, the gods granted him certain magical powers and immunities to better fight the demons.

After that, Oriador, accompanied by scholars, studied ancient works and developed numerous spells. Tholgor suddenly reappeared and built a fortress black as night.

This nightmarish place became the rallying point for a great number of demons from the lower regions. It was then that the great War of the Abyss began.

The whole earth trembled under the violence of the fighting. A large part of the world then known was annihilated, entire cities razed.

Losses were terrible despite the union of men, elves, and dwarves. The elves and dwarves suffered enormously in this war, which nearly wiped them out.

But fate at last turned in Oriador's favor, and the coalition of Good succeeded in driving the demons from this world.

As Oriador's mages worked to seal forever the metaphysical links between the infernal planes and ours.

Tholgor is said to have hidden one within a curse. Seven men of Oriador's guard were present at his death, and were cursed.

'I will return through the deaths of the descendants of those who brought about my downfall.'

Oriador cut off his head, blaming himself for not having done it sooner. The black fortress was then razed to the ground. Legend says that unspeakable horrors slept in the fortress's bowels. The foundations were therefore not destroyed, but merely buried, leaving forever a scar upon that accursed place.

The prosperous kingdom was nothing but ashes and ruins. Its lands, defiled forever, were entrusted to powerful druids, specialists of the elements. They made the earth tremble until it opened into a wide trench… which the sea filled. "

"I am an apprentice paladin… Why are we not taught this?" Darian asked, upset.

Orendil regarded him for a brief moment.

"I understand your frustration. I believe the leaders of the time thought this information was meant for scholars."

"For nearly four hundred years, humanity barely survived, because of incessant attacks from orcs, trolls, and goblins."

He went on.

"The survivors of the war chose to forget that damned region. A descendant of Oriador, Berennor, through courage and will, succeeded in uniting the human clans, who were called the Last Alliance of Men.

The War of the Great Deliverance began, and lasted nearly half a millennium. During this war, men sought to exterminate those infamous races created to serve evil.

The elves and dwarves took part only timidly, given that they had been almost completely annihilated. They had grown more aloof and were concerned now only with their own survival. "

"Do elves still exist?" Sheila asked, with a hint of excitement.

"I've always wanted to meet some."

Orendil smiled kindly.

"Yes, some still exist, but they are well hidden. I don't even know where they are... I only have a vague idea."

"Oh!" One could hear the disappointment in Sheila's voice.

"So, the Order of Calaista was created following Tholgor's fall, in order to protect peace and defend people against evil. The natural gifts were, however, lost over the generations, and probably no one today still possesses those immunities."

"By contrast, the spells developed by Oriador are still known today by our most eminent priests and paladins."

The companions looked at one another, speechless.

Only Milenna kept a neutral expression.

"My father, Svealëdor, knows these ancient legends and had already told me of them. He loves to tell this kind of story... But I think for this one, he truly believed it," Milenna explained.

"But I never would have thought the badge was connected to all this."

"Your father is very learned, and must be very wise," Orendil added.

Akennor, thoughtful, his gaze lost in the void, said:

"So then, Shaya would in a way be a descendant of one of the Seven."

"I rather think so, my friend. At least, I see no other logical explanation."

"It seems someone is trying to reestablish the links between the infernal worlds," Orendil said.

A name wanted to rise to the surface, he felt it... but something seemed to hold it back.

"Damn!" Darian exclaimed.

"Uh... I mean... It's surely some sort of ritual, isn't it?"

"Do they have to do it at a specific time or place?"

The sage skimmed a few pages quickly, then looked up.

"No. At least, there is no mention of it in this work, and I believe it complete."

"The only condition seems to be to hold the seven last descendants."

"Now that we know the reason and the aim, we must prevent the prophecy from being fulfilled," Sheila said, determined.

They went back up to the ground floor. The sun was casting its last rays.

Orendil turned to Akennor.

"Get in touch with Sathoryn. He is one of our spies in Elenshae. Recently, he observed that a dark coalition of assassins and thieves had considerably increased their operations, and that worries us. I have no more details for now; I sent one of my trusted men to investigate two days ago."

"Elenshae is a logical choice as a hideout. I'm ready to bet your abductors are heading there."

"We have indeed come to the same conclusion."

"Where can we meet your contact?" Akennor asked.

"In a den of lust, The Lady Aïcha. You will recognize him by his left eye, covered by a black patch. Be extremely careful. Tell him I am the one who sent you."

Hope had returned to the companions' hearts. Orendil asked them to join the evening meal, but they politely declined the invitation, arguing that they must not lose another instant. Instead, their reserve of rations was renewed. Orendil admired their courage, and the determination they showed to rescue their friend.

Akennor and his companions were back on their horses. The sage approached them and said:

"As for the orcs, thank you for the information. We will keep watch on the surroundings…"

"May Oriador protect and help you."

Do not let obstacles darken your hearts or break the hope that lives in you.

Darian took it as counsel meant for him and squared his shoulders. A desire for vengeance burned in his heart.

"Nor let vengeance, resentment, or hatred harden your hearts, or veil the humaneness that animates you," Orendil concluded.

Darian remained puzzled. Was he reading minds? At last, he committed those wise words to memory.

The four companions saluted him, thanked the knights of the Order for their help, and set off westward, toward Elenshae, the fair, the great. It would take them a few days to get there.

They stopped at sunset; they had been galloping since they left the fortress. Their horses were exhausted, and so were they. They prepared the fire and their blankets for the night.

Akennor managed to bring back a few hares; a hearty meal would do them a world of good. Since leaving Milenna's home, they had only swallowed the flatbreads her mother had prepared for them. They were delicious and surprisingly filling, but it was no match for good fresh meat cooked over the fire.

They had stopped in a small clearing not far from the road; a dip in the terrain meant their fire could not be seen from the track. They ate with great appetite, then after the meal, Sheila brought out the bottle of liquor bought on the day of the abduction.

"Anyone want some?" she asked, shaking the bottle. Akennor and Darian nodded, but Milenna abstained.

"You don't have to come with us, you know," Darian said to Milenna.

"I mean, we're glad you're here, but you shouldn't feel obliged or anything. Just be at ease."

"I'm happy to help; I wanted to get out, and it's for a good cause," she answered with a smile.

"Svealëdor isn't your father, is he?" Akennor asked, fixing his eyes on Milenna.

"No, indeed, I'm an orphan; I never knew or even heard of my direct parents. I was entrusted to Svealëdor when I was very young, she said, suddenly seized by a feeling of sadness; not knowing who her parents were had left a void to fill."

"But I consider him my father; he loved me as such."

"I wonder," Akennor began, "your father seemed interested in my mother's supposed people—has he ever spoken to you about it?"

"Yes, several times. He found it interesting because no one really knows it, and its inhabitants possess powers of foresight and telepathy."

Akennor went back into his thoughts; it truly intrigued him—why had his mother never told him about it?

"Gray eyes are rather unusual, but they're pretty," Milenna commented to Akennor.

"Yes indeed; most people point it out to me. Only my mother has similar eyes, which no doubt makes me a special case."

"Yes, no doubt—like each of us." Milenna looked at him with her beautiful deep blue eyes; her gaze showed restraint—she kept things to herself.

Milenna told them about the first time she transformed into a wolf. When she returned home, Svealëdor had company. Milenna resumed her normal form in front of them, but forgot that her clothes weren't there. She therefore appeared completely naked; the guests' eyes went wide, and she was very embarrassed. A few days later, her father provided her with magical clothing that would merge with the shapeshift. She laughed nervously as she told them about the most humiliating moment of her life. Her new companions laughed heartily, imagining the scene. That brief moment of laughter eased slightly the heavy fears and worries that weighed on them.

The atmosphere grew heavy after that. Akennor, Darian, and Sheila feared for their friend. Above all, they hoped she would not lose hope. For the rest of the evening they traded adventures they had lived through and various anecdotes.

Darian took the first watch; he was alert and very vigilant. Then he woke Milenna for the second watch, and she transformed into a wolf to better check the surroundings.

The night passed without incident, and they set out again the next day, at the first light of dawn.

Chapter 9 – Elenshae

In the early afternoon, Dresden and his band came within sight of the immense silver gates of the powerful coastal city. They were satisfied to have finally reached this crucial stage. Before entering the enclosure, they regrouped.

Dresden spoke:

"I will go with Parthe to the docks to find our contact. In the meantime, Deidre and Aaron will go directly to the hideout to deliver the message: we have captured the target."

"Join us afterward at the meeting point in the southern quarter."

A smile of satisfaction at a duty accomplished appeared on his lips. His companions approved. Everyone knew exactly what to do.

Shaya was utterly exhausted from being carried face down for so long. She was strapped behind Parthe like a vulgar sack. She felt like she was going to be sick, half-conscious and moaning through her gag.

"Come on, we'll meet at the docks at midday," concluded Dresden as he moved away with Parthe. They placed clothes over Shaya so that the guards would see nothing compromising. The captive was tied so tightly she had no chance of moving. Thanks to their cover as privileged merchants, they would pass without trouble. The mercenary group thus split up, confident in their two-day lead over their pursuers.

*

A voice moaned in the darkness. Akennor could not see who it was. Other more sinister voices echoed endlessly.

The sky turned blood red. Black clouds piled up, lightning flashed, sulfurous vapors erupted from the ground, and a rain of volcanic stones fell upon him. Alone in the midst of these catastrophes.

The ground shook, lava surged, the sounds of monsters and nightmarish creatures polluted the air. The earth split open, vomiting incandescent rivers, and horribly mutilated humanoid shapes emerged. The torment was unbearable; they begged for death. It was terrifying. Akennor turned his head again and again, wanting to wake up. Then he decided to think of Shaya. She had to hold on, she must not lose hope. Akennor screamed, calling out to his friend that they were coming. The sinister voices stopped their groans for a moment, before breaking into a dreadful, lugubrious laughter.

Milenna, having returned to human form, shook him abruptly.

"Akennor, come on, wake up!"

She had seen him in hs sleep while returning from her round about the camp. He was agitated and terrified. Besides, it was his turn to stand watch.

He awoke with a start.

"Huh, what? What's going on?"

Akennor was drenched in sweat. Milenna soothed him by running her hand through his hair.

"There, there. I think you had a nightmare. It's time for your watch."

Akennor caught his breath and tried to chase the images from his mind.

"Thank you... Well, that works out. Go rest, I'll be fine."

"You can talk to me about it if you want... if it helps."

Sheila had half-opened her eyes and witnessed the scene. A knot formed in her stomach. Upset, bitter, she closed her eyes again.

"Thanks... maybe later."

Akennor truly had no desire to talk about these dreams that were driving him nearly mad. In his youth, he had been haunted by them, then the nightmares had suddenly stopped. It had been so long that Akennor had come to believe himself safe from the phenomenon.

Milenna silently agreed and went to rest. They still had a long road ahead before reaching Elenshae. His breath still short, his heart pounding, Akennor felt a fear mixed with anxiety.

A sense of helplessness overwhelmed him, and he felt vulnerable. He had to calm himself. Akennor took deep breaths and watched his friends sleep. He had to hold it together, for them. His fear gradually subsided as he waited impatiently for dawn.

At daybreak, they set out again and arrived at the gates of Elenshae by late morning. It was Akennor's first time seeing the city. A great stone wall surrounded it.

At regular intervals, guard towers rose from the wall itself. The gates leading inside were covered in pure silver.

Of the six gates that granted access, only two were open in these troubled times.

Banners proudly bearing the city's emblem fluttered in the wind. The crest displayed a silver shield.

On its lower half was a sailing ship, and on the upper half, a starfish. In the background, two crossed swords could be seen. The flags flew from the watchtowers and the tallest buildings.

This great port city was renowned for its tall edifices and its harmonious, regular architecture. Here one found all the main offices of import and export, as well as the most important shipowners of the known world.

Elenshae shone through its dynamism, its thriving trade, and its devotion to knowledge. The most eminent schools of magic, commerce, naval expertise, and architecture were located here.

Even though Darian had read many books about this important city, he had never visited it. He recalled how the monastery had taught them the city's history and politics. The Order of Calaista had been, in fact, at the origin of the city's founding. The Order had instilled democratic principles there.

Every five years, the city's leaders were elected by the people. The domains ranged from commerce to industry, the army, port activity, citizen services, magic, the outer regions, and diplomacy.

This allowed the population to choose the person they deemed most competent. Darian liked this principle—that people were equal. He emerged from his thoughts as they reached the main gate. Three armed guards in armor challenged them, asking the purpose of their visit.

"We have come to visit my brother Kallo. He works as a guard," replied Akennor.

"Kallo?" asked a young guard, clearly familiar with the name.

Akennor nodded.

"Yes, that's him."

"He's a good guy, your brother, and rather funny. All right, it's fine. He's on patrol in the northeast, the richest part of the city."

"Thank you," said Akennor.

The guards let them pass, and they were able to admire the inside of the mighty city.

Near the gate were the city stables, where travelers could leave their horses during their stay. It was a clean and well-kept place. They received a safe-conduct in their names identifying their horses. The cost was one silver coin per day.

If no news came from them within a week, the city reserved the right to keep the horses. Akennor and his friends paid two days in advance and moved on.

The eastern sector of the city was the newest. Its streets were a bit wider than those in the center, located more to the west, near the docks.This part of the city consisted mainly of low houses and apartment buildings. The structures were close together. Some had stone balconies overlooking Sutaris Square, the main artery running east to west through the city. They made their way toward the southwestern quarter, the poorest and most disreputable sector of the city.

Their eyes widened at the tall chalk-colored edifices and immense stone constructions. Sheila knew this architecture well: her school was located near the city center, right beside the Tower of Sahros.

Indeed, she guided the group to pass by the school of magic.

"I'm glad to see where you live and study most of the year. It's impressive," exclaimed Akennor.

His comment lifted Sheila's spirits, and she smiled at him.

"Here is the great Tower of Sahros. It's the tallest building in the known world. It is where the elected officials and the Council of Sages, comprising the most powerful mages, sit."

Akennor and Darian gazed at it, awestruck. The Tower of Sahros seemed distant yet of vertiginous height.

It was built of solid white granite blocks taken from the seaside. They were cut, polished, and assembled with such precision that the seams were barely visible. It looked as though the tower had been carved from a single block.

"I've come here a few times with my father, mostly for trade," added Milenna, who was amazed each time she visited.

Many stone and wooden walkways linked the buildings together. People could walk across these suspended bridges and contemplate the scenery from such heights. Some buildings had slanted roofs, but most had flat roofs, ideal for observing the surroundings.

The young adventurers passed near the open-air markets of the southern sector. They offered a multitude of products, both common and exotic.

Some goods came from unknown and distant lands. The group was constantly accosted by street vendors and struggled to make their way through the dense, bustling crowd.

After a long walk and multiple requests for directions, they arrived at the Lady Aïcha. In this wretched quarter, the Lady Aïcha served as a haunt for thieves' and assassins' guilds. It was the oldest district, located near the docks. Once lively, this place was now filthy, infested with vermin and bandits.

The streets were very narrow, too tight for two horses to pass each other. A few streetlamps dotted the area, casting timid light. The Lady Aïcha was on a small street parallel to the docks. Drunkards entered and exited constantly. A group of sailors chatted loudly and laughed a little further down the alley.

Beggars drank from their bottles sitting or lying on the ground near the walls. They sometimes had to be stepped over.

Sheila and Milenna pulled their large hoods over their faces so as not to attract unwanted attention. A few sailors turned away as they entered the establishment.

Inside, it was noisy and smoky. The inn was packed with people—sailors, smugglers, and thieves. Small round tables for four filled most of the central hall. A long counter ran along the wall opposite the entrance, hosting numerous people who drank and chatted. Sailors talked among themselves while courtesans in light and provocative clothing were courted by men seeking company.

A small wooden stage stood at the back, to the left of the entrance. An old velvet curtain, red but torn in places, partly hid the stage.

There was no performance at the moment. The young adventurers looked around: the place was a real rat's nest. Darian whispered into the girls' ears to keep their hoods on and stay discreet. Akennor signaled them to move forward. Some faces were paying them too much attention, he thought. They scanned the room from every angle, searching for their contact.

Then Akennor's vision blurred as he looked toward the back of the room near the stage. He saw a great serpent coiling around an old defenseless man. The vision was brief and hazy. Akennor blinked rapidly, shook his head, then spotted the one he was seeking. A tall one-eyed man, with long brown hair tied back, and a beard of several days. He looked young, thirty at most. A scar extended past his eye-patch and slashed across his cheek; his nose, clearly once broken, was crooked. He wore black leather.

He had a sleeveless vest, fastened at the front with silver buttons. His pants also seemed of black leather, and he wore tall boots rising up to his knees, over his pants. From their shape, Akennor guessed the spy hid weapons within them as a last resort. Milenna had noticed Akennor's reaction at the moment of his vision, and it intrigued her. She understood he had seen something unusual: his startled flinch betrayed him. Akennor gestured to his companions to follow.

The establishment was a cacophony. A few musicians played a discordant tune, clearly unable to agree on the melody.

Sathoryn seemed to be talking with another man in black, but the latter slipped away before they reached him. They weaved between tables and chairs, careful not to jostle anyone.

"You are Sathoryn, aren't you? Orendil sent us, and he said you could probably help us," said Akennor. The spy remained impassive.

"I deal only with Orendil," he replied coldly, taking a swig of rum.

"We come on Orendil's behalf," insisted Darian, on the verge of exploding. He did not like this spy at all, whether he worked for the Order or not.

"Calm down, boy, I answer only to Orendil. Get lost, you're drawing too much attention."

Sheila glanced around. The half-naked women, the obscene gestures, the drunken people… all of it made her uncomfortable.

Akennor took out the badge and placed it on the table before him.

"Listen carefully. Orendil is our friend, and we are in a hurry. I'm sure you can make an effort. Do you recognize this symbol?"

At once, Sathoryn covered it with his right hand and looked at the young adventurers for the first time, his expression closed.

"Sit down. There are too many curious eyes here."

They sat around the table. Akennor sat across from the spy, Darian to his right, Milenna and Sheila to his left.

"I do not know exactly what it means, but I know that those who bear this badge have a hideout outside the city."

The young adventurers exchanged wide-eyed glances, eager to learn more.

Sathoryn took another sip of rum and continued:

"An old castle lies to the north, near the coast. According to some rumors, it has always belonged to disreputable folk… if you see what I mean."

Akennor extended his hand, and Sathoryn discreetly returned the badge. The latter furtively scanned the surroundings.

"What else do you know?" asked Akennor, looking him straight in the eyes.

"Nothing more, except that I do not advise you to cross these people—they are very dangerous."

Sathoryn held his gaze briefly before looking away.

"All right, thank you for the information."

They rose together, eager to leave that den of vice. As they did, the curtain rose. Three girls—a pretty blonde, a redhead, and a dark-haired one—began a lascivious dance.

A rhythmic tune accompanied them as they moved on stage under the light of several lanterns hung on the back wall. The dancers were scantily clad: a bra, tight panties, and translucent voile trousers.

The tempo slowed, and one by one the girls removed their bras, striking suggestive poses, to the applause and cries of delight from the audience. Sheila and Milenna were disgusted. Darian and Akennor, however, did not know if they should feel repulsed or aroused.

They found the girls very beautiful and wanted to see more, yet at the same time they were saddened that women were reduced to stripping before a crowd acting like beasts. They turned away and tried to push through the delirious crowd. Everyone applauded, thrilled with the show. The companions were cursed loudly whenever they accidentally blocked a spectator's view.

At last, they hurried out the door, determined never to return.

Akennor realized what had revolted him: it was not the sensual, charming show of the young women, but the barking and reactions of the audience, behaving like animals.

Outside, the street was crowded. As they descended the steps into the alley, thugs recognized Sheila's and Milenna's features and yanked off their hoods, revealing their identities.

"Hey, beauty," sneered the first thug, a scrawny, dirty little man.

"Where are you going like that? Don't leave, the night is just beginning."

He stepped toward Milenna, his eyes fixed obscenely on her chest. This sudden manifestation of lust drew the attention of his comrades, who turned back and delayed their re-entry into the filthy tavern. There were five of them in total: the scrawny pest, two fat ones, a giant, and another of Akennor's size.

They were dressed in filthy rags, their hair wild. They must live on the street, probably mere petty thieves, thought the young warrior.

"Yeah girls, wait! We'll take good care of you," said one of the fat ones with a lewd look.

That was all it took for Darian and Akennor to react immediately. They stepped between the thugs and their companions.

"What did you just say, you filthy vermin?" growled Darian, red with rage.

The thugs glanced at one another, then without warning, the biggest one hurled himself at Darian with a roar. Caught off guard, he had no time to draw his weapon and was slammed to the ground. Akennor's swords flashed instantly into his hands.

The scrawny man lunged straight for Milenna, his dirty hands outstretched. Just as he reached for her chest, she transformed into a wolf in an instant, growled savagely, and bit him viciously in the groin.

Despite all the atrocities this vile place had seen, never had such a scream of agony been heard. The scrawny one collapsed, desperately trying to free himself from Milenna's jaws, but in vain.

Meanwhile, Akennor engaged another opponent, while Sheila hurled a magical projectile that sent another flying into the tavern wall, leaving him unconscious.

Akennor, for his part, had no trouble handling his adversary. He feinted a high strike, blocked the counter, then slashed his foe's shoulder and thigh. The thug collapsed, writhing in pain.

Darian, meanwhile, struggled more; his opponent was visibly very strong. The two rolled about on the filthy, sodden ground of the alley. Milenna released her prey, who clutched his crotch in agony. The world spun around him, and he lost consciousness.

The crowd in the alley thickened as curious onlookers gathered. The giant thug was now on top of Darian, strangling him.

The apprentice paladin managed to free his upper body from his foe's grip by holding his wrists. Darian pushed himself upright, giving the audience a true spectacle of brute force, and smashed his head violently into his opponent's face.

The thug clutched his face, giving Darian time to get up and seize his weapon. Akennor saw his friend's face twisted with rage—there was no doubt, he was going to kill him. He hesitated. A moment too long.

"NO, Darian!" he cried.

Too late—the hammer smashed into the thug's head, hurling him against the opposite wall of the alley. Darian, panting, his mouth twisted and foam on his lips, stared at the scene. The bandit fell lifeless to the ground, his skull split open, splattering blood across the pavement and the wall.

The crowd remained silent for a moment. Akennor seized the chance to slip away with his friends. They ran at full speed through the dark, squalid alleys leading to the docks. No one followed them—truth be told, the people had enjoyed a good street fight and cared little about the one who had just lost his life.

The unfortunate man's body would remain in the alley until the city guards came to remove it. The scrawny thug died drained of his blood, and one of the fat ones was finished off by unscrupulous bystanders, hungry for violence. They stopped in the street that crossed the city from west to east to catch their breath. Milenna took the opportunity to return to her human form.

Sheila looked at her and asked with a smile:

"So, what does it taste like? Tell me."

"Not great. His last bath must have been ten years ago… maybe more," she replied jokingly.

Darian smiled too. Only Akennor did not find it funny. He was preoccupied with something else.

"But really… what got into you, Darian?" Akennor asked.

Darian shrugged, looking puzzled, and answered:
"What? He was a thief, damn it, Akennor! They attacked us without provocation!"

Akennor stepped closer, looked Darian in the eyes, and said:
"That's no reason to kill for the sheer pleasure of it, without pity or forgiveness. You didn't have to kill him. You're a paladin in the making, Darian… don't forget that."
Darian turned his gaze away, his head lowered. His friend was right—he had lost control. Darian understood the warning. Killing in self-defense was not in itself reprehensible.

No, what was serious was that he had wanted to hurt his opponent, had wanted him dead at all costs, blinded by anger and hatred. The grief and anguish he felt since Shaya's abduction weighed heavily on him. And it was influencing his actions, his decisions.

Ashamed, Darian remained silent.

Sheila and Milenna exchanged a mute glance before turning their attention back to Darian, still shaken. Sheila, impulsive herself, understood what he had just gone through.

She could not blame him: the absence of her friend gnawed at her too. Milenna, for her part, cast a new kind of look at Darian. She understood the pain of his childhood friends, but there was something in him that still eluded her.

"Let's go right away," Akennor proposed.

Chapter 10 – The Castle

Parthe prowled through the alleys of the seedy district, not far from the docks. He had contacts in Elenshae and had taken the opportunity to reconnect with old acquaintances while waiting for their ship to be ready to sail.

Dresden had ordered him not to linger, but… a more carnal urge gnawed at him. And what better place to satisfy it than the famous Lady Aïcha?

A commotion caught his attention a few steps from the establishment. Curious, he moved closer and pushed his way through the crowd. What he saw froze him in place: a true carnage. A frail, scrawny man lay face down in a pool of blood. Another had his head smashed to pulp. A third was unconscious, and a fourth was still being beaten mercilessly.

"What happened?" Parthe muttered to himself.

"A brawl between four youngsters… Two guys and two girls. Those thugs wanted the girls, but they found death instead."

The old man who had answered kept walking, indifferent. Parthe frowned and listened carefully. The whispers swirled around him: The warrior with two swords… The man with the hammer… The beautiful mage… And the she-wolf…

No… could it be…? thought Parthe, troubled.

Walking briskly, he entered the Lady Aïcha, hoping to find a valuable contact. A little later, he came back out in haste, heading straight for the ship. He climbed the gangplank and entered the main cabin.

"Ah, there you are! I told you not to take too long, didn't I?" Dresden snapped.

"You went to warm yourself at the brothel, didn't you, dear Parthe?" Deidre mocked.

He ignored them and sat down.

"The youngsters are on our trail. I just missed them."

"What! Are you sure?!" Dresden roared.

"You mean the friends of our captive?"

"Yes. But don't worry, my contact will take care of them."

"Whatever the case, we must set sail at once," Deidre growled. "We've lingered here too long."

"We're leaving soon, the captain assured me."

"Those youngsters are tough," Dresden concluded grimly.

*

Night had fallen, and the companions hoped to reach the city gates before the curfew barred their way. They quickened their pace toward the stables to retrieve their mounts. Then they headed for the northern gate, praying the guards would let them through.

"Halt! Who goes there?" called a voice Akennor immediately recognized. Their luck seemed to be turning.

"Hey! Brumir, how are you, my friend?" Akennor exclaimed joyfully. Brumir could hardly believe his eyes.

"What? Akennor! What are you doing here?"

132

"It's a long story, and I don't have time to explain. But my friends and I must leave the city at once."

"Why? The gates are closed… can't it wait until tomorrow?"

"No, it can't. Please, it's very important."

Brumir lowered his head in thought. He knew it was against regulations to open the gates, especially given the current unrest. But this was the brother of his best friend, and he had always liked Akennor.

"Wait here a moment," he said.

Brumir disappeared into the guard tower. From the shadows playing across the windows, he seemed to be negotiating with another soldier. Then he gestured for the young adventurers to come closer.

"All right. We'll lift the gate just enough for you to slip through."

"Thank you, my friend. I'll make it up to you," Akennor promised.

Once outside the protective walls, the companions made for the northwest, as Sathoryn had directed.

They moved swiftly toward the coast, putting distance between themselves and the fortified city walls to avoid drawing attention. The stars twinkled once more overhead, and soon the dark silhouette of a castle loomed on the horizon.

It was a tall structure, bristling with many sharp-roofed turrets. The central tower was high and slender, capped with a steep roof. The entire building seemed to cling precariously to the cliff's edge, its foundations partly carved into the rock.

The path leading there twisted and wound. They halted at a bend in the trail, hidden behind a low hill. The horses grew restless, but Milenna whispered soothing words only animals could understand, calming them at once.

Milenna narrowed her eyes.

"Do you see that, near the castle?"

The others squinted.

"Looks like shadows moving…" Akennor murmured.

"Yes, four people at the gate," Milenna confirmed.

"Sharp eyes, I'll give you that," Darian said.

Few trees dotted the barren landscape; guards would have a clear line of sight.

"What do we do?" Milenna asked.

"Only one entrance, and the rest looks inaccessible," Akennor observed."

"We look like fools. Should've bought rope or something," Sheila muttered.

"Let's watch quietly for now. Maybe we'll spot a less-guarded way in," Darian suggested.

Sheila smirked.

"And once inside, we politely ask a guard to show us the dungeons?"

"For now, Darian's plan is best," Akennor concluded.

But they didn't have to wait long.

Milenna, in wolf form, heard better than the others. Her ears pricked suddenly. She tapped Akennor's arm with her paw.

"Oh, how charming, she's giving paw," Akennor teased.

"I think she wants to tell us something," Darian said.

Milenna growled inwardly at their slowness, then nodded when Sheila guessed:

"Voices? Human voices?"

Another nod.

"Perhaps others are heading to the castle. Perfect—we could take their place and sneak in," Akennor said.

Three voices. Milenna tapped the ground three times.

"Three? Excellent! With our badge, that makes four," Sheila said.

"They must not raise the alarm. Quick and silent, we take them down," Akennor whispered.

"I'll take the first, Darian the middle, Milenna the last. Sheila, back us up if needed."

They hid behind boulders, waiting for the moment when the dark-clad figures were between watchful eyes. The enemies approached in single file. Akennor gripped his dagger tightly. Darian's fingers clenched around his hammer. Milenna crouched, ready to leap. Sheila prepared to cast.

Then—movement froze. The middle figure raised a staff, chanting:

"Qualin umbar-rhu!"

The others drew weapons.

Sheila fired back instantly:

"Nar anta-rhu!"

Flames burst from her hand, striking the dark mage— only to swerve aside against an unseen barrier.

"Milenna, the mage!" she shouted.

"Naira silmë-rhu!"

A blinding orb of light burst against the mage's face. He screamed in rage, clutching his eyes.

Akennor was already upon one of the warriors who advanced toward him. His opponent had grabbed a shield and a sword and was charging headlong. With a swift move, the young warrior leapt to the side, rolled, and came up behind his foe. He pivoted and struck with his blades.

The man reacted quickly, spinning his body and swinging his shield to bash Akennor. The latter narrowly avoided the blow by crouching, managing to cut into his enemy's legs. Enraged, the sect warrior gathered strength to bring down his heavy sword.

But the young fighter, quicker and more agile, anticipated the strike and dodged with ease, once again making his enemy howl in pain as he inflicted fresh wounds.

"You're dead, you little wretch!" the man growled in a deep voice.

Akennor pressed the attack, fierce, alternating high and low strikes, giving the less nimble fighter no respite. The man was beginning to tire: his moves grew clumsier. Yet his defense remained solid, leaving few openings for Akennor to land a killing blow. *No opening... he counters every strike.*

Meanwhile, Darian had engaged a tall, slim woman who was lightning-fast. She moved with feline agility and wielded her dagger and short blade with great dexterity. Swift as a panther, she leapt, rolled, and struck with both her weapons and her legs. Darian was hit on the head several times. His own blows cut only empty air: his opponent anticipated his every move. The panther-woman even managed to leave him with several shallow cuts.

How can I land a hit on her? he thought in frustration.

Milenna had heard Sheila's cry and leapt at the blinded sorcerer. With a graceful bound, she landed on her target and knocked him onto his back. She growled and bit while the sorcerer, screaming, tried to protect himself with his arms.

"Ráva-rhu!"

He managed to shout while struggling. An invisible force seized Milenna and hurled her violently aside. The wolf landed hard on the rocky ground, forcing a yelp of pain from her throat.

Sheila watched Milenna rush the mage and felt a surge of relief: he would soon be neutralized. But then the ground quivered slightly. She raised her eyebrows, confused, and turned her head. Just in time to see skeletal hands suddenly claw up from the earth.

She stared in horror, never before having witnessed such a dark spell. There were five in all, slowly dragging themselves free from the ground. Trembling, her fear flared into anger.

"Templa pilini!"

The magical projectile shot toward its target, striking it hard, tearing a skeleton apart into pieces.

One down…

Sheila screamed as a bony arm grabbed her from behind. She struggled frantically and fell on her back, but the skeleton still clutched her, while the others shambled closer.

Akennor was locked in battle when he made a mistake. The warrior took the opportunity to hurl his shield, smashing Akennor in the head and chest. The young man was knocked to the ground, dazed.

Not about to waste such a chance, his opponent charged in to finish him. The panther-woman lunged at Darian, this time flipping onto her hands and snapping her feet up under the apprentice paladin's chin.

Pain shot through him, and he fell backward. She landed astride him, her legs pinning him down, dagger and knife raised high to strike. With a cry of rage, Darian swung his hammer, smashing her arm and hurling her to the side.

He scrambled to his feet, scanning the fight, and spotted his best friend in trouble. Without hesitation, he dashed over. Just as the sect warrior was about to strike, Darian's hammer thundered against his shield. The impact was brutal, knocking the enemy off balance and driving him to one knee.

"Come on, Akennor, pull yourself together! Go take care of mine—I'll handle this one!"

Darian rained blows on the warrior, his hammer crashing against the shield until the man could no longer hold it.

Then the apprentice paladin smashed the enemy's helmeted head, denting the iron. Blood streamed over the man's face as he collapsed, lifeless. The young warrior quickly regained his footing and charged at the woman, who, battered, was struggling back to her feet.

Despite her agility, Akennor evaded and struck again and again. In moments, she was bleeding from multiple wounds. Weakened, her movements slowed. Anticipating her next move, Akennor drove both blades through her. With a sharp twist, he pulled them free, letting the woman's body fall lifeless to the ground.

Stunned and sore, Milenna rose and saw Sheila in peril against the undead. She rushed to her aid in a few bounding leaps, then shifted back into human form.

"Sirpë-rhu!"

Powerful roots burst from the earth, wrapping around the skeletons as they thrashed. Milenna stepped toward Sheila, hand outstretched, then clenched her fist. The roots tightened their grip until the bones snapped under the crushing force.

Sheila stood up.

"I'm glad to see you."

"Come on, let's finish that damned sorcerer."

Milenna nodded and turned toward the black mage.

The man had regained his sight and was preparing a spell: fire glowed in his palms.

Akennor and Darian were sprinting toward him. The young warrior hurled his dagger with all his strength. It grazed the mage's cheek, leaving a thin line of blood. *Damn…!* he cursed inwardly.

The sorcerer raised his hands. It was Darian's turn.

With a swift, precise throw, the hammer smashed full into its target's face. The black mage was hurled backward by the force, crashing to the ground.

Standing over the lifeless body, Darian grinned in satisfaction.

"Still got the touch!"

"Good thing… who knows what spell he was about to unleash."

"Still, I hate that I missed…" Akennor muttered.

Sheila and Milenna joined them.

"For a moment, I thought we were done for," Sheila admitted.

"They were tough," Akennor said, rubbing his aching jaw.

"Do we go on anyway?" Milenna asked.

"We've been tracking them for days. I want to see Shaya alive and end this nightmare. Risky or not, we have to try. I'm not here to turn back," Akennor replied firmly.

"Nor am I. Let's go, we'll see it through," Darian added.

"Let's at least rest a moment, tend our wounds," Akennor suggested.

"Gladly… I hurt all over…" Sheila sighed.

Though uncut, Milenna's fall had been brutal. They took time to treat their wounds with healing lotion and bandages.

"I was horrified seeing those skeletons rise… He must have been a powerful necromancer," Sheila said.

Afterward, they donned the clothes and gear of the three slain foes, wiping away the blood as best they could.

"Look," Sheila said, pulling out her black mage's robe from school. "That should do."

Since their victims had no horses, the companions released their own, unsure how long the infiltration might last.

Milenna caressed her horse's muzzle.

"Go, my brave Kintaro. Go to Svealëdor, and take the others with you. Be safe, my friend."

Kintaro pressed his nose against his mistress's neck, and she stroked him softly, a tear slipping down her cheek as he trotted off. The other horses followed the proud stallion into the night.

The four cast the corpses down the cliff, pinned the foul badge to their robes, wished each other luck, and marched toward the fortress—hoping their ruse would succeed.

Akennor clung to hope: surely the badge and the insignia would suffice as a safeguard within the sect. After all, no one was supposed to know it's true meaning…

Chapter 11 – The Grip of Evil

Akennor, Milenna, Darian, and Sheila arrived at the gates of the sect's hideout, those who had kidnapped their friend. The entrance of the building consisted of two heavy panels made of dark wood. Each door was supported by two large iron hinges. A small hatch, placed at face height, allowed someone to look outside. Two huge iron rings were fixed on each of the doors, allowing visitors to signal their presence.

The companions had pulled down the hood of their borrowed garb, and Akennor took charge of knocking firmly with one of the rings. The dull sound of iron clashing echoed in the air.

A brief moment passed before someone opened the hatch. They were surprised to see that it was a beautiful woman who answered them. A tall blonde, with long hair and delicate features. Her voice was soft and honeyed, almost hypnotic.

"What is it?"

Akennor showed the badge clearly.

"We are expected, and we wish to enter," he said in a firm and confident tone.

The pretty blonde woman looked at their badge.

"Oh, you must be the last team… team number fifteen, isn't it?"

Akennor, nervous, felt his tension rise.

What if it's a trap… he thought. His lips trembled briefly.

"Yes, that's right: I am Ragnor, he is Brent; here are Charlie and Helen."

The beautiful blonde scrutinized them for a moment with a piercing gaze. Her suspicious look gave way to a smile.

"Pleased to meet you. I do not know your names, but the Master certainly will. Besides, he was expecting you. Since you are late, you will see him tomorrow morning. Come in."

A loud click was heard, and the left door creaked open.

Darian was hot. He feared finding himself thus in the wolf's mouth.

What will happen to us if we are discovered? Beads of nervous sweat appeared on his forehead. Darian tried to reason with himself not to give in to panic. He already imagined himself tied up and tortured. Shivers of terror ran down his spine.

Milenna's face was perfectly impassive, despite her discomfort. This place gave her goosebumps.

What are we doing here? she wondered. All her senses were on alert, and her instinct, both animal and human, screamed at her to flee.

Akennor tried to remain calm, though he was filled with dread. He told himself that they had to succeed. They must: Shaya's life surely depended on it.

"Follow me," the women told them.

"By the way," she suddenly asked, "weren't you supposed to be three? We thought one of you had been killed."

Akennor surprised himself with the speed at which he invented a credible lie.

"Yes, well… let's just say this weakling," he said, nodding toward Darian, "he really almost didn't make it. We thought he was mortally wounded, but it was close. He's still weak… I think he even has a fever."

Darian gave a slight nod of approval, for he truly did not feel well. In fact, it seemed to him that his sweating had increased dramatically. Their pretty guide appeared to believe the story; Darian looked genuinely ill, which made the ruse all the more convincing.

The inner courtyard was very small: it took them barely a dozen steps to reach the entrance of the main building. The castle was practically devoid of windows. Only tiny openings, small but numerous, dotted the dark walls. But these windows were so narrow that little light could filter through. Akennor realized they were in fact arrow slits. The group entered the main vestibule, a large rectangular room.

The floor, made of marble, had the aspect of a checkerboard alternating with dark red squares. Black marble columns rose to the ceiling, forming a corridor all around the room. Torches, set on the pillars at regular intervals, spread a dim light.

Two large chandeliers hung from the ceiling, holding numerous candles. Akennor noticed reddish sparkles glinting.

Rubies, thought Akennor. It seemed that this organization enjoyed a solid financial source, to afford placing precious stones on its chandeliers. On each side of the room was a wide staircase of polished black wood.

On the back wall, facing the entrance, an immense fresco covered the entire surface. They could not make out the details well because of the dim lighting. However, hideous horned faces emerged from the shadows, sending chills through them.

Their guide stopped and, turning toward them, said:

"It is fairly late, and as I mentioned earlier, the Master will receive you tomorrow morning so that you may give him a detailed report on your activities of the past months. Please follow me, I will show you to your quarters."

The decor was heavy and oppressive. The air was too, filled with a strange smell of sulfur mixed with the scent of stale air. The group took the left staircase and reached the upper floor.

A long corridor ran through the castle, lined with many doors, all of the same black wood, placed on either side of the passage. A second staircase led to an even higher floor. The light, very faint, came from oil lanterns that gave off a weak glow on each side, barely enough to illuminate the place.

The lanterns were supported by humanoid arms sculpted in raw, matte metal. Between each door hung terrible paintings, illustrating horrifying acts of torture, as well as obscene scenes showing women with demons, people violated, mutilated, tortured, and devoured by monsters from the lower planes. There were also depictions of sinister figures that inspired fear just by looking at them.

The companions simply could not believe it. How could such horror exist in these places, so close to the City of Light?

Akennor wondered inwardly if these paintings reflected real events, or if they were the fruit of a morbid imagination. A shiver ran down his spine, and a deep disgust overwhelmed him.

Darian was on the verge of panic, Sheila growing more and more furious, and Milenna wore a serene expression, though inwardly filled with profound disdain. Akennor, fully aware, refused to give in to panic and fear. Halfway down, they came across a space furnished with a small wooden table, iron chairs with a brutal design, and two sofas placed on either side of the little vestibule. Funereal frescoes, depicting tortured souls and scenes showcasing demons, decorated this corner. Darian, who had once believed in man's goodness, in virtue and justice, was deeply disturbed by what he saw.

That human beings could perpetrate such sordid acts and worship such monsters... The pretty blonde stopped and turned toward them once more:

"To your right is a place to talk, read, and rest. To your left is the castle's library, containing many very old manuscripts of magic and other knowledge. Your quarters are right here, next to it."

She opened the door for them and informed them:

"The Master's office is just upstairs, at the end of the corridor, in a small tower. Be there early tomorrow, for you will leave right afterward... for you know where."

The blonde winked.

"Well then, good night."

Darian, Sheila, and Milenna entered the room, dimly lit by two small lanterns, wondering what sort of decoration it might hold.

Then came Akennor's turn, but he was stopped by a hand on his shoulder. The beautiful guide leaned close, pressed herself against him, and, in her most sensual voice, whispered:

"My room is across from the staircase, at the end of this floor. Join me… if you want."

She spoke languidly, insistently. The women slowly withdrew, moving sensually, all the while staring at him with a look that revealed her desires. The young warrior felt uneasy; never had a woman approached him in such a way. He managed to say:

"All right, maybe…" and gave her a timid smile.

The young woman walked off down the corridor, satisfied and confident that Akennor would come to their rendezvous. His three friends, who had caught fragments of the exchange, were perplexed.

He came up to them.

"What did that wench want?" Sheila asked, outraged.

"She offered me her charms for the night. Her room is across from the staircase, on this floor," said Akennor, amused.

"And you said yes? Do you think we're here to have fun ?!"

Sheila seemed truly upset… and Akennor could have sworn he detected a faint trace of jealousy.

"I didn't say yes. I told her 'maybe.' I didn't want her to insist… Refusing a woman's advances must be unusual here," he explained.

"Do you think that kind of… that kind of… woman is used to being told no? If you don't go, she'll probably come get you," retorted Sheila, stumbling over the word.

"I don't think so. She's too proud to chase after a male like that. But she's going to be very disappointed, that's certain," added Milenna.

These words seemed to calm Sheila somewhat.

"Anyway, we won't be staying here long. We need to explore the place and get out as soon as possible. Preferably before sunrise. We can't meet the Master... we'd be unmasked," suggested Akennor.

"I agree. This place is horrible... those paintings, those frescoes," said Darian. "It's as if they're watching us... I want to get out right now."

His friends sat him down on the first of the two large beds in the room. Six paintings hung on the walls, of course in the same theme as those in the corridor. Four arrow slits opened to the outside, but no light entered. The bedspreads were hand-embroidered with the same macabre motifs as the paintings, on blood-colored fabric.

"Calm down, Darian. Close your eyes and think of beautiful things," Milenna comforted him in her gentle voice.

She sat beside him and hugged him.

Darian closed his eyes.

"It doesn't change anything," he said painfully. "I feel the evil that inhabits this place... through every pore of my skin."

"We all feel it, Darian. Think of beautiful moments. Fight your dark thoughts," encouraged Akennor.

Darian managed, not without effort, to push back his fears and apprehensions by thinking of Shaya. She needed them. That thought brought back sweet memories. He recalled her disarming smile, her deep and intense eyes. Courage resurfaced in Darian's mind and chased away the panic. He could not falter.

"It's so hot in here... I feel like I'm suffocating," said Milenna. She felt a deep unease, caused as much by the atmosphere as by the heaviness of the air.

"Yes, hot... and unhealthy," added Sheila.

The companions then discussed a plan. They decided to go to the Master's office, to search for clues that might help them. If they found something… all the better. If not, they would risk exploring the castle from top to bottom, if necessary. They had to act quickly, for they all agreed: meeting the Master would be far too risky. Akennor and his friends would have to leave before sunrise.

They waited a while before acting, hearing no noise around them anymore. The group thought that probably all the residents were asleep… or busy with repulsive things. They also decided it was imperative to stay together. Akennor led the way, the others following in single file. Milenna brought up the rear.

No sound reached the young woman's attentive ears as the group advanced stealthily down the gloomy hallway, walking on tiptoe, making as little noise as possible. No floorboard creaked, thanks to the black carpet covering the corridor floor. They reached the end of the passage and took the staircase leading to the upper floor, still in complete silence and darkness. Only Milenna could distinguish anything at all.

Akennor set his foot on the last step of the landing, and a sinister creak echoed. The friends winced with apprehension and froze for a moment, on edge. Then Akennor moved forward again, taking care not to step on the defective stair.

The others carefully stepped over it. They all hoped this hadn't alerted the residents… but apparently it had not. No suspicious sound reached their ears. The companions edged around the stairwell on tiptoe, then crossed the short corridor leading to the Master's office.

The black door was ajar, which Akennor found strange. But he didn't dwell on it and silently thanked their lucky star.

It was a large room, with two small windows on each side of a wide burgundy wooden desk facing the entrance. Sheila lit the small oil lamp they had brought from their chamber, and they began to search discreetly, in silence. A blend of sulfur, leather, and paper smells permeated the room.

The wooden floor creaked faintly under their feet, making the young intruders' hair stand on end. Large bookshelves lined the left wall. An imposing fresco adorned the right wall. It depicted a great reddish demon, tinged with green, horned, humanoid in form, with a terrifying face. Its mouth was gaping open, showing sharp teeth. The demon bore an expression of satisfaction. With its right arm, it brandished the head of an old man. Another figure knelt at the monster's feet, worshiping it.

Tholgor, Akennor thought, *offering his father as a sacrifice to the demons...*

He turned away from the image, heart tight, and focused on the desk. Many papers were scattered there, and he decided to examine them methodically so as not to disturb anything. Under a few books, Akennor found something very interesting, while Sheila concentrated on the drawers. Darian and Milenna searched the shelves.

It was a very old map, judging by its condition. The edges were worn, crumbling, and blackened.

It showed a geographical description of the then-known world… except for the east, which did not appear, as it had not yet been discovered. However, a new land had been added. Akennor had never seen it on any other map.

Orendil had been right: there did exist a land to the north. The map also showed the continent as it had been before it was split apart.

Recent dotted lines indicated the fracture lines. Four points had been added: the fortress of Angrenost, a place called Marak, another called Mortgrunt, and a last one that seemed to be a port, judging by its proximity to the sea.

Akennor did not know these places, but he found the information precious. As he studied the map, trying to memorize as much as possible — since he obviously could not take it with him — he suddenly heard a cavernous laugh resonate in his head. A vile laugh, enough to chill the blood. A deep unease twisted his gut, and sweat broke out on his forehead.

He felt, in the very depths of his being, that something was wrong. The young warrior hastily put the map back and grabbed Sheila by the arm. They joined Milenna and Darian, and that was the moment when his premonition came true…

Dark, hooded figures burst into the office, led by what was probably the master of the place… and Sathoryn. Darian started when he saw them and immediately recognized the traitor.

"What? You traitor! You wretch! Scum! I'll tear your heart out!"

He stepped toward Sathoryn, but the many sword blades leveled at him quickly dissuaded him.

The one in charge of the castle stepped forward and spoke:

"So, you must be the friends of the one called Shaya… Such courage, such recklessness! To venture into the enemy's lair."

The companions exchanged a silent glance.

"So we were expected," said Akennor calmly.

"No, not really. The team that carried out the abduction merely warned us that perhaps three youths would be on their trail, but they couldn't confirm it. My friend Sathoryn, here present, was also informed of this, and he arrived a few moments ago to alert us to your presence."

But I'm being rude… We haven't introduced ourselves. I am Mortragor, master of these premises. And you are?"

"What nerve, you bastard! Where is she? Where is she?!"

Darian was seething. His fear had turned into hatred.

"Beyond your reach now. Far away. You will never see her again. There's no point insisting or wasting your time."

"Be reasonable: join us. You will be richer and more powerful than in all your wildest dreams."

Mortragor seemed sincere as he said this, judging by the malevolent gleam in his eyes and the sadistic smile revealing his pointed teeth.

"No, you're deranged!" bellowed Darian.

Mortragor made a sign, and three figures seized Darian. He tried to struggle, but in vain.

"As you wish. Either you come with us… or you suffer a punishment worse than death. Your choice."

Sathoryn gave a crooked smile and immediately left the room. He found it pointless to witness this kind of scene: the youths would be slaughtered and the villains satisfied. In the process, he would be rewarded for his loyalty.

He was the big winner in this situation.

"I prefer the punishment rather than betraying Shaya… and betraying myself."

And I believe that is the opinion of us all," declared Akennor in a determined tone. Two men grabbed him. Two others took hold of Sheila, and still others took charge of Milenna.

Darian was fuming.

"Very well, in that case… you asked for it. Ha ha ha!"

"Brainless youth, your lives will have been vain… and useless. What a pity! So much talent wasted on the wrong cause," added Mortragor.

The guards forced Sheila brutally to her knees, pushing her almost onto her belly. The tension, born of overwhelming frustration, swelled in her chest and burned within.

This can't be… this cannot happen, she told herself.

Akennor had his hands pinned behind his back. Darian was beginning to be struck. Milenna was now in the same position as Sheila.

Sheila could barely breathe. Her breathing was rapid and uneven. Her body on fire. *I've had enough. Enough.* Then her anger erupted. The burning heat inside her intensified.

"NOOOOOOOO!" she screamed.

The cry was so powerful, so piercing, that the small office windows shattered. Sheila's body became as hot as a live ember. The guards let go. She sprang up at once.

The pain of her inner fire was now almost unbearable. She stretched out her hands before her, releasing the destructive energy.

"Coron'ur!"

Suddenly, a fireball burst from her chest, passing through her outstretched hands. Their hosts had clearly not expected this. An expression of surprise, then terror, spread across their faces.

Four guards and Mortragor were struck full-on by the fireball. They were hurled violently backward, engulfed by the flames.

Darian, surprised by this surge of courage, let out a growl. He managed to bring his arms in front of him, then shoved his keepers violently—so hard that they let go and fell onto their backs.

Milenna had once again taken on her animal form, before the stunned eyes of her attackers. She turned on them and leapt at the throat of the nearest.

Akennor took the opportunity to free himself with a headbutt. His hands released, he drew his swords from their scabbards. Before one of his assailants could get back up, Darian smashed his skull with his war hammer. Then, turning quickly, he struck the second violently, sending him crashing into the wall.

The third was killed by Sheila. As the guard rushed at her, a magical projectile hurled him face-first to the floor. The mage finished him with a sword stroke.

Milenna had already strangled one. She was now dealing with another, biting and raking flesh. The victim writhed in pain, trying to shield himself from the claws… but in vain. He breathed his last in dreadful agony.

Akennor dispatched the first assailant with one blade and ran his other enemy through with the second. Another adversary attacked him: Akennor narrowly avoided a lightning-fast blow aimed at his head by ducking, and took the chance to drive his blades into the undefended body.

Cries were echoing throughout the building. Without a doubt, the fight had alerted everyone present.

"Quick! We have to get out of here—follow me!" said Akennor.

As they reached the staircase, hooded figures suddenly appeared.

"There they are!"

It was Mortragor, his face and part of his body burned. He had gone to fetch reinforcements. The companions immediately changed direction and tore off down the corridor ahead.

Arrows and crossbow bolts whistled past their ears.

"We must not let them escape!" Mortragor shouted.

The young adventurers took a nearby staircase, not knowing where it might lead. After descending one flight, an opening appeared in the wall. Without taking time to think, swept along by their momentum, they plunged through it and hurried down a second, narrow staircase cut into the stone. After a long descent, they finally reached the bottom and passed under an archway, anxious at not knowing where they were.

Suddenly, a dull rumble sounded. The floor and walls vibrated. They stood still. Then a terrible crash: a large stone fell behind them, blocking the way out. Shortly after, a vile laugh was heard. The sound, muffled, was nonetheless audible.

"Hahaha… Poor fools! Here is your punishment! No one has ever come out of this place alive. Even the oldest among us don't know what's in that hole… But be sure that horrors are waiting for you with open arms!"

The four friends were trapped. Fate had just played one of its cruelest tricks on them.

Chapter 12 – Orendil

Orendil spent the night tossing and turning in his bed, unable to find sleep. Since the young ones had departed, the sage had tried to think, to remember. Yet he had always had an excellent memory until now. In truth, only part of his memories seemed inaccessible, as if something blocked him, barring the way.

Finding no rest as the sun was about to rise, the sage decided to get up. He donned his long velvet robe of deep blue. The tips of the sleeves were embroidered with silver thread in runic inscriptions of an ancient language; the collar and hem were likewise adorned with the same symbols. He tied a broad silver belt around his waist, then went to his desk.

The old man sat heavily in his chair, as if now feeling the full weight of his years. He placed his hands over his face, trembling, his head aching more and more. Parting his fingers slightly, Orendil looked at his desk.

His eyes scanned the many documents before him until he noticed the mission order he had given one of his best men to meet with Sathoryn. That had been four days ago; the messenger should have had time to go and return. Yet no word had come back. The instructions had been clear: to communicate the gathered information as soon as possible.

A foreboding grew in the old man's mind. Doubt took root regarding Sathoryn. After all, he did not truly know him. The spy had been recommended by Berantis.

His messenger, named Baran, was loyal and trustworthy. He was supposed to meet the spy incognito in Elenshae.

He recalled the damnation of Tholgor and his prophecy about the descendants of Oriador and his guard, present at Tholgor's death. His head pounded harder, but the sage pressed on. He took paper and quill and wrote: descendants, prophecy, Tholgor…

A sudden flash of memory struck him. At last, those known for certain to be direct descendants had been hunted down and massacred. Their parents killed. These events had taken place about fifty years ago. The sage's head felt ready to burst; the pain was nearly unbearable.

Long ago, with Ardoras, his lifelong friend, he had fought a dreadful being. The torment now made him groan; his memory was barred, blocked. His temples throbbed in agony, and his skull felt like it might split. Orendil tried to break free of the bonds imprisoning his memory. He saw a terrifying face with black eyes and heard a demonic laugh. The pain was too intense, and it made him faint.

A long while later, the old sage opened his eyes weakly. The pain had ebbed, but his memory was still clouded. The effort had left him frail, his arms trembling, but he managed to straighten in his chair. He looked down at the paper with wide eyes. Before darkness had overtaken him, he had scrawled one last word with a trembling hand: "*Drendor.*"

His memory had suddenly returned.

"Drendor!" whispered the old sage. "Evil incarnate."

He was the cause of all this suffering. Did he intend to bring back the demons of old? This revelation is grave, Orendil thought ou loud.

"The young ones… those poor children do not know whom they are dealing with."

Hurrying from his study, he went to the quarters of his two finest warriors: Xantaris and Amandil. They were also good friends, ever since they had joined the Order.

The sage knocked urgently at their door. After a moment, Xantaris opened. Orendil was fond of these two young paladins. Xantaris was a warrior who had only recently become a paladin. Virtue and courage defined him. Of average build and height, he still had a boyish face and youthful features. His green eyes shone with energy and passion for justice and protecting people from evil. His short blond hair was topped by a small tuft falling over his forehead. Xantaris looked intrigued at this early-morning summons. Amandil, the second warrior, had also recently become a paladin. Slightly shorter and less robust than Xantaris, he was quicker, nimbler, more skilled. His face appeared older than his friend's, though he was in fact a little younger—perhaps because of the beard covering his chin and the mustache above his lip.

His brown hair was longer than Xantaris's, and his deep brown eyes gave his gaze an intimidating intensity.

"Good morning, Master. What can we do for you this morning? You seem weak... are you well?" asked Xantaris.

"Good morning, my brave ones... I... I have something grave to entrust to you. A mission. Urgent."

"Then come in, we're listening. Come, Amandil, the Master wishes to speak."

He entered, closing the door behind him. Amandil came forward and helped the old man sit on a small wooden chair near the entrance.

"This concerns the four young ones who came here about three days ago," he began.

"Yes, I heard about them," said Amandil.

"I fear they are in great danger, and I fear misfortune is tied to their quest."

The sage briefly recounted the legend of Tholgor, the abduction of Shaya, the quest of Akennor and his friends, his blocked memory, and Drendor.

"I believe that foul being is behind all of this. He is a fierce adversary, terribly dangerous, and without mercy. I would have you go aid them."

The two friends exchanged anxious, surprised looks. A brief silence followed. Xantaris's eyes grew bright, and Amandil spoke:

"Gladly, Master. We will do all we can to find them and help them."

"We are proud to honor our oath as paladins," added Xantaris with pride.

"Go first to Elenshae to meet Sathoryn, at the Lady Aicha, in the southwest quarter near the docks. Be cautious with this man: I have serious doubts about his loyalty. But I trust you will persuade him to aid you."

They nodded and smiled. The sage gave a brief physical description of Sathoryn. Orendil then went to the door, turning once more:

160

"I will alert the authorities of Elenshae and Kementári, as well as some friends. This matter will interest them."

He laid a hand on their shoulders, as if to give them courage.

"Good luck, my children. Be careful, and… trust no one but yourselves," he added with a kind look.

"Understood. We'll send word from Elenshae to keep you informed," Amandil added.

The Master approved and left, more troubled than ever. Each thought weighed heavier on him.

"Quite a start to the day," exclaimed Xantaris.

"You're telling me. Let's get ready quickly and go."

The two gathered their gear. Xantaris wielded a great two-handed sword, which he handled with surprising dexterity for his frame. Amandil preferred war hammers— he used two at once, shorter than regular models. Soon ready, the two friends went to the stables, saddled their horses, asked the guards to lower the drawbridge— justifying it as a patrol—and set off for Elenshae.

Back in his study, Orendil watched Xantaris and Amandil gallop away toward the great coastal city. Shortly after, the sage went to see his assistant, his right hand, named Berantis.

Berantis's parents had died when a barbarian tribe attacked their village east of Kementári, when Berantis was only four. Despite his young age, Orendil had taken him under his wing. With will and determination, Berantis quickly became a priest of the Order. In major battles, he had proven a fine strategist, and Orendil had seen leadership in him. He had made him his assistant so that one day he might become his successor. Orendil had placed much hope in him and loved him like a son.

Now he was a tall, strong man of thirty, with a face older than his years—perhaps from early misfortune.

Wrinkles already lined his cheeks and brow. A hard, short black beard covered his broad chin. His hair was short and black, and his brown eyes, beneath heavy lids, carried a constant look of sadness. That day, Berantis wore only the Order's uniform: black trousers and a dark blue velvet shirt, with silver trim at the collar and cuffs.

"What is it?" asked Berantis.

"I have troubling news for you, my boy," replied Orendil, clearing his throat.

A clatter of dishes disturbed them. They turned. A servant had entered, carrying a silver tray with a teapot and two porcelain cups marked with the Order's silver sigil.

"Ah! Please set it on the small table between the divans, Diego. Thank you," Orendil said gratefully.

"Nothing like a good tea to think more clearly," he continued, glancing at Berantis.

The latter shrugged and sat on a divan. The servant set down the tray delicately and slipped out. Orendil sat facing Berantis, poured tea into both cups, and handed one to his assistant. Berantis waited, intrigued, eager for the sage to explain. Orendil leaned back and began:

"Do you know the legend of the Damnation of Tholgor?" he asked his protégé.

Berantis looked more intrigued.

"No, I don't believe so. What is it about?"

The old sage sighed, looked into his drink, and began the tale he had told the four young adventurers days before. Berantis listened intently, without flinching.

"It seems someone seeks to fulfill the prophecy and reclaim the power brought by the demons," he said.

Berantis remained impassive, as usual. Calm and composed.

"Do you have any idea who it is?"

He sipped the refined tea. Its warmth and fragrant aroma soothed him.

"Yes, I know who," Orendil said, gaze distante.

"It is a powerful necromancer I fought long, long ago. Strangely... his name and the memories tied to him were barred from me, blocked. I cannot explain how."

"Indeed, strange. And yet you managed to unlock those memories?" Berantis asked, intrigued.

"Yes, but not without pain, believe me. In any case, it is Drendor, a powerful necromancer who damned himself long ago. I am certain it is he."

He then told of Akennor and his friends, whose story he believed tied to Drendor. He finished his cup, set it on the tray, and rose.

"We must warn the authorities of Elenshae and Kementári, visiting the rulers. We must also rally our people, that they may be ready to act. I do not know what he is planning, but I expect the worst from such a wretch. Perhaps even an invasion. That would explain why the young ones saw orcs days ago—likely a scouting party."

Berantis listened thoughtfully. He refilled the sage's cup as the old man turned away.

"I agree, Master. And we could divide the tasks to save time," Berantis suggested, handing him the cup.

He took it and sat again.

"Thank you Berantis. We'll agree on a plan and send our swiftest messengers."

The sage took another sip. But the taste was different. Bitter. Acrid. Strange. Then a searing pain gripped his chest, and he collapsed to the floor. Writhing in agony, his body convulsed. He tried to call for help, but his body betrayed him. Berantis bent over him with a cruel smile.

"What's the matter, Master? Hahaha! Don't worry—it won't be long... but it will hurt. You are clever, oh yes, too clever. But fortunately, too late. Fear not, I will take care of the Order in your... absence."

The sage now understood: his memory lapses, the growing stagnation of the Order, the decline of his health—these went back only a short time. Berantis was the cause.

Not only did his body suffer unbearable torment, but his heart broke as well. He had loved Berantis like a son...
Through the pain, he turned to look his betrayer in the eyes.

With a strangled voice, he managed:

"But... why?"

Berantis answered coldly:

"Do not trouble yourself with questions or answers that no longer matter. It is of no importance now."

The sage's last thoughts, his life flashing before him, returned. He saw again the day a paladin entrusted him with a small boy he had saved. That round little face, those bright, sparkling eyes... He saw him grow again, memory after memory. How he had loved him... *Why? What had happened?* Heartbroken, he closed his eyes.

"Be accursed."

The pain flared, sharper than ever. It felt as if his body burned from within. His lips could only release guttural groans. His body convulsed violently, ever more so. His final thoughts, full of hope, flew toward Akennor and his friends.

He wished them luck, and asked Oriador to protect and bless them. With a choking gurgle, life left him. His body went limp, his face serene, as if he had died peacefully.

"At last you die, old fool," Berantis growled.

"Formidable, Master Drendor's poison... I will send him word at once of this. He will be pleased to hear the old man is dead and that I now control the Order. What irony, hahaha!"

Berantis savored the moment, then quickly donned a mask of panic, calling for help. He told the others that the Master had suffered a seizure and collapsed. Members of the Order rushed in, trying in vain to revive him. All were shocked and saddened by the sudden loss. As he had foreseen, Berantis was appointed his replacement—until the annual assembly of the Order's sages.

Chapter 13 – Trapped

Drendor's face, cold and expressionless, bore a wicked smile. Everything was unfolding according to his plan.

Two of his lieutenants had reported to him earlier that day. First, Mortragor, from the base near Elenshae, had informed him that a group of four youths had managed to enter the castle. They seemed to be searching for "the one" who was their friend. How touching, thought Drendor coldly, but how utterly pointless.

Mortragor had added that the group was now trapped in the catacombs, a dreadful place from which no one ever returned alive. Even Drendor did not know all the horrors haunting those depths, for that part of the castle had been sealed and forgotten long ago. Long before he took control of the organization, centuries earlier. The entrance to the catacombs had only recently been rediscovered. Drendor intended to bring that place back to life, once devoted to the worship of demons.

According to Mortragor, the group had proven powerful for mere apprentices, giving him some trouble. At last, thought Drendor, the tiny threat they posed is now definitively removed. The other news pleased him even more: Berantis had confirmed the death of the leader of the Order of Calaista and taken his place. He had mentioned, however, that the sage had managed to break the enchantment Drendor had cast on him.

"The secret is complete and preserved. What a great victory we are about to achieve!" Berantis had added enthusiastically.

Drendor particularly liked this young prospect: deceitful and malevolent, just as he preferred them.

The dark necromancer slowly descended toward the throne room. Maultarg and Trumakara were bent over the large table, studying the plans.

They were discussing the final preparations when Drendor approached silently. Maultarg sensed his presence and turned.

"What news?" asked Drendor coldly.

Trumakara, the troll general, replied in his grating voice:

"All goes well, my lord. Gauldrom and Gromurh have arrived in the mountains and will soon be heading south, toward the Order's stronghold. Cartaraug left with the trolls from the Marak camp and will soon join the troops already in the mountains."

Maultarg, the half-orc, continued:

"All the teams have returned to the castle near Elenshae and await your orders. Kassef is almost with his own; he'll be there in a few days."

"Good. Very good. Maultarg, immediately order the halt of all reconnaissance patrols. We must not be discovered so close to our goal."

Drendor recalled the recent encounter between the youths and an orc patrol, a report given to him by Berantis.

"Yes, master, right away."

Maultarg strode off.

"Trumakara, you may go join Cartaraug and await my orders."

"Yes, of course, master. I believe everything is ready. All that remains is to carry out the plan."

The troll general gave a wicked smile, bowed respectfully, and left for his quarters.

"It will be a true massacre…" whispered Drendor with a sadistic laugh that echoed in the empty hall.

*

Complete darkness reigned. They were trapped in an utterly unknown place.

Darian panicked.

"Raaahhh! I want out!" he screamed, striking his hammer furiously against the stone that blocked their passage.

"No! No! It can't be!"

He kept pounding with all his strength. Small sparks flew in the dark, but the rock remained intact.

Darian had had enough of all these ordeals. Everything seemed to draw them further from Shaya forever. His throat tightened, his heart ached. He stk again, then stopped, exhausted. Sheila and Milenna approached to comfort him and held him in their arms.

Akennor spoke first:

"Come on, we have to get out of here. I don't want to rot in this hole."

"There are torches in my bag."

He fumbled and pulled out four, handing them to Sheila.

"Can you light them, please?"

She invoked her spell of light:

"Aurë!"

A glowing orb appeared, floating above them. Then she lit the torches with another spell:

"Narë-rhu!"

A flame sprang from her fingertips. Each took a torch. Darian rose again, still shaken.

"Come on, don't give up, Darian. We can get out of this, I'm sure," said Akennor encouragingly.

The combined light of the torches and the luminous sphere revealed a gloomy environment. The companions were in a circular chamber. The rough, uneven walls bore marks of ancient chiseling. The air was damp, filled with the stench of mold.

"Which way do we go?" asked Sheila.

Two tunnels opened before them.

"What about the one on the left?" suggested Milenna.

"Fine by me. Anyway, there must be many tunnels… We'll probably end up exploring them all in this cursed place," concluded Akennor.

Darian said nothing, merely nodded. They entered the left tunnel. The passage was wide enough for two to walk side by side. Akennor and Milenna led the way, with Sheila and Darian behind.

A little farther, they reached an intersection with a cross-passage. They chose to continue straight. Soon after, another crossroads appeared; this time, they turned left. The farther they advanced, the heavier, damper, and fouler the air became. The group soon entered a hall. They raised their torches high to illuminate it, but horror quickly made their arms sink.

"Oh… this is horrible!" exclaimed Akennor.

Sheila guided the orb of light to the center to see better. All widened their eyes.

The rectangular chamber held at its center two large polished stone altars. The floor was covered with sticky bones, slippery as if blood had never fully dried. The far wall was entirely built of human, elven, and dwarven skulls. Great chains hung there, with several full skeletons crucified. Eight pillars sculpted as demons supported the ceiling, with chains and bones suspended from them.

In the center of the wall was a great black metal plate engraved with silver letters — likely a dark prayer to infernal demons. The walls, ceiling, and floor were smeared with blood.

The companions gagged, imagining the horrors committed here. Darian could not contain himself and vomited.

"I was about to suggest we rest... but not here," said Akennor.

"Absolutely not! I won't spend another moment here," added Sheila.

Milenna, bent over Darian, helped him stand. They fled through the first passage they saw, eager to leave that place. It felt as if they were going in circles, but the tunnel straightened and soon led to another crossing.

From its orientation, Akennor concluded they had returned to their starting point and suggested going straight. Moments later, they faced another wall. Two new paths opened. The air from the left smelled less foul, so they chose that way. But their expressions froze: they had indeed returned to where they had begun.

In a new fit of rage, Darian pounded the blocking stone again. Sheila and Milenna sat, exhausted and disheartened. Akennor tried to reason with and comfort his friend.

"Come on, Darian, pull yourself together. I know it's hard, but..."

"Oh, what now! We're lost! Great idea, Akennor! Let's run straight into the wolf's den! See the cost now?"

Darian's tone was icy, full of bitterness. Akennor froze. How could his best friend speak to him like that?

His reply was just as sharp:

"If you had a better idea, you should have said so earlier. I thought you agreed... Unless you're just afraid. I care about Shaya, and I'm not afraid to do what it takes to find her."

Those words cut Darian deeply. With a cry of rage, he raised his hammer and tried to strike his friend. Akennor dropped his torch and drew both swords in a flash. Darian swung again, but Akennor parried skillfully.

Even as Darian seemed to lose his mind, Akennor kept his: dodging, blocking, careful not to wound his friend. The skirmish was brief.

Sheila and Milenna rushed in, restraining Darian and wresting away his weapon. Sheila laid a hand on his arm, whispering soothing words. A long silence followed. Darian sat frozen, eyes wide, realizing what he had done.

What have I done? He's my best friend... I must tell them everything. I have to.

Ashamed, he rose slowly.

"Forgive me, my friend. I wasn't myself..."

"What's gotten into you? I don't recognize you, Darian. Tell me!"

Akennor was shaken, struggling to comprehend what had just happened. Surely there was a reason, but it explained nothing.

Darian lowered his eyes.

"Forgive me for before... I lost control. This pain is deep, because... perhaps the happiest moment of my life happened just over a year ago."

172

He paused, visibly moved.

"Shaya and I spent much time together that summer. Akennor was helping his father, Sheila was working and buried in her books…"

He gazed into the distance, lost in memory.

"One day, as we watched the sunset by Lake Bay…"

Darian stopped briefly, then continued, voice thick with emotion.

"She was so beautiful that day… The sun shining on her silky, smooth hair. We looked into each other's eyes for a long time, then kissed passionately, for a long while."

He stood, throat tight, words hard to form.

"That night we slept under the stars… in each other's arms."

Now his back was to them, unable to stop sobbing. Akennor and Sheila looked at each other in disbelief. They had not expected such a confession. They rose and embraced Darian tightly.

After a moment, Akennor asked softly:

"But why didn't you tell us, Darian? We would have been happy for you…"

"We wanted time, not to rush. At the end of that summer, classes began about two weeks later… We never had the chance to tell you. We meant to, soon."

Now Akennor understood his friend's reaction and what this quest meant to him.

Sheila smiled faintly.

"So, it was you, the love of her life? Shaya told me… but never who he was. I was eager to know."

"Are you okay, Darian?" asked Akennor kindly.

"You'll see, we'll get out soon. I'll turn into a wolf and can find a way out more easily," said Milenna encouragingly.

She prepared a fire while Sheila searched the bags for food. She announced neutrally:

"Enough to eat for about two days, if we ration."

She handed out bread. They ate in silence. After the meager meal, they decided to rest before continuing.

All were exhausted, but each would take a turn on watch. Akennor kept the first, then woke the next. After a frugal breakfast, they pressed on, determined to escape this infernal place. Milenna, as a wolf, led the way, sniffing the ground and air. She took the left passage, then straight at the first branch, left at the second. They found themselves once again in the vile sacrificial hall.

"What?! We're back here?!" Sheila cried.

"Trust Milenna," suggested Akennor.

They hurried through. None wished to linger. Then they chose the right corridor. A short tunnel led them into a tall circular cavern. Stalactites hung from the ceiling, stalagmites rose from the floor. The center was darker. They approached cautiously.

"Water... it's some kind of small lake," exclaimed Sheila.

Akennor stepped closer, but Milenna bit his cloak, growling, forcing him back.

"All right... I don't like this lake either. Let's leave quickly," he said.

The path led to what seemed a vast chamber. Milenna's keen sense of smell warned her of danger. The stench was worse. Yet she pressed on, urgency driving her, and entered the hall. Another passage opened to the right. Without hesitation, Milenna guided them there. It led to a circular room with four iron tables at the center — torture tables, likely. Sinister instruments lined the walls.

Akennor thought he recognized the place.

"From the paintings... The horrible castle paintings. So... this really happened here..."

Shivers ran down their spines, Milenna's silver fur bristled. Her head swung side to side, as if hearing voices, lamentations…

"Let's get out quickly, I feel my blood freezing," whispered Sheila, horrified.

Milenna hurried ahead, the others following. Near the far end of the torture chamber lay an intersection. Recognizing their scent, she turned left. They emerged into a small empty circular room.

Three options. From the left corridor came that same unbearable stench: likely the vast hall again. The right tunnel probably led back where they had rested. Milenna chose straight ahead. Soon, a faint sound reached her ears. She disliked it.

A bad feeling grew. The noise grew louder as they advanced. Near the new chamber's entrance, the others heard it too.

"What is that? Do you hear it?" said Darian, straining.

"Sounds like… a woman crying," finished Akennor.

It was another circular chamber, with six cells, three on each side. The cells were small, completely empty. Their iron-barred doors hung ajar. Bone piles lay within each.

The sobs came from the last cell on the left, near another exit. They approached silently, peering timidly. A frail figure crouched, knees drawn up. A woman… or once a woman. Now just a pale echo of her earthly life: a ghost.

Sensing their gaze, the creature slowly raised her head. Her eyes were full of tears, lips trembling. She looked awful, emaciated; her beauty lost to grief. Darian's heart clenched. She had died of sadness, he thought.

"Have you seen my little boy? My little Bryan?" she sobbed.

"I miss him… I want to see him… I want to leave… It's so cold…"

Darian knelt gently.

"What's your name, madam?"

The ghost swallowed her tears.

"I… I think… Marianne."

Milenna tugged Darian's cloak gently, urging him away. But he ignored her. He wished to help this poor soul find peace.

"Do you know how long you've been here?"

Her gaze was lost, clueless.

"I… I don't know… A long time, I think. A very long time."

"Can you tell me what happened? Would you like to talk?"

She strained to recall.

"I was walking the streets of the New City, by the ocean, when shadows seized us. Then… darkness… these walls… My son was gone. No one told me anything. Nothing… I don't understand…"

A piercing wail cut through her sobs. Milenna grew more insistent.

"Marianne," Darian said tenderly, "I want to help you. But… your son is dead. He waits for you in the other world."

The woman raised her head.

"What do you mean?"

"You are dead too. You must accept it. Only then can you join your boy."

The truth was too harsh, too cruel. She wailed louder. Darian regretted it, but he longed for her to realize her state, to rest at last. He rose, retreating slowly.

The ghost rose too. Her sobs turned to a shrill lament, growing in anger and hate. The specter floated upward, face twisted, decomposed, empty-eyed, a vision of torment.

"It's not true! I want my child, do you hear me? I WANT MY CHILD!" she shrieked.

Suddenly, she lunged at Sheila, closest to her.

Marianne let out a hideous scream, death's messenger. Her form grew more terrifying. Milenna and Akennor instinctively averted their eyes. Sheila froze in fear; Darian too stood paralyzed. Milenna shifted back and rushed to Sheila.

Akennor dragged Darian toward the exit. Sheila and Darian dropped their torches. Akennor helped Milenna, who carried frozen Sheila on her shoulders. The ghost swirled around, spectral limbs chilling Milenna to the bone.

Akennor stayed close. Marianne screamed again, worse than before. He nearly fainted. Milenna faltered, kneeling. Akennor hauled her up with effort.

Darian sat just beyond, blank-eyed, terrified. Milenna told Akennor to tend to him. He lifted Darian and risked a glance back.

The specter stood at the threshold, unable to pass. One last shriek... then she vanished. As they staggered away, the same faint sobs echoed once more — the same that had lured them to her.

Chapter 14 – The Horror

When they heard nothing more, the adventurers stopped. Akennor sat Darian down, whose face was beginning to regain some color. Milenna gently laid Sheila on her back. She still bore an expression of horror.

Milenna rummaged in Darian's bag and lit the last torch. Akennor still had his own, which he had slipped into a holder before helping his friend.

Milenna fixed her gaze on Darian's and said:

"Why didn't you listen to me? Why? Wasn't I clear enough? Next time, must I bite you?"

She was truly angry.

"Look at her now. I hope Sheila will pull through."

Ashamed, Darian lowered his eyes.

"I'm sorry, Milenna… I don't know what came over me. That woman made me feel such pity. I just wanted to help her find peace."

Milenna's face softened.

"That's an honorable thought… but a vain one. These creatures don't even know they're dead, let alone accept it."

She paused, pensive.

"It is pitiful, yes… but nothing can be done for them. Only they, perhaps, in time…"

"What exactly was that?" Akennor asked timidly.

"A vengeful specter. A ghost... a spirit turned wicked after a very deep trauma," Milenna explained.

"These beings seek only vengeance. They want to make others pay for their death and their suffering by instilling terror."

"So she still suffers?" Akennor asked again.

"Yes. But perhaps, with time, her suffering will lessen... and she may finally know peace."

"It's unfair. Truly unfair..."

No one answered. None of them could find words, nor could they refute the statement. Akennor leaned over Sheila, whose eyes were wide open, staring into the void. He gently closed her eyelids, whispering reassuring words, happy memories in her ear. Then he held her tightly. Little by little, Sheila's body relaxed and regained suppleness. After a few moments, she blinked.

"What happened? I remember a sound... dreadful... and then nothing. I froze, I think."

Her friends laughed nervously, relieved.

"Why are you laughing?" she asked, bewildered.

"It's nerves," Akennor explained softly. "A huge relief. You scared us, you know."

"You were struck by the terror of a specter," Milenna clarified. "And it paralyzed you for quite a while, I must say."

"A specter of terror... the ghost. I was lucky," Sheila said with a shiver.

"You know about that?" Darian asked, visibly relieved to hear her speak normally again.

"Yes. We learned certain things at school about spirits and evil creatures. And how to protect ourselves from them."

She paused, then admitted:

"That's the creature I fear most. The one I never wanted to encounter. I hope there won't be others…"

A shiver ran through her at the memory.

Darian then asked:

"So… where do we go now? Does anyone have an idea?"

A nauseating odor, stronger and stronger, tickled his nostrils.

"We're in the chamber I dread the most. The one I tried to avoid at all costs," Milenna explained. "It's likely the largest in this entire labyrinth. We made a quick incursion here earlier, just before the torture chamber."

"Why do you fear it?" Sheila asked.

"Because of the smell. It's abominable… the stench of pure decay, of death. And I fear what may lurk in the shadows."

"But it looks like every path leads back here… Maybe we don't have a choice," Darian observed.

Akennor held out a small stick he had picked up from the ground.

"Do you think you could sketch out the layout?"

"Yes, I think so."

Thanks to her keen sense of smell under her wolf form, Milenna had kept a mental map of the corridors they had traveled. She knelt and, in the thick dust on the ground, drew the paths they had taken, as well as the shape of the current hall.

"This room seems to have this shape. And if there's an exit… it would probably be over there."

She pointed her torch toward a wall directly opposite the entrance through which they had entered the labyrinth.

"You're right about the smell… I feel it more and more, it's unbearable. I think I'm going to throw up," Sheila said, putting her hand over her mouth. She managed to hold back for a moment.

But a stronger wave reached Akennor, who this time couldn't contain himself. He vomited loudly.

Milenna turned away not to see, for her stomach was knotting as well.

Darian couldn't restrain himself either and retched up the flatbread he had eaten earlier in the day. Seeing her friends, Sheila could no longer hold back, and a thick viscous liquid poured from her mouth.

The smell grew even stronger, and she was seized by violent convulsions of disgust. Milenna moved closer to support her. The faint torchlight suddenly revealed a face in an advanced state of decomposition. Shreds of rotting flesh hung, its mouth twisted, teeth fully exposed, and its eyes, white and pupil-less, stared into emptiness.

"Aaaaaaaah!" screamed Sheila, opening her eyes just in time to behold the walking horror.

The creature's arm swung to strike her. But her reflexes saved her: she recoiled abruptly and cast a magic projectile. Then a second. And a third.

With a dull thud, the body fell to the ground, dismembered.

Milenna had stepped back to stay close to her friend, while Darian and Akennor rushed forward.

"What is this abomination now?" Akennor asked, exasperated.

"A walking dead. The second thing I most wished never to meet. Clearly, I'm being spoiled…" Sheila answered, breathless, trembling all over.

"And he's not alone. We're surrounded," Milenna said, all her senses alert.

The companions turned their heads in all directions. Everywhere, faces, each more hideous than the last. Their vacant eyes and gaping mouths emitted dark guttural growls. The creatures advanced slowly, arms outstretched. Some were missing large chunks of flesh.

Their clothes were stained with dried blood, greenish or yellowish fluids, and reeked of putrefaction. The circle of undead tightened around them.

Akennor and Milenna brandished their torches, waving them to keep the zombies at bay.

"Carnë-narë!" cried Sheila.

Her hands ignited, and she set ablaze the creature charging at her. The zombie groaned but kept advancing. Darian smashed his hammer onto the monster's vile head, reducing it to foul pulp.

Akennor, after handing his torch to Darian, drew his blades. He stood ready to face the horror. Milenna drew her short sword and focused.

"Above all, don't let them bite you!" Sheila shouted. "It could make you very sick... even kill you. And beware of their breath, it can poison you."

The zombies then attacked. Milenna's warning proved useful: several creatures opened their mouths and spewed a greenish cloud with an unbearable stench. The companions held their breath and fought back against the clumsy but relentless assaults of the undead.

Akennor slashed at the zombies with mighty blows of his blades, aiming above all to sever their heads. Sheila unleashed her fire spells again, letting out a savage cry, and charged into battle, followed by Darian, who finished off the wounded with hammer strikes. Akennor, isolated, began to be encircled. The zombies almost constantly spewed their pestilent breath at him, which he had to dodge while parrying their blows.

"Sirpë!" cried Milenna.

The ground trembled, the slabs broke, and long thorny roots shot forth, entwining the zombies before him. The other undead found themselves caught between Milenna and Akennor, who laid into them with abandon. Heads and arms fell from half-decayed hideous bodies. Then Akennor and Milenna rejoined Sheila and Darian, who were wreaking havoc. Zombies burned, Darian smashed bodies into pulp. But the four companions were wearing out. They were weak and exhausted, their strength waning.

Akennor realized they couldn't keep this pace much longer.

"We must charge toward the far door!" he shouted.

The companions regrouped and formed a united front. Akennor and Darian led the way, pushing the creatures back.

"Girls, slow down those behind, all right?" Darian suggested.

Milenna repeated her spell, trapping about twenty zombies in a tangle of roots. Sheila hurled magic projectiles that sent monsters flying, then set several ablaze.

"Can you do your fireball spell again, like in the castle? That was powerful," Milenna asked Sheila.

"No… I don't think I'm panicked enough yet. Maybe later…"

"Not panicked enough?" Milenna repeated, bewildered. "What more do you need?"

The undead were coming from everywhere. Some even emerged from the ground or the walls. There were hundreds. For every zombie slain, ten more appeared.

Akennor and Darian fought fiercely, managing to force their way forward.

"We have to make it... we must. We're almost there," Akennor thought."

"I see an opening!" Darian shouted. "It's not much farther now!"

The final stretch was seized at the cost of a ferocious struggle. The zombies seemed to deliberately block Akennor and Darian, as if they knew what the group was attempting.

They were pressed harder and harder against the walls. Overcome by heat, Akennor began to make mistakes. A zombie nearly grabbed his arm. Darian struggled to lift his hammer. Sheila, at her limit, could take no more. Her spells drained too much energy. Her fire had consumed dozens of zombies, but she felt she would collapse. The floor and walls seemed to spin around her. Milenna slowed the creatures with roots, cut their rotting flesh, and burned them with her torch. But Sheila finally collapsed. Everything spun. Faces blurred.

"No!" Milenna cried out, seeing her fall.

She threw herself over her to shield her from the monsters.

Darian spun around, lifted Sheila onto his shoulders, and Akennor redoubled his efforts to protect them. A glance passed between the three still standing. They understood. They had no choice left. It had to end.

With a final war cry, they hurled themselves into the fray. Darian stood at the center, shielding Sheila on his back. He had no torch, but swung his hammer with his right arm.

Akennor slashed and hewed heads with renewed vigor. Then, out of breath and strength, the young adventurers finally reached the tunnel they aimed for. The passage was short, and a staircase seemed to lead to a lower level.

He felt a diffuse dread, but he plunged in without hesitation, the guttural groans of the zombies urging him to decide quickly. Milenna turned back, her head already in the stairwell, and saw that none of the undead were following them.

"They stayed in the great hall," she announced, reassured, to her comrades.

But Darian wasn't ready to rejoice too soon. He told himself that another unpleasant surprise probably awaited them around a dark corner, and that they would likely not have enough strength to face it. The staircase was very narrow, and Darian had to take care not to bump Sheila. The steps, small and slippery, spiraled downward.

With only one torch to guide them, Akennor barely distinguished the steps and hurried along. He wanted to go further down, but the staircase ended there. The young warrior lost his balance and crashed face-first to the ground. Milenna, surprised, had no time to avoid him and fell on top of him.

The light went out abruptly. Darian, plunged into darkness, also stumbled over his companions, struggling to keep Sheila on his shoulders.

"Ah, you're crushing me..." Akennor groaned in a muffled voice.

Darian got back up and gently laid Sheila on the ground. Milenna freed herself, releasing Akennor from the combined weight of his three companions. She went to retrieve her torch, which had fallen nearby.

It still burned faintly, and as she pulled it free from the damp floor, the flame grew stronger again. Returning to the others, Milenna brought the light to Sheila's face. It was drenched in sweat, her forehead burning hot. The boys, worried, examined her body for bite marks.

"It's surely exhaustion. I see no bite, no serious injury. Just a few scratches," Akennor observed.

"Yeah, I agree," Darian approved.

"The best thing would be to rest a bit, and eat something. We don't know what awaits us," Milenna said, scanning the darkness around them.

"I'll take the second watch," she added in the same tone.

Then she took her animal form and curled up beside Sheila.

"I'll take the first watch, Darian. Rest."

"All right… I must admit I can't feel my arms anymore, they're so numb. Be vigilant, above all."

Akennor planted the torch into the stony floor near him and pulled out a flatbread his mother had prepared. He nibbled in silence, more alert than he had ever been. Nothing unusual happened. The young warrior then gently woke Milenna to take over. She yawned, revealing her sharp ivory-like fangs.

He closed his eyes and tried to find some rest. Milenna sat, ears pricked, keeping watch.

Chapter 15 – Lost

The same grating voice laughed in the dark, while thousands of other voices wailed all around. Hideous, twisted faces surrounded her. Shaya was tied to a post, burning in infernal flames at the foot of a gigantic winged demon. The vision blurred, revealing a black, devastated land streaked with rivers of blood. Then, a sudden dizzying rise was followed by an abyssal plunge into the bowels of the earth.

Akennor was suffocating, nausea rising to his throat. Darkness, again. The monstrous faces were still there. There were thousands of them. They closed in, drawing inexorably closer. Among them were Darian, Shaya, Milenna, Sheila… and two other bodies lay lifeless on the ground.

Akennor brandished his swords and screamed until his eardrums nearly burst:
"Nooooooo!"
His own cry jolted him awake with a start. Akennor leapt to his feet, drew his weapons, and swept his gaze quickly around.
Of course, his scream woke his companions, all of whom reacted immediately, believing an attack was

underway. Sheila, who had been keeping watch, rushed to calm him.

"Come now, everything's fine. You must have had a bad dream."

Akennor pulled himself together and looked at her tenderly.

"Yes... a horrible nightmare. And you, are you all right?"

"Yes, much better. I woke up during Darian's watch and took over," she answered with a smile.

"What was that death scream? I was really panicked... was that you, Akennor?" asked Darian.

"Yes... sorry. I had a dreadful nightmare."

"Well, if there are hostile beings prowling around, they won't take long to come," growled Milenna.

Sheila immediately leapt to Akennor's defense.

"Come now, Milenna, Akennor has intense nightmares he can't control. It's not his fault."

Akennor lowered his head, mortified by the incident. Even if he had never had control over his dreams, he had always feared the actions he might commit in his sleep.

"Yes, I believe that... but the damage is done. Anyway... we'll get through this. It's not serious," said Milenna, half-convinced.

"Shall we go then? Is everyone ready?" asked Darian.

The group gathered their belongings, then moved straight ahead.

"Milenna, did you catch anything unusual during your watch?" asked Akennor timidly.

Milenna sensed Akennor's discomfort and immediately softened her tone.

"Only death... It's steeped everywhere around us."

Her expression was grave, a shadow of worry darkening her features.

"We must be cautious," she added, before the silver-gray smoke enveloped her in her transformation.

Darian and Sheila had relit the torches. Each held one, except Milenna. She waited for them and, once they were ready, the beautiful wolf advanced into the corridor ahead. A gentle but steady slope led them deeper still into the heart of horror. The torches spread a faint glow, illuminating the reliefs of the walls carved in earth and hewn from stone. Soon, the young adventurers began to notice alcoves in the rock, where skeletons lay flat on their backs.

"Just what we needed…" muttered Akennor.

"Catacombs…" he added, disgusted.

"Let's hope we avoid bad encounters," said Sheila, who still felt weak and could cast only a few demanding spells.

While Akennor, Sheila, and Darian stared in horror at the human remains on either side of the corridor, Milenna followed her nose. She took a side passage to the right, for the air there carried a faint trace of purity. Focused on the scents, she realized too late that all light had vanished. Panic seized her when she turned back… only to find the passage now blocked by a wall.

A mechanism must have sealed the corridor, she thought. *But what about the others? And me, without them?*

She sniffed frantically, hoping to detect a hidden exit… in vain. Resigned, she concluded the best choice was to keep following the trail she had sensed, in hopes of escaping this place and finding her companions again.

Meanwhile, Akennor, Darian, and Sheila scanned the passage walls for any threat, not immediately noticing Milenna's disappearance. After a brief moment, Akennor frowned, swept the darkness with his torch, and looked around.

Sheila saw him growing restless and asked, worried:

"What's wrong, Akennor? Why are you so agitated?"

Instead of answering, Akennor called out:

"Milenna? Milenna! Where are you?"

The others froze in silence. When no answer came, Akennor added:

"I think we've lost her!"

"What? But how? She was just near us not long ago," said Darian.

"Let's retrace our steps—we can't lose her in this place!" urged Sheila.

Akennor agreed and lowered his torch toward the dusty ground, searching for footprints. Discouraged, Darian sat on a stone and leaned against the wall. They went back until they spotted the wolf's paw prints, disappearing into the rock wall.

"It looks like she went right through the wall!" exclaimed Sheila.

"Or else the wall closed up behind her," added Akennor, frantically searching for an opening.

But it was useless. Akennor joined Sheila at the wall of the cavern, staring in disbelief.

"I have no idea how… and I don't know how to find her. It's terrible," he lamented, dreading the thought of losing a friend in this cursed place.

"She surely isn't dead. Let's keep going, we'll find her," said Sheila encouragingly.

Akennor gave a timid smile.

"You're probably right. Let's keep hope alive. We must be extremely careful—this place holds too many surprises. We absolutely must stay together. After all, she vanished almost before our eyes."

"I agree with you. What do you think, Darian?" asked Sheila.

192

Suddenly, Akennor was seized by a strange foreboding. He spun around toward Sheila.

"Darian?" she asked timidly.

"Oh no… it can't be… oh no…"

Akennor bolted back the way they had come, Sheila rushing close behind. When they reached the spot where they had last paused, they waved their torches about, searching for the slightest clue. Darian's footprints stopped near a flat stone.

Akennor crouched down and observed:

"He sat on this rock."

Examining the relief on the stone, he added as he turned back toward Sheila:

"Darian sat on this rock and leaned against the wall."

Forgetting all prudence, Sheila screamed:

"Darian!"

The sound echoed several times on the rocky walls, Sheila's voice returning as a confused echo.

"There's so much echo it's impossible to tell where it came from," observed Akennor.

*

Darian had briefly closed his eyes. When he reopened them, the scenery had changed. It was no longer the same place at all.

Panic took hold. He leapt to his feet and shouted:

"Akennor! Sheila!"

No sound answered him. Agitated, Darian looked around in all directions and searched the wall for a way out… but it showed none.

Desperate, Darian fell to his knees on the ground.

Akennor and Sheila were now alone, lost in their thoughts.

*

How are we going to get out of here? Akennor wondered.

A soft voice answered him:

"Follow me... Come, this way!"

A silhouette of Milenna, human and radiant, stood before him. Her beauty enchanted him, and without asking questions, Akennor followed her.

After a while, Milenna quickened her pace and suddenly vanished around a turn. The young warrior, bewildered, looked around. He rubbed his eyes, frowned, turned on himself... but in vain. No one...

It was then that he understood he had been deceived, and that now they were all separated, each left to themselves.

*

Lost in her thoughts, Sheila realized, a brief moment later, that Akennor had disappeared. Incredulous, she looked around, stood up, and walked straight ahead. Panic gradually took hold at the idea of being alone in this nightmarish place.

Sheila called out, shouted Akennor's name, until the echoes disoriented her and made her stumble. She fell heavily, face down, her torch rolling a good distance away. Raising her head, Sheila saw the torch stopped by a foot — ghostly, white, almost unreal. At first shapeless, the specter took the form of a tall, white woman, slender, with piercing blue eyes, as if she could read Sheila's soul.

Sheila rose slowly, hesitant. The apparition floated, silent. Fear gradually filled her, panic intensifying. The specter suddenly transformed. The delicate features

194

twisted, deforming the beautiful face into a dreadful demonic rictus. The blue eyes turned into fiery embers, and the gentle smile revealed sharp teeth, ready to bite.

Completely terrified, Sheila cast a spell of magic projectiles. The blue luminous bolts shot toward the creature, but without effect. The specter continued to hover in place.

To see better, Sheila cast a spell to illuminate the area around her. With a glance, she saw that no exit was visible. She would have to rely only on herself against this enemy. The fury of being trapped burned inside her. Sheila's piercing gaze fixed on the creature that defied her. Pointing her hands forward, she released a formidable fireball that shot swiftly.

The fireball struck the specter squarely, but without effect. On impact, Sheila was violently thrown backward.

Shaken, Sheila painfully got back on her feet, trembling all over. She did not know this kind of creature, and therefore had no idea how to fight it.

Her thoughts suddenly drifted toward her friends who had vanished from her life without a trace. Anger rumbled again, resonating through her whole being. Sheila leapt up with a cry of rage. Attack spells followed one after another: *Templa pelini, Lácë nárë-rhu, Qualin umbar-rhu.*

The specter remained motionless, raising only its hand, as if to block the spells. The attacks bounced back and returned directly onto Sheila, who took them one after the other. Pain gave way to anger and rage. Sheila staggered, thrown to the ground by the force of her own spells.

The world faded away. Only the darkness of the cavern filled her, the cold and despair striking her with as much force as the spells themselves. She felt her spirit leave her body and travel through thoughts and dreams, before returning and awakening again. The pain still resonated, but more faintly, like an echo.

Sheila was now lying on her back. Slowly, she turned onto her right side.

Her mind drifted again toward her friends and toward Shaya. Surely, they would meet again in the afterlife. A tear rolled down her cheek. Her spirit soothed, Sheila met the gaze of the specter, which gradually changed appearance until it returned to the form from the beginning. Intrigued, Sheila rose again, this time with fewer fears. After all, the creature had not attacked her.

The ghost's expression became almost benevolent. Sheila slowly approached the apparition, driving all feelings of anger and rage from her mind. The specter's expression softened continuously, even smiling.

When Sheila was close enough for the sound of a whisper, the specter spoke in a gentle voice:

"Sheila, I'm glad you understood that anger can blind your judgment and doesn't really serve you."

"Be confident: there is more than anger that brings the right solutions."

With a smile, the specter suddenly disappeared, leaving Sheila completely stunned and bewildered. She approached the spot where the phantom had been, bent down to pick up the torch that still burned, and discovered that the cavern wall concealed an opening. Stupefied,

Sheila looked again around her before venturing into the providential opening.

The voice of the specter was heard again:

"Appearances can sometimes be deceiving, Sheila, remember that."

Sheila cast one last look at the room, now completely plunged into darkness. She swore to keep within herself the lessons of this inner battle.

*

Akennor was alone. His friends had vanished. *What to do?* Everything seemed lost. The hope of finding Shaya had left him; only the faint hope of survival still lingered.

A cruel laugh rose little by little, until it became unbearable. Akennor covered his ears with his hands. But the laughter only grew louder, until the pain forced him to his knees. A brief lull was followed by a violent tremor. The ground and the walls shook. He crouched on the floor, curled in on himself, waiting for it to stop.

At the height of the quake, to the young warrior's despair, the ground split open before him, revealing the entrails of the earth. Another tremor, and Akennor was hurled into the fissure. He screamed during the fall, which seemed endless. He landed in a flow of lava, burning yet not burned. Struggling, he clung to a stone on the bank and managed to haul himself out of the fiery river. A faint ray of light caught his eye and he followed it.

He entered a cavern, took a few steps, and suddenly found himself in the middle of a vast meadow. He rubbed his eyes, unable to believe it. What is happening to me?

Only the sinister laugh answered him. Akennor covered his ears again and ran at full speed through the tall grass, with the painful impression of not advancing. Suddenly, his foot sank into a mud hole, and he began to sink. Akennor struggled, but the more he moved, the deeper he sank. He cried out for help, but no sound left his lips.

Then came the feeling of drowning, before he crashed onto the mossy floor of another cavern. The cave was narrow and dimly lit by stones emitting a pale, cold glow.

Struggling to his feet, Akennor scanned the surroundings, worried. A dark shape stood not far away, its back turned. He remained silent, wondering what awaited him.

Then the shape spoke with a familiar voice.

"Akennor, is that you? Wonderful! I'm so happy you've returned."

Astonished, he recognized his mother's voice. *How could this be possible?* Suspicious, he approached, one hand on his sword's hilt.

When he came within arm's reach, his mother turned around screaming. Her once beautiful face was horribly mutilated: horns had sprouted from her forehead.

She had hideous, sharp teeth. Her skin was a sickly green, covered with pustules, her eyes pupil-less, grayish. Akennor screamed in fright and terror.

He collapsed, staring at the horrific thing that had impersonated his mother. He closed his eyes, but the vision remained.

"See what they did to me! Look!"

Filled with dread, Akennor replied:

"No… You're not my mother, that's impossible."

He tried to remember his true mother: gentle, always radiant and smiling.

This is only an illusion, he told himself.

It isn't real. I want the truth, he commanded.

A sudden whirlwind carried him away from the nightmarish creature, which roared in despair. He now found himself almost at the top of a gigantic tree. Akennor was aware of being present, but without a body, for he could not see himself.

He seemed to float in the air. Before him was a circular wooden platform. Carved pillars encircled it, supporting beams that formed a roof of foliage.

An old man with white hair, a long beard, and a dark blue mage's robe was there, deep in thought, sitting on a wooden bench. Shortly after, a young girl arrived. She was tall, just entering adolescence, her figure beginning to show the first signs of femininity. Her long hair was pure black. But what struck Akennor most were her eyes—the same color as his own.

She wore a robe black as night, lined with silver at its edges.

"Ah! Illawen, just in time for your lesson," said the old man in a hoarse voice.

Stunned, Akennor realized he was looking at his mother as a young girl. She sat opposite the man on the bench.

"It is now time, young one, to address an important subject regarding your many gifts."

He paused, studying his pupil closely.

"Most of us possess only a few gifts, but as you know, you have them all."

Illawen, embarrassed, lowered her head slightly in affirmation.

"You should not be ashamed of it. On the contrary, be proud. Use them for the good of our people."

"I, too, possess all these gifts. One of the most important things to master is to know how to find yourself."

Illawen frowned. The old man smiled and continued:

"You must sometimes find it hard to tell truth from falsehood, and it may feel like you're going mad, isn't that so?"

Illawen nodded again and whispered:

"Yes... it's horrible."

"You've surely noticed that closing your eyes changes nothing. We are sensitive to the thoughts and emotions of those around us."

"Far more sensitive than ordinary people. These emotions and thoughts can mingle with ours, causing profoundly disturbing visions."

The old sage straightened and went on:

"The most important thing is to find yourself in this chaos, to recover your identity and your own thoughts."

"To do this, you must focus on a true memory or feeling, one that cannot be altered. On something real, like love or friendship."

"Feelings that are undeniable, unchangeable. They are the best anchors in this world, allowing you to remain yourself. Do you understand, Illawen?"

With more assurance, she answered:

"Yes, I understand. I can't wait to try it."

"You will try it when the next crisis comes."

Abruptly, Akennor felt himself sucked away, hurled far. He was once again in the middle of a plain—but not alone.

But surrounded by rotting undead, their eyes empty, their stench unbearable. The creatures formed a wide circle around him. The sky burned red, and a humanoid figure approached. Akennor recognized the features of the demon: it was the same as the portrait in Mortragor's office.

Its voice echoed inside his head:

"You must give up, Akennor. Join me, and you'll be even more powerful."

Its lips curled into a wicked smile, revealing long fangs.

The sage's words immediately came back to him. Akennor concentrated, ignoring all around him. Sheila's gentle face appeared, and he thought of the true love he felt for her.

Memories surged, and his being took shape. Akennor emptied everything around him until only Sheila's luminous image remained, smiling softly.

Smiling back, he closed his eyes, wishing to return to where his body was. Darkness fell again. Now completely alone, Akennor stood. Exhausted, shivering, he walked on, guided only by his still-lit torch.

I will find them, he vowed.

*

The apprentice paladin gradually regained his senses. Driven by survival instinct, Darian got up. He was in a vast cavern, its vault and walls shimmering with a greenish light. Cautiously, he advanced, watching every detail the glow revealed.

A muffled groan to his right made him start. Darian drew his hammer. Taking a ready stance, he advanced carefully. Behind a large rock crouched a man, clutching his left side in pain.

Darian froze as the wounded warrior lifted his head to look at him. He was young, with a rather round face and long disheveled hair falling to his shoulders.

"Who are you, and what are you doing in this nightmare place? " Darian asked.

The young man, panting, replied:

"I was captured, but I escaped them. They caught me again in the tunnels, and they're surely still after me. And you—who are you?"

"Let's say we're in the same situation, except I started with a group, and we all got separated in these tunnels."

"I know the way out. It's just… hard to walk, and I'm afraid they'll find me."

Darian seized the opportunity:

"I can help you walk, if you show me the way out."

The young man's face lit up.

"Gladly… Argh! he groaned, trying to rise."

Darian grasped his forearm and hauled him to his feet, supporting him with his arm.

"By the way, what's your name?" asked Darian.

"I'm Yanni. And you?"

"Darian."

They resumed walking. Yanni led him through the maze of tunnels, wielding a small glowing staff that cut through the shadows and revealed hidden traps.

Yanni whispered directions into Darian's ear:

"Turn left."

"Take this branch."

Darian felt they were making progress, but he couldn't help but wonder: *How does he know the way?* A pang of worry struck him. *Maybe he's part of the sect… leading me into a trap?*

Darian sensed nothing evil from Yanni, but his unease grew at each step. They emerged into a larger cavern, its walls covered in luminous moss.

"Let's rest a bit, my friend," Yanni suggested.

Darian didn't complain and helped his companion sit. Yanni smiled.

"The exit is just ahead," he said, pointing forward.

Indeed, Darian could see a dark opening.

"We'll finally get out of this hole," Yanni added.

"That's what you think, Yanni. Hahaha!" thundered a dark voice.

Terror gripped Yanni.

Darian saw six shadows encircle them, swords raised. He glanced at his companion: the terrified look on his face.

I barely know him, thought Darian. *I don't want to die here. I must find her… but… can I really let an innocent die?*

Suppressing his conscience, Darian dashed toward the exit.

Panicked, the young man begged:

"Darian, no! It's not real… It's a trap! Don't abandon me!"

Darian kept his eyes fixed on the exit, hurrying forward. When he reached it, he turned to see if he was pursued—but there was nothing. The six figures had merged into one.

What have I done?

For Shaya, my love… I must escape.

The apprentice paladin felt faint, consumed by guilt. He heard Yanni begging for his life. The pale-faced stranger glared at him for an instant, a cruel grin spreading across his lips. He raised his sword in both frail hands and swiftly plunged the blade into Yanni's chest.

Darian wanted to scream, but no sound came.

"Darian, you… you…" gasped Yanni with his final breath.

He died staring at Darian, whose heart pounded with shame. Yanni's gaze pierced him, a mirror of his own cowardice. Disgusted, crushed by remorse, Darian turned away and left the cavern, his heart heavy.

Chapter 16 – The Stone Demon

Milenna continued her progress, constantly on guard. The path was winding, but no incident occurred. The passage suddenly widened into a vast cavern. Milenna carefully scrutinized the surroundings and made a full tour of the chamber, which contained five passages. This room seemed to be the central point of all these tunnels. So, the others should all arrive here, she thought. Milenna detected no other scent, so she was the only one who had made it so far. Sighing, the she-wolf sat in the center of the chamber and hoped the others would find their way.

Milenna waited for what felt like an eternity. She could not bring herself to remain idle.

"Something is off about this place. I must find them," she thought.

She stood and was about to shift when she heard footsteps. She stepped back toward the opposite wall, facing the openings. Relief flooded her when she saw Sheila's face, and she rushed to embrace her.

"Sheila!"

"I'm so glad to see you."

Sheila had not expected such a reunion, but it brought her great relief.

"How are you?" asked Milenna, worried.

"I'm fine, very well, but I went through a strange ordeal."

Sheila recounted her fight against the specter and the lesson she had drawn from it.

"Incredible," Milenna replied.

"Did you experience anything strange as well?" asked Sheila.

"No, I simply followed the tunnels to get here," Milenna answered.

"Milenna?" called a familiar voice from behind them.

"Akennor?" said Sheila.

"Sheila?"

The sound of running footsteps echoed. Akennor threw down his torch and seized Sheila in his arms. The contact with her fear, the scent of her hair, sent a shiver through him. He longed to kiss her.

Milenna suddenly asked:

"Darian is missing. Was he with you, Akennor?"

Akennor gently released Sheila and turned to Milenna.

"No, I honestly have no idea. I just hope he finds us."

"Did you experience something strange?" asked Sheila.

Akennor nodded.

"Indeed. I had horrible visions. I witnessed a lesson my mother endured when she was younger, in a vast forest of her homeland. Then I followed the tunnels until here."

Sheila told him of her own experience.

"Strange… this place surely has magical properties," Milenna added.

Akennor was about to comment when Milenna pressed a finger to his lips.

"Shh. Someone's coming."

They recognized Darian's face illuminated by his torch.

"Darian! cried Akennor. I'm so glad to see you."

"And I you," he replied.

"It's wonderful, you're all here."

"Did anything strange happen to you?" Sheila asked.

"Why do you ask me that?" Darian shot back.

Milenna frowned. *Why Darian sound so defensive?*

"Because we've lived through strange experiences," she answered.

"Well... I found my way thanks to a young man who helped me, then vanished as suddenly as he had appeared."

"That is indeed strange," said Akennor.

"So I'm the only one who went through nothing unusual here. And that's fine, I don't wish for it anyway," said Milenna.

"Enough of that. Which way do we go now?" asked Sheila.

Without hesitation, Milenna pointed to the passage before them.

"We've all come from the four others. This one is the only one left."

"Let's go then. I can't wait to get out of this place," added Darian.

After a long walk, they emerged into a wide cavern. The vault was high, the walls covered with gray moss, and the air smelled of dampness.

Sheila invoked her spell for light:

"Aurë!"

The cavern filled with a soft glow that reflected on the moss. At the far end stood a wooden door.

No other opening was visible. They advanced cautiously, senses sharp and weapons ready.

Pausing before the entrance, the companions exchanged glances.

"I don't know what curse lies beyond this door, but clearly we have no choice," said Akennor.

Darian looked at him.

"You can't know how much I want to get out of here. I've seen enough. Let's end this."

"Well, we have to enter now. Are you ready? I'm exhausted too; I need a bath and a proper bed," confessed Milenna.

They stepped carefully into the chamber beyond, still lit by their last torch. It was circular, resembling others on the upper floor. Empty, unremarkable.

They made a full turn and discovered, horrified, there was no exit. A heavy despair overcame them. Their thin hope of escaping this cursed place had just been extinguished.

At the center stood the only feature of the chamber: a great statue of a horned demon with a humanoid face and goat-like legs. The demon held a black stone bell in both hands.

"Damn it! Damn it all!" roared Darian. "We're trapped now. What are we going to do?"

For the first time in their quest, Akennor truly felt hopeless.

They would be prisoners of this place forever, doomed to haunt it like Marianne. He recalled part of his nightmare: Darian as a zombie, the others dead... Perhaps that was their fate.

"I can't believe it ends like this," whispered Milenna.

"It seems we'll have to face the zombies again," said Sheila.

"And go where after that?" asked Milenna.

"Where? We've tried every tunnel, every path. There's no exit. Except the way we came in—and it's blocked."

"Are you sure we didn't miss anything?" Darian asked, almost pleading.

"Yes, I'm sure. I have a keen sense of smell, Darian. I'm sorry."

Darian slumped to the floor, followed by Sheila and Milenna. Akennor remained standing a while, pacing, trying to think.

Rage boiled within Darian—rage at the failure of his trial, at Yanni's sacrifice in vain. He howled and struck the hideous statue.

The stone demon's eyes opened, awakened by Darian's blows. He froze, terrified, calling his friends' attention. They too recoiled, staring in horror as the statue spoke, its voice booming, cavernous, sinister:

"Who dares set foot in this chamber?"

"I… I am Akennor. This is Darian, Sheila, and Milenna. And you, who are you?" asked Akennor, his voice unsteady.

"I am the guardian of the treasure. Whoever enters must answer my questions—or perish."

Darian rolled his eyes.

"Oh no, you've got to be kidding me…"

The guardian ignored him.

"You must answer two questions. Succeed, and you shall receive the treasure I hold. Fail even one, and you will die in torment."

The statue's face twisted into a wicked grin.

Nervous sweat covered the companions. What kind of questions would a demon ask?

"Let's start easy. What is the name of the one who brought my kind into this realm?"

The youths exchanged glances, ensuring they agreed. Then Akennor replied, hopefully:

"Tholgor. He murdered his father to seal his pact with the demons."

"Correct, young ones. Now a harder one… good luck to you."

The stone demon's grin widened, malice radiating. Their stomachs knotted.

"What is the true name of the black prince of demons, my lord and master?"

They stared at one another, lost. They had no idea.

Milenna spoke furiously, rage in her voice:

"Typical of a demon, to set such a trap."

The statue cocked its head.

"What? What do you mean, little one?"

"I know that name has special properties. Speak it, and he might appear, for instance."

The demon smiled, impressed.

"Come now… the ties between this world and mine have been severed. That is no longer possible."

"Perhaps… but some portals may still be active," she countered.

The others looked at her in shock.

"How do you know this? You astonish me more every day," said Akennor.

"Go on, Milenna. Say it. We don't really have a choice, do we?" urged Sheila.

"Then be ready."

Milenna locked eyes with the statue.

"The true name of your black prince is Thaurgon."

A heavy silence followed. Breathless, they waited. Milenna held the statue's malevolent gaze, unwavering.

Finally, the stone demon spoke:

"Incredible. That is correct. Do I have the honor of speaking to a descendant of dear Oriador, perhaps?"

"That is none of your concern, demon. Honor your pact, commanded Milenna."

"But of course, my dear. No need to lose your temper. Here is the Medallion of Anoron. You must know what this is, I imagine?"

"I'm confuse," said Akennor, "it's not Morthag?"

"I'll let you answer", said the statue to Milenna.

"Morthag is one of his name… but the first and truly name is Thaurgon, not many people know that."

"That is correct," respond the demonic statue with a cringe.

He lifted the stone cover and presented the tray to Milenna. She had indeed heard of it—a legendary medallion long thought lost. The chain and pendant were pure silver.

The medallion was star-shaped. A large round diamond shone at its center, with six pointed diamonds on each tip. Milenna took the legendary jewel and placed it around her neck.

But suddenly the stone demon hurled the tray aside and struck Milenna hard, sending her crashing against the wall.

"Why, demon?!" Sheila cried, furious.

"We answered correctly! How dare you break your word?"

The demon sneered.

"Impudent girl. I was bound while I held the treasure. Now that I no longer do… I am free."

He lunged at them.

Akennor charged, swords flashing. Sheila fired a spell, but it had no effect. Akennor's blades clanged harmlessly against stone. Darian, enraged, roared and attacked with all his might. His hammer struck the demon's chest with tremendous force—only for the shockwave to reverberate back through him, shaking his body until he dropped his weapon and stumbled.

The demon laughed, a booming, cavernous laugh. Akennor dragged Darian away, shielding him. Sheila hurled another spell, pouring all her power into it, but the blast barely made the statue waver.

She tried again.

"Ruilë-rhu!"

Lightning arced from her fingers, striking the foe. The energy dispersed harmlessly across the stone.

Laughing, the colossus advanced on her. She leapt aside at the last moment, rolling away from the crushing blow. Akennor intercepted the monster, parrying with his swords. Sheila retreated to Darian and Milenna. But the demon feinted. Akennor dodged the first arm, not seeing the second, which slammed into his side. He slammed into the wall, nearly fainting.

Satisfied, the demon raised its arm for the final blow—

"Sirpë!" cried Milenna.

Roots erupted from the ground, binding the colossus. It struggled, roaring, but was held fast. Sheila and Milenna rushed to Akennor, lifting him carefully. Darian, still dizzy, staggered after them. Behind, the demon broke free in moments.

Sheila checked Akennor's injury. His side was bruised, ribs fractured.

"It will take time to heal," she sighed.

Akennor groaned, ashamed.

"I let myself get caught like a novice."

The demon lumbered toward them again. Sheila stood, calm now. A phrase the demon had spoken earlier echoed in her mind. She grasped the medallion around her neck.

"Demon! I order you to guard this object, which is precious to me. You will keep it until someone comes to claim it."

The jewel glowed with a silver light. To their shock, the demon knelt, gently took it, and the tray and cover reappeared in its hands.

"Very well. I shall fulfill my task, as instructed. I must guard a precious object" the demon said, in his deep rumbling voice.

212

"Look! A passage!" Milenna cried. "It's open, freed from the statue's weight."

"Quickly, before it closes again!" urged Akennor.

They fled down the tunnel. Behind them, the demon moved back toward the chamber's center.

The tunnel was long and winding, but no harm befell them. At last, they reached the exit, hidden behind piled rocks.

Night had fallen. Stars gleamed above. The young adventurers collapsed on the ground, silent, gazing at the sky they had feared never to see again. Sheila turned to Akennor, relieved he lived, though bitter at the loss of her cherished pendant.

Chapter 17 – The way of despair

The sea was rough, making the ship pitch as it tried to follow the ocean's wild rhythm. Curled up on herself at the bottom of the hold, Shaya shivered with cold. Her captors had chained her in the lowest hold, with the vermin. Her hands and feet were bound by solid chains fastened to the very structure of the hull. It felt to her as though the voyage had already lasted an eternity, though only a single day had passed since their departure from Elenshae.

Despite all her thoughts, Shaya could not understand the reason for this deed; the motive eluded her. She gave up trying to find one and instead focused on ways to escape. Thinking of her friends and her family brought her a measure of comfort; she recalled the happy moments of her life.

Her eyes were no longer covered with a blindfold, though she almost wished they still were. Despite the darkness, she could make out small glowing points nearby, leaving no doubt as to what they were. A strong smell of mold saturated the air. At first, the stench nearly made her vomit. Fear and anguish grew more and more unbearable. *What will become of me?* she wondered.

As the waves of the wild ocean tossed the ship, Shaya, prisoner in the dark hold, let herself fall into despair.

Her hands tested, without much conviction, a weakness in the iron shackles that bound her wrists. A finger brushed against the ring Darian had given her before they parted for their respective schools.

Her fingers caressed the silver engraved with elven runes, as well as the blue stone set atop it. Darian had just walked her back to her doorstep. He kissed her tenderly one last time, then pulled a small wooden case from his jacket pocket.

They gazed at each other intensely for a moment. Darian opened the case.

"Oh! It's beautiful!"

Shaya threw herself into his arms and hugged him tightly. She slipped it onto her finger and raised her hand toward the sky to admire it better. The light of the moon and stars made the runes glow with a bluish hue.

"I love you, Darian. Not once will the sun set without me thinking of you."

They embraced for a long time, then said goodbye for almost a year. Since then, not a day had gone by without her love filling her thoughts.

The harsh reality caught up to her when a wave suddenly shook the ship, throwing Shaya flat on her stomach. She painfully sat back up and cried silently. A deep distress overcame her at the thought that something terrible might have happened to her friends... and to Darian.

The thought of her love restored her resolve, and she decided to try something. Shaya focused and let herself be infused by the force of the ocean and sky. The energy of the untamed sea poured into her.

After a while, she felt the sky darken with gray-black clouds. The ocean rumbled with a low voice. The waves grew higher, stronger, lashing violently at the sides of the ship. Shaya felt this power rise within her, as well as the wrath of the sky. As the force filled her being, tingling spread across her body, which grew hotter and hotter.

Her breathing quickened, and her heart seemed to beat to the rhythm of the waves themselves. It was as though she became the ocean, her rage crashing down upon the ship that pitched harder and harder.

It was an expedition vessel, a sailboat with two main masts and a smaller one at the stern. It also had a large central cabin. It was a very common type of ship, fast, sturdy, and built for long voyages. The violent motions of the sea made Dresden curse, at the end of his patience.

"Gods, how I hate ships! Can't even eat without nailing your plate to the table…"

Deidre found it amusing to see him struggle with his meal, trying to hold it steady just to cut his tough meat. The plate slid constantly as Dresden tried to slice.

At that moment, the captain entered their cabin. He was a short, older man with a gray beard. The few teeth he had left were rotten, giving him a revolting look and breath. Rumor said he had been a notorious pirate in his youth, now infamous for his cruelty and utter lack of mercy.

"Brace yourselves, lads, a storm's brewin'."

"What do you mean, a storm? The weather wasn't supposed to worsen so fast!" Parthe exclaimed.

"Aye, well it is. And it's a strong one, too!" grumbled the captain before promptly leaving.

He struggled to close the door. The ship was rocking harder now, waves crashing over the deck.

Lightning tore the sky, and the wind filled the sails dangerously. Sailors frantically worked to tie down the canvas.

Dresden tried once more to cut his meat. Just then, a massive wave struck the vessel, making him miss and fall face-first into his plate. His companions stifled laughter, knowing his temper. Dresden rose slowly, grabbed his plate, and in a fit of rage hurled it across the cabin, sending food flying.

He turned to his companions.

"What a mess. I'm going to fetch our package. Would be stupid to lose it if the ship sinks."

"Good idea, approved Deidre," barely holding back her laughter.

Parthe and Aaron burst into muffled laughter.

Outside, a wave nearly threw Dresden overboard. He barely managed to grab a rope tied to the main mast.

"Damn it!" he swore.

He advanced slowly, clinging to everything he could. The wind and rain lashed his face and body. The ship's sway made him dizzy. He reached the descent into the holds and plunged into darkness.

At the bottom of the stairs, he groped the wall and found a torch. Lighting it with magical fire-stones, he took the ladder down to the lowest level. It was difficult not to fall with the rolling of the ship. The torch nearly went out in a draft. Dresden advanced cautiously to keep his balance. The prisoner was at the stern. He spotted her sitting calmly, eyes closed, cross-legged, hands on her knees, as if meditating. He found her beautiful and would have liked to take advantage of her, but his master would kill him. He had been strictly ordered not to harm her in any way.

Dresden jolted her from her trance with a small kick.
"Get up. Stop dreaming, we're going up."
He unshackled her feet and freed the chains from the hull, but her wrists remained bound. Dresden yanked her up by the arm and nearly lost his balance.

Shaya fell against him, and he felt himself stir with lust. Dresden shook his head, chased by sordid thoughts. This master-slave relationship stirred in him dark urges. Shaya stayed silent, dazed, as if rudely awakened.

She assumed he was taking her up because of the storm. She felt proud to have bent the elements to her will... but deeply disappointed the ship hadn't sunk.

The effort had drained her. Her head spun, her body burned. Dizzy, she could barely stand, which made her captor curse.
"Come on, slut, stand on your feet!"
He gave her a cold, cruel look, leaving no doubt what he was capable of. As he dragged her onto the main deck, the storm began to calm. The winds weakened, the rain lessened, the waves subsided. He noticed it as he stepped outside, after extinguishing his torch. Dresden watched as the weather returned to light, as if after a nightmare.

He nonetheless decided to bring the prisoner to their cabin. The ship still rocked, and he held firmly to a rope to avoid going overboard.
"In there, now!" he barked, throwing Shaya into the cabin by her hair.

She stumbled and fell face-first to the floor. Parthe bent to pick her up, sat her on a chair, and bound her firmly at the feet. Already, the sea had almost completely calmed, and the sun reappeared as suddenly as it had vanished.

"It's over? Already?" observed Deidre.

"What, are you disappointed?" Aaron muttered, weary and still seasick.

"No, I mean… it stopped as suddenly as it started." Deidre rolled her eyes.

"It calmed down when I brought her up," Dresden said, gesturing toward Shaya with his chin.

Deidre stared at her intently. Shaya avoided her gaze and fixed her eyes on the floor.

"She was meditating, wasn't she?" Deidre asked Dresden, without taking her eyes off the captive.

"Yes, she was… Are you suggesting…?"

"I think… I think we're dealing with an Elementarist."

"What? What's that?" Aaron asked.

"The name says it all, Aaron," Parthe replied.

"A druid trained in elemental control. It means she can manipulate water, wind, earth… It's an ancient form of magic, rarely practiced today, but very powerful. I had never met someone able to wield it. Interesting… very interesting."

Deidre turned her gaze back to Shaya.

"That's right, isn't it?" she asked.

Shaya stayed silent. Dresden lost patience and slapped her violently.

"Answer when spoken to!"

Shaya lifted her bound hands to her face, sobbing, and replied in a trembling voice:

"That's right…"

Inside, she boiled with fury. Her eyes blazed with hatred at her captors.

"We'd better keep her under watch. As soon as she tries to enter a trance, we wake her. If any phenomenon stirs the elements, we'll know the source," Deidre said.

The three others nodded and began discussing shifts for surveillance.

Despair overtook Shaya. The only means she had found to try to escape had been discovered, and these villains would do everything to stop her.

What will I do? she wondered.

Even if she had been found out, Shaya had achieved something great. She felt immense pride. Perhaps she could use this experience and exploit a moment of inattention from her captors.

One thing was certain: she would not let herself sink into the abyss of despair that yawned before her. She would fight with all her strength. She just had to find out how.

Her thoughts turned to her mentor. Surely, his wise advice could guide her in such a situation.

What would he tell me? she thought.

Chapter 18 – Torhon and Illawen

Torhon could finally see his home. He and Krent had parted ways a little earlier in front of the village inn, promising each other to have a drink that evening and chat with good old Josey. Josey would surely have a thousand and one questions to ask them. Akennor's father was satisfied that the journey had gone very well.

He climbed the wooden steps of the porch leading to the front door. The sun was slowly setting toward the horizon. A soft rosy light emanated from the star, giving the clouds shades of red and orange. The door creaked slightly when he entered, happy to be back with his wife and son—even if he doubted Akennor's presence.

The house was strangely quiet. Although it was dinner time, no smell of food lingered in the air. The front door opened directly into the living room. A large stone fireplace occupied the left wall. A leather-covered sofa—tanned by Torhon himself—faced a small coffee table. Two finely carved wooden chairs, also made by Torhon, completed the furnishings.

"Honey, I'm home! Hey, is anyone here? " Torhon called, raising his voice so his wife could hear him wherever she might be in the house.

Torhon looked carefully around the room and continued forward cautiously. In the narrow passageway between the sitting room and the dining room, he noticed a travel bag placed on the floor.

Two doorways connected the dining room to the living room: one directly across from the entrance, the other on the right.

It was the largest room in the house. Footsteps echoed on the wooden floor upstairs. Torhon recognized the delicate gait of his wife, which reassured him a little. The steps approached the stairs, and he waited at the bottom.

Illawen appeared. She looked troubled and worried, her eyes misty. She offered him a faint smile, but without the expected joy. Torhon's heart tightened: something was wrong. She wore her old brown leather pants, a long black coat that reached her knees, and tall leather boots—a set of clothes she hadn't worn since their first meeting. Age had slightly rounded her figure, but the clothes still suited her perfectly.

"Hello, my love... Did the trip go well? I was afraid something might have happened to you."

Illawen's voice was calm and distant.

Then, suddenly, she hurried down the stairs and threw herself into her husband's arms. She let go at last: the tension, fear, and anguish that had built up during his absence burst out in sobs. Torhon held her tight, deeply moved. He still had no idea what had happened. They stayed a long time, silently embraced.

The past few days had been exhausting for Illawen: Akennor's adventure, Kallo's departure, their eldest son, the nightmares that had haunted her for a long time—her mind and her sleep had been greatly affected.

"But what's going on, my love? I'm confused," Torhon asked softly.

"What kept you? I was so terribly worried."

Torhon suddenly felt guilty. He and Krent had decided to extend their stay in town by two more days to explore, relax, and help their son settle in.

Her sobs gradually subsided. She slowly pulled back, her eyes drowned in tears, her lips trembling. She turned her head, searching for words but unable to find them. Emotion overcame her again, the dam burst once more, and the tears flowed.

She clung to him again. Torhon said nothing. He waited. Then, after a heavy silence:

"Come to the living room… I'll tell you everything."

She gave him a shy smile, then headed to the kitchen. Torhon didn't insist and went to sit on the leather sofa, growing more impatient with each passing moment.

Shortly after, Illawen returned with a bottle of homemade wine they had prepared together from small fruits picked along the field's edge. She also brought two glasses.

She sat on a wooden chair, turned it to face her husband, poured the aromatic wine, and handed him a glass.

Illawen cleared her throat slightly, then began her account:

"About a week ago… It was the second day after you left. Akennor and his friends—you remember Darian, Sheila, and Shaya—met up that very evening…"

Torhon slowly nodded.

"The next day, they left to explore the mountains. They camped on the hill, not far from here, at nightfall."

Illawen took a sip of wine and continued:

"That's when four bandits attacked them. Shaya was kidnapped. The others immediately returned here. I treated Darian, who was in a pitiful state, then they left again at full gallop with our last horses."

Torhon was stunned, frozen for a moment. He hadn't expected such a revelation. He jumped to his feet and paced about, agitated.

"I'm sorry, dear… I didn't know how to tell you," she said, wondering if she had been too blunt.

"No, it's fine… it's fine, but why? What… ?"

Torhon struggled to find his words, unable to form coherent thoughts. Questions collided in his mind. He emptied his glass in one gulp, then handed it to his wife, who refilled it immediately.

"I don't know… The young ones didn't know either. I went to see Shaya's parents."

"And… what? What did they say?" Torhon demanded, almost losing his composure.

Illawen urged him to calm down and sit."They told me exactly what they had told Akennor."

She explained that Shaya had been adopted, under unusual circumstances.

But Torhon still couldn't understand the reason behind it all.

"But what's the link? It's too vague, something is missing."

"Yes, you're right… but that's all I know," Illawen concluded, finishing her glass. Torhon did the same, and she refilled his again.

Illawen's face grew sadder, weighed down. Torhon noticed and quickly asked:

"Is that all? No… what's troubling you?"

"It's my dreams, Torhon. They've returned to haunt me. I've had nightmares for months, and it only gets worse."

"I wake up several times a night… drenched in sweat. I'm afraid to sleep."

As she said this, Illawen broke into tears again.

Torhon caressed her hands.

"I know it's linked to Akennor, I can feel it… something terrible is going to happen. And soon."

Torhon listened intently. She went on:

"I… I've lost my gifts. Before, I could silence the visions, push away the dreams, but not anymore. They overwhelm me."

"I realize I've neglected this part of myself. And now I'm paying the price. Before, I could see further, control them… and make them speak."

Torhon timidly whispered:

"What kind of dreams are they? They must be terrible to put you in such a state."

"Oh yes… They're grim. And everything feels so real. I smell sulfur, feel scorching heat… then freezing cold."

"Voices moan in the darkness. The earth runs with rivers of blood. Undead crawl out of the ground to feed on the living."

Torhon, chilled, tried to imagine what she described.

"The worst… is when I see Akennor and his friends tortured. And Kallo… devoured by horrible creatures from the abyss…"

"I've lost something, Torhon, that I must find again. I have to understand what it means."

Her sobs resumed.

Now he understood the clothes… and the bag in the hallway. His eyes widened.

"What? You want to return to your homeland, don't you?" he exclaimed, standing abruptly.

Illawen slowly regained control of her emotions and wiped her tears. She knew it wouldn't be easy and expected the worst.

"You... you want to leave me? You want to return to your... your father—if he can even be called that," Torhon said bitterly.

"Torhon, please, what he did was wrong, but don't add more, please..."

Illawen pleaded with her eyes. He had to understand.

"I don't want to leave you. I want you to come with me."

Torhon shook his head, unsure he had heard right.

"You're asking me to go back there with you? But you know how it ended last time? You remember, don't you?"

Memories resurfaced in Illawen's mind. She remembered very well, and they were painful.

"You can't go back there. And you don't even know how your people will receive you, do you?" argued Torhon.

"No, indeed... but I still have hope," she replied.

He couldn't understand, couldn't bear the thought of her leaving. Life without her seemed impossible.

In a last attempt to convince her, Torhon added:

"And Akennor? And Kallo? If we leave... if we abandon them, what will become of them? We could still save Akennor."

Illawen knew her husband would say that. She too would have liked to do so.

"I've neglected my gifts for too long, Torhon. But there are things I'm certain of. Akennor and his friends' destiny holds trials that only they can face. I believe we can do nothing more for them. It's already too late. We couldn't catch up to them."

And I feel it:

"I must recover my powers. Otherwise, I'll lose my sanity. "

"But Illawen, you can't lose your gifts… they're part of you. They're simply asleep. You can wake them by yourself, without going back there…"

Illawen bowed her head, eyes fixed on the floor.

"I regret not teaching Akennor how to master them. I should have, Torhon. And I deeply regret it."

"None of our children have those gifts… at least, they're not supposed to. Are you sure?"

"I'm convinced. He's the only one… after all, he has my eyes."

Since Illawen had left her homeland to settle with Torhon, they had decided to leave the past behind, and she had abandoned her practices.

Even if one of them did manifest any gift, Illawen and Torhon had sworn never to encourage its development. Deep down, Torhon knew Illawen was right. Akennor had inherited his mother's abilities. He just didn't want to admit it and was lying to himself.

Illawen sensed Torhon's distress. She stood and approached him.

"I don't want to leave you. I love you more than anything, you know that, don't you?"

"After all, I followed you… I left my people for you."

Torhon raised his glass of wine and emptied it in one gulp. Their eyes met for a long time.

"Yes, I know. I love you too and the thought of losing you is unbearable."

Illawen was tired of talking. She desired her husband. She kissed him softly, then passion reignited. Their kisses became fervent, and the lovers tore off their clothes with frenzy. It had been a long time since their exchanges had been so ardent. Torhon felt as if he were reliving the very first moments of their relationship. That night, they made love passionately on the leather sofa.

Chapter 19 – The Spy

While Torhon was arriving home to find his wife Illawen again, Xantaris and Amandil reached Elenshae at the end of the day, under the last rays of the sun. They had no trouble entering the city, given their belonging to the Order of Calaista. They quickly made their way to the southern district, after having led their horses to the stables. Darkness reigned when they arrived at the Lady Aïcha.

The bodies of the bandits who had attacked the young adventurers had been removed by the city, and only traces of dried blood bore witness to the scene. The two companions had never before set foot in such an establishment and were both shocked and intrigued by the atmosphere. The air was thick with smoke. As they entered, a dance show was underway. Xantaris could hardly believe his eyes: two beautiful young women, almost naked, were performing a very suggestive dance on the small stage.

He gestured to his friend to go near the bar. It was Xantaris who first spotted Sathoryn. The one-eyed spy was deep in conversation with a man clad in a large black robe: an imposing, bald man with a golden ring through his nose. A silver dot gleamed on his robe. Xantaris quickly averted his gaze and whispered to Amandil:

"I've spotted him, back right, near the wall, with a hooded fellow. Be subtle."

Amandil observed discreetly, without attracting attention. The spy was glancing constantly around him, on his guard.

"Let's wait until the other one leaves," he suggested.

The two paladins ordered a pint of beer each and watched attentively from afar.

The dance show ended and, shortly afterward, their targets rose and made their way through the dense crowd toward the exit. Xantaris signaled to his friend. They drained their mugs and followed the one-eyed spy at a distance.

There was a crowd outside the establishment, which made the paladins' task easier. They followed Sathoryn discreetly. Then the spy and his interlocutor turned left onto the docks. With so many goods, crates, and sacks of all kinds piled high, Xantaris and Amandil were able to continue their pursuit unnoticed. The two men stopped, and so did the paladins, hiding behind some wooden crates to overhear their exchange.

"Our master is very satisfied with your loyalty, Sathoryn, and here is your reward in goods. I believe you will appreciate the gesture," said the bald man.

"It's a privilege to serve you. You are grateful, and I knew from the beginning which side it was in my best interest to serve," replied Sathoryn.

"You are very intelligent, my dear. Thanks to your devotion, the tiny threat posed by those four youths has been eliminated for good. The poor fools rushed headlong into their doom and threw themselves into the catacombs. Ha ha ha!"

The man laughed heartily. He was clearly satisfied with this turn of events. The cruel, sadistic joy on his face sent chills down the paladins' spines.

The dark figure continued:

"As I told you earlier, we no longer need you here. This mission now awaits you."

The shadowy man handed a large envelope to the spy, who quickly concealed it. Xantaris shivered. It was without doubt about the four youths Orendil had spoken of.

"Too bad, I would have liked to spend more time visiting your castle. You really have a fine view of the sea, and I would have enjoyed seeing that beautiful blonde again," declared the spy.

"She is quite enchanting, isn't she? Well, I won't delay you any longer. I wish you good luck in your new assignment."

With those final words, the shadowy figure walked away from the spy. Xantaris and Amandil were boiling with rage. Orendil had been right to mistrust him. Absorbed in listening, they did not hear the footsteps behind them. A deep voice spoke nearby:

"What are you two doing here?... Sathoryn, two youngsters are spying on you."

The man in question raised his head and walked toward the crates. Two burly sailors now stood in front of Xantaris and Amandil. One was bald and dressed in filthy, torn clothes. The other had a thick beard, wearing garments similar to his companion's. Both pointed their sabers at the paladins, who slowly rose to their feet. The bald sailor spoke:

"Come on, answer. What are you doing here, you vermin?"

Amandil swiftly drew his war hammers and assumed a fighting stance.

Xantaris responded as Sathoryn approached:

"We came to see what our dear Sathoryn was plotting."

Xantaris's tone was filled with fury. He stared straight into the traitor's eyes.

The spy smiled:

"So, I am discovered, I suppose. Orendil must have sent you, correct? No matter… you won't live long enough to report anything back."

Of course, Sathoryn knew Orendil was dead, but preferred not to reveal it to the two youths.

"Go on, attack!" Sathoryn ordered his men, who rushed forward immediately.

The sailors shouted and attacked savagely.

Amandil easily parried the bald man's assault. He blocked with one hammer, spun around, and smashed the attacker's right knee with the other. The pain was unbearable, and the sailor collapsed to the ground, rolling over in agony. Amandil seized the chance to deliver a fatal blow to the head, which burst under the impact.

Meanwhile, Xantaris dodged the bearded sailor's attack and drew his sword, strapped across his back. The paladin parried his opponent's quick strikes.

With one move, he lifted his sword high in the air and brought it crashing down on the sailor's flank. The man tried to block, but the blow was too powerful. Xantaris's blade slid down along the opponent's weapon and severed his head clean off. The body collapsed heavily to the ground.

Freed of his opponent, Amandil charged at Sathoryn. The traitor dodged the first strike by sidestepping. He aimed both his short swords at his foe's abdomen. Amandil barely parried and retreated. Xantaris joined his comrade.

The traitor didn't like this. His two men were dead, cut down easily. He was now alone against two foes. He decided to risk everything. He launched himself at Xantaris, both blades forward. The paladin managed to block one blade, but the other grazed his left side.

Taking advantage of his enemy's wound, Sathoryn fled. He judged his chances of victory nearly nil and chose to escape. Amandil had already leapt forward as the traitor struck his friend and chased him along the docks.

He was almost upon him when his left foot caught in a thick rope used to moor ships. He stumbled and fell hard on the damp, grimy dock.

The spy turned and saw his pursuer sprawled helplessly. The temptation to finish him off was strong, but the sight of Xantaris close behind dissuaded him. Sathoryn used the opportunity to vanish into the shadows.

Xantaris was bleeding. A dark stain spread across the gray fabric of his shirt. He saw the traitor retreating but chose instead to help his friend. Sathoryn was too far ahead to catch. Amandil was dazed, his chest aching. He sat up with difficulty.

"Ouch… damn, I almost had him, just a hair's breadth away. If it hadn't been for that damned rope…"

"Well, too bad for him. I think it's more important we find the youths," said Xantaris, helping his friend up.

"Yes, you're right. Anyway, he won't get away with it forever. The important thing is that he's been unmasked," Amandil concluded.

"How's your wound? Let me see," asked Amandil.

Xantaris lifted his shirt. The cut was clean, shallow.

"It's nothing serious, after all," said the injured man, relieved it wasn't worse.

"Let's send a message to Master Orendil, and afterward we'll try to locate that castle they spoke of," suggested Amandil.

They headed back into the city to find an inn for the night. They rented a room at the Travelers' Inn and wrote a message intended for their superior, to be dispatched the next morning.

Meanwhile, Sathoryn was reporting to Berantis using a magical artifact. It was a thin silver circlet, set with a diamond at its center.

As far as he knew, only the organization of the dark master — whose true name Sathoryn did not know — used this method of communication.

The diamond aligned with the "third eye" of humans, a spiritual and metaphysical point in the center of the forehead. When the stone, imbued with magical properties, made contact with this point, a vision of the interlocutor appeared. Sathoryn and Berantis thus communicated regularly.

Sathoryn placed the small circlet on his head and carefully aligned the diamond with his forehead. The vision began blurry, then Berantis's face fully appeared. His voice resonated in Sathoryn's mind:

"Any news, my friend?"

"Plenty. I was discovered by two paladins of the Order. I attacked them with two of my men, but failed. I even had to flee to save my life," explained Sathoryn.

Berantis remained unmoved. The revelation did not seem to trouble him.

"Members of the Order! Can you describe anything particular about them?"

Sathoryn thought for a moment:

"The taller one wielded a greatsword, and the other fought with two hammers. Rarely have I seen an ambidextrous paladin, Berantis. Does that help you?"

The reply came instantly, for Berantis deeply hated those two:

"Yes, I know who they were. Without doubt, Xantaris and Amandil. According to many, they are the Order's best and most virtuous warriors."

"You weren't aware of their mission, were you?" asked Sathoryn.

"No, none at all. Surely that old fool must have sent them out the morning of his death, before meeting me."

Berantis pondered a moment, then said:

"Perhaps they know compromising things. I don't know what that old fool Orendil told them, but I don't like it, Sathoryn. They must be stopped, quickly. If they discover what happened here in their absence, it could cause us serious trouble."

"Yes, of course, Berantis. I can help capture them with my men and contacts in the city, but I cannot linger long. I must soon leave for the south, on the master's orders."

"I understand, Sathoryn. Do what's necessary, and keep me informed of your progress."

With those last words, Berantis cut the connection, and Sathoryn began preparing his plan.

At the first light of dawn, Xantaris and Amandil rose from their soft beds and had breakfast in the main hall. They then went to the courier service and dispatched a letter to Master Orendil, entrusted to a mounted messenger. The missive would reach their superior in a few days.

Xantaris took the opportunity to ask the young clerk, a pretty girl with short brown hair:

"Tell me, do you know if there is a castle outside the city, not far away?"

The young woman thought for a moment, then replied:

"Yes, there is a castle to the north of the city, near the coast. It's a rather sinister place… but the people who live there are respectable. At least, from what I've heard."

"Thank you very much, miss," said Xantaris with a slight bow.

The two friends went out.

"Perfect! So, shall we go check out that castle?" asked Amandil.

"Of course, companion. Do we go on foot or retrieve our horses?"

"I think it would be more discreet to go on foot," Amandil concluded.

The two paladins left the great city and walked northward along the coast.

Chapter 20 – Reinforcements

Akennor, Darian, Sheila, and Milenna had all slept deeply for the first time in many days. The sun was already high in the sky when Akennor awoke. He was relieved not to have had nightmares during the night. Barely out of the castle's underground passages, they had collapsed from exhaustion, not even thinking of standing watch.

Milenna, already awake, looked at him with an amused smile:

"So, did you sleep well, Akennor? No nightmares to report?" she asked.

He wondered what her question implied, but merely answered kindly:

"No, nothing unusual. And I'm very glad for that."

"Then what's so special about your dreams?"

Akennor lowered his head, avoiding the intense blue eyes of Milenna.

"I don't know… I had many of them when I was younger, then nothing for years. And now suddenly, they've returned. With force. Dreams that seem very real."

"Do you think they mean something? Like a premonition?"

Milenna seemed sincerely curious. He found her curiosity irritating; he didn't like talking about it. His gray eyes met hers.

"I hope not, he replied, his tone grave, filled with anxiety."

"And you? How do you feel? You gave us quite a scare when the demon struck you, he asked, hoping to change the subject."

Milenna smiled.

"I feel much better. Just being finally out of that hell and breathing fresh air gives me strength again. But now, I'm hungry."

Sheila suddenly appeared behind them, ending their exchange.

"Good morning, you two! I slept so well last night… I feel ready for anything."

Sheila, smiling, seemed to have regained her full strength.

"Ready enough to go back into hell?" Darian teased.

"Yes, probably as much as you, Darian," Sheila retorted.

The memory of his panic and anguish sent a shiver down Darian's spine. For nothing in the world would he want to return to that infernal labyrinth.

"How are you, Milenna? You look better," Darian exclaimed.

"Yes, I'm fine," she replied.

The companions talked for a while, as if to exorcise their dreadful ordeal.

"I was really afraid. At one point, I thought I'd never see daylight again," confessed Akennor.

"That was truly the hardest moment of my life."

Darian was still trembling, his words referring to the young man Yanni.

"Those are just bad memories now, let's leave them in the past… and eat."

They ate a few cakes and set out again toward the city to resupply.

A little later, Milenna noticed two figures further along the road. She stopped her companions with a gesture and said:

"I see two individuals coming straight toward us."

"Do they have any identifying mark?" asked Akennor, worried. "They were still too close to the castle to feel safe."

"No, they're still too far away."

"We'd better hide in the woods along the road, that would be safer," suggested Darian.

The others agreed and concealed themselves on both sides of the path. Akennor and Sheila took the right. Darian, with Milenna, hid on the left.

Time passed. Milenna could distinguish the two figures more clearly. The one on the left was of medium height, with short blond hair and green-looking eyes. The one on the right was slightly shorter and seemed older, perhaps because of his beard and mustache.

Both wore the same attire: a gray shirt, black pants, and a dark blue cape fastened with a silver brooch. Milenna relayed her observations to Darian, who gave a broad smile of relief.

"They're members of the Order. I'm certain of it."

"And if it's a trap? To make us believe that?"

Darian's gaze was serious as he shook his head.

The strangers were only a dozen *maicas* away when Milenna confirmed Darian's assumption. She recognized the symbol of the Order of Calaista engraved on the silver brooch. She nodded to Darian, who stepped out of hiding and appeared a few paces before the strangers. Startled, they drew back abruptly and unsheathed their weapons. At the same time, the others emerged from the woods.

Darian raised his hands in peace.

"Come now, it's alright! If you truly are members of the Order of Calaista, then we're allies. I myself am an apprentice paladin."

The bearded man sheathed his weapons and asked:

"Were you at the fortress about a week ago?"

The companions exchanged glances, and Akennor replied:

"Yes, we were. We spoke with Master Orendil."

The two strangers exchanged a satisfied look.

"That's fantastic! We've found you. We heard you were in serious trouble," the blond exclaimed.

The companions, a little lost, didn't quite understand what their interlocutors meant. Seeing their puzzled faces, the strangers introduced themselves:

"My name is Xantaris, and this is my friend Amandil."

They bowed slightly, and Amandil continued:

"A few days after your departure, he grew very worried. He discovered who was behind your misfortunes and tasked us with aiding you in your quest."

Xantaris immediately added:

"That's right. Just yesterday, we tracked down the Order's spy in Elenshae. Orendil had warned us about him, and he was right. We discovered that he actually works for the enemy."

"Sathoryn… that filthy traitor!" Darian spat.

Akennor then recounted their adventure, from their arrival at the castle: Sathoryn's betrayal, his presence alongside them, the ensuing battle, and finally their descent into the catacombs.

Xantaris and Amandil, surprised and impressed, exchanged a complicit look. They were convinced these youths had exceptional potential.

"And where are you heading now? Do you know where your friend might be?" asked Amandil.

Akennor suddenly remembered the map he had glimpsed in Mortragor's office and explained:

"I saw a very old map in an office, just before we fell into the trap they had set for us."

"It showed a land to the north of those we know. I believe the simplest way to get there is by land, crossing the mountains."

"Are you sure she was taken there?" asked Xantaris.

"Yes, I'm sure. A fortress and two camps were drawn there. And according to the legend Master Orendil told us, it was on those ravaged lands — once prosperous — that the first pact with demons took place."

"I confess I've never heard that story," replied Xantaris.

"Nor I... but if Orendil said it..."

"In that case, let's go to Elenshae to find horses," concluded Amandil.

"It won't be easy to cross the mountains on horseback, at least not by the shortcut we intend to take. It might be better to wait and find some at Foranor. Do you have enough provisions to cross the mountains?" suggested Akennor.

"Yes, I think you're right. That'll be simpler. And we have enough food for nearly a week, if we ration it."

Amandil nodded in approval, and the group set out. Along the way, the six companions conversed. Xantaris and Amandil were very curious about their new allies and asked many questions.

For their part, Akennor, Darian, Sheila, and Milenna felt their spirits soar again. They felt reassured and encouraged, glad to have met two warriors as proud as they were skilled.

243

When they caught sight of the cursed castle in the distance, they wisely chose to skirt around it, keeping a safe distance to avoid being spotted. The sun was beginning its slow descent toward the horizon.

But in the shadows of a thicket, a young man loyal to the enemy saw them. He had gone out to gather herbs and plants for his experiments. Hearing the voices of Akennor and Xantaris — who were debating the differences between wielding a two-handed sword and the ambidextrous style — he froze.

The young sorcerer crouched behind a tree and waited for the danger to pass before reemerging. Then he ran back to the castle to warn his master. Upon hearing the news, Mortragor turned livid with rage. Foam dripped from his lips.

"What?! But that's impossible! Are you sure of what you saw?"

"Yes... yes, my lord," the apprentice stammered, trembling in fear.

"There were also two other people with them. Paladins of the Order of Calaista."

"Get out before I end your miserable existence!" roared Mortragor.

He didn't need to be told twice and fled at once.

Mortragor was deeply unsettled. How had they managed to escape the catacombs? He had clearly underestimated them. But what worried him most was how his master would react to this news.

Before informing him, he summoned his best warriors and assassins to his office. Six in total: four men and two women quickly arrived, intrigued by the urgency of the summons.

Mortragor spoke:

"You've no doubt heard of the four young intruders who entered the castle a few days ago?"

"They were trapped in the labyrinth… but they've escaped. And two paladins of the Order of Calaista have joined them. The group skirted the castle and is now heading north. Your mission is to catch and eliminate them before they jeopardize our cover."

Mortragor locked eyes with his soldiers.

"Is that clear? Any questions?"

"No, master," they all replied in unison.

"Good. You leave immediately."

The six assassins bowed briefly and returned to their quarters to collect their gear. Left alone, Mortragor, trembling with fear, slowly placed the crown upon his head to contact Drendor. Thanks to his highly developed telepathic powers, Drendor himself did not need such an artifact. He perceived any thoughts directly addressed to him.

The image of Drendor appeared sharply in Mortragor's mind.

"What is it, Mortragor? Why disturb me again? Is something slipping from your grasp?" His tone was icy, annoyed.

Mortragor tried to compose himself.

"I… I apologize, but I must tell you something grave."

"Then hurry, you miserable wretch."

"The four youths who were trapped in the catacombs…"

"Well? What does that mean?"

"They've escaped and are heading north, with two paladins."

"What?! Incompetent! Fool! Worm!" Drendor thundered, trembling with cold fury.

"What farce is this, Mortragor? Were they not meant to remain prisoners… and perish?"

"Y-yes, but… but… I think they found the exit," Mortragor stammered, petrified with fear.

"You should have made sure of it, wretch!"

"It was impossible! Everyone thought they were lost, especially since the passage was blocked. I've dispatched six of my best assassins after them. They just left," he explained, hoping this initiative would calm his master.

"You disappoint me, Mortragor. You are unfit for the tasks entrusted to you, and I do not tolerate incompetence," Drendor concluded with a sadistic smile.

"No, master, wait! I have always served you well… Aaaah!"

Mortragor clutched his head, trying to rip off the silver crown. A searing pain engulfed him, as if his skull would explode. He writhed on the floor, screaming, arms pressed to his face. Blood gushed from his ears, nose, and eyes. The torment dragged on. Drendor toyed with him, deliberately prolonging his agony. Finally, tired of the diversion, he released him. Mortragor expired in a pool of blood, curled upon himself.

Soon after, Mortragor's second-in-command — a tall bald man with a golden ring through his nose — found his lifeless body. Valros saw the silver crown upon the corpse's brow and instantly understood. He took it and placed it on his own head.

Drendor's image appeared immediately in his mind.

"Valros. Here is the situation: you will take over from poor Mortragor," Drendor announced in his rasping, icy voice.

"Six assassins have been sent to hunt down and eliminate the youths who escaped the catacombs. I expect you to see their mission through. Do not disappoint me, Valros."

"No, my master. I will prove myself worthy. You can count on me," Valros replied, bowing.

The image of Drendor vanished.

Sleras belonged to the cursed elven tribe of Carmiris. Cursed, because long ago, its members had joined Tholgor and his forces of evil. Since the war against the demons, their numbers had steadily dwindled, until only a few scattered survivors remained, feared and shunned.

He had inherited his combat skills from his father, a veteran of that ancient war. He wielded all sorts of weapons with ease, though his preference was for the straight sword and shield. His intermediate armor struck a balance between protection and agility, which he deemed essential.

Tall and lean, with pointed ears, black hair down to his shoulders, and a piercing gaze, Sleras radiated an unsettling presence. His gear ready, he headed for the entrance to join the others.

The sultry Salvara prepared for the mission. She first donned more suitable attire: rough leather pants, light armor, and a black cape with a wide hood. She carefully braided her hair, then gazed briefly into the small mirror above her furnishings.

Her thoughts wandered momentarily over the path her life had taken: from the slums of Elenshae's poorest districts to her rise within the sect. Salvara had carved her place through blades and bloodshed. A fearsome assassin, she had swiftly climbed the ranks.

Manhur waited in the vestibule, already dressed. He had first been assigned an infiltration mission in Kementári, his hometown, before being reassigned at the last moment to this one. He told himself it was just a detour. He loved that powerful, prosperous city, where his work as a thief had been very lucrative.

A longtime influential member of the thieves' guild, he held an enviable position. His interest in the sect was only financial. But lately, he had begun to grow weary of this association and wondered if he should cut ties. The dark lord's ambition frightened him. Of average height, with short brown hair and dark eyes, he passed easily unnoticed.

Not so Kathryn, who arrived shortly after and stood at his side. Manhur thought her beautiful: of his height, with full lips, large brown eyes, and long silky hair. She gave him a discreet smile.

She wore light, practical clothing: loose raw-fabric pants, a black leather vest, and a matching cape. Manhur knew little about her. Her origins were obscure, and she disliked speaking of them. But her talents as a mage were well known and feared. She had been trained by a dark necromancer in Drendor's direct service.

Salvara was the next to reach the meeting point. She stationed herself at the foot of the grand staircase, scanning the half-lit corridors. Heavy footsteps echoed on the marble. Farun, she thought, biting her lip. She remembered a torrid night.

There was something bestial about him that pleased her, especially when they made love.
What a male… she mused dreamily. He had told her he hailed from a distant, secluded people.

248

His tribe had taught him to fight and hunt all kinds of game. His preferred weapons were the bow and crossbow, though he was also skilled with a sword or even an axe.

Farun appeared beneath the dim glow of the lamps. He was taller and more massive than most, with long black hair down to his shoulders, a thick beard, black eyes, and a scar slashing across his right cheek. He wore light, functional clothing. As he stepped near her, she gave him an amused smile. He answered with a knowing wink. Sleras arrived silently and positioned himself near the staircase, slightly apart.

Rufus is missing... as always, he thought. Sleras liked him. A discreet, efficient, and deadly killer. Like himself, Rufus disliked attention and crowds. Sleras had opened up to him as he never had to anyone.

He recalled a memory, from a hot summer's day. A mission had gone wrong and ended in bloodshed. Covered in blood and sweat, they had decided to wash in a small river they came across.

The water was cool and refreshing, flowing down his muscular body. Sleras was getting dressed when Rufus emerged, his manhood erect. He moved toward him and kissed him passionately. Sleras had been surprised, almost shocked, but allowed it: he wanted it.

Their relationship was complicated. Rufus often left on assassination missions. He was a member of a guild of assassins in Colimport, a powerful southern city. Rufus had no ideological attachment to the sect: he was a mercenary.

Sleras suddenly heard quiet, almost imperceptible footsteps.

At last, he thought.

Rufus appeared, wrapped in a large black cloak, a wide hood covering his head.

His features were barely visible: dark eyes, black hair streaked with gray, a pointed nose, and thin lips.

Rufus lowered his hood. His gaze locked on him; a thin smile curved his lips.

Sleras didn't respond. But he understood.

"Finally! We are all here," Sleras said.

"Let's move!" he ordered curtly.

The group immediately set off, launched in pursuit of their prey.

They picked up the trail without much difficulty. Manhur and Salvara, both seasoned trackers, led the way, guiding their companions efficiently.

Chapter 21 – Revelations

The mountains loomed before them, like proud pillars of the sky. The group walked in silence; fatigue and weariness were slowly overtaking their strength. The forest bordering the mountains resembled the one surrounding Akennor's home village. The relatively sparse density of the trees allowed them to progress quickly and without hindrance. As night slowly gave way to day, the clouds took on a soft hue of red and gold.

As they advanced beneath the canopy, Darian's vision blurred; time seemed to suspend its course. In an instant, he was thrust back to the previous summer. He and Shaya had decided to go for a picnic in a clearing. She was waiting for him nearby, leaning against a tree, arms crossed.

"Come on, proud warrior, faster, you're too slow!" she teased.

Darian carried the backpack and struggled to catch up with her. Shaya loved to tease him this way. He rushed forward, determined to make her swallow her words. She bolted towards the clearing.

"No, you won't catch me!"

"Oh yes, you'll see, you won't escape!"

Despite the weight of the bag on his shoulders, Darian doubled his effort to catch her. She turned and saw that he was already on her heels.

"Ah!" she cried out, startled.

Just a little further, Darian told himself. He made one last effort and pounced on Shaya.

She nearly escaped by struggling, but he managed to hold on to her legs. She fell face down, laughing and protesting while fighting back.

"That doesn't count, Darian!"

"Oh yes, it does," he answered, tickling her ribs with zeal.

"No, stop! Please stop!" she laughed, begging.

Darian leaned closer to her face and plunged his gaze into her eyes.

"You see, you can't escape. You are mine," he said softly.

"And you are mine," she replied.

Shaya pressed her lips to his, and they embraced in a long, passionate kiss. Absorbed in his thoughts, Darian didn't see the stone in his path and stumbled. Amandil, who was following him, rushed to help him up.

"Are you alright, my friend? You seemed lost in thought."

Darian replied with a smile:

"Yes, in a beautiful place, where sorrow and sadness have no place. I'm fine, thank you."

The rest of the group didn't notice the incident and continued marching silently. The companions were heading northwest, nearing the coast to cross the mountain range more easily.

"We should stop for the night. I think that's enough for today," said Akennor.

"Agreed," approved Xantaris. "Let's camp here. Amandil and I will try to hunt something."

The two paladins set down their packs and went into the woods to look for game. Meanwhile, the others set up camp. Darian gathered wood for the fire with Sheila.

252

Milenna spread her blankets on a mossy patch of ground and lay down, exhausted. Akennor cut some ferns to make a more comfortable space.

Soon Darian and Sheila returned, arms full of wood. Sheila lit the fire, and soon the wood crackled under the flames.

"She's exhausted, isn't she?" Sheila said to Akennor, nodding towards Milenna.

"I think her transformations demand a great deal of energy, and she hasn't had time to recover."

"I'll wake her when the meal is ready." The three of them sat around the fire, enjoying its warmth. Milenna, meanwhile, was plunged in a deep, restorative sleep.

A long while later, Xantaris and Amandil returned to camp with three hares. Xantaris proudly displayed their catch:

"We're going to feast tonight. These little creatures are delicious."

He placed them by the fire, pulled out a knife, and began preparing them. Amandil joined him, while Sheila carved wooden skewers for cooking.

"We were lucky. This forest is full of game. It was easy to bring them down with the crossbow," Xantaris said.

The hares, carefully prepared, were soon roasting over the fire, promising a well-deserved feast. Weary, the companions spoke little, their voices barely audible over the crackling flames.

Akennor quickly dozed off. The flicker of the flames licking the meat had a hypnotic effect on him. Later, Sheila woke him gently, tickling his ear and kissing his forehead.

"What's happening?" he asked, disoriented.

"It's time to eat something, to regain strength," she answered softly.

Darian woke Milenna, who opened her eyes slowly, blinking against the bright firelight.

"Come on, eat some meat, it'll do you good, it'll give you strength," he encouraged.

"It smells wonderful," Milenna said with a smile. "That nap did me a lot of good."

The meal was shared, and the roasted hare was devoured quickly. Akennor thanked the paladins warmly:

"Thank you, Xantaris and Amandil, that was delicious… we really needed it."

"Glad to help. We should do this more often. It'll save our provisions," Xantaris replied.

Everyone agreed, since no one knew how long their journey would last.

Suddenly, attention turned to Milenna.

"How do you feel now?" asked Darian.

"I'm fine, thank you. My strength is coming back little by little."

Her words triggered a memory for Akennor, tied to their time in the sinister labyrinth.

"Now that I think about it… how did you know those details, back in the hall with the stone demon? Tell me, it intrigued me a lot."

The others looked up, curious. Even Xantaris and Amandil listened closely. Milenna sighed and straightened.

"Alright… I'll tell you. I intended to someday anyway."

She paused, choosing her words.

"You remember when Orendil told us about the damnation of Tholgor, and the curse tied to that legend…"

They nodded.

"I've known that legend since childhood. But I never imagined the insignia you found, Akennor, could be linked to it."

"The stone demon spoke the truth: I am a direct descendant of Oriador. Nine generations separate me from him. My ancestors were granted longer life by the gods. Though it has diminished over the generations, my life expectancy is still about two hundred and fifty years."

Her companions were speechless.

"But… how old are you now?" Darian asked.

"I turned fifty this year," Milenna replied with a gentle smile."

The others stared, astonished.

"You don't look it at all! I would've thought you our age!" exclaimed Xantaris.

Milenna smiled, flattered, then continued.

She told them of her parents' murder by a powerful necromancer, her rescue as a baby, and her upbringing by a mage before being entrusted to Svealëdor. She spoke of the teachings she received, her training as a druid, and the rediscovery of her ancestry.

She also revealed knowledge of the pendant guarded by the stone demon—an artifact forged by Oriador's priests to withstand demonic auras, practically indestructible.

The companions shuddered as she concluded:

"This proves there were survivors among Tholgor' disciples, working in the shadows for centuries."

Xantaris then spoke of Orendil's findings: a name whispered behind all these events.

"Drendor," he said. "An extraordinarily powerful necromancer I believe my master once faced long ago."

Akennor repeated the name, feeling an eerie resonance. Milenna's face twisted with anguish:

"It may be him who killed my parents!"

Sheila asked about his age. Xantaris answered gravely:

"Very old. Centuries. His exact age is unknown."

The conversation stretched long into the night. They eventually organized watches and fell asleep.

On guard, Darian fingered the pendant Shaya had given him, remembering her smile and their moments together. His heart ached with longing:

"I need you, Shaya…" he whispered.

Meanwhile, Akennor, tormented by dreams, saw a terrible vision: a dark figure seated on a black throne, surrounded by macabre horrors. Slowly, the creature turned its lifeless gaze upon him, baring a cruel smile of sharp, beastly teeth.

The name echoed in his mind: *Drendor.*

Akennor awoke with a start, gasping, crying out Shaya's name.

Chapter 22 – The Hunt

It was morning, the first glimmers of dawn having pierced through the layer of clouds that was gradually gathering. Akennor's cry suddenly woke his companions. Xantaris, who had been keeping watch, had even drawn his weapon, thinking it was an alarm. Amandil wondered what was happening. Milenna, Darian, and Sheila strongly suspected that their friend had once again suffered a vile nightmare.

"Are you all right, Akennor? You're sweating," asked Xantaris, eyebrows slightly furrowed, concern in his tone.

Akennor reassured his new companion:

"Yes… I'm fine, don't worry. I often have this kind of nightmare, and I react in ways I can't explain."

He wondered whether he should tell his friends about his vision and opened his mouth, when he was interrupted by Darian, once again seized with anxiety.

"We need to go now. We've already lost enough time."

He was nervous and restless. He had thought of Shaya nearly the entire night, and the idea of never seeing her again was simply unbearable.

Akennor kept silent and decided to bring it up another time. After all, it was probably just a figment of his imagination, he thought. But his attitude and mood did not escape Milenna, who watched him closely. Still, she decided not to question him for now.

*

The band of mercenaries arrived at the spot where Akennor and his friends had spent the night, only a few moments after their departure. Salvara found the remains of the campfire and examined them briefly.

"They haven't been gone long. There's still a little warmth…"

Manhur had already spotted tracks a little farther and commented:

"Indeed, it's recent, and they're heading north."

Sleras cast his dark gaze toward the mountain range before him.

"They want to cross the mountains, and I wonder why," said Manhur.

"It's obvious, I think," replied Sleras flatly. "They want to reach the fortress of Angrenost. But I don't know what drives them."

"That's madness! They'll never be able to make it," exclaimed Manhur.

"Our mission is to kill them as quickly as possible. So let's move," ordered Sleras firmly, leaving no room for argument.

Manhur and Salvara led the way, as two were needed to follow the trail, especially since a heavy rain had begun to fall.

The companions ate bread from their provisions as they walked, so as not to waste time. Darian pressed forward eagerly at the head of the group. The sky darkened quickly, and a storm seemed almost inevitable.

258

Rain began in the late morning, just as the young adventurers started their ascent into the mountains.

The trees at the foot of the range were smaller and denser. The slope, steep and treacherous, made climbing difficult.

The downpour turned the narrow trail into a slippery trap. Each of them struggled constantly to keep from falling and tumbling down the mountainside. Akennor's fractured ribs ached. His breath was short, and he occasionally clutched his side.

As he tried to grab a tree to pull himself up, his foot slipped, sending him sliding downward. His fall was brief, for he collided with Sheila, who was right behind him. He thus found himself in the drenched arms of the sorceress.

"Are you all right? Are you hurt?" asked Sheila, worried.

His broken ribs made him grimace in pain. Nearly out of breath, he answered:

"I'll be fine."

Sheila sat him down on a flat rock and rummaged through her bag. She pulled out the healing vial given by Illawen.

"You'll take more of this," she scolded.

The greenish balm from his mother warmed his aching ribs, and the healing potion soothed the pain. The companions decided to pause as well. They hadn't stopped since early morning and had marched at a brisk pace. The forest was now behind them; only a few sparse trees still stood at their height. The landscape now consisted of large rocks and a rocky ground on steep slopes.

After a short rest, and with Akennor's approval, they set out again. This time, Darian and Sheila stayed on either side of him, to prevent another mishap.

The climb was slower. Rain poured relentlessly, and the thunder's power seemed to shake the mountain itself. Lightning split the sky, illuminating it with the fury of the gods.

"We can't keep going like this, we need shelter!" shouted Xantaris, trying to make himself heard over the roar of the storm.

"Agreed—before something dreadful happens," added Milenna.

Darian seemed irritated. This would delay them again, he thought. But they had no choice: the storm was truly fierce.

Amandil, walking at the front, turned and said:

"There's a trench in the mountain. We'll be safe from the lightning, and we'll be able to keep moving."

Darian was delighted at the news and hurried to catch up with Amandil. Indeed, the group advanced into a natural passage, narrow, carved into the mountainside.

The walls rose high on either side, closing the stone corridor above their heads. While flat at first, the incline increased steadily and sharply.

The thunder still rumbled in the sky, low and continuous, its echo amplified by the stone passage. Large rocks and landslides frequently blocked the path, forcing them to climb and scramble. The stones underfoot were slick. Water streamed down their faces, seeped under their cloaks, soaking their clothes until they clung to their skin.

Suddenly the rain ceased, and the clouds dispersed, letting timid rays of sun filter through, already sinking toward the horizon. The walls of the passage gradually fell away, and the companions once again found themselves exposed.

Looking around, they realized the mountain's peak was now behind them, showing the obstacle had been overcome.

The mercenaries, however, struggled with the storm. Despite their expertise, Manhur and Salvara had great difficulty. Most of the time, the torrential rain had completely erased their prey's tracks.

Moreover, the rocky ground gave them much trouble. But the scrape marks left by Akennor's fall confirmed they were still on the right trail.

"One of them lost his footing here and slid down," said Salvara, pointing to the visible scuffs on the ground.

Night had long since fallen when Manhur and Salvara discovered the mountain passage and led their companions to the other side.

Night having replaced day, the young adventurers hurried down toward the forest to prepare a fire and take well-deserved rest. This time, Darian and Milenna went hunting, while Akennor rested and the others set up camp.

Sheila went to change discreetly behind the trees and slipped into her dark green robe. A golden belt circled her waist and fastened at the front, giving her mage's robe an elegant style.

This garment was more form-fitting than her black robe, and thus highlighted her feminine curves more. Sheila looked toward her friends and caught Xantaris watching her; his face flushed red, and he quickly lowered his head, clearly embarrassed.

Sheila smiled, then went to warm herself by the fire. The air was heavy with humidity, and a light breeze from the nearby coast lowered the temperature.

Milenna and Darian returned soon after with a small mountain stag. The group would thus have enough to eat for a few days. Once prepared and well roasted, the meal was shared with appetite among the companions, who then prepared to pass the night, all very weary.

This time, Akennor had no nightmares and slept deeply, comfortably settled. Their departure the next day was just as hasty as the day before, spurred on by Darian's growing anxiety with each passing moment.

The companions were now to cross another forest, similar to the one beyond the mountains. But what troubled them more was that they would soon find themselves on the lands of Foranor.

All the members of the group had only heard ill of this kingdom. Akennor, for his part, had often heard his father and brother speak of this people as a mortal enemy. He began to worry, and shared his apprehensions with his friends:

"When we leave this forest, we'll be on the lands of Foranor, and that worries me a little. I don't know if you've ever heard about this kingdom."

"What I know," answered Xantaris, "is that long ago, the Order helped them greatly. But I believe something happened afterward that created a rift."

"For me," said Amandil, "that's also what I know. Of course, I've heard the horror stories, but Master Orendil taught me there's a difference between truth and gossip. Since then, I judge what I hear with a critical mind."

"Soon, we'll see whether this kingdom is really so terrible. But I'm not too worried," he concluded, glancing at Akennor.

The latter thought his words deserved reflection. He hoped Amandil was right, and that they would not encounter great difficulties. Sheila and Darian had heard the same rumors as Akennor. Darian, however, had imagined all sorts of dreadful things in this land.

Milenna, for her part, shared Amandil's caution. She had never set foot there, but her mentor had. And the stories he told her differed greatly from the popular rumors.

*

The group of assassins rose very early, even before the faint rays of sunlight pierced through the thick gray clouds. These sinister individuals sought to close the gap with their prey. Sleras, boiling with rage, urged his companions to speed up.

Later, Manhur found the remains of a fire left by their quarry.

"They left not long ago. They don't have much of a lead on us," announced Salvara.

Sleras immediately signaled to resume the chase. The elf was infamous for his cunning and cruelty. No one dared oppose him, and the group advanced swiftly.

Salvara, scouting ahead as though driven by an invisible whip, suddenly returned at full speed:

"I see them. They're there, between two hills, just on the other side of this one."

Sleras immediately dropped to the ground, imitated by his allies.

They crawled silently to the crest of the hill to observe. He saw their targets for the first time, easily spotting the two paladins, and gauged the abilities of the others by their bearing.

They quickly retreated and devised an attack strategy.

"There are two members of the Order. The brown-haired girl is undoubtedly a mage. The other, I haven't yet identified," murmured Sleras.

*

After a long walk, the companions were exhausted. The sky had grown considerably darker, and the clouds again turned threatening.

"We should stop to rest and eat a little," suggested Amandil.

"We're all at our limit."

"All right, good idea. My stomach is devouring itself," exclaimed Akennor, sitting on a tree trunk.

Darian sighed, but said nothing. He was frustrated at this new loss of time. The others crouched on the ground and unpacked their bags.

"We don't have much left to eat," noted Xantaris, holding out his last travel cakes for all to see.

By pooling their remaining supplies and rationing carefully, they estimated they had enough provisions for only a few more days.

This reality struck Akennor hard. He realized they would soon need to replenish supplies. But where, he wondered, in a land wholly unknown to them? The young adventurers nibbled slowly and in silence. Each ate a travel cake, then they took a little rest.

The journey was exhausting and harsh, and it was beginning to take its toll on their morale and mood.

Chapter 23 – The Confrontation

Not far from the young adventurers, hostile eyes, hidden in the shadows of the trees, watched them. Sleras observed his enemies with great interest.

Mortragor's mercenaries exchanged hand signals, a language widely used by Sleras's banished people. The cursed elf had introduced this discreet form of communication within the sect upon his arrival. Practical for infiltration operations, this silent language became the preferred tool of spies and assassins, whom Sleras personally trained.

The youths were all lost in thought. Fatigue and weariness weighed heavily on each of them. Milenna, who could no longer stand being idle, stood up.

"I'm going to take a walk."

"Don't go too far. We'll be leaving soon... and be careful, especially," Akennor told her.

Milenna replied with a smile. She found him charming, with his piercing gaze and protective, kind demeanor. She returned to her animal form and padded away silently on her paws.

The two paladins conversed aside, while the others rested on the ground, leaning against the tree trunks.

"I hope the Order reacted quickly," said Xantaris.

"Do not doubt it," replied Amandil. Master Orendil is very alert and shrewd.

"At least our discovery will have been very useful and will likely have prevented unfortunate incidents for our brothers."

"Indeed, but I long to return to our own… There is something troubling me."

"Yes, me too, but we must… ahhhh!"

The shock was violent and treacherous. Xantaris was suddenly hurled forward, a sharp pain piercing his shoulder blades. A short metal bolt, fired from a crossbow, had lodged in his back.

Amandil rushed to his friend, now sprawled on the ground. Akennor, alerted, drew his swords and ran toward them. The young warrior scanned the woods, probing every corner, every suspicious shadow, his senses on edge.

Sheila was short of breath. Her heart clenched at the thought that unseen enemies might have them in their sights. That feeling of vulnerability was unbearable to her.

Hidden in the shadow of the foliage, Sleras allowed himself a malevolent smile. Farun's bolt had hit its target, and the group seemed to be succumbing to panic. He gave a discreet signal to Katrhyn, who in turn prepared to launch the assault.

Suddenly, a hissing voice, like that of a serpent, spread through the air. The young mage's reflexes overcame her fear. Without hesitation, she stepped in front of her companions and cried out firmly:

"Varyan-rhu!"

A shield of energy materialized around her. The magical aura, tinged with bluish-gray, deflected a dart that was speeding straight at her. But she could do nothing against the red sphere of energy that surged immediately afterward.

The impact, though softened by the magical shield, was violent enough to throw her backward. Akennor rushed toward her. Unconscious, she lay on the ground.

The young warrior glanced around: the attackers remained unseen, two of their group were injured, another unaccounted for. He realized they had to flee if they hoped to survive.

A signal confirmed that the time to flee had come. To his right, a cry of pain was followed by ferocious growls.
Milenna… at last!
The ferns shook frantically, while the growls intensified and the cries of pain faded into a death rattle.
"Go! Now! Scatter!" Ordered Akennor.
He hoisted Sheila onto his shoulders while Amandil helped Xantaris to walk. The young warrior turned to face the mercenaries and charged straight ahead. Amandil veered left, followed by Darian, who had no time to think.

Caught off guard by the wolf's attack, the mercenaries froze. Despite the agonized screams of one of their own, they did not move, abandoning him to his fate.

When her prey stopped moving, Milenna turned. She sniffed the air, the ground, the vegetation… She caught five distinct scents. Baring her fangs, she lunged at the closest, determined to exterminate all those wretches.

Rufus suddenly heard branches snapping and foliage rustling nearby. A low growl tore through the silence, then a gray mass leapt from the shadows and pounced on him. He cried for help.

The wolf gave him no chance. With one bite, she seized him by the throat and tried to strangle him. Meanwhile, Akennor, Xantaris, and Darian were fleeing through the woods.

Sleras, emerging from his hiding place, rushed toward Rufus, cursing this setback. A silvery gleam suddenly caught Milenna's attention. Thanks to this reflex, she narrowly avoided a fatal blow. The wolf leapt aside, skillfully dodging the elf's strikes.

But Sleras, furious, kept striking, his blows meeting only empty air. Little by little, Milenna was tiring. Her dodges grew more hesitant. When she heard the first words of an incantation, she decided to retreat.

The renegade roared as he saw her vanish among the trees, unharmed. He rushed immediately to his lover. Rufus's stomach was nothing but a gaping, bloody wound. He would not survive.

Sleras grasped his already icy hand.

"I'm sorry, Rufus… I would have wanted… for us to have more time."

A discreet tear slid down his cheek.

"And me too… I'm cold… hold me, Sleras…"

He trembled. But as soon as he felt the elf's touch, his body relaxed.

"There, that's better… Don't leave me… I love you… stay…"

"I'm here. I'll stay… until the end."

A lump rose in his throat and tears trickled down. Moments later, Rufus exhaled his last breath. Sleras pressed a gentle kiss on his now cold lips… and silently swore to avenge him. The renegade elf wasted no time. Without a word, he set off in pursuit of the she-wolf.

Meanwhile, Amandil supported Xantaris and desperately searched for a shelter to keep his companion safe. But already, a mercenary had taken off after them. Amandil heard his steps closing in behind.

Darian heard them too. Panting, he said:

"Go on… I'll take care of him."

The paladin nodded and continued on, dragging Xantaris. Darian slipped quietly aside, crouched low, then crawled to a pile of fallen logs. He hid and waited.

But he soon realized his mistake: it wasn't one, but two pursuers. He saw them through the foliage, weapons drawn. One wore light armor, a black cloak, and a large hood draped over his shoulders.

What a mess… Two already dead. I think I'll try to shake them off, thought Manhur. Darian instantly recognized Salvara. Hard to forget such a face. As soon as the two mercenaries passed him, he leapt out, hammer raised. He brought his weapon down on the man from behind. The impact was of brutal violence: a crack of bones echoed, and the body collapsed, lifeless. Dead on the spot.

Without waiting, Darian darted into the trees and melted into the vegetation.

"Manhur? Manhur!" Salvara called, panicked.

"You bastard… filthy coward!" she screamed after Darian.

Green with rage, humiliated at being caught so easily, she charged after him. Amandil scoured the forest in search of a refuge. He finally spotted, at the foot of a small hill, a cave hidden behind large moss-covered rocks. Some stones were tangled with thick roots, as though the forest itself sought to keep the place secret.

The hollow seemed large enough to shelter six people. He laid Xantaris there and made sure his condition hadn't worsened. Then he left immediately to find the others.

Meanwhile, Sleras pursued the wolf, but had lost her trail. Furious, he turned back and set his sights on Akennor and Sheila.

He cursed his prey, but he knew he would eventually catch up. The young warrior carried the woman on his shoulders; he would eventually weaken.

Akennor, for his part, could feel the threat closing in. His breath grew short, his arms and legs heavier and heavier. He stumbled down the hillside, avoiding treacherous roots and slippery stones, all while keeping Sheila on his shoulders.

Below, a stream wound through the trees and ferns. Its banks here were steep, lined with dense vegetation. A large, angular rock covered in moss stood to his left. A thin waterfall ran over it. Fallen trunks cluttered the watercourse, forming a natural tangle. Akennor panted, heart pounding. He swept the surroundings with his gaze, then carefully approached the edge. There, he laid her gently on the bank.

He knew the enemy was close. He had to act, fast. Then, on instinct, he bent over her, pressed his lips to hers… and plunged into the stream, Sheila in his arms. Hidden beneath trunks and branches, he held her tightly against him, breathing air into her through that silent kiss, while the sounds of their pursuers echoed just above.

On the bank, Sleras and Kathryn scanned the rippling surface of the stream. They hurriedly searched the ferns, but found nothing.

"Where did they go?" Sleras growled, beside himself.

"They can't be far!" Kathryn retorted.

Both of them stood just below Sheila and Akennor, concealed underwater. The renegade elf boiled with rage. Frustration consumed him, and he howled, unable to contain himself.

"Come now, Sleras, calm down..."

"Maybe they're hiding somewhere... or they've taken another path," she added.

Regaining his composure, Sleras replied:

"They must have crossed the stream and taken the hill. Let's follow them."

They walked along the bank and moved off toward a narrower passage. Once the danger had passed, Akennor slowly surfaced, his lips still pressed against Sheila's. Her eyes were still closed... then she fluttered her eyelids, dazed.

His gaze met Akennor's, surprised. He stepped back slightly, cheeks flushed.

"Are you... okay?" he managed to stammer.

Sheila, confused, frowned slightly. Why had Akennor kissed her?

What had happened? Why was she soaked?

Images returned to her: a red flash, searing pain, then... Akennor's kiss.

"I think I'm okay... but I feel weak. As if my limbs refuse to obey me."

"That was close. I managed to hide us... for now."

Akennor straightened, alert, scanning the surroundings with all his senses.

"We need to leave this place. And find the others."

Before Sheila could answer, Akennor hoisted her onto his shoulders and retraced his steps toward the camp, hoping to find one of their own there. The young woman's weight made the climb difficult. Holding Sheila securely, his other hand gripping trees and bushes to pull himself up, he painfully climbed the slope.

At the top, he took a few steps, then froze. Footsteps were approaching. Unsure of who was coming, he set Sheila gently against the rough trunk of a tree and motioned for silence. He hid behind another tree and waited, tense. When he recognized the tall silhouette of Amandil, two hammers in hand, he let out a sigh of relief.

Akennor jumped to his feet and called out to the paladin:

"Amandil! I'm so glad to see you!"

The paladin smiled in relief and came to meet him.

"Are you all right?" he asked with a smile, then his expression grew worried.

"Where's Sheila?"

A weak voice replied:

"Here."

Amandil approached and knelt before her.

"You're pale… but I'm glad you're alive."

Akennor followed:

"And Xantaris? How is he?"

"I found a small cave, a little farther south-east. I put him there for shelter. His condition is serious, but I'm sure he'll make it."

The news briefly darkened Akennor's face.

"Can you take Sheila to him? They'll be safe there… I have scores to settle."

"All right, the cave isn't far."

"But Akennor, don't you think it would be better if we fought them together?"

The young warrior answered his companion with a hard, uncompromising look.

Amandil understood and concluded:

"I'll find you then... until then, be careful."

Carrying the still-drowsy Sheila on his shoulders, Amandil strode away into the forest. Akennor's blood boiled in his veins. He set off after the mercenaries, determined to finish it.

Meanwhile, Milenna was tracking Farun, who left his trail deliberately visible, hounding him closely. She wanted him to know she was after him, that she was closing in.

Farun, panting, stumbled over roots, branches scratching his face. Suddenly, the she-wolf surged forward. In a few strides she was on him, then leapt powerfully to block his path. She landed right in front of him, bared fangs ready to strike.

The mercenary started, stepped back, then spun around to flee, casting terrified glances over his shoulder. Milenna prepared to pounce again... when a hammer came from nowhere and smashed into Farun's face. The impact was so brutal his skull burst. He collapsed instantly, dead, without a cry.

"Serves you right," spat Darian.

The apprentice paladin gazed a moment at the corpse, then raised his eyes to the wolf.

"Sorry for stealing your prey... but I couldn't miss such an opportunity," he added with a wink.

Milenna fixed him for a moment, then turned away. She sniffed the air, scanned the ground, tilted her head slightly.

A scent… She dashed immediately between the trees, and Darian rushed after her, pounding along in great strides.

Akennor promptly returned to the stream, determined not to waste time in finding the tracks of his enemies. They followed the watercourse for a short distance. A fallen tree served as a bridge. He crossed it in two strides and continued his pursuit.

The enemy's tracks became harder to follow on the rocky ground, but he managed to trace them. Voices reached his ears, and he pressed himself against the ground behind a large tree, hidden by the vegetation. Moments later, he heard:

"They tricked us well," spat the renegade elf. "I bet they never crossed the stream."

"We'll crush them. They won't escape us," added Salvara.

The young warrior let them pass without moving, wishing to take them by surprise, to give them a taste of their own methods. As soon as they had crossed the log, he rose and followed.

The mercenaries returned to the site of the initial clash. But as they retraced their steps, they spotted Amandil following the tracks toward the stream. Without a sound, the elf lunged at him. The paladin barely had time to dodge the sword strike and countered with his hammer, which clashed against Sleras's shield.

The elf's second blow slashed Amandil's left arm. A sharp pain forced him to drop his weapon. Sleras prepared to strike again, but his blade was intercepted. Akennor had just parried it with his swords.

He flashed a cruel smile.

"I've been looking for you… you know… I'll take pleasure in killing you."

"You've found me… and it will be your blood that spills," Akennor replied in an icy tone.

"You're dead, wretch," spat Salvara with disdain.

"You still resent me for resisting you, whore," he growled.

The elf leapt with a savage cry, but Akennor easily blocked the attack and countered immediately, bringing his right sword down violently on Sleras's flank. The traitor parried with his shield.

Akennor's left blade swung at him, but the elf barely managed to block with his sword. In a swift move, Sleras pivoted and smashed his shield against Akennor's head. The young warrior staggered back, dazed, shaking his head to recover his senses.

Salvara roared and entered the fray as well, but Amandil had reclaimed his hammer and intercepted her assault. Frustrated, she cast him a black glare, grimacing with fury and hatred. Panting, she let out a warrior's cry and hurled herself at him.

Akennor and Sleras clashed furiously. Akennor multiplied his attacks and feints, but Sleras, relentless, remained on the defensive, never allowing himself to be caught off guard. Exhaustion began to wear on the young warrior. His opponent seemed like an impenetrable fortress. The deadlock had to be broken.

Salvara, armed with two knives, attacked with murderous frenzy. She performed a macabre dance around Amandil. The paladin parried and deflected the blades, but her swift, precise movements managed to wound him several times.

The pain of the cuts and the smell of blood enraged Amandil, who increased the pace of his strikes until he overwhelmed her. Suddenly, Akennor attempted a daring maneuver.

He charged straight at his enemy, weapons raised, then ducked at the last moment, dodging the elf's blade. In the same motion, he slashed his opponent's arm. A jet of hot blood splashed his face.

The shock was terrible. The renegade elf screamed in agony and lowered his guard. Akennor seized the opportunity to drive both swords deep into his stomach, up to the hilts. The assassin, stunned, opened his eyes wide. He tried to speak, but only a stream of blood poured from his mouth, followed by the rattle of death.

Meanwhile, Amandil blocked another strike, swept his foe's legs out from under her, and knocked her onto her back. He followed with a violent blow to the belly. She lifted her torso in pain, but Amandil finished her by bringing his hammer down on her skull.

He pushed the corpse aside with his foot to free his blades. Sleras's body collapsed face down, lifeless. Moments later, Darian joined his friend near Amandil.

"They really want our heads," Akennor said without turning.

Though they already suspected the source of their attackers, Akennor wanted to be sure. He leaned over Sleras's corpse and searched his black cloak. In an inner pocket, he found what he was looking for: a metallic object that he showed them.

The sinister silver badge gleamed in his hand. Amandil took it, examined it for a few seconds, then handed it to the young paladin.

"I suppose they've been trailing us since the castle," Akennor added.

He continued his search for more clues. He found a dozen gold coins in a small leather purse on the belt of the dead man, as well as a dagger with a golden handle set with jade, carved into the shape of a serpent, its open jaws forming the pommel. The blade was thin and curved, forming a double S—elegant yet menacing.

Sheila, still very pale, had just emerged from the cave, moving slowly through the undergrowth.

"Guys, come see what I found!" she called.

Earlier, while she had followed her companion to strike at Amandil, Katrhyn had stayed slightly behind, preferring not to be disturbed so she could better support Sleras with her spells. As she focused on casting an attack spell, a furtive noise broke the silence, and a gray silhouette sprang like a shadow. She was instantly pinned to the ground, powerful jaws clamped around her neck.

Alerted by Sheila's cry, the others turned and rushed toward her. Milenna, having resumed human form, stood next to a woman in a dark red sorceress's robe, tightly bound.

"A prisoner! We could ask her some questions," suggested Amandil.

"May demons take you! I won't say a word, do you hear me? Not a word!" screamed the young sorceress.

Sheila gave her a brutal kick in the stomach.

"Shut up, and show some respect if you want your death to be painless."

Akennor, standing back, observed the scene. Sheila was recovering quickly, now that the spell's effect was fading. But anger twisted her features, and that troubled him. He didn't like seeing her this way.

"What is your name?" he asked calmly.

"That's none of your business!" spat Katrhyn, her eyes venomous.

"I just want to know who I'm dealing with."

"I don't care! Go burn in hell!"

Akennor didn't flinch. He stared straight into her eyes and continued in a calm, almost gentle tone:

"We've seen what goes on in your castle. We've glimpsed your rituals, your victims… and understood your values. But there's one thing I don't get. How did you end up here? How can one worship demons and call destruction a path?"

Katrhyn answered without thinking.

"I hate this world and everyone in it. My parents never loved me. They made my life a living hell. Then one day, I met a member of the sect, and he set me free."

A twisted grin curled her lips.

"Thanks to them, I finally found meaning in my existence. Very soon, we'll be more powerful than you can ever imagine… and this world will belong to us. We'll reshape it as we please."

"It was Mortragor who sent you, wasn't it?" asked Akennor, still calm.

Darian couldn't take it anymore. A question had consumed him for too long.

"The prisoner… the one who arrived at the castle about a week ago… Where did they take her?"

Katrhyn instantly caught the emotion in his voice. She took the chance to strike where it hurt most.

"What? That little whore!" she sneered with a venomous smile.

"I don't know. Nobody knows."

At these words, Sheila lost control. She hurled herself at the witch, kicking her furiously.

"You bitch! Don't you dare speak of my friend that way!" she screamed, beside herself.

Katrhyn laughed, panting almost, as if each blow brought her a twisted pleasure.

Akennor stepped in, holding Sheila by the shoulders to calm her. But Kathryn wasn't finished. In a provocative tone, she spat:

"It's true, she's a whore. She was raped by all the men, and she begged for more… again… and again."

Trembling, his fists clenched, his breath ragged, Darian snapped. He couldn't bear to hear such abominations. A guttural scream tore from him, raw with rage and inhuman pain. He seized his weapon and crushed the witch's skull.

The impact was horrific. Her head exploded, reduced to pulp, bone, and blood.

But it wasn't enough. The pain still burned inside.

He struck again. And again.

Until he no longer had the strength to raise his hammer.

Until his tears blinded him. No one intervened. They let him release his torment.

The silence that followed seemed to smother the entire clearing.

Darian, still trembling, stared at the lifeless body, unable to look away. His breath came in ragged gasps, his hands clutching his hammer's handle quivering slightly. The rage that had consumed him slowly ebbed, leaving a bitter emptiness, a crushing fatigue.

Akennor stood frozen. He barely recognized his best friend. Once, he would never have raised a hand against a prisoner. But he understood. He understood the suffocating grief that left no room for reason. He laid a hand on his friend's shoulder, but said nothing—he knew no words could soothe such an inner storm.

Around them, the others mechanically searched the bodies, as if clinging to routine to ground themselves in reality, before moving on.

A little later, Akennor spotted Darian, alone at the top of the hill. He walked there in silence. His friend sat with his knees pulled to his chest, eyes lost on the horizon.

Akennor sat beside him without a word, staring at the same distant line, the wind pushing his hair across his face. His friend was still crying. Silent tears carved tracks down his cheeks.

"What's going to happen to us, Akennor?" he whispered, his voice broken.

"I wish I could see her again… just one last time."

The young warrior felt the crushing weight of despair in those words.

"We're on the right path, Darian. We have to hold on."

"What that girl said about Shaya… I don't believe a word of those horrors."

Darian turned to him, his face ravaged by grief.

"Yeah… of course you're right!"

"I'm certain of it. She knew where to strike, she wanted to break us, and she succeeded. But all of that… it was only provocation."

A silence. Then he slowly nodded, without much conviction.

"Come on," said Akennor, getting back up. "It's time to move on."

Darian rose in turn, painfully, and followed him without a word. Xantaris had awakened and regained some strength. Amandil had treated him with a bit of potion and applied a salve with magical properties.

"I feel much better... Thank you, Amandil. I'm sorry, I wasn't much help."

"Don't be ridiculous," his friend retorted. "You were ambushed."

To rest and recover from their wounds, the group decided to spend the night in the cave.

"A good fire will do us good," Sheila said.

"Narë-rhu!"

The wood brought back by Akennor and Darian caught fire, and the gentle crackle of the blaze filled the space. The warmth drove the dampness from the stones and comforted their bodies, while also cooking the game Milenna had brought back.

"I've had enough," groaned Sheila. "I need a pick-me-up."

She rummaged in her bag, pulled out a bottle of brandy, and took a good swig.

"Oh! That's strong," she exclaimed, bursting into a fit of coughing.

"My turn," said Darian, reaching for it before swallowing a gulp.

"Yes! ... a good pick-me-up," he said between coughs.

The bottle went from hand to hand.

"This must also be a magic potion—I don't hurt anymore!" cried Xantaris, prompting laughter. The pressure and tension seemed to ease.

"Do you remember when Shaya stole a bottle from her father's cellar?" Darian recalled.

"Which time are you talking about? She always stole a bottle from her father!" Sheila burst out laughing.

They laughed again.

"Yes, but I mean the first time… We were sick as dogs," added Darian, his shoulders shaking with laughter.

"Oh, I remember!" cried Akennor. "We all swore—never again!"

Their laughter went on a while longer, until Xantaris asked:

"How long have you known each other?"

Sheila, Akennor, and Darian exchanged a glance. Their eyes seemed to relive entire years in a few seconds.

"I remember it perfectly," Sheila declared, her voice deeper. "It's a moment I'll never forget."

She sighed before continuing.

"It was at the beginning of primary school. I had become friends with Shaya, who lived nearby. My parents were very poor… well, they still are… and my clothes betrayed that poverty."

She saw herself again, ashamed, in the schoolyard. Some boys had blocked her and Shaya's path. They hurled insults and shoved her. Sheila lost her balance and fell face-first into the dirt, her hands covered in mud.

"Oh look! She's like a filthy pig!" one of them had shouted.

The cruel laughter of the others had echoed. As another was about to push her again, a boy had stepped in.

"That's enough, you moron!"

"What? What did you call me?!"

A second boy, blond this time, had replied without flinching:

"A moron, yes. And it suits you well."

Without a trace of fear, they had stood up to the bullies.

When one had rushed the dark-haired boy, he had grabbed his arm, twisted it behind his back, and thrown him to the ground.

"If you touch my friends again, you'll regret it," he had declared.

The boy, whimpering, had nodded.

"Those thugs never bothered us again," Sheila concluded.

She lifted her eyes to Akennor and Darian, her voice laden with emotion.

"Those two boys, it was them."

Akennor, staring at the flames, simply said:

"I couldn't just standby and do nothing."

"And I couldn't let him take all the credit," added Darian with a sly grin.

Akennor gave an amused smile.

Sheila smiled faintly before continuing:

"I also remember… when Shaya and I found a litter of three wolf pups. Their mother had been killed by poachers. I didn't know what to do, but Shaya decided we had to save them."

"They were adorable," recalled Akennor. "We raised them together."

"And it was hard for her when we had to let them go," added Darian.

Milenna spoke, touched:

"That's a beautiful thing. I can't wait until we find her… we'll get along very well."

"To Shaya!" shouted Darian, raising the bottle.

Sheila took a sip, then, more gravely:

"There are so many memories… But my parents should never have had a child. They never wanted me. I was beaten by my father and my mother… I had no refuge at home."

A heavy silence fell.

"I'm sorry," said Xantaris in a low voice. "That should never happen."

Sheila took another sip before passing the brandy to Akennor. She nodded and went on:

"Luckily my friends were there. I often went to sleep at Shaya's. Her parents treated me like their daughter. I would have liked to be adopted by them... Sometimes I slept at Akennor's or Darian's. And in the summer, when we were older, we went on expeditions. It was for fun... but mostly so I would spend as little time as possible at home."

A tear rolled down her cheek.

"Sometimes, I wanted to kill those bastards..." Akennor muttered under his breath.

"It's sad... added Amandil, staring into the flames. No one deserves that... but it brought you closer."

"Yes..." replied Sheila. "I don't know what I would have done without them. But all this anger inside me... I have to tame it."

"And you will," affirmed Milenna softly.

"Meanwhile, I'm starving, cut in Xantaris. And the meat is ready!"

They laughed a little more, then ate. Shortly after, sleep overcame them. At dawn, the group set off again. They concluded that they needed to find horses. Walking on foot was no longer enough.

As they walked in the calm of the morning, Sheila joined Darian. She slipped an arm around his shoulders and whispered comforting words to him, similar to those Akennor had said. Slowly, the young man relaxed. His heart lightened, even though a deep unease still weighed on him.

The rest of the day passed in near silence, broken only by the rustle of their steps through the tall grass.

286

They had left the forest and were now crossing the vast plains of the Foranor. The recent battle had reopened Akennor's wound, and he held his ribs, hoping the gesture alone would ease the pain.

The sun was beginning its descent, casting a golden light across the countryside. The heavy clouds had almost completely scattered. Reaching the top of a hill, the companions spotted, lower down in the valley, a small isolated farm.

The farm below consisted of a small wooden house with a sloping roof that extended to cover a wide porch surrounding the building. A barn stood nearby, and a pen stretched between the two structures, where six horses grazed peacefully.

The young adventurers crouched in the grass and whispered among themselves.

"We've found what we were looking for," said Akennor with satisfaction.

"Yes, but how do we proceed?" asked Xantaris.

"We wait until everyone is asleep and take the horses we need," declared Sheila, her face set.

The two paladins exchanged a shocked look.

"Out of the question," Xantaris growled. "We're not going to rob poor peasants, it's against our values."

"But they're bloodthirsty savages," Sheila retorted.

"Enough of these stories!" Milenna cut in. "Svealëdor has already traveled through this country, and he never told me of such atrocities."

"Then we'll go down and offer to buy horses," Darian concluded.

"And if they refuse?" asked Sheila.

"We'll deal with it," replied Amandil.

With those words, the companions descended the hill, hoping everything would go smoothly. The small farm belonged to a certain Kornis, a farmer in his forties.

He was a sturdy man, of average height, with dark skin and features worn by years of labor. He wore a short gray beard, and his equally gray hair reached down to his shoulders.

His small piercing blue eyes spotted, with surprise, six strangers crossing his land and walking toward him. Suspicious, he called his sons to his side, ordering them to come with their weapons. He himself seized a sword and stood proudly before his house.

When the adventurers were within ten *maicas*, Kornis barked a few words in his native tongue. Seeing their confused looks, he switched to the common language:

"Stay where you are! Who are you? What are you doing here?"

Akennor stepped forward, his hands clearly visible, and said in a calm and respectful tone:

"We are sorry to disturb you, we mean you no harm. We are traveling north."

Kornis frowned.

"North? People die up there. Are you looking for death?"

"In fact, we must cross the sea and reach the forgotten lands," Akennor explained.

"What lands?" The farmer narrowed his eyes, incredulous, unable to believe what he had just heard.

"There is nothing beyond the kingdom. Only a cursed mist… and the end of the world."

The farmer looked at them with perplexity. These young people seemed mad. Or else, they had been deceived.

"To be honest," he continued, "we are searching for a friend who was kidnapped, and we have every reason to believe she is somewhere north of your kingdom."

At those words, Kornis's three sons stepped behind their father, weapons in hand.

"What is it you want then?" the farmer asked sharply.

"We would like to buy a few horses from you to speed our journey." Akennor pulled a few gold coins from a leather pouch, making them gleam in the sunlight. "We can pay a good price," he added.

Kornis's eyes widened at the sight of the gold. Indeed, these young ones had appeared at the perfect time, he thought. Yet he frowned; perhaps it was too good to be true.

For two seasons, the farmer and his family had suffered a severe crisis. The harvests had been disastrous, the fishing poor, and violent epidemics had decimated the game. In the towns and villages, contagious diseases spread, killing thousands. The kingdom's economy sank into an unprecedented torpor. Many inhabitants fled to escape misery and death.

In the countryside, the situation was less dramatic: the diseases had spared most of the inhabitants, but poverty remained omnipresent.

Kornis's sons opened their eyes wide at the gold coins, as if a treasure had fallen from the sky. All three had inherited the same blond hair and piercing blue eyes, but each bore his own mark. The eldest, Akennor's age, sported tousled hair that made him look like he had just emerged from a wheat field. The youngest, frail and pale, had hollow cheeks and a glassy gaze, as if gnawed by fatigue or hunger.

The middle brother, nearly as tall as the eldest, stood straight and solid, with a healthy look and eyes that betrayed no fear.

Kornis straightened his shoulders.

"Five, and not one more. I need to keep one for work. Given the rarity of these beasts in the region, I'll let you have them for five gold coins. They are good horses, strong and in good health."

Akennor exchanged a look with his companions; they all nodded.

"Agreed, let's go see them."

Kornis invited the strangers to follow him to the enclosure. Six tall horses, proud and restless, frolicked behind the wooden fence. They looked vigorous, though a little thin.

"They are fine animals," said Xantaris. "We can take them without worry."

Kornis opened the gate and led them into the pen. He kept for himself a proud brown stallion, while the adventurers chose a black stallion, a brown-and-white spotted one, a brown mare, a black-and-white mare, and a solid black mare.

The young warrior handed the farmer twenty-five gold coins for the five horses. Kornis, a little embarrassed to demand such a sum, tucked the money into his purse.

"You seem hungry. Would you like to stay and share our meal?"

The companions exchanged a hesitant glance. The offer was unexpected, but time was pressing. Akennor spoke for the group:

"That's very generous of you, but we must continue. Every moment counts."

The farmer nodded, a faint smile appearing.

"As you wish. Be careful if you go north: epidemics are raging, and misery is everywhere."

He added, observing them intently:

"You're not from here, I'm sure of it. I don't know what drives you to go there, but you'd better turn back. There is nothing there worth the journey."

"Let's just say that love and friendships are worth all the risks… Thank you for everything," declared Akennor.

The young adventurers led the horses out of the pen. Kornis also gave them saddles, which his sons set up efficiently.

The young warrior mounted a brown stallion spotted with white, Sheila taking her place behind him. He then noticed a strange expression on Milenna's face, without being able to guess the cause.

The beasts, calm and docile, responded well to the first commands. After bidding farewell to the farmer and his sons, the companions rode across the fields. The wind whipped their faces, the tall grass bent beneath the gallop, and the landscape rushed past at great speed.

When the sun disappeared beyond the horizon, they stopped near a small wood. A river meandered nearby. The mounts were tied to the trees, free to drink as they pleased, while Milenna cut grass with her sword to feed them.

Akennor was setting out the blankets when Darian, Xantaris, and Amandil returned with firewood. When the wood was ready, Sheila lit the fire and cut the meat into pieces. She mixed in spices from her provisions, then poured a handful of brownish powder into the water of the pot.

After the meal, Milenna spoke to Akennor:

"So then, what do you think of the people of the Foranor?"

"Those we've met seemed kind to me, much more than I imagined. And I'm glad of it," he said.

"Yet this kingdom faces serious problems, observed Xantaris.

Did you see how easily we obtained these horses? Nowhere else would such animals be given away, especially by a farmer who needs them."

The companions fell thoughtful at this remark.

"You're right," said Darian. "Kornis obviously had an urgent need for money."

"I wonder what's happening here… He spoke to us of epidemics and great misery," added Sheila.

"Perhaps we'll have answers in the fishing village," concluded Milenna.

They decided to go to bed early, so they could set out again at the first light of dawn.

Chapter 24 – The forgotten village

Akennor once again had a restless sleep. In the darkness, a voice was weeping. The young warrior found himself in the middle of a vast plain covered with ashes and dust, devoid of all vegetation. Wails seemed to rise from the ground itself.

He advanced, but each step tore at him with pain. Breathing was torture, and panic rose as he suffocated. He stumbled and fell face down.

As he pushed himself up, he saw a small dark puddle, from which the cries seemed to come. Akennor bent over and leaned closer. The surface rippled and formed an image—a vision. It was Illawen, crying, begging forgiveness, her face ravaged by despair. She walked alone down a road, her expression filled with infinite sadness.

Suddenly, her features warped. Wrinkles carved into her skin, which turned grayish, and her gaze became wicked. Akennor recoiled, but the water shivered again. Another face appeared: a horned humanoid creature, with horns jutting from both sides of its skull and its chin.

He recognized it immediately, having seen it painted on the cursed castle's walls. The demon locked its eyes on his and laughed, revealing sharp teeth.

Akennor backed away, breathless, but the more he retreated, the more the face drew closer. He tried to flee, yet found himself being pulled toward it.

The puddle widened suddenly and swallowed him whole. The water rose up to his neck. He screamed, thrashing with desperate energy. The vile laughter echoed in his ears.

It was the middle of the night, and his friends surrounded him. Sheila's drawn features betrayed her worry. Akennor regained consciousness with a start, gasping, his hand wiping the sweat from his face. His whole body was shaking.

"I was the one who woke you… you had another nightmare," Sheila said softly. Still shaken, he nodded.

Xantaris, hesitant, dared to ask the question that had burned on his lips for some time.

"What do you see in your dreams? They seem far more intense than ours."

Akennor thought for a moment, catching his breath.

"I don't know… Sometimes, I see strange visions. Often, nightmares showing me horrors. I don't understand what they mean… but I wish I did."

"Since when have you had such dreams?" Milenna asked.

"For as long as I can remember, I think. They afflicted me when I was a child, then stopped. But they came back after Shaya's abduction. No doubt my mind is more troubled by this anxiety."

His friends nodded silently, except Milenna, who remained thoughtful. Once the turmoil subsided, they returned to sleep—except for Akennor, who took Sheila's watch in her place.

He never woke his relief and stayed there until dawn, eyes lost in the night. Questions destined for his parents turned in his mind. Akennor promised himself that once this adventure ended, he would speak to them at length.

Dawn finally broke, pale and timid, hidden behind a heavy layer of dark, threatening clouds. Akennor roused his companions and hurried to saddle the horses.

"Why didn't you wake me to take the watch?" Darian asked, approaching.

Akennor, bent over the straps, looked up with a faint smile.

"I wasn't really sleepy anymore. I used the time to meditate… it did me good."

"Fine… but don't make it a habit," Darian insisted. "You need rest too."

They shared some travel bread and resumed their journey north. Soon, the clouds kept their promise. A heavy, cold rain fell on them. Still, they pressed on, knowing only a violent storm would force them to seek shelter.

The fields gave way to a vast plain dotted with small woods. The land seemed deserted; not a bird's cry, not a figure on the horizon.

Suddenly, a paved road appeared, winding through tall grasses. A sign of human life—or what remained of it. They followed it, as fog crept along their trail.

The rain eased to a drizzle. The road twisted, and at the foot of a hill, a small village emerged from the mist. After several days of travel, the sight seemed almost unreal. A thick, low veil wrapped it, concealing the ground. Only a few dark, moss-covered rocks stood out.

The group advanced, their mounts hesitant. Everything felt frozen. Tall trees with blackened bark, mottled with brown patches, encircled the hamlet. Their sparse foliage gave the impression that summer had never come here.

The houses, small and alike, had stone walls and wooden roofs darkened by dampness. A warped, deserted dock lined the shore, where broken boats lay stranded— remnants of a long-dead activity.

They passed along what must have been the main street. No one came to meet them. Yet Akennor thought he glimpsed, behind a grimy windowpane, a shadow moving… but when he turned to his friends, they had seen nothing.

At the village's center stood a larger building, stone-walled and wooden-roofed. A wide double door, flanked by windows, marked its entrance.

Akennor halted and dismounted.

"Let's see if anyone's inside," he said.

His companions followed suit, tethering their horses to a beam near the entrance. All felt uneasy at the village's sinister air.

Darian and Akennor pushed open the doors, which groaned loudly. Inside was a wide, empty hall… Four large beams held up the ceiling, studded with knives and axes stuck into the wood. Deer heads adorned the far wall, and five men sat at a round table, drinking and talking.

Their deep voices resonated in the hall. Akennor caught every harsh laugh and felt relief. But Sheila froze, pale as death. The men looked to be his father's age, with weary faces and graying beards. One of them, wearing a faded apron, addressed him in a foreign tongue.

Seeing Akennor's lost expression, he switched to the common language:

"What are you doing here?"

Akennor replied calmly:

"We're only travelers. We want to buy a boat to cross the sea northward."

His companions exchanged troubled glances.

Sheila began to speak:

"But Akennor, there's no…"

Milenna clamped a hand over her mouth.

Sheila, wide-eyed, stared at Milenna, who gestured for silence. She wanted to see what would happen.

The men reacted with disbelief. Two spat out their drink, coughing.

"No one from this kingdom would be foolish enough to attempt such a journey," said the innkeeper.

The eldest added in a hoarse voice:

"Nothing exists beyond the northern sea, nothing… except death."

"Stories tell that when sailors venture too far, their ships are swallowed by impenetrable fog; fear grips them, and they wander endlessly, forever seeking their home port. That is what happens when one dares defy the gods."

"This region is cursed, you must have seen it. The trees are diseased, the air reeks, the well water tastes of sulfur, and grass barely grows," the innkeeper continued.

Another, smoking a pipe, spoke in a shrill voice:

"First, the children fell ill and all died. Then, the women vanished, carried away by monsters from the sea. The gods cursed this place, punishing us for daring to defy them."

The men's faces bore the marks of great suffering. Meanwhile, his friends watched him: he frowned, smiled at times, reacting to words they did not hear.

"We appreciate your warnings, but we must cross the sea. Here are ten gold coins for one of your boats," Akennor said, stepping forward.

He handed the leather pouch with the last of his gold to the man in the apron, who opened it with surprise.

"But this is… far too much. We cannot accept it."

"I don't think we need it. It will serve you better, to start over elsewhere. Divide it among you," Akennor replied kindly.

Darian wondered what his friend was doing, watching him leave the pouch on the table.

The men looked stunned—not only that the young adventurers truly meant to cross the sea, but at the generous gift as well.

"In that case, thank you. Please, be careful, for great dangers hide in that fog."

"A great curse," added the eldest, voice trembling.

The innkeeper slipped away briefly, then returned with provisions: bread, dried meat, sausages.

"Take these—you'll need them."

Then, they saw Akennor stretching out his arms, as if carrying something heavy. The young warrior thanked the innkeeper warmly and bid farewell to the last inhabitants of the little village. He looked at his companions and left the building.

Outside, he set the provisions on a flat stone.

"Their story is truly sad, isn't it?"

Sheila frowned.

"What story?"

Akennor smiled faintly.

"Why, the one they just told us."

"We didn't see any living men…" said Xantaris.

"Only five skeletons around a table," added Darian.

"But that's ridiculous, there were five older men drinking and talking at the table."

"You're seeing visions while awake now," Milenna concluded.

Akennor bristled; he had truly seen and heard those men. Shaking his head, he wanted to be sure. With determined steps, he returned to the inn.

The floorboards groaned. He pushed through the rotting doors. The hall was cold, reeking of dust and death. His hair stood on end, a chill running down his spine. Around the table lay five skeletons, slumped and crumbling. In one skeletal hand, the leather pouch still rested.

Sheila and Darian stood behind him, silent.

It was the young mage who dared touch him gently.

"Are you all right, Akennor?"

He did not reply, eyes roaming the room.

"I know what I saw…" he whispered.

"But how is it possible?"

"Well, young warrior, it seems you possess other gifts you are not aware of," Xantaris said. "Begin by telling us what you saw."

Akennor recounted his encounter with the spirits and their warnings.

"I think we can conclude this village has long been abandoned," Darian decided.

"This land reeks of evil… I feel it in my bones," added Amandil with a shiver.

They headed for the dock in search of a boat. The sea wind carried a thick smell of sulfur. Fog rolled in from the sea, covering the shore with a gray veil.

They walked along the only pier still standing. Blackened posts jutted from the water, remnants of old docks. The planks, swollen with salt, groaned beneath their steps; some were broken, revealing dark water below.

Half-sunken hulls knocked against the pilings in time with the waves.

At the pier's end, a larger boat with a mast and sail seemed still usable.

"Does anyone know how to sail this?" asked Akennor.

"Yes, answered Xantaris. I have some knowledge… and Amandil as well."

The latter nodded.

Sheila stared at the vessel, pale.

"Do you think it will hold? That we'll be safe in it?"

Xantaris laid a reassuring hand on her shoulder.

"It doesn't leak… and under the circumstances, it's the best we can hope for."

Half convinced, Sheila swallowed her fear. It was their only way to go after Shaya.

They loaded their gear and climbed aboard. The boat rocked, making Darian, Sheila, and Milenna grimace, uneasy on the water. Xantaris and Amandil untied the ropes and raised the sail, patched with crude repairs.

The fog swallowed them as the village vanished behind. On the shore, Akennor thought he glimpsed five silhouettes watching them… then they dissolved into the mist.

The fragile craft slid toward the unknown.

Chapter 25 – The Awakening

Torhon was still snoring, sleeping soundly. Illawen looked at him tenderly: her feelings for him were as strong as on the very first day. Then she decided to get out of bed. She slipped into a loose white dress and went down to the kitchen, where she grabbed an apple before stepping outside to breathe the fresh morning air.

The sun's rays were breaking over the horizon, and she watched it rise. Behind the house was a firepit. In the past, during summer evenings, the family would gather around the flames to tell stories or sing. Illawen had often sung for her two boys, songs she had learned in her youth.

Thinking back to her husband's words, she sat cross-legged on a broad flat stone facing the firepit. She drew in a deep breath, closed her eyes, and plunged into childhood memories.

The giant trees of her village appeared, majestic. Homes were built on the branches or carved into the trunks. Her parents' house, where the king and queen lived, rose high, surrounded by foliage. Birds chirped, and a sweet fragrance of flowers floated in the air. Leaning on the railing, little Illawen gazed down at the ground.

"Come on, Illawen, you're going to be late. Master Kellas is waiting!" scolded her mother.

"All right, I'm going," she replied.

She followed the walkways linking the suspended platforms and joined her mentor. He welcomed her with a smile.

"Here you are. Now we can begin. Sit down in front of me."

The first lessons were about meditation, the art of centering oneself. She succeeded with ease. Slowly, the next teachings flowed back into her mind like an ancient echo.

Torhon had been right: she could relearn the techniques she had put aside. Her gifts allowed her to revisit memories with striking clarity.

"Where are you, Kallo?"

Illawen focused on her eldest son, trying to sense him. She breathed deeply, recalling the child he had been, listening to her songs in wonder. Her palms tingled, and an image took form: tall buildings surrounded her, people moved about. Then the vision widened, revealing Kallo walking straight toward her, his expression stern.

She smiled, and the vision faded.

"He's alive…" she whispered with relief.

She then turned her focus to Akennor. The image was slow to come, but finally appeared: tall mountains on the horizon, a vast field, Sheila at his side, Darian slightly behind. Two young men unknown to her accompanied them, as well as a tall woman with dark hair.

"He's alive too…"

Exhausted, her head spinning, she ended the session. Yet she felt at peace: her children were alive. The next day, she tried to control her dreams and visions.

On the training platform, her mentor Kellas spoke again through her memories:

"Visions, whether in sleep or wakefulness, may foretell the future… or be mere traps meant to trouble your spirit. You must learn to discern truth."

He fixed his clear gaze on hers:

"And above all, close your mind to the thoughts of others, for they can invade you."

Illawen remembered this and practiced over the following days. One night, she had a dreadful nightmare, but managed to master it. She realized it was not just a dream, but a warning about the future. A chill ran through her body.

"These aren't nightmares… but visions of what is to come. It's terrible… what can I do?" she murmured.

"My love?" exclaimed Torhon, kissing her. "How are your sessions going? Are you making progress?

"You were right. I'm rediscovering my old lessons through my memories, and my powers are returning."

Torhon smiled.

"Perfect! No need to run to the ends of the world."

Then he grew serious.

"Illawen… I can't hold back anymore. I'm going to set out to find Akennor."

She began to protest, but he pressed a finger to her lips.

"Let me finish. You'll say I don't know where to go… but you do. Your gifts will guide you."

He withdrew his hand.

"So… you can lead the way."

Illawen stared at him for a long moment.

"I don't like admitting it twice in a row… but you're right. It's late… let's leave tomorrow at dawn."

Torhon's face lit up.

"Good. I'll stop by the inn to have one last beer with Krent and buy some supplies at the store. We'll also need horses."

He kissed her passionately before heading off toward the village.

Chapter 26 – The Cursed Lands

The ship cut through the mist before docking at the port of Nénmori, south of the orc camp of Morgrunt, on the cursed lands.

The crossing had been torment: howling winds, black waves, a treacherous fog hiding deadly reefs. The old pirate captain knew the route, but each voyage was like a gamble with death.

He suddenly burst into the cabin of Dresden and his companions.

"Here we are, lads—welcome to the black lands! he shouted with a grin, revealing the gap between his two canines."

Then he left almost as quickly as he had entered.

Dresden sighed, uneasy. He hated being in unfamiliar territory and dreaded meeting the grand master. The latter would likely be pleased with their capture and probably very grateful… but doubt had begun to creep into his mind.

"Let's pack our things and head out quickly. I don't want to keep the master waiting: he's not known for his patience."

"You're right. I'm ready to go," Deidre replied.

Parthe and Aaron prepared their packs while Dresden took care of Shaya. Bound to a small wooden chair, she was only allowed a short moment each day for her needs. Her jailers took turns feeding her.

Shaya lived a waking nightmare. Trapped in her own thoughts, she wandered through memories of her friends, her parents, and her mentor—the one who had taught her discipline.

The moments of joy with her loved ones still echoed in her mind, mingling with the grave and wise words of her instructor, urging her to reflect on the meaning of life. Dresden untied her from the crude chair, bound her wrists tightly, and hauled her to her feet without care.

"Come on, young witch. Up. We're leaving," he said coldly.

Shaya didn't flinch. Impassive, she followed her captor. The shadow mercenaries gathered on the deck, where thick fog surrounded them. The ancient stone quay, carved directly into the rock, stretched into the dark waters. On the shore, a few weathered wooden buildings, ravaged by salt and storms, looked ready to collapse.

A dozen *maicas* away, a small wooden fort stood, flanked by four corner towers and protected by blackened palisades. A large orc awaited them. Broad and muscular, his protruding lower jaw jutted well beyond the upper, two long tusks gleaming from his thick lips and dark greenish skin. His carnation, somewhere between black and dark green, contrasted with the thick mane of hair tied back.

His hollow, almost fluorescent green eyes gave him a mysterious and unsettling air. Clad in heavy leather armor, a broad sword hung from his belt, a bow over his shoulder, and a quiver full of arrows strapped to his back.

He was the first to speak:

"I am Akar. Master Drendor sends me to escort you."

His voice, clear despite the guttural accent, carried hesitation, as though searching for words.

"I am Dresden. These are Deidre, Parthe, Aaron… and our prisoner," he said, gripping Shaya firmly to display her to the orc.

Akar's eyes widened. For a fleeting moment, a primal instinct to seize her gripped his mind. Shaya stared at the creature but remained unmoved, as if he did not exist.

Introductions complete, the group set off. Akar had provided each with a horse to hasten the journey. The captive was bound tightly on a mount, placed between Dresden and Parthe. The orc led the way through the perils of the black lands.

Shaya, now aware of her destination, wished they had blindfolded her. The landscape was a nightmare: blackened, withered trees, harsh thorny grass, gray dust like ash coating the ground. Twisted plants emerged here and there, with briars sprawling like roots of some ancient evil.

The air was dry, tainted with sulfur. Silence reigned, broken only by the occasional deathlike shriek echoing across the land.

She saw snakes, scorpions, and enormous insects. Shivers ran down her spine. Fear grew within her, and she closed her eyes, retreating to memories of her friends.

The horrific visions sickened even Dresden and his companions. Their confidence crumbled as they advanced.

After a long time in this nightmarish terrain, Parthe and Aaron would have given anything to return to civilization.

They wondered what awaited them at journey's end… and why they had ever let themselves be drawn this far.

Dresden replayed the events since the monastery intrusion—and especially the paladin's words: Know this, poor child, Drendor is among the most wicked and selfish beings…

Those words now haunted him, as they neared their goal. A gnawing dread grew in his mind. Deidre, on the other hand, felt no disgust or fear. A part of her savored this morbid scenery. The young sorceress burned with impatience to meet the Master, eager to learn from him.

She was ready to give anything to follow him. His reputation preceded him, and excitement coursed through her veins. The thirst for power and the thought of carrying out the horrors she imagined sent shivers of pleasure through her.

At last, the group reached the orc camp of Morgrunt.

"There! Before us lies the camp of Morgrunt," Akar announced. "It is from here I hail, as do most of us."

Two wooden watchtowers flanked the gate, guarded by pairs of orcs. Massive wooden doors barred the entrance, the palisade rising high around the camp. Sentinels had already raised the alarm, and several orcs now advanced toward them.

The guards recognized Akar and addressed him in their guttural tongue. He presented his companions and indicated Shaya. The small cavernous eyes of the orcs widened, their growls turning frenzied at the sight of the captive.

Akar dismounted and, without hesitation, struck one guard violently across the face. He barked a sharp order, and the guards stepped back.

Remounting, Akar gestured for Dresden and the others to follow. The guard he struck shouted to the watchmen above. Soon, the creaking of the massive gates echoed as they opened, tearing the air with every groan.

Inside, austere stone buildings flanked the entrance, likely barracks. Beyond, a forge and a stable surrounded a wide pen where many horses trotted. An elderly orc hammered at a massive blade, his lighter skin and less bestial features striking Shaya immediately. She held his gaze, unsettled, refusing to admit the meaning behind what she saw.

Further on, rows of earthen huts lined the central path with military precision. The stench of rot thickened. Dresden gagged, nearly vomiting.

To the left rose a two-story building of packed earth, flanked by demonic statues. To the right, a great stone circle held an altar, looming with statues of horned demons: one with four arms and a serpent's tail, the other with pincers and a swollen, spiderlike abdomen.

Chains hung from the demon-serpent's hands, cages holding rotting humanoid corpses swarming with glowing maggots. On the demon-spider's spears, bodies impaled— one already decomposed, another a fresh victim, a young naked woman. Shaya stared through a veil of horror, anger swelling inside her like a storm.

A gust of wind made a leg wobble; it came loose, fell heavily onto the circle, and rolled to a stop at the hooves of Dresden's horse.

The assassin turned pale. The stench and the horrific sight crushed him. He retched, staggered, nearly collapsed, but Parthe caught him by the shoulder.

The other victim was recent: a young naked woman with brown hair. The metal spike pierced her entrails and came out through her mouth. Shaya watched her with a veiled gaze, as if through the haze of a nightmare. She wondered what that unfortunate soul could have done to deserve such a torment. A mute anger swelled in her, as impetuous and implacable as the ocean. She closed her eyes, trying to shut out the visions.

The other mercenaries pinched their noses to keep out the stench of putrefaction... except for Deidre, who seemed to savor that perfume of death and corruption.

A little farther to the left, a strange building emerged: it was built entirely of bones, of various sizes and lengths. It was impossible to tell which races they had belonged to. The structure formed a vast, uneven whitish dome, as if the bones themselves had fused together over time.

To the right, a large building could be made out in the mist, but it was too far for the travelers to distinguish any details. Farther on, the landscape changed: black, scrawny trees stood in sparse ranks up to the enclosure of the camp.

The other rampart merged into a small mountain range, sooty-dark, with peaks sharpened like teeth ready to bite. An opening, carved directly into the rock, led to the other side. Two wooden turrets perched on the summit served as watch posts.

The orc sentries exchanged a few guttural words, then the heavy wooden gate opened with a sinister groan. The mercenaries passed between them and plunged into a dark passage cut into raw stone.

Dresden, Parthe, and Aaron felt a sharp sense of relief: at last they were leaving that oppressive camp behind. Yet Dresden could not shake an odd impression—despite its size, the camp had seemed deserted. No doubt, he thought, most of the orcs had been sent ahead for the great operation prepared by the Master, as certain rumors had suggested.

After a while, Arak turned back to them:

"We'll soon have the troll camp of Marak in sight. Look ahead… and avoid doing stupid things like vomiting. Trolls are very sly and mean-spirited."

His eyes locked onto Dresden's, then he slowly turned his head away. High stone palisades rose before the mercenaries. On either side of the main entrance, a tower of dark earth stood like a silent watchman.

Night had fallen. The faint light cast by a dying sun behind dark, unmoving clouds had vanished. Two magical torches fixed to the watchtowers gave off a greenish glow that lit two slender silhouettes. Their scaly skin reflected an almost black green.

Their elongated heads bore bulbous yellow eyes. Their jutting noses accentuated their strange features, and their black, frizzy, braided hair fell over their knotty shoulders.

Arak stepped forward and addressed the guards in their language. His voice rang out, grating and high-pitched, very different from the orcs' low, guttural tone. The exchange was brief. The trolls cast a quick glance at the mercenaries before ordering the gate opened.

The troll camp looked much like the orc camp, except that their huts, smaller, were sunk into the ground. An equally unbearable stench saturated the air. Dresden pinched his nostrils so he wouldn't have to breathe it.

Farther on, on a large stone slab, stood four rows of six wooden posts. From the top of each post, a chain descended to a prisoner or a corpse.

On the last row, each post held a still-living human. The mercenaries—Deidre excepted—looked away at the sight of trolls tearing the flesh of the still-conscious unfortunates. A young man struggled, screaming in pain, while a set of jaws ripped bloody strips from his side. His cries, steeped in animal panic, pierced Dresden's ears. On the first row, decomposing bodies hung, skeletons nearly stripped bare. On the others, half-devoured remains rotted under the setting sun. The young man, by then half eaten, finally sagged, eyes empty, drained of blood.

Despite the darkness, Shaya could see with strange clarity. Every detail of the bloody scene etched itself into her mind. Her blood boiled; her rage surged.

Beside her, Dresden and Aaron, pale as ghosts, nearly reeled. It was too much for them. Dresden quickened his pace and urged their guide to move on.

Opposite the place where the trolls were feasting, a massive crescent-shaped building sank partially into the ground. The passage leading to its entrance sloped gently downward from the main path.

The group continued to the far end of the camp, where a heavy wooden gate barred the road.

After a brief exchange between Arak and the guards, the leaves swung open, letting out a cold breath. The mercenaries crossed the threshold and plunged into the night, into darkness heavy with dangers and nightmares.

"I'm tired," Aaron complained a short time later.

"Couldn't we stop for a bit?" he whined.

Arak turned and said curtly:

"What? Are you a man or a milksop? We stop only when we reach our destination. The Master's orders!" he bellowed.

Aaron stared, speechless. Parthe leaned toward him and murmured:

"You really want to stop? Huh? Haven't you seen enough here? Imagine what prowls in those woods…"

Aaron cast a glance around. The shadows seemed to thicken, the shapes of the trees to twist. Parthe was right. Better to keep moving. But what would the next place look like?

A cold shiver ran up his spine. He groaned inwardly and, for an instant, would have given anything to be back in the comfort of his poor mother's home.

Meanwhile, Shaya let herself be drawn into her memories. She saw herself beside her mentor, Adoron, and her three childhood friends.

Adoron was an old man with long gray hair, his white beard falling to mid-chest. Time had marked his face, but an expression of serenity softened the traces. His eyes, a limpid blue, evoked a cloudless sky.

Clad in a wide brown robe, he wore no jewelry. A straight sword always lay within reach. His smile brimmed with kindness and compassion.

The sage's words still echoed in Shaya's mind:
"You must let the energy of the surrounding elements flow through you. No force is greater than theirs. Nothing and no one can defeat a druid or a mage who soaks in the strength of nature—and who channels feeling and will to the elements."

She recalled their first meeting. The sky was overcast, the sun hidden behind a gray shroud. Adoron had brought his hands together, breathed in deeply, then raised his arms to the sky. The clouds had parted at once, letting the sun through.

Another day, during a meditation, he had confided to them:
"The hardest thing is to surrender enough—to feel the raw, untamable force of nature… and to let yourself be guided by a will that seems to surpass you."

After a lesson, he had added:
"I teach you methods, techniques to help you master the elements… but nothing confines you. Invent your own incantations, your prayers, your meditations. Nothing is clearly defined or mapped out. As a warning, know that every request has a price."

Shaya tried to let herself be infused by the elements of this devastated land. What she perceived at first was troubling: a great dark, malevolent force seemed to dominate its every parcel.

The convoy moved forward slowly in the dark. The shadow-horses, skittish, skirted invisible dangers with skill, but their caution slowed the pace.

Suddenly, the guide stopped and turned to the mercenaries. His eyes gleamed in the gloom.

"We are nearing our destination. Be attentive... if you value your lives. The Master has no patience and does not like to be crossed."

"I also inform you that you will be confined to the fortress for several days before you can leave with the next convoy. Whether you like it... or not."

His gaze went from Parthe to Dresden, then to Aaron, one by one. None of them held it. Arak set off again. Behind him, Dresden and his companions were more tense than ever... all except Deidre, who burned with impatience to meet the Master.

Soon, the black walls of the bastion rose into a sky lit only faintly by a day veiled with dark clouds. From a distance, one might have thought it a single keep. As they approached, hidden shapes revealed themselves: a tall central tower, two smaller ones flanking the main gate, and four more at the corners of the ramparts. They blended almost into the surrounding mountain landscape.

As the procession advanced, the stronghold unveiled its horrors. From the top of the walls, long iron spikes stood like sharpened teeth. Heavy chains hung down, each bearing a rotting body, their flesh sloughing off the stones in strips. At the foot of the walls, a carpet of bones and skulls bleached by time.

Gigantic magical torches cast, at regular intervals, a greenish glow that licked the walls with sickly reflections. The air reeked of sulfur and rot—an even harsher odor than in the orc or troll camps. Dresden, Parthe, and Aaron struggled to breathe.

They reached the heavy gates of black iron. Two fully armored orc guards stood on either side. Arak exchanged a few words with them, and the leaves opened in an unsettling silence.

A thick mist rose from within, and Dresden and his companions stepped inside with misgiving. Shaya opened her eyes to discover the horror before them. She felt powerful currents of energy emanating from the dark citadel.

The vast inner courtyard encircled a central building. Arak dismounted, immediately imitated by the others. Dark shapes emerged to take the horses and lead them to the stables.

A small creature, troll-like in appearance, came to meet them.

"Limzi. I'm escorting those the Master wishes to see," Arak announced, pointing to the mercenaries and their prisoner.

"The Master knows you have arrived, the creature replied. He sends me to fetch you and wishes to speak with them at once. Follow me."

Limzi lingered a moment on Shaya and gave a smile that revealed fine pointed teeth. A deep disgust seized the young woman: behind that small frame, she sensed great cruelty.

They followed Limzi through the dark corridors, climbing level after level to the top of the main bastion. There, a black-clad figure stood with its back to them, facing the horizon. A cold wind slid over the stone, raising the hairs on their arms.

Limzi approached the figure. It turned its head slightly, then stroked the creature, as if in thanks. Without a word, Limzi slipped away, vanishing into the bowels of the fortress.

Akar dropped to one knee. Slowly, the figure turned. Dresden, Parthe, and Aaron were shaken: the face before them was ravaged by time, emptied of any soul.

Shaya's heart clenched. She had never seen this man… and yet his features reminded her of something.

Drendor, the Master, glided toward them without a sound.

"Come now," Arak, rise. "You have done good work, he said in a rasping voice. You may go and rest before the great departure."

Arak rose at once, bowed deeply, thanked his master, and descended to his quarters.

Drendor stepped forward and smiled, revealing his needle-like teeth.

"You, too, have done well. Rest assured I will know how to show my gratitude. You each have a fine future before you."

The words slipped into the mercenaries' minds like a sweet venom. Fear, doubts, the visions of horror… all faded. In their place surged a flood of dreams: power, riches, glory. Everything suddenly seemed brighter.

Deidre wore an enthusiasm that bordered on indecent.

The Master approached the captive, seized her chin in a hand cold as death. Shaya shuddered head to toe at the touch. He locked his gaze with hers.

"You have caused me great trouble, Shaya. I turned heaven and earth to find you again. Nineteen years ago, I killed your parents and was about to take you… when two wretched paladins stopped me. I lost that battle, but not the war."

"And now I have finally found you. Nothing… and no one… will stop me. I am going to win at last, and nothing will prevent it."

Intrigued in spite of herself, Shaya looked up. A heavy oppression crushed her chest; air failed her, and the ground seemed to tilt under her feet. No… These were only lies meant to break her.

"You killed my parents?" she gasped, her voice trembling with rage. "But why? What did I do to deserve that?"

Anger throbbed in her voice, and the words barely emerged. She had always believed those who raised her were her real parents. The man before her, dark and implacable, repulsed her, and she hated him with all her soul. Her life was a lie; the truth had been hidden from her.

Sensing his prisoner's distress, Drendor flashed a cruel smile.

"Let's say… you are the key to a very ancient prophecy. Through you… the world will meet its end. Hahaha!"

Parthe had just enough time to seize Shaya's arm as she was about to strike. Dresden threw himself in to help, pinning her to the ground while she struggled furiously.

"Brave and impetuous… no matter. Your fate is sealed and nothing will change it. Take her to her cell! Maultarg!"

A massive silhouette emerged from the shadows.

"Maultarg, see to the prisoner while I escort our guests to their quarters."

Shaya spat hard in Drendor's direction.

The half-orc nodded, grabbed Shaya roughly, and dragged her toward the dungeons.

Drendor turned to the mercenaries.

"Your mission is now complete, and you may take a few days to rest. Come with me."

He led them to their quarters, a few floors below.

"Here we are. In a few days you will come with us and know a glory you have likely never dared dream of. Do you have any questions or requests?"

"My lord, Deidre interjected, I must inform you, we discovered she is a druid, versed in mastery over the elements."

Drendor was not the least bit impressed and burst into a sinister laugh.

"You do well to tell me, but have no fear. On this land, I control everything. She no doubt possesses great inner strength... a pity, in other times I might have tried to corrupt her."

The mercenaries entered one by one. When Deidre's turn came, Drendor stopped her by the arm.

"You have potential... and ambition... I can feel your desire. I will tell you to keep your ears open in the coming days." The Master gave her a slight wink and let her go in to rejoin her companions. Deidre entered, heart pounding.

Dresden watched his colleague go in. He had never seen her so happy—she was radiant. He frowned. We'd better stay on our guard... he thought.

Maultarg swung open the heavy iron door with its grid. The squealing hinges rang down the dark corridor. He then removed the irons from Shaya's hands and shoved her brutally into the cell, slamming the door. The metal vibrated with the impact, and he walked off without a word.

The floor and walls, slimy and damp, reeked sharply of mold, putrid flesh, and rot. The air was so foul it turned the stomach. The narrow cell contained only a frayed, filthy pallet. An oppressive silence reigned in the dungeon.

The tears she had held back until now suddenly burst forth. Her whole body convulsed under the weight of emotions too strong to bear.

The single thought that they might all be dead because of her was unbearable. The idea slashed at her soul. In that suffocating darkness, an image forced its way through: Darian. The memory of him, like a fragile flame in the night, warmed her heart for an instant. She curled up in a corner, knees drawn to her chest, and imagined herself nestled in his arms.

She remembered when they were near Lake Bae. The air was mild there, the surface of the water rippling with the wind. They were huddled together, Darian's hands stroking her hair.

"I'm going to miss you terribly," she whispered.

"I'll miss you too," Darian replied, placing a gentle kiss on her lips.

"I hope nothing will change between us."

"Why would it change?"

He took her delicate face in his hands and looked into her eyes.

"Don't worry, nothing will change… least of all, my love. I'll write to you. I'll think of you every day. You'll always be with me."

"I love you."

They held each other for a long time, kissing until the sun had set.

Silent tears rolled down her cheeks at the memory.

"I love you, Darian…"

Shaya lay down on the grimy pallet. The cold bit into her skin, but in her dream, she was once again by the lake, held tight in his arms.

The boat sailed on the calm waters of the Sea of Mercy. The youths had been silent and pensive since leaving the abandoned village. A breeze from the south swelled the sails and swept away some of the dense fog.

Darian, exhausted, had fallen asleep at the stern. Sheila dozed too, crouched on the starboard side. Milenna, thoughtful, gazed out to sea. Xantaris held the helm, with his friend Amandil beside him. Akennor, seated midship, scanned the surroundings anxiously.

"Why is there so much fog?" he asked, pensive.

"It's the Veil of Oblivion," Milenna answered in a neutral tone, eyes on the horizon. "Svealëdor told me about it a very long time ago. The gods separated the land and raised the Veil of Oblivion so that no one could see the cursed lands."

A long silence settled, broken later by Xantaris, who wanted to be done with his questions.

"Tell me, Akennor, what exactly do you see in your dreams?"

"Visions that seem premonitory… It's been getting more and more intense lately," Akennor answered with a deep sigh.

"What is it? Some sort of gift?" Amandil asked, intrigued.

"I'd say it's a gift… and at the same time a curse," Milenna interjected.

The others were surprised—Akennor especially. Milenna clarified:

"A gift you can't control can only become a curse."

Akennor nodded.

"I think you're right, my dear. If it's a gift, I don't know how to use it or control it… and it's ruining my life," he said wearily.

"Akennor, if you have other visions or dreams, don't hesitate to tell us," Amandil added.

Akennor dipped his head shyly. Milenna stretched and announced she would sleep a little. Xantaris suggested Akennor do the same, assuring him that he and Amandil would mind the helm and the boat.

Sleep was not very restorative for Akennor. As his conscious mind drifted off, his unconscious awoke… He found himself standing on the fishing boat, naked and alone. The wind blew hard, carrying a nauseating smell. Suddenly, everything flipped: the craft was sucked into a whirlpool and sank into black, icy waters. Countless decomposing bodies drifted around him, some staring at Akennor with empty sockets. He recognized among them men, elves, and dwarves.

The descent quickened, and he ended up face down on the ground. Before him, Elenshae, the splendid city with silver gates, burned, entirely encircled by hordes of orcs and trolls. Akennor blinked, refusing to believe it. The wind carried the weeping and dying screams of the inhabitants, while a cold, high, piercing laugh filled the air.

He shut his eyes, clapped his hands over his ears… and felt a force shake him. Sheila gently woke him, pulling him from the nightmare.

"I've had enough," he said in a frustrated voice.

She held him until he gathered himself. Milenna and Darian were still asleep, Xantaris too, but Amandil watched at the helm. Sheila and Akennor sat for a time by the gunwale of the small craft.

"What was it this time?" Amandil asked.

"Elenshae was burning… Monsters encircled it… People were dying…"

The paladin shivered.

It was the second day at sea—days that felt like an eternity. The companions spoke little. All were exhausted. Akennor stared forward, lost in the thick white fog. A dizziness made his head spin. Rocks, like a giant stone jaw, rose from the water, ready to clamp their fangs on the frail boat.

He shouted, grabbed an oar, and rushed to the bow, the oar thrust out ahead of him. He managed to cushion and deflect the impact of a rock with knife-sharp sides. Akennor grimaced under the strain. The hull scraped hard along the submerged face of the rock, making the wood creak.

Sheila, who had jumped up after Akennor, was thrown forward and fell heavily. Amandil clung to the helm, which kept him from going overboard. The others were jolted awake from their peaceful sleep. Darian shook his head, still groggy.

"What's happening?"

"We nearly rammed a rock head-on. We'll have to be very careful from now on," Akennor replied.

Xantaris leaned over the side near the rock to get a better view of the threat.

"I think we should lower the sail and use only the oars," he suggested.

"Good idea," Amandil agreed. "And I propose one of us stay at the prow, oar in hand, to watch for dangers the fog might hide."

"By the way, Akennor… how did you see that rock in such dense fog?"

Akennor said nothing. He had seen the danger clearly and had thought the others saw it too.

"I don't know… Some kind of premonition, maybe… I'm not used to it."

"The important thing is we avoided it."

Akennor took the first watch. Milenna came to stand beside him.

"You listened to your instinct… good," she said.

Her gaze seemed fixed on nothing.

"It feels… easier, somehow. Evil emanates from everything around us. I feel like my senses are sharper… The sense of danger is stronger in me."

Milenna patted him on the shoulder before returning to her place.

A very long time went by. The companions rowed in silence, all senses alert. Akennor, still forward, parted the fog with his oar and avoided several hazards. The hull sometimes scraped the rocks, but without serious damage.

Suddenly, Milenna's keen hearing caught an unusual sound drawing nearer. Unable to identify it, she left her spot and joined Akennor.

"Slow the pace a moment, I hear a strange noise."

The boat lost speed in the thick curtain of mist. The sound swelled until they all heard it. No one dared speak; each one focused.

Akennor still scanned the rocks emerging from the fog. The rumbling grew, and worry spread among the young adventurers. No one noticed the rise in temperature until sweat beaded on their foreheads.

Suddenly, an imperceptible resistance tugged at the oar in his hands. He yanked it back. A gust swept the fog aside, revealing the horror waiting for them.

Akennor cried out in surprise: his oar was aflame, facing a gigantic flow of molten lava gushing from a gaping rift in the earth, and the seawater boiled into scalding vapor where it touched.

"Back water, fast! Row!" he shouted, setting the example.

Milenna stood transfixed, hypnotized by that open wound in the earth letting an incandescent blood pour out.

Their progress toward the burning shore halted. Akennor stopped rowing, and the others followed suit at once.

Xantaris and Amandil, at the stern, had seen nothing.

"There's a fissure in the earth… and lava is pouring from it," Akennor explained, still shaken. "I think it's what's creating all this fog."

Darian and Sheila had glimpsed the scene for only an instant, but it was enough to chill them. Xantaris, for his part, had noticed only the burning oar and struggled to understand how that was possible in the middle of the sea.

"We're close to shore. Better to follow the flow west; it can't stretch on forever… at least, I hope not," Akennor added.

The little boat swung around and set a course westward. Akennor and Milenna stayed alert: he at the bow, she aft near Xantaris.

The sizzling of water on lava told them they were nearing the coast, but they kept a prudent distance. Little by little, the crackling faded until it vanished. Akennor then asked that the craft be steered toward the shore.

As the companions maneuvered, the bow bumped gently against sand. Akennor leaned down, brushed the ground with his fingers, then straightened:

"That's it… We've made landfall."

Smiles appeared, mingled with deep sighs of relief. At last, the hostile sea and its traps were behind them. Akennor jumped overboard and steadied the boat while the others gathered their things to set foot on the inhospitable land. Darian and Xantaris helped him haul the craft beyond the reach of the tide. They spotted an old wooden post, blackened by time, and moored the skiff there in case they needed to return.

Single file behind Akennor, the companions entered a fog still thick, advancing cautiously. The young warrior swept his oar ahead to sound the terrain. The flat ground was covered in small jagged rocks that made walking painful.

Little by little, the mist thinned, revealing a landscape worthy of the worst nightmares. Akennor, who normally disliked walking blind, would almost have preferred to see nothing.

Milenna, Darian, and Sheila wore looks of disgust, while Amandil remained impassive, as if he had expected such a sight.

Xantaris, more emotional, let out:

"How ugly… so… awful."

"It looks like another world, completely different from ours," Sheila exclaimed.

Before them stretched a meager, dreary forest of shrubs and trees black as if charred. Thorny brambles snaked over the rocky soil. Everything was black, gray, and bleak, stripped of life and soul. Dark clouds covered the sky, though it was likely midday.

"We should rest a bit before moving on," Darian suggested, his mood dark at the thought that Shaya was somewhere on this dead land.

They shared some waybread and drank the last mouthfuls from their gourds. Akennor, eyes on his, warned:

"We'll have to ration water. I doubt it's plentiful here."

"And avoid any contact with the ground's plants. I'm certain they're poisonous," Milenna added.

"In fact, we should distrust everything in this land," Amandil concluded.

Darian turned to Akennor, his voice drier than usual:

"Which way do we go, according to the map?"

Akennor, surprised by the tone, chalked it up to fatigue and anxiety. He recalled the map he had glimpsed on Mortragor's desk.

"Hard to say… But I think we should head northwest."

Soon after, the group set off again: Akennor in the lead with Sheila, followed by Milenna and Darian, with Xantaris and Amandil bringing up the rear. No sign of life, apart from a few repulsive insects and thorny roots that seemed to gnaw at the earth like a parasite at its host.

With their eyes glued to the ground to avoid those traps, they did not at first see what Milenna spotted in the distance. She caught up to Akennor and Sheila:

"Wait… I can make out a thick black smoke straight ahead."

"You can tell that from the dark clouds? Well, I'm impressed," Darian said mockingly.

"Yes, and there are dwellings. Let's stay cautious."

The others agreed. Soon, they all could make out the wooden towers of the orc camp of Morgrunt.

"There's an orc posted up there, a lookout," Milenna said to her companions, who could not see the figure at that distance.

As they drew near, Darian tried to move closer to Milenna. As he quickened his pace, he set his foot on a flat stone... which gave way. He pitched into emptiness and crashed hard onto rough, sandy ground.

Xantaris and Amandil, right behind him, saw him vanish before their eyes.

"Wait! Darian's fallen into a hole!" Xantaris cried.

Chapter 27 – The Survivors

They edged closer around the hole, incredulous.

"Darian, you okay? Anything broken?" Akennor shouted down, leaning over.

Sore all over, Darian pushed himself unsteadily to his feet and rubbed his lower back.

"Nothing serious… a bit dazed, but I'm all right," he said, glancing around.

"I'm in a sort of cavern. Throw me a rope."

Akennor rummaged in his pack and pulled out the rope he'd brought. Darian was still rubbing his back when, out of nowhere, a black shape lunged at him, slamming him hard to the ground.

Milenna heard the attack.

"What's happening, Darian?"

Only a groan of pain answered her. Without hesitation, she dove headfirst into the cave. Akennor followed at once, telling the others to stay topside until they knew more.

The young warrior landed lightly and drew his swords. Milenna, now a wolf again, stood beside Darian, hackles raised, growling into the surrounding darkness.

A hooded figure burst from the shadows and rushed Akennor, sword in hand. He caught the blow at the last instant with one blade and, in a perfectly timed motion, disarmed his attacker with the other.

For a heartbeat the assailant lay pinned, immobilized, while Milenna's fangs hovered inches from their face. The figure froze, staring at the animal in terror. With a sharp motion, Akennor tore back the hood.

The surprise was total: the attacker was a young blonde woman with brown eyes, a delicate face, and a slender frame. Her slight build seemed at odds with the place. Akennor stiffened, afraid she belonged to the cult. They were likely in the bowels of an outpost.

He set his sword point to her throat.

"Who are you? What are you doing here?" he asked, voice firm.

Despite the fury in her eyes, the woman answered steadily:

"My name is Savannah. I'm the daughter of the lord of the Foranor. And you—who are you?"

Savannah had taken them for agents of the Shadow, but she noticed they wore no badges. And they clearly didn't recognize her—even though she'd been hunted for a long time.

Akennor wondered whether to believe a story like that.

"Sure… and I'm the god of flowers. All right then— where's your badge, and who's the traitor who sent you?"

Stunned, the young woman shook her head.

"I'm telling the truth! I thought you were assassins from the black fortress… they've been after me for a long time."

"Years ago, I was kidnapped from my father's castle while he was away on a diplomatic mission to Elenshae."

Akennor sensed no lie in her words. Her tone stayed steady; her gaze never wavered. At last he lowered his blade and offered his hand to help her up.

Milenna had shifted back to human and stood beside Darian. Savannah started when she saw her.

"What! You're a woman too? How is that possible?" she said, plainly impressed.

"It's a form of magic," Milenna answered with a crooked smile.

"Then who are you, and what brings you to these accursed lands?" Savannah asked.

"We're looking for a friend taken by a dark order that worships demons," Akennor said.

Savannah's eyes went wide and her hand flew to her mouth. Darian spotted the reaction.

"What? What is it? Do you know something?"

She looked at them, hesitating.

"Maybe… My sources say a convoy passed through the Morgrunt camp: four shadow-mercenaries, an orc guide… and a prisoner with long brown hair."

Darian's and Akennor's hearts skipped a beat.

"What? It's true?!" Darian cried.

He dropped to his knees and wept with relief. Knowing she was alive—and that they were on the right trail—rekindled his hope. Milenna bent to comfort him.

"It's her, I'm sure of it," Akennor said. "How long ago?"

"A few days," Savannah replied, her voice tinged with sadness. "They must have reached the fortress already."

"Hey! You all right down there? What's going on?" Sheila called, worried.

"We're fine, Sheila. One moment, okay?" Akennor answered.

"We have to leave for that fortress at once. What's the safest way?"

"Underground. Tell your friends to come down and I'll show you the route," Savannah said with a thin smile.

"Come down!" Akennor shouted up to Sheila, Xantaris, and Amandil. "We've had an unexpected encounter."

The three climbed down at once, and Akennor made introductions.

"This is Savannah, daughter of the king of the Foranor."

The paladins took her hand and knelt on one knee.

"We're honored, my lady. But how did you end up in a place like this?" Xantaris asked.

"It's a long story... I was abducted by a band of mercenaries. Then we traveled by boat and I was taken to the Morgrunt camp not far from here," she replied.

"And... I'm not the only one. Please follow me—I'll explain."

Akennor leaned toward Milenna and murmured,

"Think we can trust her?"

She knit her brow.

"I don't know yet... Let's stay on our guard."

Savannah took the lead, the companions close behind. It was very dark, but after a while a faint light appeared ahead. The cavern narrowed into a tunnel hewn from stone. The walls, smooth and even, formed perfect angles. Akennor ran his fingertips over the polished surface, impressed.

"Do you know who shaped these walls, Savannah?"

She turned her head.

"From what we've found, they were made by the enemies of the demonic forces. But we don't know much more than that."

"The orcs don't know these passages exist, and we use them as shelter."

The young adventurers understood who had built this, and were awed to behold such a piece of their world's history.

Savannah lifted two torches from brackets on either side of the passage and handed one to the young warrior.

"We mustn't leave obvious signs these places are inhabited—just in case the orcs discover them."

The tunnels formed a true labyrinth. Savannah led them corridor to corridor until they were completely lost and disoriented. She alone seemed to know exactly where she was going.

"I hope we haven't made a huge mistake…" Akennor whispered to Milenna.

"Don't worry, I can track our way by scent," she whispered back.

A little later the tunnel widened into a vast chamber carved in the black rock. Numerous torches lit the space, revealing every detail.

Akennor and his friends stared, wide-eyed. The cavern, perfectly circular, was dominated at its center by a broad stone dais. Around it, six immense columns, evenly spaced, held a ceiling that rose a good ten *maicas*. Ahead was another passage; to their right, a broad opening.

Savannah had told the truth: she wasn't alone. About ten young women sat cross-legged around a fire, talking softly. Farther off, four old women watched them, eyes empty— as if all life's spark had gone out.

Seeing Savannah return with six strangers, the young women sprang up and reached for their weapons.

"Don't be afraid," Savannah called. "They're from our world. They come from the realm of Elenshae… Isn't that right?" she added, turning to Akennor.

"Yes, that's right," he answered shyly. He felt awkward, wondering why so many women lived in such a place.

"I present to you Akennor, Darian, Sheila, Milenna, Xantaris, and Amandil," Savannah told her companions.

The young women sat again, and Savannah invited the newcomers to join her at the fire.

Once everyone was seated, Savannah began, eyes fixed on her guests.

"As I said before, I was taken from my family and brought here—like all the women you see… and those in the cavern over there."

She paused, lowered her gaze, then added gravely:

"There are also hundreds still imprisoned in the Morgrunt camp."

At this revelation, the companions traded looks, unsettled. A shadow crossed Milenna's eyes; a thought had come to her, one she refused to believe.

Savannah went on, her voice trembling.

"You must be wondering why… Why women, when men—stronger—would make better slaves?"

She sighed.

"The answer is simple—and obvious. During the Great Deliverance wars, the orcs were almost wiped out. A twisted mind gathered them on this cursed land and set about repopulating them."

"But there was a problem… We learned they weren't numerous enough and needed fresh blood to keep their children from being born with grave deformities. So those monsters began to raid the continent… to steal women."

She clenched her fists.

"The Foranor's proximity meant almost all the captives were ours."

Beside her, Amandil felt his heart clench. He guessed what she would say next and wondered how the gods could allow such sacrilege.

Savannah's voice broke:

"Once in the camp… the women are…"

She drew breath, shook, then forced out:

"Raped. By orcs. Again and again… so they'll get pregnant as fast as possible."

She lifted her eyes to the stone vault, as if to draw strength to continue.

Darian ground his teeth, heart in shreds. Imagining what they'd endured was unbearable.

"Those who are infertile are killed… and eaten. As soon as they grow too old, they meet the same fate."

Tears streamed down Savannah's cheeks. Her voice shook as she poured out these horrors to Akennor and his friends, frozen with shock. Around them, the other young women had wet eyes; some clung to one another for silent comfort.

The young adventurers were shattered by the revelations. Milenna had guessed, but hearing it from Savannah's lips was more than she could bear.

Sheila, furious, clenched her fists. She wanted blood. Her whole being burned with a single desire: to avenge these women.

Overwhelmed by rage, eyes wet, Xantaris was first to find his voice.

"I… I'm speechless. I could never have imagined such horror. It's a crime against everything that exists—against honor, against virtue, against life itself. What monster could devise something so vile?"

The young paladin trembled. His blood boiled. On the spot, he would have slain the one who had orchestrated all this suffering—the shadow reflected in these women's eyes.

"It's the same one who took our friend... No doubt he's been preparing his plan for a very long time," Akennor said, throat tight.

"You're right. From our elders' stories, the scheme has worked for several generations. Today the orcs are numerous enough to sustain themselves," Savannah replied.

She went on, eyes dark:

"They now breed among themselves, and the number of human captives is falling. Their goal is to restore the purity of their race. From what we've learned, half-orcs are more rebellious, more intelligent, and less willing to submit to authority."

"There must be a real army in that camp. How many are there, would you say?" Amandil asked.

"I don't know exactly... I'd say several thousand. And I've heard there are other camps, even larger, farther north—populated only by pure orcs."

"These are grim revelations... and they pose an immense threat to everyone on our continent," Xantaris said thoughtfully.

Savannah continued:

"Morgrunt is almost deserted. At most a few hundred orcs remain. The rest marched out a few weeks ago... and I know they were heading to the ships."

She paused, then added:

"Hundreds of vessels coming and going, loaded with orcs... for weeks."

"What?!" Akennor exclaimed.

He looked from face to face. The same astonishment and dismay were written on all of them.

"They mean to invade our lands! We have to warn the realm so it can prepare. We have to act!"

Akennor already saw the enemy's plan: a surprise attack, cities caught unawares—and Elenshae vulnerable to such a tide.

"I suppose trolls are moving with the orcs," Sheila said bitterly. She loathed those creatures.

"The trolls, yes—that's what the orcs call them," Savannah answered. "Huge beings, covered in small green scales.

They came through the camp a few days before the orcs left. Fewer in number… perhaps a few thousand soldiers."

The companions grimaced at the figure. Amandil voiced what everyone thought:

"No kingdom could withstand an assault of that size. Not the Foranor, nor Elenshae, nor Kementári."

Darian sat with his face in his hands, in despair. Milenna stared into space, thinking of her adoptive father and fearing for him. Sheila burned to fight. Akennor thought of his family, dreading disaster—they lived so close to the great city.

Xantaris and Amandil, for their part, thought of warning the Order of the threat. And although Darian thought of his family too, his mind kept circling back to Shaya.

"What do we do now?" he asked evenly. "Maybe we should split up—one group to warn the realm, the other to free Shaya."

"I'm going on," Akennor said with resolve. "I won't leave Shaya in a monster's hands without doing something."

"Me too. I'm not quitting when we're this close," Sheila growled.

"Though it worries me… I said my farewells to my father, and I hope nothing ill befalls him. I'm staying with you. I won't let you down," Milenna declared.

"I think the best way to bring down an organization like this is to strike the head. Kill the leader and they'll be in disarray," Amandil added, firm.

"Yes… all right. I trust our brothers—they won't be easily surprised," Xantaris concluded.

"Besides, Orendil must be on alert since we exposed the spy. He may already know of this threat."

"So we keep going together, all the way," Akennor told Darian who was so relieved he smiled.

"Can you guide us to the fortress?" the young warrior asked Savannah.

She nodded.

"Of course… it would be an honor. But in return, I'd like to ask your help. We want to free the women who haven't yet been impregnated—perhaps forty. As for those already with child… it's impossible.

They're too closely watched—especially to keep them from harming themselves. But since the camp is nearly empty, it's the perfect chance. Afterward we'll flee to the continent."

The companions exchanged a look.

"You have a plan?" Darian asked.

Savannah nodded.

"Yes. It'll be quick, I promise."

"I'm in. It won't delay us much anyway," Darian answered.

The others agreed—especially since the thought of thinning the orcs' numbers pleased them greatly.

"That's very kind of you," Savannah said, visibly moved.

"In that case, we leave tomorrow. That will give you time to recover and prepare what you need," she added.

Savannah stood and moved toward the entry of the stone-hewn dwelling, the young women following.

"I can't wait to cut down those orc scum," Sheila said, rubbing her hands.

Chapter 28 – The Prisoners of Morgrunt

The companions were chatting with the women of Foranor when Savannah approached, a kind smile on her lips.

"You must be hungry. Would you like to share our meal?"

Xantaris courteously replied:

"Gladly. Our provisions are nearly gone… but we don't want to take advantage of your hospitality."

"It would be our pleasure."

She gestured, and six young girls stepped forward, each carrying a wooden bowl. The adventurers breathed in the aroma wafting out.

"That smells amazing," exclaimed Xantaris. "A hot meal would do us a world of good."

Inside the bowls, pieces of meat swam in a thick brown sauce, fragrant with herbs.

Milenna took hers reluctantly, staring at it with disgust. Embarrassed, she stammered:

"I'm sorry, but I'm not really hungry. My stomach is unsettled."

"All the more reason to eat; it will help you," encouraged Amandil.

Akennor, on the other hand, was starving. The journey had forced them into strict rations. He grabbed the bowl, seized the lead spoon, and swallowed a juicy piece of meat. Closing his eyes, he savored the flavor.

"Mmm… what a delight," he thought.

When he opened his eyes… everything changed.

"AHHHHHHHH!"

He leapt to his feet, hurling the bowl across the room and spitting out the half-chewed bite. In his hands, instead of the dish, lay the severed head of a young blonde girl, her delicate features framed by blue eyes.

Everyone stared at him — the women of Foranor as well as his companions — frozen in shock. Trembling, Akennor sat down again.

"I'm sorry… I have visions, and they play tricks on me."

"What did you see this time?" asked Amandil, intrigued. Sheila sat beside him and wrapped an arm around him.

"Probably the face of a young woman," answered Milenna.

"What? But… what does that mean?" exclaimed Xantaris.

"Where do you think this meat in our bowls comes from?" asked Sheila, pale. She put her dish on the floor, nausea rising.

Savannah flushed, clearly uncomfortable. She stammered:

"I… I'm sorry. I should have told you… but I never thought you would figure it out."

Xantaris and Amandil exchanged a stunned look, then set their bowls down at their feet. Darian followed suit.

Ashamed, the other women of Foranor quietly slipped away, leaving Savannah alone with her guests.

"As I told you earlier… when a woman grew too old or was infertile… the orcs ate her," she explained, eyes fixed on the ground.

"And… that's how they fed us. We found out by accident."

She paused, still staring at the floor.

"I know what you must think. We are ashamed of it. It's unnatural… but we had no choice if we wanted to survive."

Her voice broke. Savannah sobbed. Akennor stood and held her in his arms. He searched for words… but the horror choked him.

The image of the young woman's face lingered in his mind, making him gag. He stepped back, fighting nausea.

"I do not judge you… you did what you had to do to stay alive," said Milenna gently.

Little by little, Savannah regained her composure, though her eyes were still filled with tears.

"These trials sometimes make me fear what I've become… who I am."

"Trials are meant to be overcome. They may change certain parts of us, but never our true nature," answered Amandil with a warm smile of compassion.

"Rest now. I'll find something else for you to eat. I won't ask you to make this sacrifice… you don't have to bear it."

With these words, she vanished into a corridor.

Darian slipped away discreetly to vomit up what he had eaten, disgusted at the thought of having found it good. Sheila, flushed and dizzy, lay down on the cool stone floor.

"What did she mean by "this sacrifice?" asked Darian, still shaken.

"To give up a part of her humanity," Milenna answered, glancing toward the corridor where Savannah had disappeared.

"What a horror!" exclaimed Xantaris. "I feel so much sympathy for these women living in hell… I hope Elarána will envelop them in her light."

"Elarána, cálë aicollion, envinyata ómartainna, hlára naicëntassë."

"That's beautiful… what does it mean?" asked Darian.

"Elarána, hear their suffering and heal their souls," Milenna said, wiping her tears. "I know a few words."

Xantaris gave her a tender smile. She held his gaze for a long moment, noticing his blond hair and piercing eyes. When he met her eyes, she quickly turned her head, cheeks flushed.

After a rather short night, the rescue group left the great cavern of pillars. Savannah led the way, followed by Akennor, his friends, and about twenty women.

Soon, the tunnel began to change: it narrowed, its roughly hewn walls lacking refinement. Savannah stopped and declared:

"We're here. Right now, we are just beneath the northwestern section of the camp, where the women are imprisoned. As you must have noticed, we dug this extension of tunnel to reach this point."

"The plan is simple: we must enter the building where they are held, then escort them to another secret exit on the far side of the mountain," she continued.

"Why not just go back through this tunnel?" suggested Darian.

"Because we don't want the orcs to discover its existence. We'll collapse it once we're out. The other path will mislead them, buying us safety. And… we must lead you there so you can continue your journey," she explained.

"Sounds like a good plan," Darian approved.

The tunnel sloped sharply downward. At its end, a wide stone slab, propped by two wooden beams, blocked the passage. Savannah drew her sword, one she had found in the great cavern of the ancient empire.

"At my signal!"

Her sisters unsheathed their blades and braced themselves, while two others seized the beams.

"Go!"

The beams were pulled and the heavy stone crashed to the ground with a dull thud. Savannah dashed forward, followed by Akennor, his friends, and half the women. The others stayed behind to erase all traces of the tunnel.

It was night, and the camp seemed eerily quiet: no sentries appeared alerted. Ahead loomed a large building with only one entrance — a massive wooden door.

Milenna shifted into her beast form and crept forward. A guard suddenly appeared on the left; spotting silhouettes in the dark, he opened his mouth to sound the alarm. Milenna was faster: his cry died in his throat. The path was now clear. Akennor and Darian took positions on either side of the door.

"On my signal…" whispered Akennor.

Darian nodded. Akennor signaled the paladins. Milenna reared up, ready to pounce.

"Now!" he shouted.

Together they burst through the double doors, which gave way more easily than expected. Xantaris, carried by momentum, stumbled and fell flat, while Milenna leapt over him, searching for prey.

Sheila and Savannah followed closely, the other women hanging back to guard the rear. Only one orc was inside, stunned at the intrusion. Quick as lightning, Darian vaulted onto a filthy table and smashed his hammer down on the monster's skull, shattering it in one blow.

Savannah grabbed the keys from the corpse and rushed to a nearby iron door. Her hands trembled, making the keys clatter. Darian covered her hands with his, and together they turned the key.

The door opened with a sinister creak. Milenna charged in first, followed by the rest. Two torches flickered on the walls, casting a dim light. The companions recoiled in horror at the sight: four rows of straw pallets, about forty in total, filled the room. Seven orcs loomed nearby, preparing to assault the chained women.

Milenna's blood boiled. She launched herself at the closest orc. Caught off guard, he had no time to react.

She leapt on his back, biting his neck and raking his spine with her claws. The orc screamed and collapsed.

Akennor's eyes gleamed with murderous fire. He lunged at another. The orc barely drew his sword before Akennor's blades flashed — his head rolled to the floor. Fueled by rage, Sheila roared and unleashed a jet of flames, hurling an orc against the far wall. He ignited, and she finished him with a magical projectile.

Darian faced the fourth. Raising his warhammer high, the apprentice paladin crushed the orc's jaw, sending him sprawling. Xantaris charged another.

The orc raised his blade, but Xantaris dodged and plunged his sword to the hilt into the beast's body. Face-to-face, Xantaris grimaced with savage fury before shoving the corpse away. Amandil rushed his opponent. The orc stood ready, but the duel ended quickly: Amandil knocked aside his blade with one hammer, then caved in his skull with the other.

The last fell to Savannah. With a bestial scream, she stabbed him through the chest. The orc gasped a few words in his tongue before dying, but Savannah ripped her blade free without hesitation.

Akennor approached cautiously.

"You knew him, didn't you?"

Savannah glared.

"Yes. He was the one who raped me at the start… Why?"

Akennor lowered his shoulders.

"I'm sorry, I didn't mean to…"

"I'm relieved to have killed that filth. Now hurry, we must go."

The imprisoned women recognized Savannah and rejoiced at her return. They rose eagerly, ready to follow. Amandil and Xantaris broke their chains.

Their numbers swelled to forty as they fled northward, toward the mountains. But drums, horns, and hunting dogs soon echoed behind them. The alarm was raised.

They reached the base of the range, but the orcs closed in.

Savannah directed five warriors to guide the fugitives into a ravine. She then rejoined Akennor.

"We'll distract them. Follow me quickly. We must avoid a fight."

Orcs on black steeds appeared in the distance, dogs leading the chase. A horn's echo filled the valley.

The group plunged into the ravine, the hounds snapping at their heels. Ten orcs managed to descend as bolts whistled overhead.

Akennor slew the first dog with his sword. Sheila blasted another with a spell. Darian smashed the last with his hammer.

Still they ran. Pursuers closed in until Savannah veered suddenly right and vanished into the rock.

The companions followed and discovered an illusionary passage.

"Silence. Follow me," whispered Savannah.

Inside the mountain, they could still hear the enraged orcs outside.

When the danger passed, Savannah turned:

"Thank you for your help. We've saved many lives. Follow this passage straight through; you'll emerge halfway to the troll camp of Marak. Avoid them. Once past, you'll be only half a day from the fortress."

"This is where we part ways. I hope to see you again. Be safe… and good luck."

"Thank you, Savannah. It was an honor to help you," smiled Akennor.

They exchanged farewells. Savannah slipped into a side passage, rejoining her people.

"Let's go too, we've a long road ahead," said Sheila.

"*Aurë!*"

The ball of light appeared, floating before Sheila and spreading a soft glow around them. The walls of the mountain, carved with great precision, revealed that this passage dated back to an ancient time.

The procession advanced in silence, each lost in their thoughts. Some pondered battle plans, strategies to counter the orc and troll threat; others, thoughts of love. But all were haunted by dark reflections.

The trials they had endured so far had taken a heavy toll, both morally and physically. Beneath the mountain, they moved forward by pure automatism, one foot in front of the other, carried by exhaustion.

348

After a long while, a light finally appeared at the end of the tunnel. Before risking stepping outside, they decided to use the shelter of the passage to eat and rest a little.

Akennor's sleep was restless once again. Images raced through his mind until the whirlwind and the fog gave way to a clear vision.

He was standing on a small hill in the middle of a ruined city, overlooking an immense crowd that all walked in the same direction. The gray, desolate figures advanced with slow, steady steps, their empty eyes filled with crushing despair. The human tide stretched as far as the eye could see, encircling the hill.

Suddenly, a bright brown mane of hair caught his eye. He thought he recognized that distant silhouette, swept away by the crowd. Without hesitation, he leapt into the mass and tried to force his way through, pushing bodies aside with his shoulders. To keep her in sight, he leapt regularly, but the shine of her hair dimmed more and more as she drew away.

He screamed with all his might, but no sound left his lips. Frustration consumed him, anger rumbled within like thunder echoing across the mountains. Ahead, people fell into a vast abyss, marching toward nothingness without the slightest resistance.

Panicked, Akennor redoubled his efforts, striking and shoving the figures to move forward. The precipice loomed dangerously close: he had to reach her before it was too late.

As the woman with the long hair was about to topple into the endless chasm, Akennor screamed her name. This time, his voice filled the sky:

"SHAYA!"

He caught her arm at the last moment. Hearing her name, she turned slightly. Their eyes met, her pale gray gaze locking onto his. Her face suddenly lit up, color returned to her skin, and a radiant smile erased the shadow that had darkened it.

A great wave of relief washed over Akennor: he had saved her. Without speaking, she sent words into his mind, like a breath in his soul: *I will not give up.*

The void collapsed, and Akennor was suddenly pulled back, reentering his body.

He woke with a start, drenched in sweat.

"Are you alright, Akennor?" Sheila asked, worried, while the others still slept.

He wiped his brow with a trembling hand.

"Yes… I'm fine. I… I saw Shaya in my dream. It was strange, unreal… but with a troubling sense of reality. I hope she is safe," he added pensively.

Sheila sat beside him and rested her head on his shoulder.

"So do I. I long for this nightmare we're living to end."

Chapter 29 – On the Land of Horror

Shaya tossed in her sleep, her mind troubled. She found herself in the middle of a crowd with empty, sullen faces. She felt uneasy, yet let herself be carried along. Hope had abandoned her; she had no desire to go on. Not far ahead, a wide precipice swallowed the people of the crowd who cast themselves into it without making any attempt to escape.

She too was about to let herself be engulfed by the void, when a familiar voice called her by name. A strong hand grasped her arm. She turned and plunged her gaze into Akennor's.

The worried face and the kind expression of her friend comforted her. She knew at that moment that her companions were not dead, contrary to what Drendor had insinuated. Without speaking a word, he transmitted to her inwardly: It is not over.

Hope was reborn within her, and a smile blossomed, lighting up her face.
She woke with a start, her heart pounding furiously.
"They're not dead…" she murmured.

Determined to free herself and help her friends who were coming to save her. Sitting cross-legged, she closed her eyes. Her thoughts turned to her master, and she recalled his teachings, his calm voice filled with wisdom.

"The incantations I taught you are the foundation… but you can create your own upon this base."

Shaya intoned one of the formulas she had learned and continued her memory:

"Let go of your will and your instinct; the incantation will follow the path traced by the spirit."

A long breath. Her hands trembled. The prayer took shape on its own, carried by her breath.

*

Drendor coldly scrutinized the pale, gloomy faces of his chief advisers.

"Summon the Black Guard!" he ordered.

The members of the Black Guard resembled their master: eyes streaked with blood-red veins, bulging and almost devoid of iris; pointed teeth; bald skulls most often hidden by a wide black hood.

According to rumor, these humanoid creatures came from infernal regions, sent by the lord of darkness to serve Drendor.

In truth, three of them had once been men, the fourth an elf. It was said that these powerful necromancers had long since renounced their origin and their race. Years of dark magic, practiced to increase their power and prolong their life, had disfigured their appearance.

Drendor had found them one by one, in the course of his many journeys to the far corners of the world. The youngest necromancer was named Kalimder, the renegade elf bore the name Tromorgul, the slyest among them was called Bregor, and the most powerful answered to the name of Morutha.

Morutha spoke:
"The preparations are almost complete, Master. Everything will be ready in time for the next full moon," he said in a grave, tomb-like voice.
"Excellent! Everything is in place. I will give the order to the troops to attack, and when we seal our victory in blood, men will know their punishment."

Drendor savored the thought, like a fantasy soon to be fulfilled. Shaya was in a trance, striving to reach the elements that surrounded her in this land steeped in darkness. The roots of evil coursed through sky and earth, keeping the elements under their grip, enslaved.

The dark master had almost entirely subjugated the natural forces of this hostile land, reshaping it according to his desire and will. As she continued to call upon the power of nature, a memory surged. The atmosphere of that day returned with clarity: it was their last lesson of the year.

Her master was old, though no one knew his exact age; some claimed he was as ancient as the world itself. His thick bushy eyebrows overhung a long gray beard streaked with white. He wore a brown robe, like packed earth.

The memory of Shaya remained vivid in her mind. The wise man sat upon a large flat rock, aided by his long wooden staff. Adoron made himself comfortable, then surveyed his students in silence. He looked over each one, lingering longer on Shaya. He gave her a smile, seemingly satisfied with his group of pupils. Taking a deep breath, he began:

"I will not be long today. I will leave you to a well-deserved rest. You have learned so much this year, and you need time to absorb it all."

He blinked before continuing:

"When you channel the energy of nature, you must let yourself be imbued with its strength. You must feel like a fire: fanned by the wind, it becomes stronger, more threatening."

"But remember that a fire too fed by the wind consumes itself quickly. The greater the powers you ask for, the more energy is required."

At that moment, Adoron fixed Shaya straight in the eyes, and she understood perfectly what her master meant.

A long silence… then a howl rose from the depths, long and tearing, resounding abruptly in the darkness of the dungeon. Shaya jumped and broke from her trance. She searched around, but saw nothing. As she closed her eyes again, a second, sharper cry tore through the silence.

After a brief lull, came a torrent of screams, supplications, and moans. Shivers ran down her spine. She wondered what torment the man at the origin of those cries had endured.

A nasal voice rose before her:

"The scream of a specter… memory of a distant past."

She turned and saw a small creature. It resembled a troll, but far smaller. Shaya fixed the hideous being with disgust, sensing the cruelty radiating from it. She stepped closer, repulsed:

"His suffering must have been immense, for even the reflection of his presence remembers it."

Limzi blinked, excited.

"Oh yes, oh yes! He was tortured by Master Drendor himself. His soul will never know rest."

Shaya stared at him with deep scorn.

"You must be truly twisted to delight in such misery."

The creature inspired her with visceral disgust, and anger surged within her like a wave. Limzi flashed a wicked smile, cruelty gleaming in his eyes.

"To see strong people broken, denying their ideals and their faith to escape pain… it is satisfying."

That was too much. Shaya wanted to see him suffer in turn, to see him beg. She raised her hands and whispered inaudible words. Limzi stared, incredulous, unable to grasp what she was attempting.

A dull vibration rose from the ground, a low rumble swelled… then, with a sharp crack, a stone spike shot up, stopping inches from his face. Limzi froze, mouth agape, but had no time to react: a second point sprang up beneath his feet. He leapt backward, narrowly escaping impalement, then fled headlong without looking back.

Shaya opened her eyes, a satisfied smile on her lips, and watched the puny silhouette scurry away at full speed. The stone spikes retracted into the ground as quickly as they had appeared.

Her breathing was short, her head spun. A searing pain crossed her chest. She lay down, waiting for the physical pain to fade, but her heart remained oppressed… for her thoughts were turned toward Darian.

*

The companions breakfasted on a piece of travel bread and were now ready to leave their underground shelter to continue their route. The tunnel's exit was concealed in the same way as the entrance, camouflaged.

Outside, twisted trunks cast their blackened shadows.

Beneath their steps, gray dust rose in curls, stinging the throat. Each snapping twig resounded too loudly. Yet nothing disturbed their advance. Akennor and Sheila led the way, followed by Darian and Milenna; Amandil and Xantaris brought up the rear.

They advanced in silence, each attentive to the gloomy landscape enfolding them. Their steps were lit by the gentle glow of a magical sphere conjured by Sheila. Later, they perceived a faint light through the thick gray clouds: day had broken.

Soon, the dark wooden palisades of Marak appeared before them.

"Here we are, within sight of the troll camp," announced Akennor in a neutral tone.

"Yes, and we must cross the forest to bypass it. Let's be cautious," declared Amandil.

They veered to the right to avoid being spotted by the guards perched atop their towers. Once at what they judged a safe distance, they plunged into a sparse forest, populated with trees whose bark was blackened, like charred. The ground was covered with a grayish dust resembling ash.

The trees, with their twisted silhouettes, seemed haunted by a malevolent force. Fortunately, nothing disturbed their progress — the companions took great care to avoid anything suspicious.

They stopped for a while to rest before continuing north. Veering slightly left, they realized they had skirted the troll camp. A silent relief passed through them: the trolls had not noticed their presence.

The rugged terrain forced them to stay vigilant. After a long trek, a dark silhouette appeared on the horizon. The fortress slowly revealed itself, its jagged lines blending into the landscape to conceal its vastness.

Akennor fixed the lair of Drendor, thinking that somewhere in that hell Shaya was imprisoned. Darian's heart pounded wildly. He longed to shout his beloved's name so she would know he was near. An irrepressible urge pushed him to charge headlong, to tear her from evil's claws.

"Here we are, my friends... at last, the goal of our journey," Akennor said pensively.

"Shall we storm it?" asked Darian, eager to end it once and for all.

His friend looked at him, incredulous.

"We know nothing of this place, nor of the dangers that await us. What we do know is that monsters of unmatched cruelty dwell here. That alone is enough to understand we must remain cautious," judged Amandil.

"He's right. We should make a plan, observe and try to see what is happening inside. With luck, that will give us some idea," added Xantaris.

Darian stamped his foot, unable to contain his frustration.

"So we'll just wait patiently... while Shaya may be suffering the worst torments!" he almost shouted. Anger burned in his eyes.

"Darian, calm down, please. I know you want to save her, as we all do, but we must act wisely. What will happen if we're captured? Do you think things will go faster? If we fail, it will be the end," concluded Sheila, fixing him intensely.

He turned away, face darkened.

"You're right…" he admitted after a brief silence, regaining his senses.

The group pulled back behind a rocky embankment and a few withered trees. They organized guard shifts in pairs: two would rest, two would watch, and the others would discreetly scout the area to observe the fortress's comings and goings.

Akennor went with Sheila, Milenna with Xantaris, and Amandil accompanied Darian. Akennor and Sheila advanced close enough to make out the ramparts. Dismal sounds — the dry crack of tree branches and long laments of pain — polluted the air, fraying their nerves.

Iron spikes, tall as towers, speared toward the gray sky. The wind moaned as it rushed through them, making chains rattle. Only then did they discern what hung there: emaciated silhouettes, human without a doubt. Some dangled by their wrists, swaying like broken puppets. Others had been impaled, frozen in eternal agony.

"What cruelty… I can hardly believe this is not a nightmare," whispered Akennor.

"It's dreadful. Such evil has no place in this world," added Sheila.

They encountered no obstacle during their patrol and found nothing significant. Back at camp, the others awaited them anxiously.

"So, did you see anything?" asked Darian.

"No, not really… sorry. I hope you'll have better luck than us." His voice was low, heavy with discouragement.

"Well, let's go, Darian."

The paladin and the apprentice went off in their turn, seeking information.

Meanwhile, Xantaris and Milenna slept peacefully. Akennor sat on a flat stone near Milenna. Sheila came to sit beside him.

"I can't ait for this to be over," she sighed in a weary voice.

"These past weeks have been trying."

"Things never happen as we want."

"What do you mean by that?"

Sheila gave a shy smile, torn between what her heart urged and what her reason dictated. She said nothing, let a few silent tears flow, and nestled against Akennor.

His heart beat fast. Gently, he lifted Sheila's face. She stared intensely at him, and he found her more beautiful than ever. A shiver ran through him. Slowly, he inclined his head until his lips brushed hers. She returned his kiss, and they kissed passionately.

A kiss, soft and tender… The world vanished around them; nothing else mattered. They remained thus, entwined, until Darian and Amandil returned.

"So?" asked Akennor, curious.

"No… not really. Sorry," Darian replied, visibly dejected.

Milenna and Xantaris were then awakened for their watch. Akennor and Sheila took a few moments of rest, still nestled together. Darian, lost in thought, seemed to notice nothing. Amandil, however, observed the scene, though he said nothing, a grin upon his face.

"It's about time!" He thought.

*

In the throne room, Maultarg appeared, summoned by Drendor. The half-orc knelt before his master.

"You desire, Master?"

Drendor motioned him to rise.

"My dear Maultarg, it is time for you to leave. You will join the trolls stationed in the mountains of Kalandor. I also want you to give the order to the orc armies to put the plan into motion. The trolls must attack as soon as possible. You leave now, accompanied by Arak to the port. Is that clear?"

The half-orc raised his head, squaring his shoulders proudly.

"Yes, Master, it is very clear and it will be done. I will give the orders as soon as I am on the ship, and I will ask the trolls to leave a battalion to wait for me."

"Good... our day of glory approaches swiftly, Maultarg, and you will be richly rewarded," declared Drendor with a shadowy smile.

Maultarg left the throne room and gathered his belongings. In the courtyard, Arak already awaited him with two horses.

"Here is your mount, Maultarg," he announced, handing him the reins of a proud black stallion.

Drendor's right-hand man mounted the animal.

"Forward!" he cried enthusiastically. "The coming days will be filled with battles, massacres... and blood."

*

For their watch, Milenna took on her wolf form, her senses instantly sharpened. Xantaris followed close behind. She halted, ears pricked, muzzle twitching. With a supple leap, she slid behind a large rock bordering the road leading to the fortress. Xantaris imitated her, panting, hiding as best he could.

Soon, the two huge iron gates of the main door opened. Two orc riders burst out, whipping their mounts.

The taller shouted loudly in the common tongue, berating his companion. The horses thundered down the road, passing so close they felt the vibrations in the ground.

They continued their exploration. Milenna sniffed the air vigorously, searching for any trace. A damp breath, heavy with a musty smell, reached her muzzle. She lifted her head, sniffing frantically, then followed the invisible trail carried by the wind.

Xantaris ran behind, struggling to keep up. Milenna led him to a crevice resembling a trench. They advanced for about thirty *maicas* in the narrow ditch. Behind a large stone, the entrance to a passage was revealed, half-hidden.

The wolf sat, waiting for her companion. Xantaris, out of breath, rested his hands on his knees and caught his breath.

"Well, I don't know what you smelled, but I had trouble keeping up with you!"

Raising his head, he saw the mouth of a cavern. He turned his eyes to Milenna:

"Do you think this could lead inside?"

The wolf tilted her head in affirmation.

"In that case, let's hurry back to warn the others."

The paladin stroked her head with a teasing smile

"Good work."

When they returned, the rest of the group, already awake, awaited them impatiently. Milenna resumed human form and declared, before anyone could question her:

"We have... discovered something."

All turned to her.

"We saw two riders pass on the road southward, and we found... an entrance... a tunnel that seems to lead inside the fortress."

"Messengers, no doubt," supposed Amandil.

"A secret passage!" exclaimed Sheila.

"Secret or forgotten," wondered Xantaris.

"Perhaps both," added Akennor.

"So, let's go! We can't just wait until they bring Shaya out – if they ever do..." said Darian impatient.

"Yes, we're going to save our friend!" added Sheila.

"I agree," concluded Akennor.

"Before we continue, I'd like to settle something," announced Milenna, producing the Anoron pendant. She clutched it in her palm, as if still hesitating. Then she removed it from her neck.

"I don't need it... not as much as she does."

She turned to Sheila and held out the star.

"I propose to entrust it to Sheila, since she is more vulnerable during battle. And we will surely need her spells in the coming fight."

"I approve, seconded Amandil. That's a good choice."

Milenna placed the star of Anoron around Sheila's neck.

"Thank you... it's an honor," rejoiced the apprentice sorceress, touched by the gesture that reassured her.

The companions gathered their belongings and set off, guided by the she-wolf who sniffed the ground. Upon reaching the entrance of the tunnel, Sheila cast a spell of light, and they plunged into the depths of the cursed earth.

*

For what seemed like an eternity, Shaya meditated, endlessly calling upon the earth and the sky. She managed

362

to communicate with the elements, but too weakly to break the evil bonds that chained them. She would need much more energy… or more time. But time was what she did not have.

Without warning, a stocky orc suddenly burst open the door of her cell and stormed inside. The creature seized Shaya in both arms and forcefully dragged her out of the room.

The orc shoved her roughly through the shadowy corridors. Abruptly, he stopped and hurled her into a vast, icy hall. The air was heavy, and the atmosphere so terrifying that a chilling shiver ran down her spine.

Before her, Drendor sat upon his throne, flanked by four hooded black figures, two on each side.

"Ha ha…" he sneered in his dark voice.

"It is time. Your miserable existence, along with those of your kind, will give way to something far greater… and glorious."

Drendor rose and snapped his fingers. Instantly, an orc stepped forward to fasten her wrists with heavy iron shackles. Sweeping her eyes across the hall, she noticed six other captives: three boys and three girls. Their hands were bound, their eyes empty, and a chilling resignation marked their faces.

They seemed to have been imprisoned for many years. Most of the young women had lost their hair, their faces aged by suffering, appearing decades older. Their emaciated bodies bore the imprint of countless wounds and scars.

"Forward!" ordered Drendor, striding with solemn steps, followed by the four shadowy figures.

The black silhouettes glided behind him. The orcs seized the captives, pulling on the chains that clattered through the hall. The procession began: Drendor at the head, his acolytes at his side, the prisoners behind, surrounded by a dozen armed guards. The pounding of footsteps on the stone slabs resounded like a funeral knell.

A subtle vibration coursed through her senses, like a foreign breath brushing her mind. She lifted her eyes, searching for the invisible source. Nothing.

Yet the sensation persisted, insistent. Shaya inhaled, closed her eyelids, and folded in on herself, extending her spirit toward the forces that surrounded her.

Chapter 30 – Drendor's Rage

His army was ready to sweep across the world like a raging wave crashing against a docile shore. Cartaraug was satisfied: he had finally received the order from Maultarg to attack, without quarter, without mercy. He was also to leave a battalion behind to wait for the half-orc.

At once, the troll lieutenant prepared his troops for the offensive. The camp would be entirely dismantled by nightfall, and their first target would be reached by the middle of the night. All around him, Cartaraug felt the feverish excitement of his warriors: the trolls ran and barked their thirst for blood in their bestial language.

*

"Come now, tell me everything!" begged Josey.

Torhon was sitting at the counter, sipping a beer, accompanied by his friend Krent and the kind-hearted innkeeper. Josey liked the young men and worried about what might have happened to them.

"I heard from Ben that their daughter Shaya had been kidnapped by bandits, but I don't know much more. They left shortly after," he mumbled.

"That's what I know as well," replied Torhon, taking another good swig.

"The bandits attacked them on our lands, not very far from my home, can you believe it? My wife treated Darian, who was wounded... and that's all I know. They then went off in pursuit of their assailants."

Josey could hardly believe it: their village had always been a peaceful place for so many years. Krent, Torhon's best friend, had also been surprised and deeply shaken.

"I'm very worried, my friends, and I feel like going after them. I can't stay here doing nothing. Fortunately, I've convinced my wife to go search for them. We'll leave early tomorrow morning."

"I'll go with you, my friend. Your quest will also be mine," Krent said with sincerity.

"Thank you, Krent, but you'd better stay to watch over your family."

"My family is fine. Every one of them is safe and not in danger."

Torhon smiled at his friend, knowing full well that nothing would change Krent's mind.

The three of them—Torhon, Krent, and Josey—drank to the health of the missing ones. When Akennor's father finished his beer, he rose from his stool.

Suddenly, the door burst open. A man, armed with a sword and a blood-stained shield, staggered inside. His clothes were in tatters, revealing numerous wounds all over his body. His gaze was shifty, panicked beyond measure. He screamed:

"We were attacked by... by trolls!"

Stunned, Torhon's blood ran cold, sensing that this event was connected to his son and his friends. His wife's words echoed even more strongly in his mind. *I know it's linked to Akennor. I know it, I feel it deep inside. Terrible things are coming, and soon.*

Dread grew as the wounded young man approached.

"I come from the village of Vendaras, a little north of Arhanar."

Panting, short of breath, he continued:

"We were attacked by surprise. We tried to resist, but it was hopeless. There are thousands of them. Even their severed limbs grow back. We fell back here, hoping to find brave men to help us fight these monsters."

"AAHH, aaargn!" he groaned.

A searing pain gnawed at him from within, and he collapsed to his knees. His face streamed with sweat. A fit of coughing shook him, and blood spurted from his mouth.

The young warrior collapsed onto the wooden floor, convulsing violently. Torhon and Krent rushed to his side, but could do nothing… the young man died, his last words drowned in a bloody gurgle.

Krent looked at his friend holding the warrior in his arms.

"Poor boy… Dead as a true warrior, felled by his wounds. May Númellon guide your spirit to the other world." Torhon gently laid the warrior's head down and closed his eyes.

"He was poisoned. The trolls coat almost all their weapons with poison. It's a miracle he made it this far," Torhon added.

"How do you know that?" asked Josey, stepping closer.

"I had experience with trolls… a very long time ago…"

Krent raised an eyebrow, surprised. Never had his friend spoken of such an adventure. Other customers had gathered, forming a circle around the dead young warrior.

In the distance, horrible groans resounded, along with the metallic clash of weapons. Already, cries of terror echoed from afar, mingling with the clash of blades.

"Grab torches! Fire is far more deadly to them than steel!"

The villagers drew their weapons, snatched the torches hanging from the beams, and rushed outside.

Torhon followed, side by side with Krent and Josey, fire and steel their only defenses against the night. Violent fighting raged in the village streets. Most of the inhabitants fought shoulder to shoulder with the refugees from Vendaras.

A troll leapt before Torhon, roaring, arms outstretched, eyes bloodshot. Consumed by frenzy, it was nothing but a beast. Torhon dodged its clumsy strike and thrust his torch straight into its face. The creature howled in agony, flailing to extinguish the flames… in vain. Soon, it was nothing but a living torch.

Seizing the momentum, Torhon set a second troll aflame.

"Gather together! Burn them!" he shouted. The villagers formed a large circle.

Peasants armed with bows lit their arrows and loosed them toward the enemy. Blazes rose everywhere, illuminating the pitch-black night.

But the trolls struck back in turn. Their poisoned arrows rained down. Torhon knew many would not survive.

"We must retreat, or we'll all perish!"

Their group was surrounded, cornered. Suddenly, an immense flash lit up the sky. A fire spell struck a cluster of trolls, obliterating them in a blazing explosion.

Torhon turned his head and saw the frail silhouette of the village's old sorceress. She smiled at him.

"Go! Run!" he bellowed. "NOW!"

Seeing hope, the survivors rushed through the cleared path.

"Rally the men!" he cried again.

But Krent was kneeling by Josey, struck by an arrow.

"Come, Krent! We must save our families!"

Tears streamed down the blacksmith's face.

"Save yourselves... quickly..." Josey murmured with his last breath.

Torhon seized his friend's arm and pulled him away. They fled into the forest, leaving their torches behind. The trolls pursued, seeing perfectly in the dark. They had gained some distance, but as Torhon turned to gauge it, he slammed into a tree or a stone. Everything went black.

Krent ran on. All he heard was the pounding of his own steps. He stopped, turned... and realized he was alone. He retraced his steps to find Torhon. Suddenly, a hiss sliced through the night, followed by searing pain in his leg. He staggered: a poisoned arrow had struck him. Ahead, ominous pairs of yellow eyes pierced the darkness.

Limping, Krent forced himself onward through the forest. Behind him, the creatures halted. They knew: their prey was doomed. The poison would do the rest. Tears blurred his vision. Krent wept for his lost friend, his doomed village, the sacrificed families. But he could not collapse. Not yet. He had to save whoever he could still reach.

Despite the pain, he ran. He could: he had the endurance of blacksmiths, forged by years of toil. But his strength waned, his vision faltered. Soon, a veil fell over his eyes.

Still, he pushed on. His friend's house was near. A light shone from the balcony. Exhausted, Krent climbed the steps and collapsed into the arms of Illawen, standing on the threshold. She had been watching the distant glow of the burning village.

"Krent!" she cried. "What is happening? Where is Torhon?"

He tried to answer, but his thoughts blurred. Only a few syllables escaped:

"Trolls… Torhon… dead…"

Illawen's eyes fell to his leg: the wound was black, the poison already at work. She did not hesitate. She knew this affliction, passed down among her people for generations.

She helped him inside, laid him down. She quickly returned with a vial of greenish liquid, acrid-smelling. She lifted the wounded man's head and poured the potion into his mouth, then applied it to the wound, after removing the arrow.

She bandaged it with clean cloth and let Krent rest.
Time passed.

At last, Krent opened his eyes. Lying on the floor, he saw Illawen sitting nearby, legs crossed, her gaze serene.

"Well? Do you feel better?"

Krent propped himself on his elbows and looked at her, perplexed.

"How… how is it that I'm not dead? I don't understand."

Illawen gave a faint smile.

"You were on the brink of death… let's say my potion brought you back."

Krent sat up a little more.

"Tell me what happened. Where is Torhon?"

Illawen's expression grew pleading. Krent drew a deep breath.

"We were drinking with Josey when a young man arrived, panicked. He told us his village had been attacked by trolls. He didn't survive: the poison killed him before our eyes. Soon after, the fighting erupted, right into our streets."

He shut his eyes a moment.

"We fought. But we were too few… We had to flee into the forest. Torhon ran with me. Then suddenly, he was gone."

Realizing he had lost his best friend, a tear slipped down his cheek.

"I tried to find him, retraced my steps, only to realize we were still pursued. I was struck, but managed to get here.

"I'm sorry. I couldn't find him. I thought I would die."

Illawen embraced him silently, tears streaming down her face. Her nightmares were coming true, one after another.

He nodded, stood. His leg burned, forcing him to limp. Before leaving, he turned:

"You can come… if you wish."

She shook her head gently.

"No. Thank you, Krent. I still have something important to do."

"Then… be careful. Thank you for everything. Torhon was like a brother to me. I will avenge him."

She hugged him one last time. Then he descended the steps slowly and vanished into the night, still hoping to find his people alive.

Illawen watched his silhouette disappear into the darkness. Then she returned inside, took a travel bag, and packed a few clothes and useful items.

As she was about to close it, a wave of grief overwhelmed her. She wept for her husband, her sons, her nightmares.

She screamed her anguish:
"Torhon... my love... where are you? You've been torn from me."
She focused all her energy on finding him, sensing him. But nothing—no image came, even when she drew on all her memories.
"No... he cannot... he must not... Torhon, where are you?"
Sobs wracked her body. Only after a long time did reason return. She rose, seized her bag, and left the house never to return.

The night was silent. In the distance, towering flames rose to the sky, lighting the moonless dark. She approached the village. On the way, mutilated bodies of men, women, and children littered the ground. Her throat tightened, her heart clenched.

Only the crackling of fire disturbed the silence. The monsters had already vanished. She fell to her knees, hands over her face. The roaring flames seemed to demand more blood. The stench of burnt flesh hung thick in the air, nauseating. Not far, a house collapsed in a sinister crash. All that remained of that home were ashes and glowing embers dancing in the night breeze.

A family had surely lived there once, happy and fulfilled. Illawen rose, staggering. Each step was an effort. Her path would be long, solitary, scarred by pain—just like in her dreams.

Crossing the village ruins, she saw bodies riddled with black arrows. Charred trolls lay in ashes. The battle had been brief, but fierce. From the tracks, the creatures had headed toward Elenshae, no doubt to hunt the few survivors. But Illawen was not alone. Hidden in the shadows, several pairs of yellow eyes watched her silently.

Her beauty enthralled them. Yet the trolls saw only an object of lust. In their twisted minds, Illawen was to be captured, offered to their master, and broken.

Guttural growls rose. They exchanged words in their foul tongue, then stepped slowly from the shadows, claws outstretched, eyes gleaming with excitement. Their pace widened as they neared.

Illawen sensed them before seeing them. Their vile thoughts invaded her. In their minds, she saw herself chained, humiliated, tortured. Her soul shuddered in horror.

The trolls were within reach. Their claws were about to seize her…

…when a light erupted.

A blazing sun rose, taking its place high in the sky, driving away the shadows and the dark thoughts of the monsters. Their brief jubilation was replaced by sheer panic. Shrieks of horror filled the night, echoing off distant mountainsides.

The trolls loathed the sun above all. They cursed the star of light and damned it with all their wretched souls. Illawen walked on silently as the trolls shrieked and wailed.

Though the creatures raised their arms to shield from the searing light, they watched in horror as their skin ignited like straw. Total panic consumed them, drowning what reason they had left. The heat was stifling, the light blinding, the pain unbearable.

Though flames devoured their flesh, the creatures did not burn away. The panic in their minds was stronger than anything

Driven mad, they clawed themselves, tore at their own bodies, hoping to end the torment. But the flames persisted. More than punishment, it was an eternal sentence—one reserved for those whom malice would never leave.

Illawen, impassive, kept walking. Then she stopped, glancing back. The trolls writhed on the ground, screaming, their faces twisted in terror. Once, she would have savored their suffering.

But not tonight.

She felt neither satisfaction nor pity. Her pain was too deep. Her rage, too raw. Illawen felt nothing… nothing but emptiness. She resumed her path, leaving behind her old life, once full and happy. Now, only solitude remained.

Illawen followed the tracks left by Akennor and his companions, weeks earlier. Behind her, the night filled with the atrocious lamentations of trolls in agony.

*

The atmosphere at the fortress of the Order of Calaista was tense. Since Master Orendil's death, a veil of grief had hung over the place. To restore some cheer, Berantis had decided to host a great feast, with food and drink aplenty.

The general enthusiasm was palpable: it had been a long time since they had allowed themselves any merriment. The stress of recent events, combined with mourning, had severely shaken morale.

Long wooden tables were set in the castle's inner courtyard. Paladins and priests from across the region gathered, laughing heartily, relieved for a time of their burdens.

But Turanis, a young paladin recently promoted and close to Xantaris, had no heart for celebration. He wandered alone through the stone corridors, deep in thought. He could not believe their beloved master could have died so suddenly, he who seemed still so robust. And more troubling still, the arrest warrant against his friends Xantaris and Amandil, accused of desertion, left him perplexed.

He knew their loyalty better than anyone. Never would they betray the Order. Berantis, who also knew them, should have understood that. Yet he had sown doubt, insinuating their sudden departure hid something. Despite the indignation of many, his arguments had silenced any opposition.

Turanis suspected another truth. Perhaps Orendil had entrusted them with a secret mission. After all, Xantaris and Amandil were the two most valiant warriors of the fortress.

Lost in thought, Turanis climbed the ramparts above the main gate. It was pitch-dark, but the cloudless sky let the stars shine with gentle light. In the distance, a glow caught his attention.

Metallic reflections, like flashes of armor, then small flames, moving slowly toward the fortress.

Suddenly, a movement right at the base of the wall made him start. A massive, dark-skinned creature was watching him. Its protruding fangs gleamed in starlight. Its nose was crushed, its lower jaw too wide for its hideous face.

The being wore crude iron armor, a thick wooden shield, and an oversized sword.

Turanis widened his eyes, breathless

"An orc…" he whispered.

The swelling lights and metallic glints awakened his instincts: the Order was in danger. Turanis rushed toward the watchtower, ready to sound the alarm with the horn.

But his run stopped abruptly. A violent blow struck him, throwing him to the ground. Dazed, he looked up… and found Berantis, standing before him, a sinister smile on his lips.

"Berantis!" Turanis gasped. "Orcs… thousands of orcs are coming! We must sound the alarm!"

He scrambled to his feet, but the Order's master's arm held him back.

The icy bite of the blade pierced his side.

Turanis, stunned, felt blood rise in his throat. His eyes met Berantis's, and the truth struck him: Orendil's death, Amandil and Xantaris's disappearance, even the feast… it all made sense.

"It's you…" he breathed. "Why?"

"That would take too long to explain," Berantis replied, leaning close to his ear. "And besides… it's no longer your concern. Rest in peace, brother."

His voice dripped with treachery. With a cruel laugh, he drove the blade deeper. Turanis convulsed. Then, with a brutal shove, the traitor hurled him into the void.

The young paladin's body crashed at the base of the ramparts with a dull thud. Berantis signaled an orc scout hidden in the shadows. Moments later, he himself lowered the drawbridge and raised the portcullis, delivering the fortress to the enemy.

A bestial howl rose into the night: the orc army, until then massed before the walls, surged forward. Inside, the members of the Order, still feasting, had only a few moments to realize they were under attack.

The slaughter was swift. Berantis's betrayal and the overwhelming numbers of the orcs crushed the defenders. In only a few moments, it was over. Soon after, Gauldrom, the orc general, entered the traitor's office.

Berantis stood at once, a broad smile on his lips.

"Gauldrom, I presume? I am Berantis, the Master's contact within his enemies."

The massive general, silent and imposing, studied him at length.

"I have heard of you. You have done well. Almost too well. My men found this attack… strangely easy."

"I am delighted to hear it," Berantis replied with a sly grin.

"I will leave two battalions here. The rest of the army marches on toward Elenshae. The fortress is yours."

"Perfect. I believe our Master will be very pleased. Everything is unfolding as planned."

The traitor laid a falsely brotherly hand on the general's shoulder. Together, they left the room, behind them only the ashes of a shattered Order.

Chapter 31 – The Shadow of the Past

The tunnel was narrow. Often, they had to walk sideways to make progress. The air, saturated with humidity, exhaled a rancid, moldy stench. The ball of light they carried barely pierced the darkness, as though the shadows themselves absorbed its glow.

The winding corridor twisted and turned endlessly, without a single branching passage. The group advanced in silence. Soon, the air grew heavier, and the hair on the young adventurers' arms bristled. Suddenly, the tunnel widened.

A lugubrious sound rose—a muffled howl, mingled with a cry of pain. Instinctively, they stopped, every sense on alert. Silence fell again. Xantaris felt an evil presence lurking somewhere in the shadows. No one dared to move or speak.

Akennor turned his head in all directions, scrutinizing the gloom. Suddenly, as he brought his gaze back forward, a hideous face appeared: a specter in advanced decay. Its translucent body, tinged with green, wore the armor of Oriador's ancient soldiers, just as described in the engravings he had seen.

The ghost fixed him with its gaze for an instant. Akennor, seized with terror, dared not move or speak.

Wondering if his companions saw the same thing, he remained frozen. The creature stepped back, then released a shrill scream that froze their blood. It drew a greatsword and raised it high, ready to strike.

By reflex, Akennor shouted and shoved Sheila aside, narrowly dodging the phantom blade. The others screamed in horror and stumbled backward in panic.

The specter pressed its assault. Akennor drew his swords and tried to parry, but the spectral weapon passed through his blades as if they did not exist, then pierced his thigh. His eyes widened as an icy bite spread from the wound.

Pain surged through his leg. Clutching his thigh, he felt the cold seeping into him like a spreading gangrene. The specter sneered and raised its weapon again, poised to deliver the killing blow.

But Sheila leapt to his side, driven by instinct and courage. She interposed herself, facing the ghost. Her Anoron pendant suddenly blazed, flooding the cavern with brilliant light. The specter froze, stunned, then let its sword fall. It shook its head as if waking from a nightmare and dropped to its knees before Sheila.

From its mouth came a voice from beyond the grave:

"The Star of Anoron... I lost it, while hunting the priests of Tholgor in the dungeons. They ambushed me... and cursed me. I am condemned to wander these tunnels for eternity..."

A deep sorrow imbued the specter's cavernous voice. In Anoron's light, its appearance slowly transformed: its face returned to what it once had been—that of a young man in the prime of life.

Sheila, moved by his despair, asked softly:

"Is there anything we can do to help free you from this curse?"

The young man smiled radiantly.

"You have already done it, brave souls. To see the Star of Anoron again makes me light… free. I no longer need to wander this earth. It is time for me to rejoin my kin, who wait for me."

The specter rose and turned his gaze toward Akennor, who still clutched his leg, grimacing in pain.

"It will fade… Rest now. If you continue straight ahead, you will reach a great hall, an important place of this fortress. I do not know what brings you here, but… may Oriador watch over you."

Milenna, after a moment's hesitation, dared to ask:

"Knight… what is your name?"

As his image slowly dissolved into the air, a distant voice resounded:

"Ferennor."

The Star of Anoron went completely dark the moment Ferennor's spirit vanished.

"Does it hurt?" asked Sheila, kneeling beside Akennor. She examined his leg: no wound was visible. But when her hand brushed the spot where the blow had struck, his skin was ice-cold.

"Ahh… gently, please… It's almost unbearable."

The companions sat around him.

"Imagine if it had struck your chest!" exclaimed Milenna.

"I would be dead…" he replied. "Thank you, Sheila. Without your courage, I wouldn't be here anymore…"

She held him tenderly for a moment.

"I think a bit of rest will do us good, said Darian," his gaze distant.

"We are close. Soon, we will see the end of our journey," he added.

"Yes… lie down, Akennor," said Amandil. "We will make a small fire. Perhaps it will help your leg recover faster."

The paladins lit a small fire with a few pieces of wood they carried. Milenna covered Akennor with a blanket, while Sheila remained by his side. Darian, exhausted as well, lay down and fell asleep almost instantly.

Before long, only Milenna remained awake, keeping silent watch over their makeshift camp. When Akennor opened his eyes again, he met Sheila's tender gaze fixed on him.

"I was so afraid," she whispered. "I thought… it was the end."

"My heart froze too," he replied. "I felt all hope slipping away."

Sheila smiled softly and pressed a kiss to his forehead.

At last, sleep also claimed Milenna, until Akennor woke her a little later.

"Come on, up you get. I'm better. My leg is alive again."

Milenna rubbed her eyes as she rose.

"I'm glad for you. Now we can continue."

Soon after, the companions resumed their progress. The dark corridors stretched on, narrow and twisting. As the specter had said, they pressed straight ahead.

At last, they reached the heart of the fortress. A vast hall opened before them, supported by countless pillars—each carved with the effigy of a different demon. At its center stood an imposing altar, and seven pillars arranged in a half-moon rose before it, standing like silent sentinels.

Chapter 32 – The new alliance

The altar, carved from black rock, formed a large cross with sharp edges. At its center, a pentacle surrounded by ancient runes seemed to snake toward the edges of the slab. Four other identical stars, rigorously oriented, marked the cardinal points.

Drendor slowly turned toward the prisoners and, in a cavernous voice, ordered his servants:

"Tie them, each to an arch."

Immediately, the orcs stirred. One of them brutally grabbed Shaya by the wrists and pulled her mercilessly. She stumbled, nearly collapsed, but barely managed to keep her balance.

"Move, bitch!" roared the orc, violently throwing her against a stone arch.

The shock tore a cry of pain from her. Without waiting, the orc detached her wrists, fixed them to iron rings sealed into the structure, then chained her feet on either side of the arch, immobilizing her completely.

Meanwhile, Drendor climbed the steps of the altar and placed an old grimoire on a worn pedestal. The four hooded figures, dressed in long black robes, took position in the pentacles drawn on the ground, at the foot of the altar. They turned toward their master in a chilling silence.

Soon, a lugubrious chant rose, deep, resonating like a murmur from the depths.

Hearing this sound, Shaya distinguished the long, sharp teeth of the necromancers. Their mere presence froze the blood. Around her, the six other prisoners did not react.

Their eyes fixed on the ground, they seemed absent, broken long ago by torture and humiliation. Hope had left them years before.

When all the preparations were complete, Drendor raised his arms. His guttural voice rose, chanting an ancient invocation, supported by the hoarse murmurs of the necromancers. The orcs, motionless, guarded the arches with vigilance.

Drendor's face was carved with deep wrinkles, sculpted by time and darkness. His spirit was taut to the extreme. He now spoke the ancient tongue of the demons, drawing his words from a cursed work, written by Tholgor himself and his disciples, according to the teachings of the lord of the abyss. This grimoire had once escaped the hands of Oriador and his allies, stolen by a powerful dark mage. Drendor had crossed the world, braved cursed lands, and faced a thousand perils to recover this forbidden treasure of impious knowledge.

The companions then arrived, just in time to witness the scene. Frozen in terror, they hid behind cracked pillars and larges blocks of rock, their eyes fixed on the altar.

As the incantation progressed, a supernatural fire suddenly burst from the ground before the altar, mixing green and blue flames that writhed like serpents.

"We must go now!" said Darian, his voice charged with urgency.

"Yes, I think you're right," agreed Xantaris.

"Don't worry, Sheila, Anoron's pendant will protect you from their spells," explained Milenna.

"I also know protective spells. I'll cast one on all of you, it will help."

"If demons appear, as I fear, by using the bodies of the sacrificed, they won't have all their powers at first. That will be the moment to strike," she added.

Akennor then spoke:

"All right. I'll rush Drendor with Darian. Sheila, cover us. Milenna, do as you judge best. Amandil, Xantaris, clear the orcs around us!"

All nodded silently, determined.

"*Dûlu-rhu, Dûlu sairina!*"

Milenna closed her eyes and whispered an incantation in an ancient tongue unknown to the others. A soft blue light surrounded them, passed through them.

A sensation of warmth and strength filled them. In an instant, fear vanished from their hearts, replaced by a serene confidence.

Shaya could not break the occult chains that bound the elements to Drendor's will. She wept with helplessness, frustration, and grief, knowing she would likely never see her loved ones again. Not even one last time to say farewell.

Her thoughts turned to Darian, the man she loved deeply. She relived that blessed day when they had promised each other sincere love. Her heart clenched. Never again would he hold her in his arms. Never again would their lips meet. Love had been cut short — stolen without justice, without goodbye.

Before the altar, the green flames danced more and more violently. Drendor's incantation was reaching its climax. The dark master raised his hands. The four necromancers then stepped forward, knives in hand, toward the prisoners aligned in a half-circle. Shaya, at the center, watched them, breathless.

The necromancers slowly lifted their knives above the victims' heads, then lowered the blades before their faces with ritual precision... before plunging them down in a sharp thrust into their hearts.

As life drained from the sacrificed bodies, a jet of flame erupted from the altar and struck each corpse. The fire seeped into their flesh, triggering a horrifying metamorphosis: skin split open to reveal massive muscle, the bodies grew taller, horns sprouted from their skulls, and their once-innocent faces twisted into infernal expressions. Membranous wings tore out of their backs. Their skin hardened into red and green scales, while their fingers and toes transformed into curved, razor-like claws.

The demons screamed — a cry of both agony and exultation — rejoicing at finally returning to this world that had been forbidden to them for centuries.

Shaya, horrified, trembled at the thought of what awaited her. The transformation of the first victims now complete, two of the necromancers were already approaching the next prisoners.

On the altar, Drendor laughed madly, a demented laugh that echoed through the entire hall. He exulted, celebrating the return of Tholgor's demonic servants.

"SHAYA!" Darian roared, hurling himself into the assault, body and soul.

The cry snapped her out of the haze clouding her mind. She lifted her eyes… and her heart leapt. She saw him, running straight toward her, hammer raised, the features of his beloved face twisted in explosive fury.

At his side, Akennor charged with both blades drawn. Sheila ran just behind them. At the sight, tears burst from Shaya's eyes: a surge of joy and courage filled her. Like a ray of light in the darkness, hope returned.

"WHAT!? What is this!?" Drendor shrieked, pale with rage.

"My demons, attack!" he roared. "Show them the power of the darkness!"

The creatures broke their chains and rushed at the intruders. Shaya felt panic seize her. She knew her friends stood no chance against such monsters.

Deep within her soul and heart, Shaya understood the sacrifice she had to make. The incantation, the prayer whispered to the elements, subtly shifted. At that moment, immense energy coursed through her body and radiated outward… her call was heard.

She released her emotions, her deepest desires merging with her breath. The wind rose in fury, clouds gathered, and the sky thundered in anger. The air grew heavy, and the earth trembled violently, throwing the necromancers and demons off balance; even Drendor fell from the altar to the ground.

The quake tore open a vast fissure in the ground, carving a wide chasm between Shaya and Drendor.

The columns holding the stone dome collapsed under the force of the tremors. The entire fortress shook with violent convulsions.

There was a brief pause — both the attackers and the demons frozen. Then, as the demons regained their footing and advanced again, rumblings rose from the depths of the earth, vibrating beneath their feet, intensifying as if the shockwave itself were drawing closer.

Enormous mounds of soil erupted, hurling stone slabs aside, taking the shape of giants. Four elementals of earth and stone emerged, facing the demons. Their roars rumbled like avalanches as the entities clashed with colossal force.

The impact of their blows shook the very ground. The companions, stunned, were seized by a surge of hope. Amandil and Xantaris rushed past Akennor and Darian, charging straight at the orcs who tried to intercept them.

This vision of elemental giants fighting the demons galvanized them all. Without hesitation, Amandil and Xantaris stormed forward, sweeping through the orcs like a storm.

Xantaris dodged the blade of his first opponent and drove his sword to the hilt into the creature's chest. With a violent push, he shoved the orc into a second one approaching. Instinctively, the second caught his companion—an error that cost him his life, as Xantaris brought his sword down in a crushing strike that split the orc's skull in two.

A third attacker charged. Xantaris ducked under the swing of a massive hammer and slashed low, cutting both legs at the knees. The beast collapsed in a guttural howl, writhing on the ground.

On his side, Amandil was fighting no less fiercely. He caught a sword blow on one of his hammers, then swung the other down hard, smashing the orc's skull. A second came at him, shield raised. With a grunt, Amandil slammed his left arm into the shield, knocking the orc back and off balance. His right hammer came down savagely at the base of the neck, snapping bones in a grisly crunch.

Another orc tried to strike, but Amandil blocked the attack, then, roaring, swung his hammer in a brutal arc. Bone shattered. The orc gasped, collapsed to his knees, and Amandil finished him with a rain of crushing blows.

Meanwhile, Akennor and Darian had almost reached Shaya. Two of the four necromancers had managed to cross the fissure and stood in their way.
"*Templa pilini!*" cried Sheila.
A magical flash surged across the hall, striking Kalimder, who flew through the air and crashed farther away. Bregor, enraged, raised his hands to cast, but Akennor was faster. With a great leap, he was upon the necromancer and sliced his head clean off. The spell died in the dead man's throat.

Darian overtook Akennor and charged the necromancer staggering back to his feet. He swung his hammer with explosive force, sending the dark sorcerer crashing against the stones in a spray of black blood.

Outside, thunder roared even louder, bolts of lightning tearing through the thick blanket of clouds. Another tremor ripped the chamber; part of the ceiling caved in. Stones crashed to the ground with deafening thunder.

Drendor, in the middle of casting, barely dodged a massive block by reflex, though a smaller stone struck his skull. He fell to the ground, unconscious. The battle between elementals and demons raged on. The abyssal fiends were stronger, and the elementals weakened with each clash.

Milenna rushed to aid them.

"*Aista turma sairina!*" she cried.

An orange light burst from her palm, striking one of the demons square in the chest.

The monster snarled at her, its voice cavernous:

"I thought the bastard kin of Oriador were extinct…"

The spell drained its strength. The elemental sensed it at once—its strikes now landed with devastating impact.

Milenna drew her blade and slashed at the demon's legs and torso as the elemental grappled it. Staggering, the beast faltered. Milenna leapt, driving her sword into its heart.

The fiend shrieked with a piercing cry, thrashing violently, but after moments of agony, it collapsed face-first into the dirt.

Pulling her sword free, Milenna turned toward the next demon. The elemental it had been fighting had just crumbled under a fiery onslaught.

The monster raised its claws and invoked a spell:

"*Urë-Falampa!*"

Flames erupted from the ground in a massive wave, engulfing the elemental and blowing it apart in a shower of molten rock. Milenna herself was scorched and hurled violently aside.

The demon advanced quickly on her. A sudden roar, then a fireball struck the beast in the chest. The blast made it stumble but caused no damage. The fiend laughed—creatures of the Abyss feared little of ordinary magic.

Milenna pushed herself to her feet, raising her hand. Her fingers glowed with pure radiance. She whispered one of Oriador's lost incantations—a gift of the gods meant to shatter the defenses of abyssal beings.
"Let's see if you still laugh, abomination," she hissed coldly.
"Templa Aista turma sairina!"
The air trembled as Milenna cried out:
"Now, Sheila—again!"
A bright beam of white light split the darkness, slamming into the demon's head. The impact boomed like thunder. The fiend staggered, stunned, just long enough for Milenna to dash forward and cut it down.

The last demon struck an elemental with such force that the creature shattered apart, its body collapsing into rubble. Freed, the abyssal fiend wasted no time. Its cavernous voice thundered:
"Ungwaleros!"
A blinding beam of purple light burst from its hands and struck Sheila.
Stunned, she saw the energy absorbed into the pendant of Anoron at her neck.
The demon roared with fury:
"Naurë ringa, urco-nárë!"

Flames erupted from the ground in a blazing wave, engulfing Milenna, Amandil, and Xantaris. They were hurled back, their bodies seared, rolling on the ground to extinguish the fire.

The monster bore down on Milenna, raising a claw for the killing strike.

"Not her… demon, stay away from her!"

"Templa pilini!" screamed Sheila.

A blue bolt seared into the fiend's face. It staggered back, blinded and howling in rage. Snarling, it lunged at Milenna anyway. One brutal strike sent her flying, her limbs limp as she crashed to the ground.

Xantaris and Amandil, their bodies still smoking, charged once more. Amandil, gasping for breath, hammered relentlessly at the beast, forcing it to falter. Seizing the moment, Xantaris drove his sword full into its belly, up to the hilt.

The demon bellowed and backhanded him away with crushing force. Sheila unleashed another blast, this one slamming into the monster's skull.

Amandil, seeing the opening, roared and rained down his hammers. Each blow smashed bone and scale until the fiend reeled.

"Urë-nor!" cried Sheila.

Flames surged from her hands, searing its face. The beast toppled backward.

Xantaris, already on his feet, sprinted forward. With a cry, he plunged his blade deep into its heart. He twisted the sword, and the demon gave a final, gurgling roar.

Black blood poured from its mouth before its massive body collapsed in a heap.

Tears streamed down Shaya's face. Relief, joy, and love overwhelmed her as Darian and Akennor rushed toward her. But her strength was gone, her eyelids heavy, her body yearning for rest.

Darian reached her first. With a mighty swing, he shattered her chains.

She fell into his arms.

"Shaya, it's me... I've missed you so much," he whispered, weeping with joy.

She opened her eyes, gazing at him tenderly, and smiled faintly.

"I missed you terribly too. I thought I'd never see you again."

Darian held her close, convinced the nightmare was finally ending.

"It's over. We're together again. Everything will be all right."

But her expression shifted—sorrow clouded her face. Her body burned with unbearable pain. She trembled in his arms.

"What's wrong? What's happening?" he begged.

And then, beside her, stood Adoron. No one else could see him. His kind eyes shone with pride and sorrow. His voice resonated within her mind:

"Every request demands a sacrifice. I am proud of you. Go in peace, child. Let the wind carry you to a better world."

His image faded.

Shaya looked at Darian one last time. Her lips trembled. "I love you...so much... kiss me..."

Darian bent down, pressing his lips to hers.

Her body arched in agony. Fire seared through her, shredding her nerves, devouring her life. She clung to him, her face frozen between love and unbearable pain. As life was leaving Shaya, her skin turned grey, her body stiffened, and slowly, her form disintegrated into ash.

A breeze swept through the broken dome, carrying her away. Darian held her until only a handful of dust remained in his palms.

He collapsed, sobbing soundlessly.

The pain… this pain that tore his soul apart… so intense he could not even scream, could not even breathe. In that absolute silence where time itself had stopped, only his eyes wept — bleeding the very blood of his soul.

The companions stood around him, broken. Nothing could soothe the void left by her passing. Then a low growl echoed.

They turned—and there was Drendor, his face twisted in rage. He had survived.
"He's back…" Akennor muttered.
Darian's grief twisted into fury, into a pure and unquenchable thirst for vengeance. His knuckles whitened around his hammer.
With a roar, without thinking, he charged Drendor.
"No! Darian, stop!" cried Akennor.
But it was too late.
The master of darkness raised his hands and shouted:
"Ungwaleros!"
A blast of purple fire slammed into Darian's chest. His scream tore the air—then his body convulsed, and he felt lifeless to the ground.

"NOOO!" Akennor bellowed. His mind shattered with memories of laughter, battles, friendship—now torn away forever.

Drendor's sneer froze on his lips. With the desperate strength of the doomed, Akennor's dagger flew, a streak of silver and grief — and struck the dark lord in the throat.

Two blue bolts followed, Sheila's magic. The impact hurled the dark master backward into the fissure.

Akennor dropped beside Darian, turning him over… but it was too late. He closed his friend's eyes with trembling fingers. His teeth clenched. The grief of losing both Darian and Shaya in one day was beyond bearing.

He rose, his body quaking with fury, ready to throw himself into the abyss to finish Drendor—

But Sheila blocked his path, tears streaming.

"No, Akennor… We cannot defeat him here. He isn't dead. You know it."

He tried to push past, but she clung to him desperately.

"I've lost my sister. You've lost your brother. But I cannot lose you too. Please… live. We will avenge them, I swear it. If it takes our entire lives."

Milenna, Xantaris, and Amandil joined her, each laying a hand on Akennor's shoulders. Their eyes spoke what words could not. Together, they turned back, leading the wounded survivors out of the collapsing fortress.

Chapter 33 – The Escape

Suddenly, the pounding of hooves echoed in the distance, caught by the companions' attentive ears. They turned in alarm and saw Savannah, the daughter of the Foranor, emerging with a dozen warrior women.

Encouraged by the appearance of these unexpected allies, they rushed to meet them.

"Savannah, what a wonderful surprise!" exclaimed Amandil, relieved.

"What happened?" she asked.

"We'll tell you everything, gladly, but later," replied Milenna, quickening her pace and her tone.

Each took a horse that had been assigned to them. As they galloped at full speed to flee that cursed place, bolts of lightning split the sky and struck randomly among the riders. Savannah was hit squarely and thrown violently from her mount. Two other warrior women were also struck, but for them, the impact was fatal.

Without hesitation, Akennor wheeled his horse around and galloped to Savannah's rescue. Once he had hoisted her across his saddle, he spurred his mount again to rejoin the others.

As he rode, his vision blurred for an instant. He saw a stain of bright red blood on the ground just ahead. Trusting his instinct, he yanked on the reins to avoid it.

At that very moment, a vivid red lightning bolt struck exactly where he would have passed.

Savannah, unconscious but still alive, lay across his horse's back. Carried by the wind came a roar of rage: it was Drendor's voice. The horses tore through the darkness, the group galloping relentlessly until dawn finally dispelled the last of the shadows.

*

"RAAAAHGN!" roared Drendor, smashing everything within reach of his fists. He vented his fury on the lifeless bodies of orcs, mutilating them with blows while hurling insults at their incompetence.

In a fit of rage, he slammed both fists down on the stone altar, reducing it to rubble. Carried away by his madness, he struck Tromorgul and Morutha as they approached. The renegade elf glared at his master with fury: he understood the frustration but was not a man to be humiliated without consequence.

Drendor eventually pulled away, fearing he might kill them in a sudden rage — he still needed their services.

Morutha rubbed his bruised cheek and declared:

"Master, in anticipation of the disaster that loomed, Tromorgul and I performed a special rite…"

Drendor stopped, though he did not turn around. Sensing he had his master's attention, Morutha continued:

"We have managed to preserve certain links between this world and the lower planes…"

He felt that Drendor had calmed and pressed on more confidently:

"These links, Master, will allow us to summon demons to our service. Not as powerful as what you had originally intended... but still possible."

Drendor slowly turned. A cruel smile stretched across his blood-streaked face. He seemed on the verge of madness. Approaching his necromancers, he burst into uncontrollable, demonic laughter. Tromorgul and Morutha stood frozen, unsure whether to be pleased or terrified. Incredulous, they watched their master in silence.

At last, Drendor regained composure. He had thought the bridges with the infernal planes destroyed forever. Yet, though his great design had failed, the situation was not as desperate as he had feared.

Placing himself between his two acolytes, he spoke coldly:

"Good. Bring some forth as soon as possible. And I want the death of those young fools. They will pay for their insolence. I will send hunting parties after them."

Drendor and his servants left the ruins at a brisk pace. As he walked, the Dark Master activated his telepathic powers, contacting the chiefs of the camps of Marak and Morgrunt to warn them that humans on horseback were heading their way. He also alerted the fortress garrison, ordering all available forces to pursue them.

The adventurers had anticipated their enemy's reaction and had circled widely around the troll camp, hoping to escape the sentries' vigilance. Yet, a large group of trolls eventually spotted them as they neared the mountains.

Guided by Diana, Savannah's right hand, they managed to outdistance their pursuers and slip into a cleft in the rocky wall.

But on the other side, their respite was brief: a band of orc patrols was nearby, and a clash became inevitable. Akennor, more skilled fighting on foot and fearing to further injure Savannah during the ride, leapt from his horse to face the enemy on solid ground.

Sheila wasted no time. She hurled a fireball toward the orc group ahead. Panic spread instantly. Some tried to wheel their horses around to avoid the blast, while others threw themselves to the ground in hopes of escaping the explosion.

The fireball struck dead center among the enemy. The explosion was spectacular, sending plumes of flame in every direction. Several orcs were engulfed in fire and shrieked in agony.

Akennor rushed in to finish off the burning monsters. Drunk on rage, he hacked relentlessly, cleaving limbs, reaping lives in a macabre, blood-soaked dance. Behind him lay a true carnage.

From the saddle, Xantaris brought his sword crashing down on the skulls of nearby foes. Amandil swung his hammer with brute force, smashing enemies from atop his mount.

Milenna had resumed her animal form, sowing terror among the enemy horses, scattering them until their riders were thrown. The moment an orc hit the ground, she was upon him, tearing his throat without mercy.

Meanwhile, Sheila shielded her friends with magical bolts and lightning, striking down the most dangerous opponents.

The battle was brief but ferocious. The orcs were all slaughtered, and the youths immediately resumed their frantic ride southward. Out of caution, they circled far around the camp of Mortgrunt once more.

Soon, it faded behind them. The sun set, and the last pale light filtering through dark clouds vanished. Exhausted, they could barely stay in the saddle.

"We must rest, or we won't make it," Amandil called out over the pounding hooves.

The group halted a little farther on, believing they had shaken off most patrols. Danger seemed to recede, at least for the moment.

They lit no fire and organized watches by pairs. Akennor gently laid Savannah on a blanket and checked her vital signs.

"She's breathing. Her heart is steady. She should pull through and wake soon," he told his companions while dressing her wounds.

Seeing Diana approach, he asked:

"Why did you come? What happened?"

"Savannah and we felt we owed you a debt. So we all decided to join you in your quest. At the port, we fought orcs, defeated them, and seized a boat. Our sisters are safe now, near the shores of our homeland," she replied calmly.

"Your arrival was a miracle. Without you, our fate was sealed. I'm glad to hear your sisters are safe."

Diana and the other survivors of Mortgrunt knelt around Savannah's body. Together, they joined hands and prayed silently.

Moments later, Savannah's eyes fluttered open.

"Oh… what happened?" she asked, rubbing her head, still dizzy.

"You were struck by lightning." Akennor brought you back, just in time, Diana explained, embracing her friend with relief.

"I owe you yet another favor," Savannah said, turning to her savior.

"I'm sure fate will give you the chance," he replied with a wink.

Akennor took the first watch with Sheila. Sleep would not come; his mind was haunted by recent events, by all they had endured… and all they had lost. Sheila, sensing his torment, came closer and sat quietly at his side.

"Quite unexpected, isn't it?" he murmured. "We chased mercenaries… fought monsters…"

He sighed, eyes lost in the void ahead.

"All of it to save our friend, and in the end, it was she who saved us."

He was devastated. The loss of two of his closest friends weighed heavily, leaving a bitter scar on his heart. This adventure, instead of granting victory, had stolen a piece of himself.

Sheila nestled against him. Helpless, she had witnessed the tragic deaths of Shaya and Darian. Rage boiled within her like a storm waiting to break.

"She was my best friend… more than a friend. I've known her since I was so little… I have so many memories with her…"

Sheila broke into sobs. Akennor slipped an arm around her, stroking her gently, wordless.

Milenna appeared and quietly sat nearby. She studied them for a moment, then spoke softly:

"I couldn't sleep, and I heard you."

She met their eyes directly.

"Do you really think all this was for nothing?"

"Well… it seems that way! And you? You think it was a success?" retorted Sheila, her tone sharp.

Milenna did not flinch. She remained calm, her voice gentle, soothing the tension.

"Yes, and far more than you realize. Tell me, Sheila… could you have forgiven yourself for abandoning Shaya without a fight?"

Sheila lowered her eyes. She knew Milenna was right. She could never have lived with that weight.

"No… I couldn't have," she whispered. Her tone had softened, anger giving way to sorrow.

"You know… we witnessed a miracle," Milenna explained.

Akennor and Sheila exchanged a glance, uncertain of what she meant.

"Shaya sacrificed herself to save us… and to prevent evil from tightening its grip further on this world. She unleashed a force unimaginable, enough to break, even for a moment, the power of darkness over these lands. That is what allowed the elementals to appear and fight for us."

She paused, then added:

"Now the demons have failed. The ancient bonds, once broken, can never be restored. A colossal burden has just been lifted from the shoulders of this world."

They sat in silence, reflecting on her words. And in that silence, their grief grew gentler, less sharp.

"And Darian… his life would have had no meaning without her. He faced evil with courage. We owe them respect, gratitude… and though their absence wounds us deeply, they did not live — nor perish — in vain."

Milenna gave them a faint smile, rose, and returned to her place on the rocky ground.

Akennor and Sheila remained in each other's arms, silent, until their watch ended. Violent lightning and rolling thunder tore from the sky, rousing those who had managed a little rest.

A torrential rain lashed at the group, the wind whipping their faces without respite. Soaked through, the adventurers gathered their belongings and pressed on at a gallop, braving the storm.

The rocky soil, less muddy than the plain, was still treacherous. The horses moved cautiously to avoid slipping. Soon, the air grew heavier, thick with mist. They all recognized it instantly: the Fog of Oblivion — that strange supernatural veil forever concealing the accursed land they were about to leave.

"Well… here we are at the coast. That's good news, but no one thought to mark where we left the boat, right?" Akennor muttered, half-irritated, half-amused.

"We shouldn't be far now," replied Amandil.

"I think so too. A bit further east," added Milenna. Her animal instincts gave her a remarkable sense of direction.

Trusting her, they followed the shoreline eastward. The regular lapping of waves against rock was suddenly drowned by the sound of a horn, followed by savage cries and the clatter of metal through the mist.

The orcs burst forth without warning, charging to block their escape.

"Stay together!" shouted Akennor, leaping from his horse.

He sheltered his mount behind a boulder, drew his twin blades, and awaited the enemy. A hideous face loomed out of the fog. The orc lunged, but Akennor dodged and drove his sword to the hilt.

Xantaris and Amandil, still on horseback, fought confidently against those who drew too near. Their weapons flashed in the mist, lit by lightning.

The dense fog forced Sheila to use close-range spells.

"Carnë-narë!"

She rubbed her hands together, which burst into flames. She hurled fire onto the nearest orcs. Screaming in torment, they burned like living torches. Their shrieks and the light of the blaze illuminated the fog, granting them better vision.

Yet the orcs kept coming. Dozens fell, endlessly replaced. The attackers slowly tightened their net.

"We must push east before they surround us completely!" Akennor cried to his comrades.

The daughters of the Foranor, driven by a ferocious rage, fought with a savagery born of vengeance against those who had inflicted such horrors upon them.

They closed ranks and forced a breach eastward. Amandil seized Akennor's horse's bridle and pulled him forward.

While the paladins, Milenna, and Sheila cleared the way, Akennor and the warrior women protected the flanks and rear. A gap opened in the orc assault, and the young adventurers surged through, fleeing at full speed. Akennor, straggling behind, was suddenly seared by a burning pain in his thigh. He let out a guttural cry as his leg gave way. He collapsed, pressing his bleeding thigh. A crossbow bolt had sunk deep, nearly piercing through.

Nearby, two screams rang out. Two of Savannah's warrior women had fallen, dragged into desperate combat.

Akennor looked up — and froze. A massive troll, skin scaled and greenish, loomed before him. Its narrow maw split in a vile grin, revealing a forest of razor-sharp teeth.

The beast grinned, its crossbow aimed at him, another bolt already in place. Suddenly, a wild roar broke the night, followed by a burst of blue lightning. The magical bolt struck the troll square in the chest, hurling it back violently.

Sheila's horse reared. She dismounted at once, ran to Akennor, and hauled him onto her saddle.

"I came to see why you were lagging behind," she teased, mocking even in crisis.

She spurred her horse and quickly rejoined the group, who were beginning to worry at their absence.

"You took your time!" Milenna called. "Quickly, I see the ship just ahead!"

There, stranded near jagged rocks, lay the old fishing boat — their final hope. They dismounted, hastily gathered their gear, and threw themselves aboard.

Akennor struggled to walk; his legs were numb and heavy. Amandil and Xantaris each grabbed an arm, dragging him forward.

Once everyone was aboard, Xantaris, Amandil, and two of the Foranor women shoved the boat into the sea. Exhausted, half-immersed in water, the paladins had to be helped aboard in turn.

Sheila and Milenna settled Akennor as best they could, then examined his wound.

"It's a poisoned bolt... and the venom is strong. It's already spreading," Milenna said grimly.

"I'll pull it out," Sheila declared, rummaging through her bag for her mother's potion.

Bracing her legs, Milenna took a deep breath and yanked the bolt free in one swift motion. Akennor barely reacted — his body was already numb, drifting in a fog.

Sheila found the greenish potion and handed it to Milenna. Carefully, she widened the wound with her knife and poured a generous dose directly onto the raw flesh. Then she helped Akennor drink the remainder, down to the last drop

Milenna and Sheila exchanged a worried glance.

"I hope that will be enough…" Milenna whispered.

"So do I…" Sheila murmured. She lay close to him, watching anxiously for signs of life.

Meanwhile, wary of reefs along the coast, Amandil stood at the bow, oar in hand, peering into the mist. Xantaris held the tiller while the Foranor women rowed steadily, Milenna among them.

At last, the fog began to thin. Amandil left his post and raised the sail. Akennor was still unconscious. Sheila leaned over him, tenderly wiping the fevered sweat from his brow.

*

After the youths' escape, Drendor summoned Dresden and his band into the throne room. The mercenaries entered warily — all except Deidre, who seemed almost delighted to see the Dark Master again.

Drendor sat upon his throne, his two necromancers flanking him like shadows.

"I summoned you because you succeeded in capturing the one they call Shaya. But tonight, her friends intervened… and ruined the ritual," he thundered in his cavernous voice.

He paused, then added:

"I order you to pursue them at once. Refusal means certain death. Immediate death."

"What? But… that was not our agreement! Dresden protested. Our mission was to find her and bring her back, and we did."

He had no intention of chasing them again. Weary of endless ventures, Dresden only wanted to rest… and enjoy his share of gold. Drendor's expression did not change, but fury seethed beneath

Dresden dared meet his gaze. Bad idea. A violent telepathic surge struck his mind. He screamed and collapsed, clutching his head. The pain was unbearable. Blood poured from his mouth, eyes, ears. Moments later, his convulsing body went still.

Drendor's eyes swept the survivors.

"Well? Your answer? Or rather… your choice?"

"I would be honored to obey, Master," Deidre said without hesitation.

Parthe and Aaron nodded reluctantly. They did not wish to share Dresden's fate, though they were far from eager.

"Good. You leave at once. They headed south, no doubt to cross the sea. The orc and troll garrisons at Morgrunt and Marak are already after them. Call on whatever aid you need. I want them alive… or dead. But alive would be preferable. I have torments for them to discover…"

The mercenaries hurried off to the stables. Once alone, Drendor motioned for Morutha and Tromorgul to approach. The two necromancers knelt, tracing cabalistic symbols on the ground. Around the circles, they inscribed occult runes, ancient and menacing.

They took their places outside the markings and began a chant in the abyssal tongue — the very language once used by Tholgor himself to summon demons.

A cloud of gray smoke slowly rose from the ground. As the voices grew in intensity, the smoke thickened, charged with electricity, and flames burst forth within the circles.

Two demonic forms emerged from the blaze, shrieking as if they had never believed they would set foot in this world again.

Their bodies, massive and misshapen, were covered in green scales streaked with red. Two great horns jutted from their skulls, while three smaller ones protruded from their chins. Their hands and feet ended in enormous black claws, gleaming with dark magic.

Drendor advanced slowly, imposing, his gaze shining with cruelty.
"Welcome to this world... a world where everything can be yours. I shall let you taste human flesh."
The demons roared with delight. For centuries, they had dreamed of invading and subjugating the frail race of men.
The Master's call tore him abruptly from his sleep
Something was wrong.

Maultarg felt it deep within himself. A commanding force dragged him out of his slumber. Rising from his cot, he seized his silver circlet and placed it upon his brow. Drendor's image instantly filled his mind. The Master looked exhausted... displeased.

His dark, resonant voice flooded the half-orc's spirit:

"Maultarg, the band of young fools... the friends of the last sacrifice... have sabotaged the ritual. You are my greatest warrior, Maultarg, and I order you to pursue them. I believe they have taken to the sea and will most likely land north of the Foranor."

"Take your best warriors and hunt them down. I have already sent other emissaries in pursuit. I want them alive, Maultarg... I wish to massacre them with my own hands."

"They sabotaged the ritual? But how?"

"Do not concern yourself with that! Go... and find them!"

"Very well, Master... But how many are they? Do you have a quick description to give me?"

The Master allowed a cruel smile to spread across his face. With a mere gesture, he projected visions into the half-orc's mind. Violent images flooded Maultarg's spirit. The action was deliberately slowed so he could observe each target in detail.

He first saw a tall warrior with black hair and strangely colored eyes — pale gray. He wielded two swords with remarkable agility. Maultarg understood immediately that he would need to be wary of this one.

Then appeared a striking woman, with jet-black hair, clad in pale gray garments — who transformed into a fierce wolf.

Next came a sorceress, her brown hair flying wildly as she hurled a devastating fireball. After her, a paladin of Oriador — Maultarg recognized the uniform — wielding a hammer in each hand.

Finally, the last warrior also wore the Order's armor and carried a massive two-handed sword.

412

The visions faded, leaving Maultarg alone once more, the images still burning in his mind.

He sat cross-legged, thinking for a moment. Without further hesitation, he rose to his feet… the hunt had begun.

Chapter 34 – The Return

Akennor stood on a high hill overlooking a vast, dark forest. A narrow path stretched before him, plunging into the vegetal gloom.

When he turned around, he saw behind him a sea of fire rushing forward at great speed. The sky was covered with thick black and red clouds, as if soaked in blood. The earth trembled violently, and balls of lava crashed down heavily onto the ground.

Suddenly, a figure passed abruptly in front of him without stopping.It was a tall woman, draped in a wide black cloak, her face hidden beneath a drooping hood.
A soft, familiar voice echoed in his mind:
"I am sorry, my son... I failed you."
Akennor instantly recognized the silhouette.
"Mother! Mother, wait for me!" he cried.
But she did not hear him. She continued her march, imperturbable, without turning back.
He rushed forward to reach her, but every step was a struggle.
It felt as if all the despair of the world clung to him, weighing him down like a ball and chain.

His mother did not slow down and disappeared into the forest.

As she passed near him, he heard her murmur in a resigned voice:

"All I have left are my origins. I must make peace with my past."

He raised his head slowly: a long dark road stretched out before him. Akennor fell to his knees and struck the ground in frustration.

Akennor saw his mother move away. Tears streamed down his cheeks.

He would have needed her so much… her help, her love, in this dark moment of his life.

A flash of lightning lit up the sky, pulling Akennor from his troubled sleep.

Sheila was still leaning over him, her eyes filled with relief.

"Akennor… finally! You are back!" she said, her voice trembling with emotion.

Confused, he looked ahead and behind the boat, still seeing the dark path. His vision slowly cleared.

"We were so afraid for you," added Milenna with a smile. "The dart contained a very powerful poison… but your mother's potion worked wonders."

Despite the pouring rain and the gusts of wind lashing their faces, everyone wore a genuine smile, relieved to see him awake.

The sky was still covered with heavy clouds, and the fog lingered.

Akennor tried to sit up, leaning on his arms.

Out of the haze of his nightmare, he managed to say:

"How long have I slept?"

"Since our departure, a little more than a day," estimated Amandil, nearby.

"We can't be very far from the coast now," added Xantaris.

It had rained without respite since they had left the shores of the cursed lands, making navigation difficult.

The sea remained rough, and the boat rocked violently. The wind blew against the current, forcing the crew to row relentlessly since the start of their return.

It seemed as if an invisible force was striving to keep them from fleeing the lands of horror. The daughters of Foranor, exhausted, struggled to sustain such constant effort.

None of them were used to such physical strain, and the foul weather had denied everyone any rest or restorative sleep. Akennor tried to stand to grab an oar, but a brutal dizziness forced him back down at once.

His head spun, and nausea overwhelmed him.

"Stay seated, Akennor. You are still very pale, and clearly unable to make the slightest effort. Rest," Sheila advised softly.

He nodded, resigned, and lay back down at the bottom of the boat, now filled with cold water that bit his skin.

A little later, the boat struck a rock barely above the surface.

"Ah no! Not reefs again!" snapped Xantaris, on the verge of breaking down.

Fortunately, the impact caused no serious damage.

Amandil rushed forward and pushed the boat free with an oar, releasing it from the rocky trap.

"No damage, but let's stay vigilant," he said, returning to his place.

The rain gradually eased, and the wind fell. The boat drifted slowly over the dark, icy waters. The fog lifted, revealing threatening shapes lurking around them.

Amandil scanned the horizon, guiding Xantaris and the others to avoid the last obstacles.

"We are almost there! The shore is close!" he shouted, his voice vibrant with enthusiasm.

The boat ran aground softly on the wet sand of an unknown coast. The paladins jumped ashore and steadied the boat to allow the others to disembark. Akennor was helped by Sheila and Milenna, each supporting him by an arm. Once the whole group had gathered on the shore, a collective sigh of relief rose:

They were finally out of danger.

The clouds slowly brightened, allowing the first pale rays of a weakened sun to filter through. The rain ceased. Night was falling.

Exhausted, the companions decided to stop there. The next day, they would resume their journey back to their homes. In his heart, Akennor knew he would go and find his kin.

Xantaris and Amandil would return to the Order to warn their brothers of the peril still looming. Milenna would return to her adoptive father. And Sheila... she would walk by Akennor's side, wherever he decided to go.

📖 To be continued in Volume II, The Grip of Darkness

Please take a few minutes to leave a review. You can follow me on Amazon and Facebook.

Upcoming Releases

End of 2025
The Last Light Trilogy
Book II – The Grip of Darkness
The shadow thickens over the world, as Drendor, the
Master of Shadows, extends his dominion.
As kingdoms falter, alliances collapse, and the flames of
his vengeance spread, a handful of broken heroes still
hold on.
How can one fight an enemy who pulls the strings from
the shadows, manipulating both the living and the dead?
The Dark Master has plotted everything in secrecy,
imposing upon
the world his sordid dream.
In this second volume of the trilogy, darkness advances…
and not all will see the light again.

First Quarter 2026
The Last Light Trilogy
Book III – A Light in the Night
Akennor and Sheila are determined to uncover the secret
of their
enemy, a quest that will carry them into an epic struggle.
Torhon and Krent, loyal friends, seek to unravel the
mystery of an
artifact.
Illawen will infiltrate the very heart of the enemy.
The mighty city of Kementari faces an unprecedented
threat. And the enemy will stop at nothing, calling upon
both the living and the dead.

The final battle between darkness and light, between the dead and the living.

Release Date to Be Determined
Drendor – The Birth of Evil

This volume will explore the origins of the antagonist, revealing his path, his corruption, and the quests he undertook.

About the Author

F. Dubay is a Québecois author passionate about dark fantasy, mythology, and epic worlds.

After years of creation, he publishes his first trilogy The Last Light, a saga weaving together magic, war, and tragic destiny.

When he is not writing, he enjoys traveling and celebrating life in good company.

Printed in Dunstable, United Kingdom